ORDER OF THE SHADOW DRAGON

STEVEN MCKINNON

Cover design by www.trifbookdesign.com

First Edition

www.stevenmckinnon.net

2019 list. Safe to say that I'm seriously excited for what comes next. **9/10**" Emma Davis, *Fantasy Book Review*

"*Wrath of Storms* is a masterpiece in storytelling and establishes Steven McKinnon as the heir to Joe Abercrombie's throne. **5/5**"- Phil Parker, author of *The Bastard From Fairyland*

"Very well written and flows really well. The ending kept me on the edge of my seat. So damn good. **5/5**" - Super Stardrifter

"A high-octane, action-fantasy adventure laced with dry humor, a diverse cast of heroes and villains, and an infectious case of 'just-one-more-chapter' syndrome. **8.8/10**" - Adam Weller, *Fantasy Book Review*

ORDER OF THE SHADOW DRAGON

Get The Raincatcher's Ballad prequel novella, ***The Fury Yet To Come***, absolutely FREE by joining the author's Mailing List!

Visit subscribe.stevenmckinnon.net to download NOW!

'Fortune Find You!'

For Henry McCourt.

I miss you, Granda.

A NOTE ON THE TEXT

This book takes place after The Raincatcher's Ballad trilogy
but can be read independently.

Order of the Shadow Dragon was written in the United
Kingdom and utilises British English, such as 'colour' instead
of 'color', 'armour' instead of 'armor', 'mum' instead of 'mom'
and the suffix '-ise' instead of '-ize' etc.

THE VOW

I am a knight of the Shadow Dragon
I am its tool, its servant, its sword
My deeds are measured in a flash of the blade
I bow to neither king nor lord

I am a knight of the Shadow Dragon
I will fight until my dying breath
I know no glory and shall rest in a nameless tomb
In deference to death

I am a knight of the Shadow Dragon
I know only the eternal fight
To defy the kingdom of the worm
That place which knows no light

ADRIAN

The scream wrenched Adrian Navarro from a dream. Weak light from a bedside lantern cast stretching shadows across his small, cramped room, like dark fingers reaching out for him. Wind moaned through the tiny house, whispering Adrian's name. He pulled the cover over his head and clenched his eyes, willing himself to sleep. If he slept, then the shadows would go away. If he slept, then the monsters weren't real...

I'm not scared of the dark.

I'm not scared—

Another scream, louder this time.

Frost settled on Adrian's skin.

He eased one foot onto the cold floor, then another, heart beating hard. The bare, wooden floorboards creaked. With trembling fingers, he clutched his lantern and made his way toward the red bedroom door. The room didn't belong to him, not in the dark. When he eased the door open and stepped into the hallway, another scream tore the silence apart.

It came from his father's room.

"D... Dad?" The word sounded muted in the hallway, as if

some phantom had stolen Adrian's voice. He held his lantern up; the shadows swayed, breathed.

A thin curtain fluttered, revealing a world of darkness outside. An eclipse blinded the sun and left a circle of fire in the sky. Sol's Kiss, they called it. Adrian didn't understand what it meant.

He inched toward his father's room. Steeped in darkness, the hallway stretched on forever—but he had to be brave. He was ten, now, a child no longer.

I'm not scared of the dark...

Hugging the wall, the floor creaked with each step. Fear made his heart race, but he had to be brave—Father always said so.

Mumbling sobs gurgled from his father's room and dull red light seeped out from beneath the door.

He had to be brave.

Reaching, Adrian teased the door open. "Father?"

The next scream burst from Adrian himself.

His father was pinned against the wall, arms outstretched, chin tilted up, blood bubbling from his lips.

"Father!"

Adrian darted forward but his father tumbled through the air and hit the wall at the other side.

The lamp slipped from Adrian's fingers and shattered. Light stuttered and the room blinked in and out. His father was on the floor, then against the wall, like a child's doll being flung from side to side.

The light flared bright and his father soared to the ceiling —and stayed there.

His anguished eyes fell on Adrian. "Run!"

Adrian could only stare as his father thrashed on the ceiling, fighting against some invisible force. Garbled words tumbled from his mouth. *"Run!"*

Crack.

His father screamed as one of his legs bent outward, then

the other. His left arm twisted and snapped, fingers scraping across the ceiling. He reached out to Adrian, muttering gibberish and—

One by one, his fingers broke.

"Adrian!"

Adrian tried to move, to reach up—tried to be brave—but fear rooted him to the floor. Pain flared in his chest, stabbing, piercing. He could only watch as his father died before him, his mouth twisting in horror.

Light flickered and the shadows convulsed—slick and black, like oil. Then a face formed within.

Twisting and stretching, a black skull with empty, hollow eyes, its mouth a cavern of howling emptiness, grinning at Adrian, grinning and...

Laughing.

A shrill, piercing laughter from a thousand demented voices, unseen and everywhere.

Words choked and died in Adrian's mouth.

The sound grew louder, and louder—a sickening, buzzing giggling as the very darkness mocked him.

Screaming, his father's mouth widened—a terrible grin stretching, stretching until his jaw cracked.

Adrian cowered and covered his eyes, but his father's howls pierced him like a thousand needles in the darkness—that harsh, terrible darkness...

Nine years later

Adrian's sword painted silver swirls.

Ramiro struck fast, but too practised—too textbook; Adrian swept his blade away and spun behind him, kicked him in the back of the knee and touched the point of his sword to his back.

"And that's how you die. Again."

They practiced for another twenty minutes, their blunted blades clashing and ringing.

"Not sure I see the point of this," Ramiro groused when Adrian lifted him from the floor for a third time. He cut a dashing figure, with his blonde hair and boyish looks—the very stereotype of a gallant knight. "No-one uses swords these days."

Every soldier—whether an initiate or a veteran—voiced the same complaint. "Never know how long the ignicite crisis will last," Adrian responded. "Could be fighting the next war with sticks and stones."

"C'mon, let's get this over with." Mara strode onto the training hall's wooden floor and eased a crick in her neck. If Ramiro was the picture of a gallant knight brought to life, then Mara was the reality: Muscular, strong and keen to get her hands dirty. She wore her brown hair in a single long braid and wielded a two-handed sword as if she'd been training since she was a toddler.

Adrian readied his short sword.

Growling, she struck first—fast, savage, powerful. Adrian let her attack, dodging only when he had to; they circled the training hall, Mara lunging and swiping at Adrian like she hated him.

Maybe she did; she feinted and Adrian fell for it—she twisted and battered the flat side of the blade into his ribs. Pain exploded but dissipated just as fast.

Mara towered over him, one corner of her mouth curving sharper than any sword. "And that's how *you* die."

"Is it?"

From a pouch concealed in his sleeve, Adrian tossed a pinch of powder at Mara. It crackled in her eyes and fizzed bright blue.

Blinded, she drove her sword down—but struck nothing.

Adrian stood behind her, his sword at her neck. "Don't get cocky."

Ten minutes later, the two rookies stood before a mirror and adjusted their midnight-blue dress uniforms. Ramiro puffed his chest and raised his chin. "Really ought to get a portrait done."

Adrian had last worn his dress uniform at his own graduation ceremony. He didn't look half so prideful. But then, he hadn't joined in with the traditional parade through the taverns of Phadra the night before being knighted, either—and that very much seemed to be Mara and Ramiro's intention.

Mara turned to him, hands on her hips. When she spoke, her voice ground like churning gravel. "You cheated."

"Reckon your enemies will always follow the rules of engagement?" Adrian picked blunted weapons from the floor and set them away. "We use whatever tools we have at our disposal to achieve our objective; my objective was to beat you."

"Not talking about your sparkpowder—parlour trick." She narrowed her dark eyes at him. "I struck you hard enough to fell an ox and you didn't so much as blink."

"Got a strong constitution."

"Yeah. Not half."

"Thieves, assassins and knights who resort to low cunning." Ramiro ran a comb through his golden-blonde hair. The purple in his irises glinted. "No wonder the Order of the Shadow Dragon fell by the wayside."

"Or is that what we *want* you to think?" Adrian countered.

"You gonna sign us off or what?" Mara said.

And that's what it came down to—the formality of training with every military order to attain their knighthood. Adrian didn't care; he didn't need allies. Not for his fight.

"We're shipping out to San Sira tomorrow, Sir Adrian, as

soon as we're knighted." Ramiro slapped Mara's back. "Pride of Phadros, we'll be. Glory awaits!"

Mara grunted. "Not much glory in helping the victims of an earthquake on foreign soil."

"You don't think we should be helping?" Adrian asked.

"I'm for helping whoever needs helping—just reckon that sending in the might of the Phadrosi military might cause more trouble than it's worth."

Adrian didn't disagree; no-one knew what exactly had caused the recent earthquake in San Sira, but it was clear that King Harnan wanted to capitalise on it.

"Maybe the Mages' Guild told Harnan to do it?" Ramiro said. "I heard they've been sniffing around the palace. What's the king want with them?"

"You hear a lot of things," Mara said.

Ramiro fastened a belt with his ceremonial sabre hanging at his leg. "Still, unusual, eh?"

"Reckon the king's looking to learn a few tricks himself." Mara cracked her knuckles. "The refugees from San Sira talk of monsters."

Ramiro laughed. "The Mages' Guild have about as much magical power as I do. Anyway, he's the king; he has *us* to fight for him, no? What do you reckon, Sir Adrian? Has King Harnan lost his marbles?"

Adrian's short sword danced as he performed more drills. "If monsters caused the disaster in San Sira, then we should put 'em down. The king wants the Mages' Guild to turn him into a wizard? Then he should be put down, too."

Ramiro's smile faltered at that.

"Don't joke about that," Mara said. "Might not be us who hear you next time."

Who's joking?

Ramiro cleared his throat and slapped Adrian's back. "Got to take time off at some point, Sir Adrian. Join us!"

"No."

"The girls in the gaming dens love our uniforms! The San Siran girls *especially* love us. What's the use of being a knight if you don't take advantage of free beer and women, eh?"

"As noble as it is to swear an oath to the Crown in order to chase vulnerable women, reckon I'll give it a miss." Adrian thrust again.

Ramiro laughed. "We're knights of Phadros and they've got us on relief efforts, man! How exactly will your sword drills help the poor San Sirans?"

"Leave him." Mara dragged Ramiro to the door. "The gamblers are getting pissed and I've coin to take from 'em."

"We'll return from San Sira as heroes!" Ramiro yelled back. "Phadros shall sing of us! Who'll remember you if your blade never leaves the training hall?"

When they left, amber light pulsed through Adrian's sword.

Let the others have their fun—he had work to do.

The sun sank into the clouds, washing Phadra in copper. The song of the street thrummed—shouts, laughter, cries. Protestors filled the centre of Upper Phadra, crowding around Esperanza's Tower, the bell tower commissioned by Esperanza the Angel Queen to commemorate the hundreds of thousands killed by Phadrosi conquistadors in centuries past.

Its bell tolled and the protesters choked the road to the palace, chanting about the ignicite shortage and King Harnan's dismal attempts to house refugees displaced from San Sira. *An earthquake*, the broadsheets said. *San Sira riven in two.* Just the excuse King Harnan needed to send troops in and leave San Sira with a colossal debt to pay, right in the middle of a fuel crisis. Phadrosi kings had tried to annex the city-kingdom before, but they'd accomplished nothing beyond becoming bloody footnotes in the history books.

Now, Harnan might seize San Sira without shedding a single drop of blood.

Adrian stuck to the wider avenues where he could, keeping the sinking sun at his back. Horses trotted on roads once filled with motorcarriages. All over town, the beer and coffee houses were packed with common soldiers and knights alike. Most of them would muster out in the morning, so tonight would be their last opportunity to show off their shiny buckles and their King's Shilling, the ceremonial coin worth a hundred aerons, stamped with the soldier's name and identification number so that no two were identical. Mara and Ramiro would be among them, no doubt.

Adrian felt the weight of his own shilling in the pocket of his long, light coat. How quiet would the city be tomorrow, after the relief efforts marched south?

In the distance, the stepped pyramid of Phadra's royal palace perched on a squat, rocky hillock overlooking the city. Three months since Adrian had last set foot in it—three months since his graduation ceremony.

Three months since severing ties with Lord Lucien.

For centuries, the bodies of Phadros' dead monarchs would be taken to the top of the pyramid and a bloodletting ritual performed. Gutters would carry the monarchs' blood to the base of the pyramid and into the palace walls and the soil of its grounds. A blessing to keep Phadros pure and to retain the wisdom of its kings and queens for the monarchs who would replace them, apparently. Why they couldn't simply leave a note for the next monarch, Adrian couldn't say.

He marched towards his quarters. Per the king's recent decree, butchers passed parcels of meat to San Siran refugees as they swarmed towards the registrar's buildings. Most of the men had barely set foot in the capital before finding a King's Shilling pressed into their palms.

He cut through a throng of people and into a dark alleyway. Tenements rose up and blotted out the sun; no street lamps with candles here. Mosquitoes jostled inside Adrian's stomach. He sped up towards the alley's exit, fingers gliding over the rough walls until he reached the safety of the light. Ahead, in the sandstone tenement block across the road, he spied the anonymous entrance to the Dragons' Lair, the unofficial name for the Order of the Shadow Dragon's headquarters.

Rusty hinges squealed as Adrian pushed the old door open. He descended a dark staircase that led to a basement. Adrian unlocked a door and, once inside, lit a candle; it illuminated waltzing motes of dust and shed weak light over piles of books and useless equipment. Adrian Navarro's great inheritance—command of the Order of the Shadow Dragon and everything that came with it: Obsolete instruments, out of date texts, and the mocking disdain from every other knight in the kingdom. Even their great library of ancient and forbidden texts had been taken to rot away in some anonymous aristocrat's private collection.

No sound emanated within the Dragons' Lair. Clusters of extinguished candles littered the room. A single ignium lamp would light the entire room, but times were tough. Dragons —in the hierarchy of Phadrosi knights—were regarded with less respect than a common watchman. Fifty years ago, the Dragons were housed in the palace with the other orders, until they squeezed them out to make space for the knights they actually gave a damn about. Now the Order of the Shadow Dragon called a basement of an old tenement home. No-one believed in magic any more. No-one believed in monsters.

No-one except Adrian.

He stepped over a pile of alchemists' textbooks; he'd known they'd prove useless in revealing the secrets of magic, but that didn't stop him from stealing them from the Order of the Ivory Dove's library.

He eased himself onto a battered chair. The city grew more chaotic with each hour as more victims of the catastrophe in San Sira poured in—and so too did the rumours of monsters roaming the countryside and forests.

And for most people, that's all they were—rumours. People liked to invent fairy tales to distract themselves from reality, all the better to convince themselves that their enemy was something intangible, something they could *blame*.

But Adrian knew better. Some monsters were *real*.

And if the rumours are true, now the king's engaging the Mages' Guild.

Liars and charlatans the Mages' Guild may be, but any attempt Adrian had made at accessing their resources had been met with a wall of silence. Maybe he'd try again tomorrow, after the bulk of the military had moved south.

He lit another candle and set it into a lantern, then another, filling the Dragons' Lair with light. Adrian leaned back in the chair; he'd halfway formed a plan to climb the Mages' guildhouse walls and sneak inside when he noticed an unopened letter on his desk. It bore the seal of Defence Minister Lord Lucien.

With a stone in his stomach, Adrian peeled it open—and immediately wished he hadn't.

Night encroached and dark clouds turned the silver glare of the waxing moon into a smudge of grey. Still, the royal palace stood out like a glittering gem atop a mound of mud, illuminated by powerful ignium lamps.

In contrast, Adrian watched an elderly lamplighter scurry from street to street, climbing streetlights and igniting candles encased in lanterns. Before the fuel crisis, ignium gas hissed through the streetlights and bathed the cobbled roads in white and orange—candles offered only a hint of that.

Adrian followed him across the Bridge of Bone, a stone

bridge that cut through the centre of Phadra. Beneath it, the waters of the Rio de Sangre rustled. Returning conquistadors during the Age of Exploration would parade down the bridge with the spoils of their victory, earning the street its name.

Not much to celebrate these days.

Adrian passed the old lamplighter, his own lamp clutched tight and his eyes fixed on the palace. Ahead, voices rumbled like far-off thunder. Rounding a corner, Adrian saw the purple flag of Phadros wafting in the wind, held aloft at the head of a procession.

His stomach fell. *The Sons of Belios.*

The procession slid through the streets like sewage. Two days since the earthquake in San Sira, and the Sons' message of hate had grown harder to ignore. How could Phadros cope with thousands of refugees when the fuel crisis had rendered half of her own people starving?

Valador Ramos—the Sons' leader—wanted a seat at the council, so that the people of Phadros had a voice—or so he claimed. Rumours of back-alley deals and political promises had spread through the barracks faster than bloodlung in a brothel.

The Sons' chanting filled his ears, their hate and racism packaged into easy-to-remember rhyming couplets. Adrian recognised faces from the barracks among them; one day, the soldiers sang of putting down "half-blooded dogs" and the next, they were being sent to rescue them. It was like how the historians referred to Phadros' conquests as the Age of Exploration and not the Age of Bloody Murder—people swallowed stories of bloodshed easier when the main ingredients were chopped up to the point of being unnoticed.

Adrian struggled through the crowd; the palace wasn't far now but the main streets were choked—better to go through the alleys and—

A window smashed.

Two brawlers spilled out of a pub and into the street, crashing into the procession. Adrian slipped into the alley behind the pub, lamp clutched tight. His feet slapped the concrete, rounded a corner and—

And tripped over a boy huddled by the wall, knees drawn to his chest.

"Careful," Adrian said. The boy met his eyes; he looked skinny and weak, no older than thirteen. With his golden-brown, umber skin, Adrian figured him for San Siran.

"You okay, kid?"

The boy said nothing.

"I'm not gonna hurt you." The bruises on the boy's arms were more than a day old. "From San Sira, right?"

The kid nodded.

Adrian set his lamp onto the ground and bent low. "My name's Adrian. I'm a knight. You with anyone? You have parents, family?"

Staring at nothing, the boy shook his head.

"You're gonna be okay."

The words sounded hollow. The knightly orders were good at training soldiers how to use weapons and keep their mouths shut during torture, but less than adept at helping the people they saved.

"You have a name?"

"Nerris," the boy whimpered.

"Okay, Nerris. There are healers in the palace—come with me, they'll look at you and—"

"There's the little shit."

Adrian stood. One of the brawlers from the pub stumbled towards him. He was big, stout and wore his hair cropped short, like all rank-and-file soldiers. The stench of stale beer rolled from him.

Adrian clenched his fists.

"There's the little San Siran shit," the big soldier muttered again. "Been wondering where you got to. You got a friend now?"

"Name's Sir Adrian Navarro." The drunkard didn't look like he'd respect the chain of command, but pulling rank was worth a shot. "And I'm ordering you to piss all the way off."

The drunkard frowned. "A knight? Which order you belong to?"

"The Order of the Shadow Dragon."

He laughed. "Thought you was someone important. Kid, come out—I ain't gonna hurt you—just gonna take back what's mine."

Adrian squared up to him, pulse quickening. "You really want to do this?"

"Little shit stole a ration pack from me."

"I'll take much more if you go near him."

"He…" The thug stopped when he noticed Adrian's eyes. "Thought your kind were extinct, hey?"

"Happy to disappoint you."

"A half-breed. You're worse'n the San Sirans."

If the Sons of Belios were to be believed, a Phadrosi with two violet irises carried the blood of the Gods; any Phadrosi who didn't have purple eyes was considered impure. Worst of all were people who had one purple iris and one of a different colour—they were half-breeds, traitors and pretenders.

Adrian Navarro—in an early demonstration of the sort of luck he could expect to live the rest of his life with—was born with one purple eye and one grey.

The drunkard spat onto the ground. "Tell you what, mate —you piss off and I won't break your face."

Adrian's heart pounded with excitement. "That's one way this could go."

The thug punched but Adrian dodged. Wearing his most infuriating smirk, he said, "Gotta be quicker."

Spittle flying from his mouth, the thug's fists blurred. Adrian spun and twisted, as intangible as smoke.

The kid said something but Adrian wasn't done yet. Hands on his hips, he said, "You're what passes for a Phadrosi soldier, now?"

The thug had the scent of blood. Like a bull, he charged.

Adrian spun and sent his elbow into the back of his head.

The drunkard spun but found his footing. He lunged and shouldered Adrian into the wall.

"Know what trumps strength? Not being a cocky little shit." He punched Adrian and bright dots filled his head. Pain flared but then numbed into nothing.

The thug punched again and again; Adrian slipped the third attempt, slid through his legs and kicked the back of his knee.

Staggering, the bastard shattered Adrian's lamp and snuffed the light.

In the sudden darkness, Adrian froze. The soldier seized the chance.

He flung Adrian into a wall and rained punches. Though he felt no pain, he did taste copper.

Adrian kicked out and caught the thug in the groin—after that, he loosened his grip.

Adrian slipped away again but the thug came at him. "How in all hells are you still standing?"

Adrian ducked and swept the bastard's legs away, then punched him into the dirt, breaking his nose. The thug grunted and reached up.

Adrian kicked him. "No, really—don't get up." Heart racing in the dark, Adrian spat blood and dusted himself down.

"Sorry about that, kid—let's…"

But the boy had gone.

·   ·   ·

"You summoned me, my lord." Adrian put his hands behind his back.

"Sir Adrian." Lord Lucien's voice sounded flat. He sat behind a large, ornate desk of varnished oak, shuffling papers and signing documents. Adrian heard every sheaf of paper, every scrape of the lord's signature, and every creak in the floorboards of the lavish office.

Gods above, say what you need to say.

As if reading his mind, Lucien pulled his spectacles off. "Never had to wear these before. It's the candlelight—never had this problem with ignium lamps."

Grey peppered his black hair and beard, and the bags under his eyes told Adrian he hadn't slept. He stared at Adrian for a long moment. "It's good to see you again."

Adrian shifted from foot to foot. "My lord."

"No time for reminiscing, I'm afraid; the king is meeting with a delegation from Idaris, and he insists that I be in attendance."

"The Idari are here?"

"You must be the only soldier in Phadra unaware. Always too focused on your dusty tomes, Sir Adrian—you need to get out more. Yes, the Idari are here. King Harnan wishes to negotiate with them—he calls it trade; I call it appeasement."

A trade deal with the Idari wasn't the worst idea in the world, Adrian figured; the Idari had always shunned ignicite —who better to ask for assistance during a global fuel shortage than those who'd never relied on it in the first place?

"There are many in Imanis who still wish to wage war with Idaris," Lucien continued. "While Tarevia, Mercuria and Ryndara yell at one another across tables, the Idari emperor sharpens his knives. The pieces that make up a fractured Imanis will shatter before the might of a single, unified Idaris." Lucien glided towards his big bay window and looked down upon the city. He'd lost weight since Adrian had last seen him. "War is inevitable. Only King Harnan wishes to ally with the Idari—he's considering the global ramifications of no ignicite, while the streets of Phadra are choked with refugees from San Sira."

"You reckon he should be focused on local problems?"

Lucien pinched his nose. "I don't envy the king's position. The Sons of Belios are calling for the refugees to be turned back and half the Watch are siding with them. All the while, King Harnan sees the disaster in San Sira as an opportunity."

Lucien stood there in contemplation of his own words, unmoving like the silhouette of a tombstone.

"Do you see that statue?" Lucien asked. "Phadrosi and San Siran alike crowd around it. You must have passed it on your way in?"

"Sol and Lunos. Yeah, I passed it."

Phadros boasted many monuments to itself, countless statues of conquistadors and kings, yet none more pompous than the statue depicting the Sun God, Sol, and Lunos the Moon Goddess entwined with one another—Lunos in black marble and Sol in white. Following their union, so the story went, Lunos gave birth to Phadros. A couple of things made that difficult to swallow; one, most accounts agreed that they were brother and sister, and two, the story of the Indecim— the eleven Gods—was only two thousand years old. Phadrosi empires had risen and fallen a hundred times before the advent of the Gods.

"Like you," Lucien started, "most people believe it depicts Sol and Lunos in an embrace. And like you, they are wrong."

Adrian wanted to ask why he'd been summoned for a debate on statues, but he swallowed the words. Instead, he said, "My lord?"

"Phadros is an old country. Ancient. We conquered the world bit by bit, found favour with the gods that time forgets."

"Niamat and Zirun. The Old Gods." Every kid in Phadros

knew the story of how Niamat—Goddess of Darkness—and Zirun—God of Light—both favoured Phadros over every other kingdom, and how that made Phadrosi special. Adrian figured every country in the world had a similar legend to explain why life existed before the Indecim. "Weren't they brother and sister, too?"

"Niamat and Zirun," Lucien repeated. "Lunos and Sol. Shadow and light. Phadros rose to power again during the Age of Exploration. History repeats itself over and over. We'll never uncover all of history's secrets, but myths often possess a kernel of truth. And that means they can be moulded to fit whatever narrative suits. People like something to believe in—it gives them strength... And makes them blind. There's a lesson in that, I think."

"If this is you trying to get me to leave my order—"

"No." Lucien turned, and his face grew sterner. "Harnan sees the destruction of San Sira as a gateway to the old Phadros; I fear he allies himself with the Idari to achieve that."

"Isn't he sending relief to San Sira?"

"Oh, yes—the might of our military. Don't believe everything the broadsheets tell you, Adrian; it wasn't an earthquake that tore San Sira apart."

Adrian frowned. "Don't tell me it was *us?*"

"What I'm about to confide in you must remain secret—that is the purview of the Order of the Shadow Dragon, yes? Secrets and subterfuge?"

"When we're not doing very important work like training recruits on how to use weapons they'll never use, yes."

"The world may have evolved, but some things come back to haunt us. Tell me—what did Amos teach you about magic?"

"That it's evil." Adrian raised his chin. "That's all I need to know."

The bare hint of a smile played on the lord's lips. "We are

of a like mind. Yes, magic is a corrupting force—a blight long thought extinguished from the world. But our complacency has betrayed us." Lucien held Adrian's gaze, as if weighing his words. "Magic bleeds into the world once more. Wielders—those skilled in its use—are sprouting like weeds all over Phadros, sowing chaos and discord. They must be stopped."

Ice expanded in Adrian's chest.

A face formed in the shadows... A black skull with empty, hollow eyes... Twisting and stretching, grinning...

"What?" he managed. "How?"

"No-one knows for certain. So far, we've managed to keep it quiet—but San Sira's cataclysm has forced our hand."

Adrian's heart pounded. "*Magic* destroyed San Sira?"

"Every San Siran survivor has a conflicting account and there has been no word from their archduke. King Harnan wishes to keep the cause of the devastation quiet, but rumours are spreading. Whoever these Wielders are, they command great power. Some may have slipped into Phadra under the guise of refugees already."

Adrian flexed his fingers. How many books had he obsessed over, scouring each page for a hint of evidence that magic existed? Maybe now he could get the Shadow Dragon's confiscated materials back—and finally put his training to good use.

"This explains why he's consulting with the Mages' Guild."

For once, Lucien looked surprised. "How did you know that?"

Adrian permitted himself a smile. "Didn't 'til now."

Lucien shook his head. "I was never the best at poker."

"I'll root the Wielders out of the city," Adrian proclaimed. "I'll find 'em."

"Oh, I have something more important in mind for you. Adrian… The king grows isolated and paranoid. I no longer have a seat at his table and he plans to replace me as Defence

Minister. This, and seeking the counsel of the Mages at the same time as a mystical strike on our most bitter rival is too much of a coincidence for me to ignore."

"What are you saying? That the king sent Wielders to destroy San Sira?"

The creases in Lucien's face deepened. "The truth is, I don't know what to think. Our intelligence is... Spotty. But numerous accounts agree on one thing: Just before the earthquake, a woman murdered a dozen men with some form of scorching light. Burned them in an instant. They call her the White Death. Her whereabouts are currently unknown—Adrian, she *must* not reach Phadra."

"How do you know she's not here already?"

"I don't, but the Confessors are interrogating every San Siran who has crossed the border. They'll divine truth from deceit."

Adrian arched an eyebrow. "They have my sympathies."

"If King Harnan is truly responsible for this, then I need to know. Rivalry or no, war with our closest neighbour would be catastrophic." Lucien placed a hand on Adrian's shoulder. "You are young and untested—it grieves me to say so, but as Commander of the Order of the Shadow Dragon, this crisis falls squarely on your shoulders. It's a heavy burden and not one to be taken—"

"I'll leave now."

Lucien laughed. "Your enthusiasm is admirable, but what have I told you before?"

Like a child before an angry schoolmaster, Adrian's stomach knotted. "Think before I speak."

"A whisper in an ear is more effective than barking at a crowd. Between recovery operations, the ignicite shortage, and Idaris posturing for war, our military resources are spread thin. Gods, we're enlisting men in their eighties to teach schoolboys how to sail first-generation airships. We're desperate and we're running out of allies."

"I don't need an army."

"Fortunate, since you don't have one. I'm stalling Harnan's plans, but it won't delay things forever—he has the scent of blood and won't be deterred."

"I'll need supplies, transport, writs of passage—a covert operation without the king's consent is illegal."

"But necessary. I can provide you with a letter confirming that you're on state business, but the details will be scant. I have no available transport—I can't put you with the Doves or Lynxes without fear of the king finding out. You'll need to find your own way into San Sira, Adrian. In short, you're on your own."

"Suits me."

"Go to San Sira—investigate these rumours. End this war before it begins."

His heart pounded harder and harder. "And if I find the White Death?"

"The Order of the Shadow Dragon is charged to neutralise the threat of magic—I expect you to do your duty."

Chin raised, Adrian said, "I will, my lord. For the Crown."

For my father.

For vengeance.

DANTE

"I'm hearing the name… Alejandro." Dante opened one eye; no reaction. "No, not Alejandro… Alex… Alan… Al—"

"Alberto?" the old woman at the other side of the small table offered.

"Yes! Alberto." Dante swept a hand through his mop of black hair. The soft candlelight made his bare room seem even smaller. "He was your hus—"

"Brother?"

"—brother, yes!"

"Where is he?" A note of panic rang in the crone's voice. "Is he in pain? Alberto, can you hear me?"

"Yes, yes, he can hear you. He says to tell you… that…" Dante's eyes fluttered and his body stiffened.

"Dante?" the woman said.

Dante let out a long sigh and said, "Not at the moment."

The woman gasped. "Al… Alberto? Is it you?"

"Yes," Dante whispered. "It's me, dear sister… I have returned."

Tears glinted in the woman's violet eyes. "Oh, Alberto… I've missed you. Tell me, are you in pain? How did… How did you go?"

Dante's heart spiked. "It... doesn't matter. All that matters is that I am safe. And content."

A smile smeared over the woman's face. "Is Celina with you?"

"Yes, she is... But not right now."

"Alberto... Answer me honestly. Why did you take it?"

Dante froze. When he spoke, he kept his voice leaden and the words clipped. "Because. I had to."

The woman wiped a tear. "I understand."

"I must go. Now. But know that I am safe. And happy. And not in pain."

The woman sobbed, though light filled her face. "Good-bye, Alberto."

Dante blinked and released a slow breath. He leaned close to the woman and placed a hand on her cheek. These were the moments he lived for—the comfort in the customers' eyes, the smiles, the appreciation. And people tipped better when they were happy. "Don't you feel better?"

The woman sniffed. "I do. Thank you, Dante tal Arata. Thank you. You're a lovely boy, and two purple eyes, too. Blessed by the Gods, you are. You've earned your forty aerons—see that you spend it on something to eat, put some muscle on those bones."

"I appreciate that."

The old man next to her crossed his arms and said, "My sister might be easy to fool, but not me—Alberto didn't show an ounce of remorse in his life. Let's get this over with."

"Patience, old man." Dante's words brushed as soft as a feather.

"Old? As long as you're alive, you're young," the man countered. "But that don't mean I have time to waste. Get on with it so I can go."

Dante shifted on his hard, wooden chair. He'd use the old man's coin to buy a cushion. "Let me concentrate—I can only step into the spirit world if I'm invited."

"Then knock on the door."

Dante bit his tongue. He'd been a child prodigy, the toast of every stage from here to Ryndara—who was this old man, rushing him? *Nobody.* Had he seen Dante play Sir Cristo the Boy-King in *He Who Sewed Stars Upon the Fabric of Night*, he'd have more patience. Gods, he wielded that prop sword like a conductor with a baton! A decade had passed since then, but Dante knew that the performance lingered in the minds of the audience.

It had to.

The old man offered a theatrical cough.

Dante flinched. "Sorry. I'm channelling my powers." He wished he had a sword right now. "It's the upcoming eclipse, you see; the walls between our world and the spirit plane are thinner, makes it harder to divine with whom I converse."

Bullshit, of course, but it sounded plausible enough. Sol's Kiss, as the eclipse was known, occurred every nine years. Phadra hosted carnivals and celebrations, and the travellers it brought always lined the pockets of men like Dante tal Arata.

Though some customers were more discerning than others.

Dante pressed his thin fingers onto the table and peered through the crystal prism before him. The old man warped and contorted through it. "I'm seeing a girl... No, a woman..."

The old man crossed his arms, face blank but for his furrowed brow.

"She is saying... 'Don't be disappointed—have faith.'"

"She obviously never paid forty aerons to see you."

A pearl of sweat rolled down the back of Dante's neck. His fingers danced over the prism as though manipulating a puppet. He closed his eyes and sang one of the many prayers in the Book of Musa—they were always the most musical, and that suited his soprano voice.

"The spirits like music," he explained. "It soothes them."

"I find whisky better for that—and for forty aerons, I can buy a decent Glenfortoshan."

Dante slapped the table. "Georgio!"

That startled the woman, but not the old man.

"Young man," he started, "I gave you my name when I came in."

"*Georgio*," Dante whispered. "It's me. Your. Mother. I've been watching you, Georgio. I've seen your secrets."

That silenced the old man.

Dante leaned forward and kept it up. "And I must say. I am sorely. Disappointed. I cannot fathom—"

"Funny how every spirit sounds the same."

Words caught in Dante's mouth. "What?"

"Every spirit who speaks through you talks with the same stop-start voice."

"I… It's not… It's complicated, Georgio—I can only—"

Georgio's chair scraped back and he stood. "We've wasted enough time and money, let's go."

The old woman stood with a hunched posture, refusing to meet Dante's eye.

Dante reached out. "No, wait, I, I—"

"You're a fraud," Georgio snapped. "And worse, *not a very good one!*"

The old man slammed the door behind them. Dante swept the prism onto the floor and shattered it, then flopped into his chair. Natural disasters and uncertain times were supposed to be *good* for business!

Mrs. Herrera burst into the room. "Keep the noise down!"

Ancient and withered, it never ceased to amaze Dante how someone so small could barge into a room with the force of a hurricane.

"And remember your rent," she snapped. "It was due two weeks ago!"

"Oh, shove it, Mrs. Herrera!"

"No, no, none of that talk or I'll have you out, *out!*"

"Chuck me out, see if I care, you old bat!"

"Ungrateful swine, after all I've done for you! I ought to call the Watch and have them throw you into jail for the lies you peddle."

Dante shot to his feet. He towered over the old woman, though that didn't mean much to her.

He clenched his eyes shut. "I'm getting a message... From the other side. Your husband! He's burning, Mrs. Herrera. Oh, how he burns!"

She gasped and turned, muttering something and swearing to throw Dante out in the morning.

"You should hear his screams!" Dante followed her into the hallway. "Nyr herself has him! Oh my, but he's been a very naughty boy!"

Mrs. Herrera stomped upstairs. "One of these days, you will get what you are owed, Dante tal Arata!"

He cupped his hands to his mouth and yelled, "Well it's about bloody time!"

"*Rent!*"

Old bat. If it wasn't for Dante, she'd have no-one. *Who else would pay to stay in this rat-hole?*

He closed his eyes and massaged his temples. "Keep calm, keep calm. Better than being on the streets."

"At least then we only had to answer to ourselves."

Low and heavy, the voice sounded familiar—*very* familiar.

"Could it be the dead really do commune with me?" Dante opened his eyes, and sure enough, Adrian Navarro stood before him. "Or is the ignicite-infused absinthe finally catching up to me?"

"Hello, Dante." Adrian wore a long, hooded black cloak, and a sword hung at his side. He looked like a kid playing an olden-time knight.

Dante crossed his arms. "The military kick you out?"

"They've given me a mission."

"Hardly surprising—the whole city's buzzing around like bees in a hive. Why are you here?"

"Can I come in? I'd like to sit."

Dante wanted to sit, too, but he'd be damned if he was going to let Adrian Navarro into his home.

"You can stay in the hallway."

"Need your help, Dante."

Now Dante wished he was sitting down. "*My* help? What do royal knights need with a psychic?"

"Ain't the Crown that's asking—it's me."

"You must be desperate."

"I'm headed to San Sira. Off the books."

Dante frowned. "What does that mean?"

"Means I'm travelling alone. In secret. Means sneaking aboard an airship and risking the Lynxes throwing my ass overboard, or finding another way—and you know every thief and smuggler in the city."

Dante crossed his arms. "No, I don't."

"Who's the best, these days?"

"Piss off, Adrian."

"Every aerial vessel's been requisitioned. Not enough igneus to fuel 'em anyway. The roads are choked—but the port's wide open. Who do I talk to?"

"Keep quiet!" Herrera barked from the top of the stairwell.

"Bat," Dante shifted his weight from foot to foot. "Two hundred aerons. No, *three* hundred."

For a moment, Adrian said nothing. "Deal. When I'm back."

"Now."

"*When I'm back.*"

Dante put his hands on his hips and stood straighter. "*I've* got the upper hand here, Adrian."

The young knight cocked his head and peered into Dante's apartment. "Doesn't look like it."

Dante put a hand onto the door frame to block Adrian's view. "Half, then."

"No."

"A quarter?"

"I'll square you up when I'm back, then you'll never have to see me again—or I'll get my information from someone else. Someone *cheaper*. Up to you."

Dante scratched the back of his head. "Fine. You want Pedro—captains the *Solnadar*. Crown has him ferrying San Sirans too sick to walk, but he has a storied history of smuggling all sorts of wonderful goods. He sails the Phadril Sea but sticks close to the Bronze Coast. Does the trip a couple of times a week—leaves at noon, takes all night."

"I appreciate it." Adrian offered a curt nod before leaving.

Dante cupped his hands around his mouth and yelled, "Money!"

Pain thumped in his head and harsh light flowed into his eyes.

"Hmm? What?"

Mrs. Herrera called something.

Groggy, and eyes sticky with sleep, Dante swung out of bed, toppled, and fell straight back onto it. Bottles clattered on the floor.

Damn, but he'd made a valiant effort to drown his sorrows last night. Seeing Adrian again, the reminder of what the little bastard had done...

Three bangs struck his door, *thud, thud, thud.*

Who comes to a man's door at the ungodly hour of...

Dante glanced at his pocket watch.

Eleven forty-five in the morning?

"I'm asleep!"

"It's the City Watch, open up!"

"I'm busy."

Thud.

"I'll ask you once more—this is the City Watch!"

"Do what you want, see if I… Wait, *what?*"

The door convulsed and Dante sprang up.

She did it.

She really did it!

Dante staggered, bottles rolling under his feet, arms flailing wild. "Um, just a minute!"

"You're *out!*" Herrera screeched. "No underhand deals in my property. Out!"

"Open up, by order of the Phadra City Watch!"

Damn.

Shit.

Damn and shit.

"Uh, uh, yes, just a moment!"

If the Watch turned his room over and saw his wares, he'd never see the outside of a cell again.

But where could he go? Who would take a man like Dante tal Arata in?

"Gods damn it."

He yanked clothes from the floor and stuffed them into a case. the door thumping all the while.

"Be with you in two seconds!"

Shirt, trousers, make-up, lens case...

He stuffed them and more into a tattered rucksack. With great effort, he yanked the window up in its frame, hooked one leg out and—

His bedside drawer.

Dante swept beads, necklaces, and various religious charms out of the way and clawed at the false bottom.

Beneath, lying flat, were half a dozen King's Shillings. He scooped them up and bundled them into his case.

The door splintered.

"Blasted door, caught in its frame!" Dante called. "Give me a moment and I'll get it!"

He stumbled back to the window, peeked out; it wasn't a big drop, and if—

He vomited onto the pavement.

Then the door crashed open.

Damn.

Two burly watchmen barrelled towards him. Dante half-jumped, half-fell through the window and hit the pavement. He bolted and tumbled through a knot of San Sirans huddled on a street corner.

"After him!" a watchman yelled.

Phadra flew past.

Acid lurched into Dante's throat and his stomach threatened to empty whatever else was still sloshing around inside.

"Stop!" the watchmen called.

They were gaining—but no-one knew Lower Phadra like Dante, the slums, the shortcuts. He ducked into an alley, and then another, traipsing over drunk soldiers and Gods-knew-what else.

He barrelled further down, through twisting streets, the screech of Watch whistles growing louder.

There—sails in the distance.

Go, go, go, go...

Sweat poured from him and his body odour left a lot to be desired, but still Dante pushed himself towards the harbour, the coppery flare of the sun in his eyes.

Go, go, go, go...

Esperanza's bell tolled.

Noon.

No, no, no, no...

People crowded the harbour, busier than Dante had ever seen it before. Families cried their farewells, maidens wept and children tugged at their parents' clothes.

Lungs burning, Dante stopped and scanned the horizon.

There!

Relief turned his muscles to jelly. Dante squeezed through the crowd, towards the *Solnadar*—towards Adrian.

"Wait! Wait for me! Adrian—!"

A paw gripped his shoulder and brought Dante to the ground.

"Dante tal Arata," a purple-eyed watchman recited, "you're under arrest for being a debtor and a con-man—and once we've scoured your apartment, likely one or two other things."

"Gods, your breath is worse than mine."

The watchman raised a fist—

"Let him go."

A silhouette filled Dante's eyes.

The watchman stood. "This man is under arrest, boy, by order of the Phadra City Watch."

"This man is in my custody," said Adrian, "by order of me, Sir Adrian Navarro, Commander of the Order of the Shadow Dragon."

"Thank Aerulus," Dante muttered. "Or whichever deity just saved my ass."

"Order of the Shadow Dragon?" The copper stifled a laugh. "That lot still around?"

Adrian handed a piece of paper to the watchman. "Ask Lord Lucien."

Grumbling, the officer scanned it. "Son of a..." He glared down at Dante. "We have our eye on you."

Adrian extended a hand and pulled Dante up.

"Thank you—you saved my peachy bum."

"Not from light bruising, I reckon."

Dante wanted to laugh, the way they always had, but he stopped himself. "You can drop me off somewhere nice." Clutching his suitcase, Dante followed Adrian onto the boat. "Can I get a sword?"

CASSANDRA

The pleasant, scouring scent of the sea wafted through the narrow window and cleansed the back of Sergeant Cassandra Diaz's throat. Months of reduced ignium usage had let nature gain a foothold in the city; a murky, bronze cloud still hung over the harbour, but it receded more each day and let the sun in.

Cassandra fixed her sword belt, pulled a long, light coat on, and slipped her Watch badge into her pocket. By rights, she should leave the brass emblem in the back of a drawer, but it brought her comfort—and these were uncertain times.

Almost noon.

She tied her russet-brown ringlets into a ponytail, arranged her notebooks into a neat pile on her plain desk, then slung a small rucksack around her shoulder. She took a final glance at the collection of novels bursting from her bookcase; her fingers ran across the spines and temptation tugged at her, but she pulled away.

Back straight and chin raised—like any good copper— she glided down the warren of staircases that connected the lower part of the city. During her training, she'd run from the harbour to Upper Phadra; it'd take over an hour. These days, she did it in forty-five minutes, breaking every record in her Watch house. Not that anyone cared about the achievements of a half-San Siran woman, of course, but she didn't do it for them; working twice as hard for only half the recognition fuelled the fire in her, a fire that she needed.

Lower Phadra sprawled open beneath her, dozens of thin tenements and boxy buildings pressed together. The lower part of the city skirted the edge of a crescent beach, and—separated by a defensive wall—the upper city flourished. Across the bay, golden domes and spires glinted with sunlight, turning the city into a glimmering sea of gold. Phadra, the Golden City, the jewel in Phadros' crown—built by the bloodstained treasure of Phadrosi conquistadors. As a girl, how many hours had she spent staring up at the stepped pyramid palace, looking up at the Watch flag fluttering before it? That was the innate genius of housing the Watch headquarters in the palace—it meant the Arch Vigil—commander of the City Watch—looked over everyone. It meant that no-one could hide from the gaze of justice. Her heart swelled with pride each time she pinned her badge to her chest. Even now, tucked away in her pocket, it still lent her a sense of purpose.

Towering over Upper Phadra, Queen Esperanza's bell tower gleamed in the sun, its belfry painted in pristine white with golden edges. *If only she was still alive.* Queen Esperanza, the Angel Queen, had been Phadros' first monarch to publicly apologise for the atrocities committed against the kingdom's San Siran neighbours. The names of thousands of murdered San Sirans were inscribed in the bell tower's bricks. *In every brick—and it's two hundred feet high.*

The sun glared at her and followed her down the stone steps, and kept glaring at her. Unease tugged at her.

But she had a mission to do.

Her fingers brushed her coat, feeling the brass badge

inside. It wasn't right, concealing who you were, but she had a duty to her home—*and* San Sira.

She passed through a gatehouse, through Upper Phadra's defensive wall, then squeezed through a narrow alley choked by a cart with a broken wheel, where the sounds and smells of the lower city assailed her senses. Men whistled at her and shouted but she paid them no mind; how differently the citizens of Phadra regarded her when they couldn't see her Watch badge.

The sun watched her with every step through Lower Phadra, like the judging eye of Aerulus God-King himself. San Siran refugees filled the streets and alleys, begging, pleading. Cass wanted to reach out, to explain that she was one of them, that they had a voice in the Watch...

But that wasn't the mission.

Some coppers delighted in concealing their badge, treating it like a token in a game to be brought out and taken away at will. They were the kind who relished entrapping a suspect, bullying them into some minor infraction just to arrest them; the Arch Vigil insisted such tactics were a means to an end, that they had quotas to keep—but for too many watchmen, it was *fun*. It was about power, and ego. Half the Watch was made up of little boys brandishing their shiny badges when it suited them—little boys who were too dumb —or too smart—to enlist in the army.

Not Cassandra.

Ahead, bobbing between two larger vessels, she spotted the *Solnadar*. Her captain was a smuggler, taking advantage of the Cataclysm; it galled Cass to let his crimes pass.

Yes, the badge weighed almost nothing, but the responsibility it bore weighed as heavy as a millstone—and hiding the badge meant hiding from that.

The cargo hold had been fashioned into makeshift passenger

quarters. The room smelled stuffy and damp, but sweet as well; empty barrels carried the crest of the Phadrosi royal vineyard. Sergeant Diaz never drank wine—just one of the many things that isolated her from her comrades. Bedrolls lay crowded together on the floor and hammocks hung between wooden pillars. All used, all filthy.

She unhooked her sword belt. Watch blades were thin and light—long obsolete, but she liked having it around. It reminded her of fencing lessons with her grandfather, where they'd dance upon a sun-kissed lawn, darting between lemon trees, swords clashing.

From atop the stairs, Captain Pedro yelled, "Leaving in five!" A broad man with a craggy face and a permanent scowl, he didn't seem pleased with her presence. The Watch had that effect on the guilty.

Cassie's first partner—a skinny, silver-haired tyrant named Inspector Mila—had always said, "You trap flies with honey, not vinegar". She'd taught the young Cass how to stay awake during stakeouts, how to follow a target unseen—and how to leverage knowledge against someone. Mila had lost all her money gambling with cut-throats in the Beaming Bull tavern, but she'd also garnered a lot of intelligence. Cassie had considered such tactics to be dirty, to go against what the brass badge of the Watch stood for—but a speck of dirt was an easy thing to ignore if everything else remained unblemished.

And Captain Pedro had racked up a considerable debt to Inspector Mila over the years; and this morning—when he'd brought her into the Beaming Bull before its doors had even opened—he'd hoped that his whispers of a knight sneaking into San Sira on some illegal operation would clear the debt. Cassie had never leapt Phadra's stone steps so quickly on her way to the palace...

The stairs into the hold creaked and a young man wearing a thin, plain black shirt, trousers and boots glided down. Around his back hung a hooded cloak, the kind that was fashionable a hundred years ago. A sword hung at his side, not much better than her own, judging by its plain hilt. Curious; most knights took every opportunity to display their insignia and prance around like peacocks. And while the Watch still carried swords these days, the knights only used theirs for ceremonial purposes.

"Hello." Cass held out a hand.

He offered a curt nod and walked past her. He had one purple eye and one grey; she put him at nineteen or twenty, just a couple of years younger than herself.

She dropped her hand and cleared her throat. "I'm Cassandra Diaz, sergeant in the City Watch."

"Adrian." He busied himself by organising his gear.

"Not many Phadrosi going *into* San Sira, eh?" She nodded to his sword. "Are you with the military?"

"No."

"The Watch doesn't know I'm going—I've family in San Sira that I haven't heard from. Going for my own peace of mind, more than anything."

"You're San Siran?"

"On my mother's side." For once, Cass appreciated the question; most Phadrosi saw her dark skin and simply assumed she was from San Sira. "Not every San Siran is grateful for Phadrosi assistance; I'm hoping I can loosen lips, get some more information."

Adrian grunted.

"Is that why you're going? To find out what's really happening?"

"Something like that."

Gods, trying to make conversation with this man was like asking a drunkard to burp Aurien tal Varaldo's 8th Symphony.

"Not the nicest accommodations," she started, "but plenty of space for the two of us."

A lyrical voice floated down the steps, belonging to a wiry, rake-thin man.

There was only supposed to be one. "A friend of yours, Adrian?"

"Certainly not!" the new man said. Unkempt, sweat-matted black curls crowned his head, and the clothes he wore might have been considered fashionable a decade ago. "Sir Adrian has no friends, madam." With a twirl of a hand, he bowed. "Dante tal Arata, at your service."

Cassandra frowned. "Are you drunk?"

"Only half as much as I plan to be."

"I see. And *Sir* Adrian? You *are* a knight."

Adrian eyed her, though without expression.

"Pedro didn't say anything else about a third passenger," Dante said. "We'll appreciate the company."

"I suspect Captain Pedro keeps a lot of details to himself."

"Oh, yes." Dante's violet eyes sparkled. "That's why I like him."

The ship shuddered and creaked, and they set off.

They sat in separate spaces in the hold. The journey would take hours—until dawn the following morning—but neither man seemed keen on talking. They knew each other, it seemed.

Hours passed without another word—night would soon settle over Phadros. Gods, but sea travel was slow. It was even more boring than being on duty aboard a Watch airship, where the other officers shunned her. Still, there was a certain freedom, a certain *wonder*, to being a warden of the skies.

"There's more music to these machines than any instrument, girl—all you need to do is listen..." Her grandfather Luís had said that a hundred times or more as he showed off his various contraptions. Most were broken and rusted, but he

made them shine. He loved machines more than foil and sabre.

Especially his Bride's Code transmitter.

The brass plates and fittings of his old bricode machine always gleamed; Cassie loved it, too. Boats and airships would talk to each other through bricode machines, in simple codes of dots and dashes. As a child, she imagined herself as a co-pilot, looking at maps and charts and communicating with rhythmic whirs and bleeps, tap-tap-tapping and transmitting messages.

"Used ignium lamps for Bride's Code before the machines came along," Grandpa Luís would tell her. "Or they'd lash a man to the deck and give him flags to communicate with!"

Little Cassie never asked if that last claim was true, and she refused to look it up even now; it'd ruin the magic. That's where ignicite-derived technology and human ingenuity worked in harmony, to open up communication, to bridge gaps, to bring people together.

Now, Phadrosi eyed San Sirans with suspicion. The world seemed more divided than ever.

Cassandra sat beneath a lit lantern, enjoying the sway of the vessel, where she could just as easily be sailing across the clouds. Dante slept in a hammock, snoring like a content baby, mumbling in his sleep. Sir Adrian, on the other hand, lay on the floor between two lit lanterns. *Is he asleep or awake?*

In a swift, deft movement, she slipped a hand into her coat pocket. She'd been looking forward to stealing a moment to indulge in her guilty pleasure ever since setting off…

She pulled out her battered copy of *Captain Crimsonwing and the Mad Baron's Mechanical Menace*. She'd read it a dozen times, of course, along with all the other *Crimsonwing* books, but this was her favourite. As a child, she'd relished escaping into the captain's adventures, loved how he overcame every obstacle and defeated Baron Midnight at the end.

Her sister Mariana had hated Cassie for that—for having something that she loved. Every year on Wintercast morning, Cassandra would tear her gifts open with glee. And every year, she was happier with her new Crimsonwing book than Mariana was with whatever piece of expensive jewellery she'd begged of their parents.

One summer, after a Watch cadets camping trip, Cassie had returned home to find every page of her entire *Crimsonwing* collection torn out and spread over her bedroom floor. "It's time to grow up," Mariana had said with a cruel smile. "They're stupid books and they're all exactly the same."

Cassie was despondent for weeks, even if the criticism rang true; who cared if stories followed the same beats and formula? There was something to be said for a tale that felt at once familiar and fresh.

She'd spent hundreds of aerons over the years reforming her collection, even buying multiple copies and different editions. Her original copy of *Captain Crimsonwing and the Mad Baron's Mechanical Menace* was the book she'd taken to camp that year, and the only one that had survived her sister's wrath. Even now, reading it was an act of rebellion.

"Can't sleep?" Dante asked, just as Cassie reached the part where Crimsonwing used a dagger to slide down the sail of a pirate ship.

She snapped the book shut. "Just killing time."

"Don't let me interrupt you."

"No, it's fine," she said through pursed lips.

Dante sat upright. "You're not enjoying it?"

Cassie cleared her throat. "No, I am. It's... a guilty pleasure."

"No pleasure should ever leave you feeling guilty—especially books."

"Everyone loves Captain Crimsonwing," Sir Adrian chimed in.

"Thought you were asleep," said Cassandra.

He didn't respond.

She cleared her throat. "I hope your sword is enough protection, Sir Adrian; I heard there were bandits roaming the countryside, stealing from the refugees coming north. The going rate for passage on a boat is five hundred aerons—greedy captains gouging the needy."

"Bastards." Dante shook his head in disgust. "Clever bastards."

Adrian crossed his arms. "I'll be fine, Sergeant."

Cassandra wasn't convinced; she'd done basic sword drills, but she'd never used a gun before; with the military's obsession with repeater rifles and weapons of mass destruction, it was plain to anyone that the world was in an age of mechanised warfare, especially after Idaris' failed attempt to invade Dalthea. The ignicite crisis had slowed all that, and Cass hoped it'd stay that way—put a gun in someone's hands and they'd find a reason to use it.

That said, two swords between three people seemed less than efficient.

"My superiors don't know I'm travelling to San Sira," Cass started. "At least, they don't know why."

"You said you're looking for your family?" Adrian said.

Cassie avoided his eye. "I, I am, but the Watch is aware of… rumours. Of strange phenomena. But they're ignoring them."

Navarro sat up and met her eyes. "What kind of phenomena?"

She glanced between the two men. "Magic. *Dangerous* magic. My bosses dismissed the stories but I want to investigate. I want to help."

"What, specifically, have you heard?"

"I heard that a woman made of fire scorched San Sira. You probably think I'm mad."

"I don't."

"No? Is… Is that why you're here?"

The knight took a while to respond. "Looks like we want the same thing, Sergeant."

Dante clapped. "Glad to see we're making friends."

"We're still outnumbered," Sir Adrian said. "I can't protect you both if we run into Wielders."

"Sir Adrian," Cass began, "I'm perfectly capable of looking after myself."

"Well, three is better than two," Dante said. "Means you two can do all the fighting while I run and hide. That'd make a change, eh, Adrian?"

Again, Adrian didn't respond. Cass made a mental note of that.

Dante opened one of his bags and shovelled salted almonds into his mouth. "You'd never think we were close as brothers once, would you, Sergeant? Becoming a knight changed him."

Cass had heard the rumours—heard how the various orders of knights made cruel men of their recruits, as though that made for better servants. The Watch houses were rife with stories of initiates forced to undergo merciless induction rituals, like beating the weaker members and imbibing strange potions—all designed to purge the humanity from them. Even knights of the Order of the Ivory Dove—Phadros' order dedicated to the Gods—were always stoic and churlish. Cassandra was no stranger to the folly of trusting too much, but to stifle one's emotions?

The Shadow Dragon knights of old were renowned for stepping out of darkness and killing a target unseen. Some said they got their powers by sacrificing a loved one to Nyr, God of Death; others said they themselves were dead. The Crown didn't keep records of Shadow Dragon operations, so no-one knew what was real and what was false. And why were Wielders automatically evil and knights always pure and gallant?

That's why she preferred having the rule of law—it

offered clarity. Things were black and white. Morality didn't come into it; you were either right or wrong. It was easier to sleep at night knowing that no matter what happened, she had the law to protect her.

Cassie turned her back on them both. They made for an odd crew; a San Siran watchwoman that no-one liked, a rookie knight, and… Whatever the hell Dante was.

Her fingers brushed over her Watch badge. It wasn't right, lying. It wasn't honest. But in uncertain times, one had to work towards the greater good.

As the ship bounced on the waves and sleep refused to come, Lucien's orders played on her mind.

"Thank you for coming to me, Sergeant Diaz. The king grows desperate and when he goes, I'll see that his sycophants follow. A new age dawns and we can no longer cling to the past; the Arch Vigil has allowed corruption to fester within the Watch for too long.

"The Order of the Shadow Dragon is the same; it attracts thieves and liars and has sown the seeds of the Crown's darkest ambitions for centuries—it is a relic of the past and must remain there. Sergeant Diaz, when the White Death has been neutralised, arrest Sir Adrian Navarro—and I will ensure the Watch flourishes under your leadership."

ADRIAN

Three months ago

The stench of cheap rum and sweat rolled out of Commander Amos' pores. He lay beneath a ragged blanket, like a felled oak tree covered in moss. A mess of curls crowned his head, more grey than black these days. When Adrian had first met him, his arms and legs were thick with muscle. Now…

"Why waste your time here, boy? I've given you all the Order's secrets. Today's your pledging, aye?"

"Yeah. Lord Lucien's got me a comfortable position with the Order of the Golden Griffin."

The old man laughed, cold and bitter. "Soldiers of fortune, loyal only to money."

"A good living, though."

"But not a good death, giving up your life to save some nobleman's shipment of silk." Amos wheezed. "The night before my pledging, I drank until the sun came up and cavorted with any woman who'd have me. Near missed the damn ceremony. You should be out with the rest of the young'uns."

"Not interested."

"Too single-minded, that's your trouble. You ever hear the phrase, 'as long as you're alive, you're young'? Well, I reckon you could stand to act your age a little."

"Lucien says the order will be disbanded."

Amos coughed into a rag, leaving a pale, pink stain. "I have to die before that can happen."

Adrian glanced to the corner of the room, to the walls of books and other trinkets. "What will happen to this place if they close us down?"

"The bloody Mages' Guild will take it, like they have with everything else. Listen to me, lad; no-one can know what's behind our walls. No-one can know what's in our vault."

"Then I'll pledge to our order."

"No, you bloody won't. You do that, they'll lock you here forever. Everything I've taught you, all your gifts... All of it will go to waste. The Order of the Shadow Dragon takes our enemies' strengths and uses it against 'em. We work in secret —don't matter what uniform you wear or which order's badge is pinned on your chest. No, don't put a target on your back—pledge to the Griffins but keep everything you've learned, keep the weapons hidden and—"

A hacking cough cut the rest of the sentence off.

Adrian poured water into a glass and handed it to his commander. "Does it bother you?"

Amos sipped. "Having you make a fuss over me? Take a guess."

"Imanis is gearing up for war against Idaris, boss—you're First Sword of the Order of the Shadow Dragon and you're stuck here. We should be out there."

"No—the Order of the Shadow Dragon has a job to do, boy, and Amos says that's sacred. The Order of the Amethyst Lynx fights our wars abroad and the Order of the Ivory Dove shields the Fayth; *we* are sworn to defend against darkness and magic and… monsters." The old man's breathing grew more laboured with each word. "The minute we… blur those lines, Amos reckons, we make ourselves weak."

Adrian had no desire to go off and fight the Idari, either—but a disused sword was prone to rust. "Commander, let me help—"

Amos held a finger up. "You're the only initiate who stuck it out, boy. The only one. The rest come in here, treat me like a joke, and I sign their writs all the same. But you…"

Amos convulsed in a coughing fit, red-brown blood soaking his rag.

"Gods above, let me do something."

He batted Adrian's hand away. "Boy… I ain't got much time left, so listen up: The Doves, the Griffins, the Lynxes… None of 'em would lift a finger to help us… The… The only person you can rely on… is *yourself*."

Adrian mopped sweat from the old man's brow. "Sounds like a lonely life."

"Millennia ago… The Order of the Shadow Dragon was the only defence Phadros had against corrupting magic… Don't forget your vow, boy—and not the worthless pledge that Lucien will make you speak—the *real* vow."

"Amos—"

"*Listen!* You've heard the rumours; dragons spotted off the coast of Ryndara… Idari sorceresses controlling people's minds… Dead men stalking the streets of Dalthea…" Candle-light danced in Amos' blue eyes. With weak fingers, he grasped Adrian's wrist. "Darkness is bleeding into the world —and we need warriors to defend it. *You*, boy. Let Lucien shut us down. Pledge to another order so no-one suspects you. *Are you listening?* Warriors can have no limits. No friends. No weaknesses."

Even as he died, the conviction remained in Amos' eyes.

· · ·

"Before King Harnan and the Indecim, to which order do you pledge your life?" Lord Lucien asked the initiate kneeling before him.

Adrian stood in a line at the top of the Hall of Aerulus, looking out at an assembly of men, women and representatives from each order. An immaculate, vaulted ceiling rose high above the crowd, and twisting, white marble pillars reached up like crooked fingers. Whatever the architect's intensions, Adrian always had the impression of walking between the bones of a long-dead monster.

"I pledge my life to the Order of the Ivory Dove," the initiate answered.

The lord tapped a sabre to the boy's left shoulder, then his right. "Arise, Sir Edwyn Santos—knight of the Order of the Ivory Dove."

And so it continued. "I pledge my life to the Order of the Amethyst Lynx," the initiates spoke. "I pledge my life to the Order of the Golden Griffin."

Pledging was a formality; the commander of each order had already accepted their new recruits—this was just the final step, and pledging to a different order than that which had already been agreed was considered a great offense.

Parents hugged their sons and daughters, comrades slapped each other's backs, and—with a few words—initiates became knights of Phadros.

And then Lucien's shadow fell over Adrian.

"Adrian Navarro." A soft, genuine smile played on the lord's lips. His words were warm, warmer than when he'd spoken to the other rookies. "You are a man grown and an initiate under the command of the Phadrosi Crown. Before King Harnan and the Indecim, to which order do you pledge your life?"

"I pledge my life..." A stone settled in Adrian's stomach. *Darkness is bleeding into the world... No friends. No weaknesses.*

If he did this, there would be no going back—no forgiveness.

But if he didn't, he'd never find answers, never find the monster that had killed his father.

"...To the Order of the Shadow Dragon."

For a split second, the veneer in Lucien's façade cracked. "Adrian?"

Adrian cleared his throat. Clearer, he said, "I pledge my life to the Order of the Shadow Dragon."

With stiff arms, Lucien's sabre tapped Adrian's shoulders. "Arise, Sir Adrian Navarro. Knight of the Order of the Shadow Dragon."

Now

Grey clouds obscured the sun and a morning mist hung low on the Phadril Sea. The *Solnadar* trudged through choppy water, as if sailing through mud. Its engine chugged low and steady and belched plumes of amber-brown smoke. The metallic smell of recycled igneus clashed with the salty, natural scent of the sea.

Adrian stood at the bow and stretched his arms.

The boat slipped between jutting rocks and through narrow lanes, skirting the edges of glowering cliffs. The Bronze Coast, named after the towering, rocky ignicite that pulsed with amber and gold. For centuries, sailors praised Terros, God of the Earth, for gifting them the Bronze Coast, a glimmering beacon to guide their way even on the darkest of nights. A hundred years ago, the Phadrosi Crown decreed that the ignicite within the Bronze Coast should not be mined, except when the ignicite expanded too much. It was the jewel of the nation, a radiant reminder that the Gods favoured Phadros above all else.

But now the cliffs were grey as granite, drained of their former majesty.

Guess the Gods got tired of us.

Overhead, two first-generation airships floated towards Phadra, patchwork envelopes hinting at their age. Adrian had never seen one outside of a museum before, let alone two. Boats with crowded decks sailed north, forlorn and hungry faces staring out.

Half of Phadros and all of San Sira heads to the capital to escape the disaster, and we head straight towards it.

Adrian stood on the deck for another half hour, watching as the sun brightened the world. The Bronze Coast dissolved into flat land and pebbled beaches—and revealed trains of people. The wind carried a chorus of yells as they spotted the *Solnadar*. Crowds waved out to the vessel, hands holding children aloft, or wads of aerons—but Adrian could only stare back.

A man dived into the sea, swimming for his life—he disappeared within the mist, and whether the tide caught him or he made it back to land, Adrian couldn't say.

Despite the rising sun, the morning mist grew into a thick fog. Adrian's fingers tightened around the handrail as the *Solnadar* bounced and juddered. White water sprayed onto the deck.

Then out of nowhere, storm clouds gathered, black and angry. Lightning split the sky and thunder growled, jolting the vessel.

"Inside!" Pedro yelled. "Now!"

Adrian turned—the vessel leapt and he lost his footing.

Stumbling, he crashed into the rail and almost tipped overboard, into the dark depths of the swirling, black sea…

"Adrian!" Sergeant Diaz grabbed him and hauled him back.

Clouds collided and unleashed thunder. The boat spun, pulled by the wind and sea. Diaz dragged Adrian into the wheelhouse. There, Pedro gripped the steering wheel with white knuckles. "Hold on! Never seen a storm hit like this in all my days o' sailing."

Thunder detonated. The sea threatened to capsize the boat. Tools and instruments flew from the wheelhouse walls and skittered over the floor. A wall of white water rushed up and battered the deck.

"Are we safer here or in the cargo hold?" Diaz asked the captain.

"Depends where you wanna drown!"

Wind hammered the boat. Lightning burst and thunder boomed like a cannonade. The fog grew so thick that Phadros disappeared, leaving the *Solnadar* spinning through an empty, fathomless grey.

Adrian's heart pounded.

"Not natural," Pedro muttered. "Not natural."

Do the Wielders know we're coming?

Was the White Death watching them, even now?

And then a blade of sunlight cut through the fog.

The mist melted away and the storm calmed as if it had never been there at all. The sea opened, green and blue and bright.

Diaz wiped sweat from her forehead. "That was... Something."

Pedro still clung to the wheel. "Ain't natural."

"Everyone okay?" Adrian asked.

Diaz nodded, but again Pedro said, "Ain't natural. All my years o' sailing, all the storms I navigated, never seen one hit so sudden, nor disappear so quick."

"Well, thank the Gods we're in one piece," said Diaz.

"Damn the Gods," said Pedro. "This is as far as I go."

"Captain," Adrian started, "I know this journey ain't easy, but—"

"Don't talk down to me, young'un—I've spent more of my life on the sea than on land and I'm telling ya, this ain't right.

48

You reckon I'm superstitious? Few things I'm scared of, but an uncertain sea is one of 'em."

"We had a deal. You're taking us to San Sira."

Pedro arched an eyebrow. "Got that in writing?"

"Captain, I—"

"My name ain't stamped on a King's Shilling, and I didn't swear no oath to griffins or dragons or whatever the hell you lot do—I pray by Irros Ocean-Lord, and Irros says this ain't right. I'm turning back."

Adrian rubbed his forehead. "We'll secure alternative transport to San Sira. Take us to the nearest landing—can you do that?"

Pedro chewed on that. "Aye."

"You'll be here when we get back, Pedro. Give us seven days. Give us until Sol's Kiss."

"Only sailing for four—got family o' my own to take care of."

"Oh, I wouldn't worry about them—they can visit you in the palace dungeon after you explain to Lord Lucien why you disobeyed a knight of Phadros and reneged on the terms of our arrangement."

The creases in Pedro's face deepened. "Our *arrangement* was four days."

Adrian let a smile sneak onto his lips. "Got that in writing?"

Pedro's face soured. "Seven days. Meet me at Bermeja Port—it's at the other side of the forest. You ain't there in seven days, I'm gone."

"Agreed."

Dante stumbled into the wheelhouse, yawning and rubbing his eyes. "Morning, all! Did I miss anything exciting?"

"Remember: Seven days," Captain Pedro barked.

Adrian stepped onto a beach and slung his pack over his shoulders. His sword hung at his side. "Seven days."

He climbed over a rocky hill. A blue sky stretched overhead, bright and brilliant with nary a cloud in sight.

"We follow the coast south." Adrian stepped to the crest of the hill. "We'll make camp come nightfall Or…"

"What?" Dante asked. "What is it?"

At the foot of the hill, a field of tents pressed together like the slums in Lower Phadra.

Diaz pressed a finger to her chest and drew an eleven-pointed star, the symbol of the Fayth. "Didn't realise it was this bad."

"Let's see what we can find out." Adrian started forward. "Dante, you can disappear here, or make your way back to Phadra."

"So the bastard Watch can pick me up? No thanks. No offence, Sergeant."

"None taken," she said.

"Sergeant," Adrian began, "question the San Sirans, get as much info as you can—with luck, you'll find your family here. Dante… Try not to steal what little coin they have left."

"Next pick-up is due in an hour!" a Phadrosi soldier yelled. She wore the white uniform and winged insignia of the Order of the Ivory Dove. She stood firm against people clutching bundles of aerons. "Be patient!"

Adrian slipped through a tight, muddy avenue lined with relief tents. Men and women lay on cots, moaning in pain. The putrid odour of stale blood and filth hung in the air.

"These people…" Diaz shook her head. "Are we sure they've only been here a few days? Do we help the Doves?"

"Can't risk my mission."

Forlorn faces stared at them as the three marched down the muddy avenue. A young, thin boy followed them and kept peeking out from between tents; Dante stuck his tongue out and made faces at him.

"We stick out too much," said Diaz. "We're the only ones with fresh faces and clean clothes."

"We should split up," said Adrian.

Dante blew raspberries at the boy. The kid giggled and ran past Dante, bumping into him.

"I'll question the healthy," Adrian continued, "those who aren't being looked at too closely by the Doves or—"

"*Stop!*" Diaz grabbed the boy by his collar and pulled him around. "Give me that."

The kid gazed to the ground and held up a red apple.

"That doesn't belong to you."

"It's mine." Dante put his hands on his hips and frowned down at the boy. Then he winked and patted his head. "Keep it. And save it 'til you're hungry—never know when you'll eat again."

The kid smiled and scampered off.

"Keep moving," Adrian commanded. "Don't draw attention."

"Foolish," said Cassandra. "He'll steal again."

"I should hope so," said Dante. "He needs to eat to live."

"The law is the law."

"Just because something's *legal* doesn't make it *moral*."

"Just one person ignoring the rules makes it harder for the rest of us."

"Apologies, Sergeant—did you believe that all villains wielded pitchforks and twirled their moustaches while tying helpless damsels onto train tracks? We're not in the city any more. These folk are fleeing natural disaster. Famine, disease, looting—how far d'you reckon the law will protect them?"

"It should," the watchwoman muttered.

"'Should' doesn't come into it. Everyone *should* have enough to eat. Everyone *should* have a roof over their heads."

"There's help available."

"If you can afford it. If money went where it was needed most, we'd all be laughing. Laws are full of loopholes for the rich and powerful. Why do you reckon so many poor folk are locked up? The rich don't need to steal to eat."

"If they don't commit crimes, then they won't get locked up."

"And if prisons worked as a deterrent, they'd all be empty."

"One rule for one person and a separate rule for another is *not* a system of justice."

"Could not agree more!" Dante said with a grin. "If your mum stole an apple, Sergeant, would you knock on her door and... Hang on a minute..." Dante halted. "Sergeant Diaz... Gods above, you're not... You *are*, aren't you?"

Diaz stood still and put her hands on her hips. "I'm what?"

"Cassandra Coldheart! You're the copper who arrested her own mother, aren't you?"

Diaz's fingers balled into fists. For a moment, she looked like she'd respond, but she kept quiet.

"Enough," said Adrian. "If you two don't stop biting at each other, I'm gonna let the White Death kill you before I take her out."

Dante offered a mock salute. "Sir, yes, sir."

"Focus on the mission. Speak to the people and listen to what they say."

And speak to the people Adrian did, but information didn't come easily—or, rather, it came *too* easily; every evacuee offered a single fragment of what happened to San Sira, or else a different story altogether.

An earthquake ruptured San Sira City.

A volcano formed out of nothing and spewed white-hot lava.

A comet thundered through the sky and punched through the world.

But no-one had seen the White Death. No sign of sorceresses, or Wielders—or even so much as a mage in a fancy outfit conjuring pennies from people's ears.

"This is getting us nowhere," said Diaz.

"With such keen observation skills, no wonder you're prized among the Watch," said Dante.

"At least I'm trying." She cocked her head. "Remind me why you're here again?"

"Three reasons." Dante counted off his fingers. "One, I know how to talk to people, unlike the mindless automatons the Watch churns out—or Adrian, who's just mindless. Two, I know every town, village and inn from here to the end of San Sira. And three, I'm *much* better looking than the two of you, and any band of adventurers must have *some* sex appeal."

"Four," Adrian said, "you're wanted by the Watch and don't have any other choice."

That knocked the wind out of Dante's sails.

"Time's running out, we're miles from where we thought we'd be. What's the first thing we did after a heist, Dante?"

"Lie low, wait for the heat to pass."

"A *heist?*" Diaz said, aghast. "You're a knight!"

Adrian ignored her. "If you're a Wielder and all Phadros is looking for you—the Watch knocks on every door in the country and rounds up all their informants—what do you do?"

"Tell my friends different stories to buy time and then go underground." Dante clapped his hands. "Literally. Have you ever been to Oro Lengua?"

"No."

"It's a mining town, near the Bermeja Forest. Used to be popular on the theatre troupe trail—lots of coming and going. Lots of loose lips and underhand deals. Rav loved it there."

"Who's Rav?" the copper asked.

Dante drew a hand through his hair. "Uh, nobody.

Anyway, these days, Oro Lengua's a ghost town—the perfect place for a criminal or an evil Wielder to lie low. Hazardous terrain, sandstorms—no-one goes there unless they have to. It's dangerous."

Adrian set off. "Then that's our next stop."

Accompanied by the soft song of the sea, Dante led Adrian and Diaz over endless, rolling, yellow hills.

"I've been to Oro Lengua once," Dante said. "Hid out there after a fireball show."

"Fireball show?" Diaz asked.

Light twinkled in Dante's purple eyes. "A fireball show, my dear Coldheart, is when a travelling troupe or carnival is so strapped for cash that they advertise the most obscene, the most lascivious, the most *extreme* attractions to get people frothing to come inside."

"And people pay for that?"

"Oh, yeah—they *love* debauchery."

"I don't understand—why not just have that as your normal act if it brings in coin?"

"That's the beauty of it, Sergeant; we sell the *promise* and—"

"Once they're through the door, they pick their pockets and fleece 'em as quickly as possible," Adrian finished. "They pass free moonshine and watered-down whisky, get folk nice and drunk. By the time the town wakes up the next morning and realises they've been conned—"

"We're well on our way!" Dante clapped. "The trick is to advertise your outfit under a different name, to keep one's reputation intact."

"That's disgusting," said Diaz.

"Nothing like desperation to push creative boundaries."

"Saw a fireball show when I was a kid," said Adrian. "They had a man-eating chicken. Scarred me for life."

"No wonder you want to kill monsters," said Cassie.

Adrian couldn't resist the smirk creeping over his lips.

"What?" the copper demanded.

Dante couldn't stifle his giggling. "And don't get me started on the woman with three tits or the man with two cocks."

The copper frowned. "I don't…" Then realisation dawned on her. "Wordplay. The man-eating chicken was a man, eating chicken. And the man with two cocks—"

"Had two birds," said Dante. "You catch on quicker'n most coppers. It's all in how you sell it. *I* was good at that. As a boy, I'd have the audience eating out the palm of my hand, marching across the stage and regaling them with tales of the gruesome man eating chicken behind the curtain. 'Dare I pull it back?' I'd ask, fear and horror in my voice. Or, 'If every one of you sticks ten aerons into a bucket, I think I can convince Auntie Gertrude to show you her three tits!' And she did— the blue tit, the willow tit, and the crested tit. It's all about massaging the truth. The audience would be in an uproar once they found out, of course—but I convinced them to see the funny side. 'Want to get one over on your friends and neighbours? Then send them here and don't tell 'em a thing!'"

"It's dishonest."

"*Technically* not lies, though. Not that the rubes would listen to logic; it's called a burnout show because they'd never let us back in. Only to be used in desperate times."

An extreme measure for desperate times... Such as sending a single knight into a foreign territory to assassinate a sorceress.

"Thought we'd have seen more San Sirans on the road," Adrian said half an hour later. Rocks and hills dotted the landscape.

"Me, too," Dante agreed. "Maybe that's a good thing?"

"Yeah… Maybe."

"What happens if we run into outlaws? Desperate citizens

make for easy prey, and I'd be half-tempted to let them give you a kicking."

"Yes," Diaz muttered, "desperation makes people vulnerable—a fact you're acquainted with, seer."

"Ha, yes, very droll."

"We deal with 'em," Adrian said. "Help who we can. Chances are they're just refugees who've banded together."

"I'll place them under arrest," Diaz said. "They may be desperate but they're still bound by the law."

"Splendid," said Dante. "And while you're bleeding out, Adrian and I can run away. Or perhaps…" Dante stopped before a rushing river and scratched the back of his head. "Sorry, I, uh… I don't recall the river being this wide."

Diaz groaned. "Are we lost?"

"Oh, only in the literal sense."

"We've walked in a straight line since the tent city." Diaz wiped sweat from her forehead. "How can we be lost?"

"Through mystical intervention," Adrian said. "The storm. Remember what Pedro said? That he'd never seen a storm come so fast or disappear so quickly? That man's been a sailor for about six hundred years."

Diaz frowned. "What are you saying?"

"I'm saying that we can't trust the environment. Spontaneous storms, the Cataclysm itself… Dante, you know every hiding hole, secret basement and false wall in Phadra; you once danced through every street in the city in alphabetical order with a blindfold around your eyes. If we're lost, it ain't you."

"Thank you, Adrian—but to be fair, I did cheat."

"You're not suggesting Wielders reformed the landscape?" Diaz shook her head. "Gods above and below, we're out of our depth."

"We can't cross this river, Dante—what's the next best way to Oro Lengua?"

"Through the Bermeja Forest."

Adrian looked east, to the dense, dark treeline. "You want to cut through the forest? That takes us off of our path, away from the roads."

Dante started towards it. "Better than getting lost while walking in a straight line, no?"

The woods closed around Adrian and the afternoon sun threatened to dip beneath the treetops.

For over an hour, Dante led them through forest paths, over streams and across crevices. Strings of small ignium lamps showed the way—not illuminated at this hour, and probably never would be again, but Adrian liked knowing they were there.

"My people hung them." Dante pointed to the lights. "Well, not *my* people, but travelling bards and entertainers. Used them as a path to navigate the great Bermeja. Every troupe would follow a specific line of lights so as not to encroach on one another. At Wintercast, three or four troupes would band together and throw a week-long carnival."

"Fascinating," said Diaz. "And how many people did you fleece out of their coin?"

Dante rolled his eyes. "People pay for entertainment—and by the Gods, they got it. You've never lived until you've heard Dante tal Arata sing sweet arias."

If Lucien had told Adrian that he'd have to put up with constant griping between these two, he would've renounced the Order of the Shadow Dragon there and then.

"How do you two know each other?" the watchwoman asked.

The question came out of nowhere; Adrian ignored it.

Dante, on the other hand, clapped and said, "That's a story for the ages! We met on the streets, after I'd severed ties with Rav and his mongrels. Adrian and I were the best of friends, brothers of a different blood, thick as thieves —literally."

"Dante—" Adrian started.

"Oh, what have you got to worry about? Our Adrian was the most naturally gifted pickpocket I'd ever seen—including me!"

"You were both thieves." Diaz rolled her eyes. "Why am I not surprised?"

"One day, Adrian picked the pocket of none other than Lord Lucien himself."

"*What?*"

"Oh, yes. Any other boy would be picking pockets with one hand after that, but not Adrian Navarro. Lucien sponsored him, gave him a cushy place to stay and a knighthood to go along with it. After that, *Sir* Adrian didn't have much time for his old friends. He got the knighthood; I got six months in a hole. Hardly seems fair, does it?"

"Less talking," Adrian said. "More walking."

Where Dante and Diaz had to stop for breath, Adrian kept his pace. He had the training to thank for that; Amos had neglected his training drills and lived overweight and slow before the bloodlung got him; Adrian wouldn't face the same fate. Phadros might have no need for his order, but Adrian would put its teachings to good use. He'd studied swordplay and poisons, subterfuge and stealth. He'd learned how to survive on his own, learned the most efficient ways to kill a man without being seen and how to disappear within shadows and reappear leagues away.

He didn't know how to track demons, but he knew how to make a man give up his secrets—and he looked forward to making Wielders talk.

"Well, then." Dante sighed. "I'm afraid I hear the call of the forest. *Pee*," he added at Diaz's look.

Adrian set his pack down. "Me, too." He found a secluded

tree—and then Dante slapped his back. "Do you have to stand so close?"

"No," Dante said, "but I enjoy making you uncomfortable."

Adrian stared ahead; the Bermeja Forest stretched on forever, deep and far and steeped in shadow. Insects buzzed and scuttled, and the trees themselves seemed to throb with noise. At this hour, the sun's descent would be swift. *And when the darkness comes, the shadows laugh...*

"Having a little trouble?"

"What?"

Dante arched an eyebrow.

Adrian cleared his throat and adjusted himself. "Let's go."

"It's okay, y'know," Dante said at his back. "Of course, my experience with stage fright is *literal*, but nerves creep up when you least expect it."

"I'm fine."

"If you say so."

"You two are whispering like schoolboys poring over a dirty picture book," Diaz said. "Where exactly is Oro Lengua?"

"Not far." Dante marched onwards. "If the trains were running, it'd take a few hours. As it is, we'll need to spend the night in one of the tourist villages—Ignarribia's closest. The Bermeja Forest is full of settlements. A pity no-one had the foresight to cut the damn trees down, though, or getting to them would be much easier."

Diaz tutted. "Don't you know anything? There's an ancient law that states the Bermeja should be left to flourish; this is a *holy* place. Lunos and Sol themselves coupled beneath the moon here during the first ever eclipse. That's why they call it Sol's Kiss. Their union gave rise to the forest."

"Nyr's tits, it was just a joke," Dante muttered.

"Wait," Adrian said. "Look ahead."

A plume of grey smoke wafted over the treeline. Adrian strode towards it, fingers on the hilt of his sword.

The forest grew denser with each step, but its song receded—no birds wheeled in the sky and no leaves rustled.

If the forest is silent, it means there's a predator nearby.

But sometimes the predator is you.

He stalked through the treeline—and a sudden, icy chill ran through the air.

Adrian stopped.

Above, the sky shimmered like a heat mirage. The air fizzled and warped like it had been ripped apart and sewn back together, leaving a scar in the sky.

Magic is bleeding into the world...

"Just an optical illusion," Dante said. "Right?"

"C'mon." Adrian pressed forward and came to a burned and blackened shell of a building.

"It's a church," said Diaz.

"Dedicated to Irros," said Dante. "I stopped here many a time. Gods above."

"Recent, too. The fire's not been extinguished for long."

Dante muttered a prayer to Irros, then asked, "Who'd do this?"

"Wielders," Adrian answered. "To break people's spirit. Show 'em who has power."

Diaz shook her head. "Don't form conclusions without evidence. Could have been bandits. Could have been an accident."

Could've been a scary witch who can set you on fire.

Heart rate rising, Adrian marched forward. "Let's check it out."

Debris smothered the church and scorch marks scarred its stonework, but there were no bodies inside.

Diaz examined the floor and walls. "No signs of a struggle. If anyone was here, at least they made it out alive."

Brow furrowed, Dante said, "So it was an accident, then?"

Adrian met his eyes. He thought for a second before speaking. "Most likely. Let's go; whoever did this is long gone."

But as darkness enveloped the forest, Adrian sensed it watching him.

"Not as big as I remember," Dante said.

Where once the walls of Ignarribia lit up the surrounding forest, now they stood as a grey-brown smudge with only a smattering of flaming torches hinting at the settlement behind.

"The absence of light does that," said Adrian. "Makes everything feel smaller."

No stars ventured into the sky tonight, and the moon glinted like a tarnished silver coin.

Adrian followed Dante through a large, unmanned gate. The town looked like it had been frozen in time for the past two hundred years; winding, cobbled streets meandered this way and that, a symptom of the city spreading unplanned. Watchmen unpacked mules and horses and candlelight flickered within windows.

"Used to perform in an old wooden theatre," Dante explained. "Built by Lucas Salvarado himself when he marched south during the Age of Exploration."

"There's an inn," said Adrian. "We stay the night, leave at dawn."

Blunted swords, daggers and other weapons filled the walls of the Seven Sisters Inn; the name and choice of décor were no doubt inspired by Belios, the God of War, who'd fathered seven daughters.

Candlelit lanterns offered a gentle, pulsing ebb of warm light, and the aroma of stewed meat and thick, sweet beer filled Adrian's nose. But the patrons' voices were hushed and no music shook the rafters.

"All the young folk enlisted," Dante said. "King Harnan offered a pretty penny for the recovery operations."

"Sit where you like," the brawny barman commanded. "We don't got much."

An old man eyed Adrian's sword and chuckled. "Got kids with toothpicks fighting for us now. Harnan's lost his mind. That thing'll serve the country better hanging on the wall!"

His friends laughed.

"We're not going to get much information from this lot," said Diaz.

"Oh, who cares about that?" Dante clapped his hands. "I'm *starving*."

"You lot, it's six aerons for a beer." The barman placed his hands on the bar and leaned forward, glowering at Diaz. "Eight for her."

"Nyr's tits," said Dante. "If that's how much a beer costs, then Gods know how much a room is."

"It's me." Diaz's chin drew down. "They don't like me."

"Because you're a copper?" Dante said. "Seems fair."

"Because I'm *San Siran*."

"Ah. Well, for the love of Belios, do *not* tell them you're a copper as well."

"I have a writ from Lucien," Adrian said. "The Crown will settle any tab."

"No, no—I have a better idea." Dante marched to the bar and slapped the counter, which didn't endear the barman to him one bit. "I note that you have a stage and no band; in exchange for three rooms and a hot plate each, I'll have this sorry lot dancing and drinking in no time."

"Piss off."

"I'll have your patrons parting with more coin than a drunk at happy hour. My name is Dante tal Arata—perhaps you've heard of me?"

"No."

"What's he doing?" Diaz whispered to Adrian.

Adrian clenched his fists. "Getting us kicked out."

"Tell you what," Dante continued, "and I'm cutting my own nose off, here—that fiddle you have collecting dust on the stage? Give it to me and we can negotiate after. Deal?"

"Give him a go, Javes," one of the old-timers said. "Could do with a laugh."

"Do what you want—but if you screw up, you and your San Siran friend are out on your arse."

Dante smirked and bowed before making his way to the stage. With cautious fingers, he picked the fiddle and bow up.

He's nervous.

Dante stood there, frozen on the stage. Candlelight danced in his wide, violet eyes.

Shit.

Adrian got up to move, but an instant later, a note rang out.

At first, the fiddle cried a sweet, sorrowful melody before Dante launched into a frenzied gallop. He danced like he was born to it, in perfect step with the sudden time changes. The patrons didn't slap their thighs or clap, but nor did they take their eyes from him.

For ten full minutes, music rolled out of Dante. Raucous rhythms shot out of the fiddle like cannonballs; Adrian forgot himself for a moment and almost bobbed his head.

Almost.

Then a note screeched out of the instrument like drawing a saw across its strings.

Dante froze.

Laughter murmured among the patrons. Dante cleared his throat and offered a half-hearted bow. "Well, it's, it's been a while, and, uh, I'm a touch rusty. But music has a strange hypnotism—doesn't it draw us together? Do be generous with your coin at the bar, folks—take it from me, the only way to navigate the dire straits we find ourselves in is to do so *together*."

Silence.

Empty, cavernous *silence*.

Then one of the patrons yelled, "An ale for the pure-eyed dandy!" and tossed aerons at the bar. Others followed.

"S'pose you and your friends can stay. Donna!" Javes called to a young serving girl. "A room each for our three guests. But you pay double; the Doves are offering free shelter and stole my customers."

Dante muttered his thanks and stepped off the stage, bowing and holding a hand to his heart.

He threw himself down next to Adrian. "Well, that was bloody awful."

"What are you talking about?" Diaz asked. "You did well!"

"*Well* doesn't cut it. Or, at least, it shouldn't. I'm supposed to be a professional."

Diaz waved his concerns away. "You're being too hard on yourself. No-one judges a small mistake."

"I do. But what's one more, eh?"

"Dante—"

Dante crossed his arms. "I know, I know, I'm being dramatic—can't help it. Should've left me where I was, Adrian."

"To get picked up by the Watch?"

"*Do* keep throwing that back in my face."

Adrian leaned forward, fingers splayed on the rough, wooden table. "Look, the sooner we find what we're looking for, the sooner I'll have you back home—Lucien'll pardon you and you'll never have to see me again."

"That's the best plan you've come up with yet."

"Let's focus on the mission, shall we?" Diaz said. "I don't know you but we all want the same thing, yes? They'll talk to you more than they will a San Siran, Dante. Let the ale flow a while longer and—"

Dante held a hand up. "Made a fool of myself enough for

one day. No, I think I'll retire to my room—not much of an appetite after all."

"After what you just did, you're in a prime position to get intel—everyone will want to talk to you."

"Yes, Cassandra." Dante's chair scraped back and he stood and stalked away. "That's the problem."

Adrian watched him disappear, exchanging silent nods and empty words with the patrons. They didn't see the slump in his shoulders, but Adrian did.

Cutlery scraped on plates and laughter murmured throughout the bar. A small but warm fire crackled, keeping the shadows at bay and painting the room in soft, fuzzy orange. Dante might disagree, but Adrian knew that he'd done his part.

"What's our next move?" Sergeant Diaz asked.

"You want to find your family, right? We can part ways here, if you want—place like this is bound to attract travellers. Might even have a bricode machine. The road Dante and I are on is only gonna get harder."

"I don't think it's safe for me here. I'd rather stick with you, if it's all the same."

Adrian didn't argue.

"Why *is* Dante here?" she asked. "He's not a knight. Not a soldier. You said the Watch wants him. Do your superiors know that he's here?"

"What Lucien doesn't know won't hurt him. Anyway, it's not like *he* does everything by the book."

"What do you mean?"

Adrian met her eyes. "This operation isn't exactly… Legal."

"Meaning?"

"Meaning neither the king nor the council has signed off on it—it's all Lucien. No writs. No warrants. That's why I need Dante; he's been smuggling, thieving and conning his way across Imanis his whole life. If the San Sirans catch us, I can't protect us—but *he* can take us wherever we need to go without being seen. Dante tal Arata can lie his way out of a locked room."

Diaz crossed her arms. "I see."

"Anyway, we've wasted a day, Dante's in a mood, and we're nowhere near San Sira. You got a plan, Sergeant, now's the time."

She glanced at the bar. "Screw it. If you want a job done right…" She got up and strode towards the barman.

Shit.

Adrian joined her. The big man didn't glance up from the open broadsheet on the bar. Its pages were soaked with spilled beer.

"…storm kicked up out of nowhere, never seen anything like it." The barman tapped the paper. "These Wielders are to blame."

"Wielders?" Adrian echoed without thinking.

Javes glared at him. He peeled the front page over; it was the evening edition of the *Dias Cetro*, Phadros' most popular newspaper. Its headline read:

San Siran Tragedy Uncovered!
Black Magic Wielders to Blame!

"Crock of shit," one of the patrons said. "Magic ain't real."

"Just the paper trying to sell copies," Javes agreed. "But King Harnan himself is calling 'em out, huh? And you know what they say about the Idari; cannibals and savages. Anyone got the stones to destroy a whole country, it's them. Anyway, says here that Wielders are responsible—whether they use magic or not don't really matter."

Adrian grimaced. *The world knows about Wielders.* That would make his job harder. The *Dias Cetro* sensationalised even the most anodyne of stories; it counted a member of the Sons of Belios as a senior investor, and many—including

Adrian—blamed the rise of the Sons' popularity on the paper handing them a platform.

What does Harnan gain by revealing this? Is he still in league with the Mages' Guild? Or the Idari?

Gods knew what Lucien made of it all... If he was even still Defence Minister.

"But Sir Vega's the finest soldier in the kingdom, no doubt he'll steer 'em right," Javes continued. "Heart swelled with pride when I saw the *Judgement* sailin' overhead. Majestic, she was. Vega'll show these Wielders who's boss, then we'll finally annex San Sira. For their own protection, mind."

"You saw the *Judgement?*" Adrian asked. "The Amethyst Lynx is here?"

Javes turned his nose up. "What's it to you?"

"Oh, we mean no trouble!" Diaz cut in. "Only, we were caught in the storm you spoke of, just trying to find our way back home. To Phadra."

Javes narrowed his eyes at her. "You're from the capital?"

"Oh, yes." Diaz set her Watch badge onto the counter. "Our ship got caught in the storm and blew us miles off-course—we're headed north, to the refugee camp."

Javes crossed his arms. "You figurin' on arresting 'em?"

"If I must—the Doves are running things, and you know how they are—more likely to escort a horde of San Sirans straight into Phadra and give 'em free food and a place to stay at the expense of good Phadrosi folk."

A smile brushed Javes' lips. "Aye, we had a lot of 'em pass through on their way north. Thank the Gods the Doves weren't here or I'd have to give up even more space."

"You gave them room and board?" Adrian asked. "Did they tell you what happened to San Sira?"

"Like hell I did. But don't let it be said that Javes ain't charitable; I do my bit. I let 'em sleep in the stables."

Diaz forced a smile. "Of course."

"They come in here, ranting about some bright, blinding

light in the sky. An explosion, I reckon, like what did Dalthea in a few years back. Tell you, if it ain't these Wielders, it's the Idari."

"A bomb?" Diaz shook her head. "That's all we need, a refugee smuggling weapons into Phadros."

"That's what *I* said! Might be bullshit, o' course, but San Sirans always were a bit slower than the rest of us."

Behind her back, Diaz curled her fists but her expression betrayed nothing.

"Did they mention a woman?" Adrian pressed. "A white witch? Or where they came from?"

Javes cocked his head. "Her, I like. You, I don't. You know what they say about folk with one purple eye and one not, huh?"

That we're a cast-off of god and man, more mongrel than human—but that still makes me twice the man you are.

Adrian left the retort unsaid; when you grew up among bullies every day, what was one more but a drop of rain in a storm?

Diaz nodded. "Thank you, Javes."

The big man peeled his eyes away from Adrian. "Just doing my bit. The Sons o' Belios got it right, you ask me. Charity begins at home. Gotta look after your own before you can look after others." Donna slid two plates of piping hot pork across the bar. "I'll send your friend's to his room. Always happy to look after an officer of the Watch— you do the Gods' work. And well done for coming to *our* side."

"Our side?"

"Oh, meaning no offence! I can just tell you're San Siran, is all. Enjoy your supper."

To her credit, Diaz's smile didn't falter. "Thank you, Javes."

"You played that well," Adrian said when they were back at the table. "Using his… *patriotism* against him."

"Call it what it is: Racism." Diaz thumbed the corner of the dog-eared book poking out of her pocket.

"Fair enough. If you'd rather while the time away with Captain Crimsonwing, I understand."

Diaz blushed. "Sorry. It's a habit, when I'm thinking."

"You're embarrassed. No-one should be ashamed of reading, Diaz."

She tensed. "Call me Cassie. Or at least Sergeant."

"Cassie. And don't bother calling me 'sir'."

"Okay." Cassie started eating. Bloody gravy oozed over her knife. "So, we still don't have any hard intelligence—you think Oro Lengua is the right place to go?"

Adrian nodded. "And watch out for the Lynxes. The biggest warship in the fleet won't be too difficult to find— let's pray the San Sirans don't see it as an act of war."

"Is Harnan so heartless that he'll attack a country on its knees?"

Between the Mages' Guild and the Idari, I'm not sure whose side Harnan is on.

"It's a show of strength," Adrian said. "Posturing. But it doesn't change our mission. You'll get the information you need, Cassie, and I'll use it to eliminate the Wielders. I just hope we find the White Death before the *Judgement* does."

"You make it sound easy."

"Easy? No. But it *is* simple. They need to be removed and only I can do it. We might have an igneus-fuelled warship on our side but for all we know, the White Death can bring it down with a snap of her fingers."

Diaz shook her head. "They should have given you more men."

"I don't need more men—I only need to find her."

"If she's powerful enough to bring down a warship and tear a country in two, what can you possibly do?"

Adrian cracked his knuckles. "I just need to get close. That's all."

"I wish I shared your confidence."

"We all have a role to play. I'm Commander and First Sword of the Order of the Shadow Dragon—I'm trained to combat magic and monsters."

And a ton of other things that no-one believes in.

"You sound like you hate them. 'The only good Wielder is a dead Wielder'—the Sons of Belios say the same about San Sirans."

"It's… complicated."

"Doesn't appear to be."

"We're not talking crystal balls and guardian angels—this is dark stuff. *Dangerous* stuff. You spend your days arresting thieves and beggars, but the *real* threat is out there, in the shadows."

She looked offended at that, but why should Adrian care? Bitter truths were better than sweet lies.

Diaz leaned back. "I once saw a blind artist use magic to produce astonishing works. She sensed the colours and the patterns though she couldn't see them. She painted vistas in hues much prettier than those found in the natural world."

"Then she played you for a fool."

"I believe what my eyes and ears tell me. I believe in facts. Evidence. But I recognise that some things cannot be explained by facts alone; some say Aurien tal Varaldo's greatest symphonies were the result of magic—of peering toward the stars and listening to the planets sing."

"Sounds like Aurien tal Varaldo took a lot of drugs."

"You made a deal for Dante. Saved him from the Watch. He's a thief and a conman, but you saved him all the same."

"There are shades of grey between black and white. Dante's a good person."

Diaz met his eye. "But Wielders can't be?"

"I…"

What could he say? That he'd watched his father get ripped apart by a shadow demon? That he still heard the crack of his bones when he closed his eyes? That he still heard the hateful, serrated giggling every night when darkness came?

Adrian pushed his plate of untouched food away and stood. "I'm going to bed."

Without another word, he marched to his room, locked it, and set his sword onto the bed.

Diaz wouldn't understand. Neither would Dante. How could they? They hadn't seen what he'd seen.

The world had moved on from weapons like swords and axes, from horse-drawn coaches and pistols that fired one shot and took an age to reload. But in the new world—a world reliant on a now-depleted fuel source—there was still a place for elements of the old.

Adrian removed his shirt and stripped naked. In a dirty mirror at the far side of the room, he glimpsed the black tattoos slithering over his chest and limbs: Spears of black ink drew down over each shoulder towards his chest, six in total, and merged into a single point in the centre, like six black blades meeting point-to-point. Similar blades of ink ran down his legs and the sides of his arms and ended at his biceps. On his back, two lines of ink slashed up between his shoulder blades and joined the spears on his shoulders. Adrian still remembered the pain when the tattoos were applied; burning, corrosive.

But worth it.

He blew the room's solitary candle out. Darkness enveloped him like a cloak of black ice and made the hair on his arms stand on end.

Though his fingers tremored, he took time unsheathing the sword. Nightsbane, Amos had called it.

Adrian let the darkness wash over his bare skin; here, alone, he invited shadows into his mind—exposure to build his resistance to them and strengthen his resolve.

His heart quickened.

He heard the shadows now; his father's screams, the breaking bones, the mocking laughter…

Adrian held Nightsbane high; the ignicite within the steel shimmered like sunshine upon a stream. Adrian channelled his strength into it, and a soft, amber glow caressed his skin, glowing brighter and brighter.

The glow didn't diminish as Adrian practised his drills until the sun came up.

The late-morning sun shone bright and coppery, and a refreshing breeze sang through the towering, fractured cliffside looming before Adrian. The cliff splintered into three peaks, worn smooth by wind and sand.

"There we are!" Dante called. "Who said Dante tal Arata doesn't come through in a pinch?"

"No-one," Diaz answered. "No-one's talked of you at all."

Adrian wondered if—for someone like Dante—not being spoken of at all was worse than being criticised.

Dante cleared his throat. "Well, anyway—these are the Three Teeth." He bounded up the stairs carved into the side of the cliff. "Oro Lengua isn't far."

Adrian followed. Atop the cliffside, a squealing, rusty sign wavered with the breeze: "Welcome to Oro Lengua: Pop. 1200".

"This way," said Dante.

Sand danced through silent streets and empty homes.

Oro Lengua—Golden Tongue—once brimmed with people and commerce. Unlike the Bronze Coast, the Phadrosi Crown had no issue with mining the veins of ignicite here. The town had thrived for decades—the Small Capital, they called it, for the money it brought in. But as with so many other places, the state-owned mining corporation got greedy. Ignicite required time to regenerate, and that meant a slower influx of money. A month, a year, a decade—

no-one knew for certain how long a vein would take to regenerate.

But the miners in Oro Lengua were instructed to keep mining. Deeper and deeper they dug, and eventually, they found the core—the pulsing, throbbing amber heart of every ignicite vein. Adrian had never seen an active core, but he'd heard how mesmerising they were to behold—mesmerising, and volatile.

The miners struck the core and ruptured the vein. The core had imploded, the land had collapsed, and most of Oro Lengua disappeared under the dirt, killing hundreds and thrusting Phadros into an economic recession.

"A ghost town," said Diaz. "Is this the best way to San Sira?"

Wind moaned through empty windows and abandoned streets.

"Oh, yes," said Dante. "Until we find an unattended motorcarriage or airship lying around. Let's hope we don't run into a sandstorm, hey?"

Dante led them through the broken landscape, and—as if Aerulus God-King himself had heard his words—the wind grew angrier with each step.

Dust and sand lashed the ground and whipped Adrian's skin. "How long?"

"The mine is just ahead!" Dante called above the wind.

Sure enough, monstrous mining platforms resolved behind the sandstorm.

Diaz shielded her eyes from the sand and said, "I've never been in a mine before! Should be inter—"

She screamed and plummeted, but Adrian wrapped his arms around her waist and pulled her close.

"Watch your step," he commanded. "Place is riven with fissures."

"Th-thank you. I didn't see… Thank you."

"You did the same for me on the *Solnadar*—we're even!"

"This is where deep-mining gets you!" Even in the sandstorm, Dante's teeth gleamed. "Still, shouldn't complain—a godsend for smugglers!"

Dante pointed to the entrance of a narrow tunnel cut into a cliffside and disappeared inside. Adrian followed, the wind howling at his back.

"There we are." Dante pointed to a large, rusting red door. Chains wrapped around it, held in place by a padlock.

"Dante?" Adrian asked.

"Yup?"

"Did you lead us to a locked door?"

"Yup."

Diaz groaned. "Seriously?"

"Oh, ye of little faith!" Dante bent over the padlock. From his pocket, he produced a lock-picking kit—and in an instant, the chains jangled to the floor.

"You're either remarkably talented," Diaz started, "or remarkably lucky."

Dante winked at her.

"It was already unlocked, wasn't it?"

"Yup."

"Give me a hand with the door," Adrian said.

With some effort, the rusted, red door shrieked open.

Beyond, darkness filled the mine, thick and black and vast. The ceiling disappeared within shadows, as if steeped in black ink. The darkness leered at Adrian.

Dante cupped his hands around his mouth and yelled, "Hello!"

The echo resounded in the black, a chorus of ghostly voices greeting them.

Adrian's hand fell to the pommel of his sword; did the darkness laugh down here, so deep in the earth? Would Adrian hear that sneering, creeping giggling?

Would it come for him again, so far from home, so far from childhood?

He held his breath, waiting, waiting, but nothing—

Shrieks pierced the silence and a teeming storm of bats gushed out of the darkness.

Adrian screamed and drew his sword, slashing at nothing but air.

"They're gone." Diaz put a hand on his shoulder. "They startled me, too."

Heart racing, Adrian shrugged her away. "Let's move."

He followed Dante through narrow corridors and squeezed through collapsed shafts. His hand glided over rough stone and smooth, hewn rock. His heart beat like a drum and a stale, light, caustic smell carried through the honeycomb tunnels.

"You'd think there'd be plenty of ignium lamps in an ignicite mine," Diaz said.

"The abundance of ignicite provided its own light," Dante pointed out. "Less need for lamps. But still, I agree."

Their voices sounded louder in the depths; Adrian preferred it to the sound of his heart.

Deeper they delved inside the mine. The air grew more tense with each step.

Diaz cleared her throat. "So, um, you just keep a lockpick kit on you?"

She feels it, too. The tension.

"Mrs. Herrera changes her locks a lot," Dante answered. "Adrian, here."

He followed Dante into an antechamber and lit a candle lantern lying on the floor. Warm light washed the chamber in fuzzy orange, illuminating bulky, dormant machinery. Adrian's muscles relaxed.

Dust coated the silent machinery, and all around, the ignicite remained black and dead.

Monuments to arrogance.

"It regenerated at some point." Diaz ran her fingers over

jagged, dark rock. "But it's hardly distinguishable from stone, now."

Dante lit more lanterns and examined corners and crates. "Let's see, let's see... Ah!" He found canned vegetables and dry-cured pork. "Lunch time."

Diaz frowned. "How long has that been here?"

Dante tore off a piece of meat and chewed. "This lasts a year, or longer—you learn how to dry-cure, keep things in brine, *all* sorts of things when you're a traveller and never know where your next meal is. Or how long you need to lie low."

"Same as the military." Adrian scanned the shadows in the ceiling. "Never waste an opportunity to eat or sleep."

"*You're* not eating."

Adrian met her eyes but said nothing.

"All the more for me." Dante grinned and pulled more meat apart with his teeth. "My old troupe kept supplies here; we used an old theatre ship to bring joy and stories and mirth to the provincial towns. A small craft, to be sure, so we had to leave caches of supplies everywhere."

Diaz put her hands on her hips. "Do you think my head buttons up at the back?"

Dante frowned. "What?"

"Do you think I was born yesterday?"

"I don't—"

"You didn't leave supplies, you left *plunder.*"

"Well, yes, of course—smuggling *is* illegal, you know. Keep hot property here until it cools off and then sell it."

After Dante and Diaz ate, they ventured farther into the mine. At once, tension filled the air again and the darkness thickened. Dread filled Adrian's stomach like tumbling scree.

"Dante," he started. "Are we going *uphill?*"

"Um... Yes. So many collapsed shafts and caverns. Nothing to worry about. Nothing to worry about."

"You *do* know where we're going, yes?" Diaz asked.

"Oh, yeah. Yes."

Minutes crawled past in silence and still the path climbed and climbed. Then Dante stopped by the lip of a sheer drop. But rather than look down, he pointed up. "Look—light."

Adrian stood alongside him. Sure enough, thin spears of light pierced the ceiling...

And shone on the devastation below.

The light illuminated mounds of rubble—and things Adrian recognised. Homes, a church...

Bones.

"It's the rest of Oro Lengua."

"Sweet Musa." Diaz traced an eleven-pointed star on her chest. "May Nyr bring them peace."

The three stood there in silence, staring down into the dark pit. The light above only served to highlight the darkness shrouding the rest of the pit. What horrors did the shadows conceal?

Adrian stared at the darkness, and the darkness stared back.

His father had told him a story once, about a mariner who'd spent his life on the seas, sailing alone in his small boat, his feet never meeting land. During one voyage—on a moonless, starless night—the mariner took his evening meal onto the deck, as he always did. The wind didn't wail and the sea remained still—so still that the mariner could not tell where the black sea ended and the sky began, even with his decades of experience.

For hours, the mariner stood in silence and stared into the fathomless darkness, as if in a trance.

"After a while, without a word, the mariner climbed up on the taffrail, peering down into that dark nothingness... And leapt in."

His father's voice had dropped to a whisper, but Adrian was a boy of eight and not afraid.

"So who told the story?" he asked.

He remembered the puzzled look his father wore.

"If he sailed alone," Adrian pressed, "then who told the story?"

The look on his father's face turned from puzzled to sullen. "The darkness whispered the tale to the world as a warning: If you stare at something dark, and deep, and empty for long enough... Sooner or later, it will invite you in."

"Um..." Dante cleared his throat. "The exit is this way."

A face formed in the shadows... A black skull with empty, hollow eyes... Twisting and stretching, grinning...

If you stare at something dark, and deep, and empty for long enough... sooner or later, it will invite you in.

Adrian had never believed his father on that score, but seeing the enormous, dark pit with only a weak island of light, he recognised the truth of it.

Wind whistled through tumbled stone and the sun speared through gaps. Adrian scrambled through and climbed down. The sandstorm had dissipated and left a stillness in its wake. Adrian let the sunlight linger on him before assisting Dante and Diaz down.

Diaz stretched her arms. "Finally, we can breathe again. Where are we?"

"Asedro Valley." Dante swept his hands out and took a deep breath. "This way." He forged ahead, whistling and swaggering.

Adrian watched him go, and a pang of guilt stabbed his chest. He'd forgotten how much he'd enjoyed Dante's company.

"You coming?" Diaz asked.

In silence, he followed.

Adrian had never appreciated Phadros' landscape, but as Dante led them through bubbling brooks and across hissing streams, he couldn't help but be awed. So much space, so much natural grandeur. The dark, narrow alleys and cloying filth of Lower Phadra might as well be a world away.

The Asedro River snaked between sandy canyons, and ahead, a forest full of beech and fir trees loomed.

"The woods ahead…" Dante frowned.

"What?"

"Asedro Forest… Looks different. Ruptured and upturned, or… I don't know. So many forests in Phadros, I'm likely confusing them, eh?"

Dante stepped forward but Adrian held a hand out. "Wait."

"What is it?"

"Smoke, above the treeline."

"I swear to the Gods," said Diaz, "if we find that church of Irros and it turns out we've gone in a circle…"

Adrian dashed into the treeline, eyes scanning the shadows, hand on Nightsbane's hilt. Broken trunks and fallen trees littered the forest floor. The metallic smell of burning igneus hung in the air.

The White Death.

He crouched low and prowled through the trees, a predator with the scent of blood in its nostrils. Deep gouges and twisted steel scarred the ground.

But instead of Wielders, he found soldiers—Phadrosi soldiers, surrounding a hulking mass of metal.

Adrian's heart sank. "Not Wielders," he said when Diaz had caught up.

"You sound disappointed."

Adrian recognised the soldiers' purple uniforms—the Order of the Amethyst Lynx. "It's the *Judgement.*"

He stepped forward, Diaz and Dante close behind. Soldiers surrounded it, ferrying crates and making repairs. Holes and scorch marks riddled the warship's hull, and its ruptured fuel lines snaked into barrels to gather escaping liquid igneus.

"You ought to put up a defensive perimeter," Adrian said.

At once, the soldiers raised their repeater rifles.

"Um, Adrian?" said Dante. "I could do without getting shot."

Adrian held a hand up. "I'm here on behalf of the Phadrosi Crown. What happened?"

Their leader pulled away from the map he was staring at and strode forward—Adrian recognised him straight away: Sir Talan Vega, the Lynxes' First Sword. At over six feet tall, he towered over Adrian. A tight nest of auburn curls crowned his head, and he wore a neat moustache. The violet in his eyes glinted brighter than Dante's. "Name yourselves."

"I'm Sir Adrian Navarro, Commander and First Sword of the Order of the Shadow Dragon. What happened?"

A smile played on Vega's lips. "For a moment I thought you were someone important."

"What are you doing here?"

Vega regarded Adrian like he was shit on his shoe. "Recovery operations—not that it matters to you."

"What happened to your vessel?"

Vega pulled his gaze away from Adrian's and scratched his cheek. "Technical malfunction."

"Bloody big malfunction," said Dante.

Through tight lips, Vega said, "Sir Adrian—since you're here, you will assist with our repairs. Speak to my engineers, they will direct you."

"No."

Vega frowned. "Excuse me?"

"As Commander of a Phadrosi military order, I outrank you. I have my own mission."

Vega bristled. "Then don't let me detain you any further. What do you think, lads? Should we let the Order of the Shadow Dragon concentrate on its very important mission?"

Vega's men laughed, but then one of them shouldered past his crewmates.

No, not one of them.

He wore a gold uniform with black trim. "Maybe one of us should go with them, sir? You know, to keep an eye on them?"

Vega glared at his man. "Name?"

"Sir Ramiro Alvarez."

Vega cocked his head. "Well, Alvarez, since you're wearing the colours of the Golden Griffin and are therefore about as much use to me as tits on a kipper, *you* can go with them."

Adrian welcomed the decision—Vega was hiding something and it wouldn't take much effort to get Ramiro to talk. Couldn't shut him up, most of the time.

"Sir." Ramiro wore relief as plain as the griffin on his uniform. He nodded to Adrian but didn't let Vega know that they were acquainted.

"Hold on," Vega said. "Alvarez, where's your babysitter?"

Ramiro paled. "Sir?"

"The one you follow like a lovesick puppy."

Ramiro's friend Mara stepped forward, Grease and sweat glistening on her skin. "Sir."

"Go with your boy-toy—see that he doesn't bring the good name of the Amethyst Lynx into disrepute—like he has with his own outfit."

Mara's lips pursed. "Sir, my place is here."

"Oh, it is?" Vega put his hands on his hips. "What do you reckon, lads? Is it a coincidence that the *Judgement* crashed as soon as Lucien let women join the Lynx?"

Again, the men laughed.

"Off you go, Sir Mara. That's an order."

To her credit, Mara didn't strike the smug bastard then and there. She offered a curt salute and said, "Sir."

Adrian turned to Vega. "I wasn't kidding when I said you need to set up that perimeter, Sir Vega—that's an order."

"Gods, what an asshole," Dante said when they'd cleared the woods.

A gale swept over the open grassland, cold on Adrian's skin. "Alright, Ramiro, what in all hells happened?"

Ramiro opened his mouth to speak, but Mara cut him off. "Airship crashed. Pretty obvious."

"Ramiro, that your assessment, too?"

The young knight couldn't meet Adrian's eye. "Yes."

"Don't think we're hanging around," Mara said. "We ain't Shadow Dragons."

"Good, 'cause we don't have the supplies for you. Dante, where can they get passage back to the capital?"

"Alma-Condenar's a day or two's walk, it's on the troubadour route," the actor said. "Travelling carnivals stop there to replenish their supplies. There's half a dozen villages between here and there, so you might get lucky, but most folk will be in Phadra for Sol's Kiss."

"Right—Mara, Ramiro, accompany us 'til then."

And in the meantime, you'll give me answers.

Adrian crossed a stone bridge that straddled a foaming stream. Black mountains glowered at him, absent of the ignicite that once pulsed through them.

"Um, thank you," Ramiro said to Adrian.

"For what?"

"Being there when you were. To think I cheered when my commander seconded his men to the Lynx. Sir Vega's a legend but he's... Not easy to get along with."

"Reckon most military legends are assholes."

"Goes double for the Order of the Shadow Dragon," said Mara.

Adrian didn't argue—his order courted controversy back in the day, most of it justified.

"I thought you were the sole member of your outfit?" Ramiro asked.

"Oh, we're not with him," said Dante. "Well, we are, but not really."

"You'll have to explain your situation sooner or later," Sergeant Diaz said.

Mara looked the watchwoman up and down. "Who the hell are you?"

"She's with the Watch," Dante answered.

"And who the hell are *you*?"

"*Not* with the Watch, which makes me more trustworthy than her."

"*Mara*," Ramiro urged. "They're on our side."

"Ain't on mine—I belong to the Amethyst Lynx." She nodded to Adrian. "He your commanding officer now?"

"He's of the Shadow Dragon, Mara—if anyone can help us, it's him."

"Okay, enough." Adrian stopped. "What happened to the *Judgement*?"

"Not here." Ramiro eyed the sky. "Indoors. Safer."

It didn't take long to find an inn by a crossroads village, the Travelling Troubadour. It had been commandeered by the Order of the Ivory Dove and used as a checkpoint and resupply station for those heading north.

A long queue of people spiralled towards a Bride's Code transmitter; the device let anyone send and receive messages to loved ones. A knight of the Ivory Dove explained that some people had been waiting two days for a response. Sergeant Diaz glanced at it and looked away.

She's worried for her family.

The watchwoman asked a lot of questions but didn't offer much about her own personal life. *Probably for the best. Friends make a warrior weak.*

Cutlery chimed and men and women shared stories and laughter. In here, the troubles of the outside world didn't seem to matter.

"Dozens of villages like this, all over Phadra," Dante explained. "All left to rot after air travel became commonplace. It's people like me—entertainers, singers—that keep them alive. Stories are the lifeblood of mankind, don't you think?"

Mara glowered at him from across the table.

The Doves ministered and read passages from the Fayth Codex to San Sirans seeking shelter, but they had welcomed Adrian and his allies with open arms. They offered food for free but Adrian donated fifty aerons.

Dante and Diaz ate a meal of monkfish and rice seasoned with saffron and garlic, but Mara and Ramiro could only pick at their food; normally the two rookie knights were inseparable, but here they sat apart.

Adrian had no food. He sipped water from a battered tankard and said, "Talk."

Ramiro pulled a small pewter hip flask from his tattered golden jacket and set it onto the table. "Vega…"

"Ramiro," Mara growled. "You owe 'em nothing."

"No, Mara, we do. The *Judgement* was attacked, Sir Adrian. By monsters."

"Monsters?"

"Darkness. Smoke demons."

The din of laughter receded into nothing and the only sound came from Adrian's hammering heart.

"Keep going."

"We thought it was a storm cloud at first." Ramiro shook his head. "The instruments went haywire… We thought other craft were attacking, maybe the Idari, so Vega commanded the gunners to open fire… Gods, the sound. It was like thunder. But there were no other vessels. The sky turned black and burned, then tore open… Shadows spilled out of the hole and into the airship. Shadows with *faces*." Sweat beaded the young knight's pallid skin. "They melted through the bulkheads, dark and translucent and... They attacked us with swords of smoke. Our steel passed right through them. I, I tried to fight, but it was useless." Ramiro stared at his hip flask. "Useless."

"What happened next?" Adrian leaned closer. "Ramiro, *what happened next?*"

"A shade of a man... He stalked through the corridors and slaughtered our soldiers." In trembling fingers, Ramiro held his flask and stared at it. "A gift from my father, this. 'To Sir Ramiro Alvarez.' Glenfortoshan, twenty-one years old. He bought it on the day I was born. I'd intended on saving it, enjoy a dram after a glorious return from every mission." Ramiro laughed but the sound had no humour. He drank.

Adrian understood. His own most prized possession was a book of fairy tales that his father used to read from. Adrian loved the story of Dalil, a boy who tricked his master and summoned a djinn, and the tale of the Sleepless Knight. He hadn't opened it since the night his father died.

But right now, none of that meant a goddamn thing. "Keep going."

Ramiro tilted his head in curiosity. "A strange thing... The flickering shade wore expressions on his face, like a man... The darkness smiled at me, Sir Adrian."

Stare at the darkness for long enough, and it'll invite you in...

"He had a crown," Ramiro continued. "At least, the flickering shadows resembled the tines of a crown. We fought back. *Tried* to fight back. Ha! Sabres did nothing. Repeater bullets sailed through them, maimed more of our own men than anything else. All our training... The Shadow King wielded a huge sword of shimmering black. It cleaved through men like butter. He hacked them to bits, severed limbs, cut bodies in half... But by the time they hit the ground, they were old and rotted and cold and shrivelled and…" Ramiro tipped the flask to his lips again, though his trembling fingers spilled more whisky than he drank. "It stole the light from their eyes. I'll never forget the expressions on their faces, Navarro; frozen in anguish, empty eyes staring at me… They'll follow me forever."

Dread seeped through Adrian's stomach like the sewage in Lower Phadra. "I know it's difficult, Ramiro, but I need to know everything."

"The shade came for me. I carried a repeater but I couldn't even lift the damn thing let alone fire… He raised his sword, and…"

"I pulled Ramiro away." Mara's voice sounded as heavy as a tombstone. "And we ran. Hid inside the boiler room. No wonder Vega kicked me out."

"We listened to our comrades die. Then the strangest thing." And here, Ramiro met Adrian's eye. "A storm came out of nowhere. Wind and lightning and white light filled the sky. The lightning struck us. I've been on an airship struck by lightning before—normally, it's harmless, but this… This was different. It tore the thrusters and rotors, burned the emergency ballonets. Then scorching light, bright as the sun. When it faded, the demons, the Shadow King, the hole in the sky… All gone. The sky shook, like a mirage. An invisible scar, like—"

"Like it had been sewn back together." *Like the scarred sky above the church of Irros.* "Then what? Think carefully."

"We crashed," Mara said. "The storm's what brought us down. We ploughed through the earth. Reckon the King of Shadows was a distraction. In under ten minutes, Phadros' greatest warship was taken out."

"That's not all. After the crash…" Ramiro tipped the flask to his mouth again.

"What?"

Candlelight shimmered in Ramiro's glistening eyes. "A unit of Doves came to help. They were escorting civvies from a village—probably here. Vega told them to hand over their weapons and supplies. When they refused, he executed them—the Doves *and* the San Sirans. Said that if they disobeyed, it was because they're conspiring with the enemy. Sir Talan Vega committed an act of war."

The dipping sun washed the world in crimson. Flat country turned into mountainous terrain. Adrian pushed on, accompanied by the song of nightjars and crakes. Tributaries met and formed a rushing river. White froth washed over his dark clothes as he leapt from one rock to another.

The shade of a man.

A king of shadows.

He's here.

The thing that killed my father...

He's here.

How many times had Lucien told him that the shadow figures were his imagination? How many times had Adrian told *himself* that the images were the result of a young boy's trauma, nothing more?

But they're real.

They're all real.

And only I can stop them.

Ramiro hadn't spoken since his revelations, and Adrian had told Dante and Diaz to stay with the Doves in the Travelling Troubadour, but the Doves had no beds to offer.

Adrian stood at the other side of the river, waiting on the others. Mara arrived first; she eyed Adrian with naked suspicion. "You're gonna get 'em killed. You know that, right?"

Dante flailed and plummeted into the water. Diaz helped him to solid ground but not without an insult.

"I'll kill the White Death *and* the Shadow King."

Mara looked far from convinced. "Night's coming. We need shelter."

They followed the winding river, clambering over rocky inclines and staying close to the shore.

"There." Dante pointed to a yawning cave. "That's our digs for the night. Once, I—"

"Stayed there during a tour," Diaz said with a sigh. "And no doubt the spirits of the dead convinced their loved ones to fill your pockets with coin."

"Okay." Adrian looked to the sky; the swelling moon shone bright. "We rest here, set off at daybreak."

Ten minutes later, they were around a campfire on a stony beach. The nameless river brushed over the rocky shore; Adrian didn't hate the sound.

A warm breeze passed but Ramiro sat hunched over, with Mara's light cloak over his shoulders. He stared into the fire. Dante and Diaz shared their rations of dried fruit, crackers, and salted meat from the stash in Oro Lengua. The darkness of that place lingered on Adrian like smoke after a fire.

Mara nudged sticks and the fire brightened. "Running low on food."

"Alma-Condenar is the next town," Dante said. "We'll restock there. It's the last big settlement before San Sira."

"You didn't hear?" Mara asked. "Alma-Condenar's empty."

"What?"

"Aftershocks from the Cataclysm."

"The town's destroyed?" Adrian asked. "The Cataclysm struck this far from San Sira City?"

"Way I hear it," said Mara. "Abandoned, anyway. Lucien's head must be up his ass if he didn't tell you."

Dante frowned. "Oro Lengua all over again."

Ramiro cleared his throat. Still peering at the fire, he said, "You're a seer, Dante. Could you... Would you mind performing a séance? I... I want to ask the spirits about the shadow demons."

The words hung there like a poisonous fog.

Dante shifted. "Ah, I'm a touch... Out of tune."

"Should've seen him play the fiddle in Ignarribia," said Diaz. "At that, at least, he's very talented."

"Forget fairy tales, we need to take inventory," Mara said. She kept her repeater rifle close; it was the only firearm among them.

"One gun, three swords," Diaz said. "And whatever Dante has up his sleeve."

"A pack of playing cards and a Glenfortoshan miniature," the seer said.

Mara stuck her bottom lip out. "Least we won't get bored."

"The whisky's for me and the deck of cards is missing the two of harps and the seven of daggers." A wide smile revealed Dante's gleaming teeth. "But I always seem to have a spare ace of crowns."

"Not much to go around," Mara grumbled. "Weapons, I mean." She nodded to Adrian's sword. "Who in all hells still uses swords?"

"The Watch," said Sergeant Diaz. "In these trying times, more officers than ever are strapping a sword to their hip."

"Feels like the world is stepping back," said Dante. "The ignicite crisis has a lot to answer for."

Adrian shook his head. "The world never should have relied on a single resource for so long."

"That's a point, though." Ramiro looked up from the fire. "With the Crown keen to press the San Sirans into service, the army's growing so big it's a wonder they're not armed with wooden swords."

"Can do a lot of damage with a piece of wood," Mara said. Adrian got the impression she spoke from experience.

Ramiro took another drink. "And poor Carmen must be working flat-out in the recruiting halls."

Cassandra frowned. "Who's Carmen?"

"Carmen Caro," Ramiro explained. "The singer."

"The *caricature*," Mara muttered.

"Real as any woman I've seen." Ramiro managed a smile. "She tours the country with the King's Shilling between her lips and promises to make a man of any boy who enlists."

"One kiss to sign your life away," Dante said. "Hardly seems worth it."

"You've obviously never seen her."

Cassandra held her hand up. "Wait, wait, wait… She'll *kiss* any boy who signs up?"

Mara crossed her thick arms. "More'n that, if you believe the talk in the barracks."

Diaz's eyes bulged. "She's a… *whore?*"

"Consider the men who sign up to lick the king's arse for a kiss and a shilling," Dante said. "Who do you think's being screwed more?"

"Dante," Adrian started, "you've taken more shillings than half the army combined."

"A falsehood!" Dante grinned, and his purple irises snatched light from the moon. "Dante tal Arata has taken no King's Shilling. Other men with my face and different names may have taken them, who can say?"

Adrian unsheathed his sword, set it on his lap and ran a cloth over the blade. Moonlight flowed over the steel like a rushing river. "You should all rest. I'll take the watch."

"All night?" Ramiro held his flask out to Adrian. "Then you'll need this."

Without looking up from the blade, Adrian said, "No."

"Ramiro, you're forgetting he's First Sword *and* a commander." Mara stood and unpacked her bedroll. "He's afraid he'll spill it and stain his shiny sword."

Adrian admired the polished steel one last time before sheathing it; it'd get plenty stained soon.

The red gates of Alma-Condenar stood lopsided on their hinges. Rubble and debris smothered the ground where walls once stood, and smoke lingered in the air. An acrid smell burned Adrian's nose.

"A fight," Mara said. "Recent."

Adrian unsheathed his sword. "Everyone, stay close behind me."

Adrian pulled on the red door. It screeched open and revealed devastation beyond. Fog clung to the air like a rough, woollen blanket and a light drizzle swept over Alma-Condenar's toppled walls.

A scorched stone path wended through the destruction, as if the ground had been pounded by artillery. The black stone of Alma Fortress bore smashed walls and broken turrets; it once stood proud, and tall, and mighty, with walls as tall and thick as Upper Phadra's. Where the city of Phadra had expanded and spread, Alma-Condenar *rose*—a fortress upon a fortress upon a fortress; and as it did, so too did the town that sat in its shadow.

To the south, fractured cliffs and hidden caverns invited incursions from San Sira, who—if the stories were true— came in the middle of the night to slaughter Condenar's men and steal the women and children. The fortress had put a stop to that. At least, that was the story Sir Lucas Salvarado, the great Phadrosi hero, peddled to justify building walls around the town.

Not a million miles from Valador Ramos and his justifications.

Adrian prowled forward and the hair on his arms stood on end. Half a dozen grey towers rose throughout the town, each connected to the fortress by a stone bridge. If one of the towers fell into enemy hands, then the defending force could destroy the bridge and isolate the invaders.

All proud, all mighty—all gone. Did the Wielders take over each tower and starve the occupants?

"It's like a jigsaw of a town," Dante said. "Except all the pieces are jumbled."

Ramiro pointed. "The stone's scorched."

Fire raged through Adrian's veins. "The White Death."

"Damn shame," said Mara. "This was a fortress during the Age of Exploration—a symbol of our strength. Defended Phadros for centuries. Now look at it."

Without a word, Adrian climbed over rubble and onto the fractured road. Small fires flickered and wind moaned through the streets.

The mist thickened, making ghostly outlines of the toppled ruins. In one deserted avenue, in pristine condition, stood a statue depicting Sir Lucas Salvarado astride a rearing horse, sabre raised. Its inscription read, *"I am the Sword of Phadros; I am Belios Incarnate; look upon my deeds and tremble."*

Nothing lasted forever. Empires rose and turned to dust, men and women faded from memory, and gods who were once worshipped fell into half-remembered myths.

Like Zirun and Niamat. History repeats and only the details change. How will history remember the Sons of Belios? Or the White Death? Or San—

He stopped. Like a heat mirage, the air before him shimmered.

"You see something?" Mara asked.

Adrian stopped and held a hand out. The air rippled, almost imperceptible, like sweeping fingers through a pond.

"Is…" Ramiro cleared his throat. "Is something there?"

The air shimmered and warped. *A glamour?*

"The Wielders are concealing themselves. They're close."

"Cowards." Mara released the safety catch on her repeater. "Could be watching us."

"We should turn back," said Diaz.

"Sir Adrian?" Ramiro started. "What do we do? If the King of Shadows is here…"

Adrian faced him. He looked younger than his twenty years—younger than Adrian, even. His skin paled.

"Stay here. Stay with Mara."

"You can't do this on your own," Diaz pleaded. "We should turn back."

"I have a duty, Sergeant; I leave now, I'll never find 'em again. Wait here. All of you."

"Like hell," Mara spat. "These assholes brought down my ship, killed good men."

"I'll give 'em your regards."

An icy wind breathed over Adrian as he stepped through the invisible barrier. Sword readied, he prowled through the still mist and deep into the town's shattered stone streets.

Silence filled Alma-Condenar, absolute and dense. The peaks of towers glowered down at him, lopsided and crooked. Vines crawled over the roads and cobbled stone with thorns as sharp as steel.

A glint in the hallway of an abandoned home caught his eye—a flame, orange and dying, clinging to a tapestry hanging on the wall. Adrian stared at it; the flame didn't flicker, didn't dance, didn't climb the fabric—it remained still.

Scanning the long thoroughfare before him, Adrian approached the flame and held a hand out. Heat radiated from it, but it remained still as stone, frozen in place.

He put the frozen flame to his back and advanced down the thoroughfare, hugging walls and sticking to cover.

Tangled together, thorned vines twisted through the shell of a tavern, like a snake coiling through a skull. Stone and slate tumbled from the tavern's roof…

Except they didn't tumble.

They hung there, frozen in mid-air.

What the hell is going on?

Smashed buildings and mounds of rubble surrounded him. Adrian rubbed the gauntlet on his right forearm. *Need higher ground.*

Adrian looked up at the closest tower and held a fist out.

From his forearm, a thin, hooked rope snaked out and lodged into the stone.

Adrian shot up and climbed. The grapple loosed and retracted again and again as he ascended one tower and swung through the mist to the next.

He passed a spotless starling leaping from the edge of a window, wings outstretched—but instead of soaring high, it remained stuck in place.

What sorcery had the Wielders employed here? Would Alma-Condenar be left static forever, unmoving, unchanging? *Find the source of the magic, find the Wielders.*

The grappling hook snaked out and Adrian swung to the next tower and scaled, hands and feet gliding over footholds and gaps in the stone. Perched on the battlement like a gargoyle, Adrian scanned the surroundings. Fog made visibility poor, but in the stillness, he only had to listen.

It didn't take long.

Without the howling wind, laughter resounded nearby —*human* laughter. Adrian climbed down and followed the sound; it took him to two men, one small, one huge.

He stalked them, swift and silent, using low walls and debris to cover his approach.

The smaller man was the older of the two, with wisps of grey hair and wrinkled skin. The other was a mountain of a man with long, wild black hair and thick arms. They moved with easy confidence—no fear, no trepidation.

This is their territory.

Adrian stalked them through Alma-Condenar's deserted streets, for once grateful for poor sunlight. The silence of the city made their footsteps sing.

His heart pounded with each step. What were they looking for?

How many were there?

What could they do?

The Wielders passed a cracked stone fountain. Water rose from it, frozen in place.

The two targets stopped and laughed over some joke. Laughed, like friends.

Like *people*.

The older one stopped and sat on the edge of the fountain, wiping sweat from his papery skin, while the bigger man strode down a silent street.

His hand brushing the hilt of Nightsbane, Adrian crept closer and closer…

The Wielder had no idea; he stretched and got up from the fountain, taking his time.

Adrian steadied his breath. Strike now, or wait for the old man to lead him to the bigger one—to the White Death?

His fingers tightened around the hilt. One unsuspecting Wielder would be easier to deal with than two. Adrian picked up the pace.

He'd never get another chance…

For my father.

For vengeance.

He charged, Nightsbane primed. Adrian closed the distance and—

Slashed at nothing.

Five yards in front of him, the Wielder ran ahead.

How did he get so far?

Adrian darted after him and attacked—and again struck only air.

Steel flashed and flicked like a snake's tongue, but each time, the Wielder ducked and weaved, blinked this way and that.

Adrian roared and pressed the attack. Hate gave him strength. Hate fuelled him.

But the Wielder moved fast and dodged Adrian again and again.

Adrian lunged—the Wielder staggered back and tripped

over a thick tree root bursting from the road. He tried to stand, slipped, then hit the ground again.

Get up!

Lungs burning, Adrian pounded forward.

Get up so I can put you back down.

Squirming on the ground, the Wielder punched out—a ring of air struck Adrian—but it did nothing.

The Wielder's mouth fell open. Adrian pounced, the point of Nightsbane pressed to the Wielder's throat.

Frozen in fear, the old man paled, eyes wide.

But breath caught in Adrian's throat. Doubt wormed in his stomach.

The Wielder didn't waste the opportunity; in the blink of an eye, he slipped from Adrian and reappeared to his left.

Nightsbane sheared the ground and bit the air as the old man disappeared again.

Then Alma-Condenar awoke.

Wind howled and mist rolled. Birds fluttered, stone tumbled and the fountain gushed.

Adrian spun, heart racing. *Where—?*

"Boo."

The old Wielder kicked Adrian's leg away, blinked in and out of existence, smirking and hitting Adrian in the face each time.

Though feeling no pain, Adrian spat blood. He growled in frustration as the old Wielder flicked here and there, dodging Nightsbane like a fly avoiding a swat, blinking, slipping, flickering—

Then the snap of gunfire ripped through the air in a steady *boom-boom-boom*.

With a smirk, the Wielder wove between the gunfire.

Mara.

Ramiro sprang out of nowhere and lunged with his sabre —an instant later, the old man was on Ramiro's back, punching his head.

Adrian grabbed the Wielder, but again he slipped through his grasp.

"Behind!" Mara roared.

Adrian ducked—Mara fired.

The old man held out a hand and the air rippled.

Mara's bullets hung there, suspended in mid-air. The Wielder stepped out of the way and let the bullets strike a wall behind him.

And still he wore that smile.

Ramiro retrieved his sabre and attacked; the Wielder laughed and then the sword was in his hand, poised towards Ramiro.

Adrian lunged. The old man thrust a hand at Adrian—the air flickered, but again nothing happened.

Swords clashed, Adrian driving the Wielder back, dodging and deflecting. He slashed the old man's arm—blood seeped and his sword fell to the ground. He disappeared, but this time, Adrian anticipated it; he ducked as the old Wielder pounced at his back, grabbed him and tossed him to the ground.

Before Nightsbane ended him, the world trembled. The earth quaked and rubble exploded.

The big raven-haired Wielder stood in the street, hands outstretched. A gale tore through the town. Roots as big as tree trunks punched out of the ground and rose between the old Wielder and Adrian, hard as stone.

Mara levelled her weapon and took aim but her bullets sank into thick foliage, harmless.

"Lay down your weapons!" the black-haired Wielder yelled.

Adrian's grip tightened.

The big Wielder scowled. Roots and vines snaked behind him and two cocoons punched through the earth. Inch by inch, they opened—and revealed Diaz and Dante, wrapped in vines and trapped.

Mara swivelled her repeater and took aim at the Wielder.

"No!" Adrian yelled.

Too late.

A thorny vine flicked out and stabbed her in the chest. Mara screamed, and fell to one knee as blood leaked from the wound and stained her uniform.

Ramiro darted towards her but vines burst from the ground and wrapped around his legs. He thrashed and yelled but couldn't get close to her.

"Drop your weapon," the big Wielder said again. "Or I'll water the soil with their blood."

Shaking with rage, Adrian set Nightsbane onto the ground, where the living foliage swallowed it.

With Mara's dying screams raging in his ears, Adrian stood, legs wide and fists raised, mind racing with ideas.

But before he could act on any of them, the roiling mist parted. A grey shadow drew through the fog and resolved into a woman. She marched towards Adrian, her ice-blue eyes bearing down on him, tresses of silver-blonde hair whipping in the wind.

CASSANDRA

T rapped, all Cass could do was listen as Mara's screams turned into whimpers, then to nothing.

Her heart raced and her body ached but when she moved, thorns pricked her skin and drew blood. The four of them—Cass, Adrian, Dante, Ramiro—were all trapped in thorned prisons.

"Help her!" Cass urged. "Someone!"

The White Death flitted past like a ghost, indifferent. Like the other two, she wore adventurer's garb: Dirty boots, a loose white shirt strapped with belts, and forearm greaves. No dirt blemished her porcelain-white skin.

The White Death walked with slow purpose, making eye contact with each of her captives. "Who are they?" she asked the black-haired Wielder. "Guild?"

The big man shook his head. "Not clever enough."

"Help her!" Ramiro struggled in vain. "She's *dying!*"

The White Death craned her head toward him. "Stop—you'll only hurt yourself."

"*I don't care!* Please, just help her."

"You care for her?"

Through clenched teeth, Ramiro said, "*Yes.*"

"Say nothing," Navarro commanded.

The witch gave a curt nod to the black-haired Wielder, and in an instant, the vines holding Ramiro in place receded.

Ramiro spilled out and tumbled towards Mara. He ripped her jacket open—blood bubbled from the stab wound in her chest. "Gods, oh Gods…"

The white-haired woman towered over Mara. "I can help her."

"Your people *did* this," Adrian snapped.

"Defending themselves." The White Death looked Adrian in the eye. "You're the leader?"

The knight hesitated for a second before saying, "Yeah."

"Not with the Amethyst Lynx," she said. "Or the Mages' Guild."

"It makes no difference!" Cass yelled. "She needs help."

"She does," the witch replied, eyes still locked on Navarro. "Whether she lives or dies is up to you. Who are you?"

"I'm telling you *nothing*."

"Then her blood is on your hands."

"Adrian!" Dante urged. "Let her help, man!"

"Can't."

"Adrian!" Diaz roared. "She's *dying*."

"Can't trust 'em."

"Screw your mission." Ramiro turned to the sorceress. "We're knights of Phadros—different units. He commands the Order of the Shadow Dragon."

"Thank you." The White Death bent low and gripped Mara's forearm with pale, slender fingers. Cass noticed sweat bead the witch's forehead.

"What are you doing?" Ramiro begged. "What's happening?"

Faint light, like golden threads, flowed through the Wielder's veins and into Mara's. All around, the roots and vines turned from green to brown. Plants withered and died.

Then Cass saw it.

Mara's wound closed over and her skin wove together. Flesh reformed over bone and her fingers twitched. Her eyes fluttered open and she gasped for air.

Then the witch stood and faced Adrian. "You're welcome."

Cass could only look as Ramiro comforted his friend.

The big Wielder raised his hands. His fingers moved as if manipulating a puppet; at once, colour bled back into the withered plants and flowers, vibrant and strong. "What next?" he asked of the White Death.

She put her hands on her hips. She was pretty, pale of skin save for a sprinkling of freckles over her nose and cheeks. She looked the same age as Sir Adrian. *Barely grown up.*

"They come with us." Her accent sounded lyrical and creamy, soft on the ears—Aludanian, maybe? "Varl."

The vines holding Cass in place slackened and receded into the ground. She smeared blood away and massaged her wrists. "You're just going to let us go with you?"

"Of course not."

Cass didn't understand—she stepped forward and—

And found that her hands were bound with rope.

What...?

Navarro and the others were the same.

"Come if you're coming—you don't wanna get left behind." The white witch marched forward. "There are monsters out here."

"Where?" Sir Adrian demanded. "Where are you taking us?"

The White Death glared at him. "To San Sira."

"Hurry up," the big, dark-haired Wielder commanded. Sir Adrian's sword hung at his side.

A trophy. Sir Adrian won't like that.

The forest only grew denser. Trees swayed and shifted, paths disappeared and reformed.

They survive by altering the terrain. Is that how they triggered the Cataclysm?

Cassie had been stripped of her sword, of course, but she didn't mind; her chief weapon was her brain. So many of her peers in the Watch misunderstood the job; they were thugs with badges, at best halting crime in its tracks but never preventing it, and never working to solve anything more complicated than a scuzz addict snatching a purse.

Cass wanted to solve cases, regardless of how complicated they were or what echelon of society the victim belonged to. She wanted to *investigate*; to discern the patterns, the variables. Numbers didn't lie—boil everything down to a number and you found the truth. How else to prevent future crimes? After this—after giving Sir Adrian to Lord Lucien—she'd see to it that the investigators within the Watch were given resources and taken seriously. Hells, with the advent of Wielders, a new squad would be required, a team that she could lead. She'd recruit the best, the most honest, the most loyal—just like Lucien had done with her.

But first she had to survive.

The White Death led them through mountainous jungle, up muddy slopes and through tight passages. The black-haired man walked by the sorceress's side, waving a hand any time they came to an impassable obstacle. The jungle bent and swayed as if in deference to him, but it took a toll—more than once, Cassie noticed him sweat and take deep breaths after using his power.

They have limits. Good to know.

Knowledge was a copper's best weapon—knowledge, and the sense to know when to use it.

But they were heading towards San Sira. Why? Weren't Wielders seeking to infiltrate Phadros? Why go the opposite direction when you had prisoners you could bargain with? Surely three knights and a copper were worth *something*?

Maybe worth more dead than alive. Send a message. But why heal Mara?

There were more pieces to this puzzle… And Cassandra Diaz relished the challenge.

"Go by the stream," the White Death said to the big Wielder. "Give 'em water."

Grunting, he nodded and took his prisoners to a rustling, sapphire-blue stream. He put a wooden cup to Cassie's lips and let her drink. The others, too.

No-one said a word for another hour. Were they observing, the same way Cass was? Or just too humbled by their defeat?

Sir Adrian's stupidity had almost killed them all. He was too young for command, too bull-headed. Cassandra stole a glance behind her; he kept his head low. Mara, on the other hand, didn't seem any different. Still tall. Still strong—as though she hadn't been moments away from dying.

The elderly Wielder kept scouting ahead and returning, but only for a few minutes at a time.

The sorceress can heal, the big one can manipulate the environment, and he can disappear and reappear at will.

But how did they bind Cassie's wrists?

The big Wielder held a curtain of vines open. "Watch step. Roots are hard as rock." His voice crunched with the low, harsh rumble of an eastern Imanis accent, probably Tarevian.

"Friend!" said Dante. "I wonder if this would be easier if our wrists weren't bound?"

"I am no friend."

"Well, if I call you 'arsehole', you'll hit me. What's your name?"

The Wielder gave Dante a sideways glance. "My name is Varl."

"Thank you, Varl!"

"You stay bound. Trek gets harder from here. Keep up."

Varl didn't lie; Cassie's legs ached as she clambered over a steep incline. Wind lashed and filled her ears. Dirt and stone broke away with every movement, each step threatening to bring her down.

"Careful here." Varl extended a hand.

Through clenched teeth, Cassie said, "I'll be fine, thank—"

She slipped and slammed into the mud, her bound fingers scrabbling for purchase.

Varl grunted and hauled her up, a mocking smile on his lips.

Cass felt her skin burn. "Thanks."

She stared straight ahead. Her sister would've punished Cassie for embarrassing herself like that for days. She heard her voice now: "That embarrassed *me* more than *you*. Can't you learn to be careful? You're so *stupid*."

And when you grew up with Mariana Diaz, being stupid was the worst crime in the world.

"I'm sweating my tits off," Dante said. "No offense."

Cass sighed. "None taken."

The sun beat down and Cassie's sweat-ridden clothes clung to her. "Where exactly in San Sira are you taking us?" she asked Varl. "Do you have a safe place?"

"Talk to Caela."

Caela. I was right—Aludanian. Aludan, the land of rolling highlands and Glenfortoshan whisky. And where men wore colourful skirts.

Cass asked Caela the same question.

"Don't ask questions—just think about ways to stay useful to me."

After another hour of rocky terrain and bubbling brooks, Caela let them stop. Varl offered Cass and the others more water. "Ten minutes, then we go again. Stay within treeline."

They sat in silence; Adrian stood rigid and fixed his gaze over a cliffside. He looked even smaller without his strange sword at his side. His hood cast a shadow over his features, like a stone statue carved in permanent misery.

"You're quiet," Cassie said.

"Often a side-effect when you've nothing to say."

"Nothing at all? After everything we've seen?"

He didn't meet Cassandra's eye.

"I know you're military, Adrian—stiff upper lip and all that. But you can't keep everything bottled up."

"I'm not; I'm just refusing to get too close to our enemies. You might consider doing the same, Sergeant."

"She saved Mara's life."

"One good deed doesn't absolve anyone's sins. Or did they forget to teach you that in Watch school, in between showing you how to beat on the homeless or make scuzz addicts dance naked for a penny?"

Cass frowned. "Those examples are *very* specific."

"I grew up on the streets of Phadra. The Watch ain't the heroes you want 'em to be, Diaz." Adrian stalked off. "All we have is ourselves."

Dante slid over to Cass. "Leave him be, he's not worth the time. Did you see what the witch did to Mara?"

"Pretty hard to miss."

"How did she do that?"

"Magic." Saying the word out loud felt strange—but how else to describe it?

"Yes, but *how?*"

"You sound excited."

"You're not?"

How could Cass be excited when this meant that Lord Lucien's warnings were true? Wielders existed. *Magic* existed, and more than likely it had been used to rip San Sira apart.

Yes, *this time* it had saved Mara, but what were the consequences? What would the White Death expect in return? Could she steal life as easily as gifting it? What other powers did she possess? And Mara… So close to death, so close to Nyr's judgment, and nothing?

Cassandra followed the Fayth of the Indecim—the Eleven Gods who had vanquished the evil Orinul and saved humanity; did she dare ask Mara what she'd seen? Or did Nyr Death-God, in her wisdom, know not to send for Mara's soul?

So many questions when a copper needed *facts*.

A few minutes later, they were on the move again.

They crossed a swaying rope bridge and followed a dirt path through a jungle dotted with vibrant pink and purple flowers.

"Are you from Tarevia?" she asked Varl. "How did you end up in Phadros?"

"No more talk."

Adrian halted. "Why are we going to San Sira?"

"I do not answer to you, little man."

"Let the others go." Sir Adrian stepped closer to Varl. Even with his hands tied, he squared his shoulders and kept his stance wide. "I'm the one who attacked you. Take me. Let them go. Kill me if you want."

Caela exchanged a glance with Varl and chuckled. "Oh, brave sir knight!" she said. "How gallant of you to save face in front of your friends by nobly sacrificing yourself. Will that make knowing we kicked your arse feel any better?"

If Caela's jibes offended him, he didn't show it.

"We're not in the habit of killing in cold blood," Caela continued. "We're not the Amethyst Lynx."

"Let Dante and Diaz go," Sir Adrian pressed. "They're not soldiers. *I* brought Dante, and Sergeant Diaz only wants to find her family. She's San Siran."

The White Death met Cassie's eye. "That true?"

Cassie forced her eyes to stay on Caela's. "Yes."

"Then you're best sticking with us. Believe it or not, we want the same thing you do."

"You attacked the *Judgement*," Mara growled. "Near killed me."

Varl's eyes narrowed. "I'll try harder next time."

Mara started for him.

"Stop!" said Ramiro. "Gods above, Mara—just *stop*. You know what happened. Vega will say it was an accident but it wasn't. He ordered it. He opened fire on the Doves and the refugees."

"We both saw the King of Shadows, Ramiro—for all we know, he's one of these assholes."

"I am not Talan Vega." Caela squared up to Mara. "I am not a shadow demon. I look after my people—we don't kill unless we need to."

"Demons attacked the *Judgement* and slaughtered dozens of men—you telling me that ain't Wielders?"

"Caela destroyed the demons," Varl said. "You say we attacked your warship, but I summoned storm to save lives."

The storm that brought down the Judgement *and nearly capsized the* Solnadar *from miles away... He's powerful.*

Mara shook her head. "Black magic don't save lives—it's a *weapon*."

Varl snorted. "It is person who is good or bad; magic is indifferent."

Cass caught Navarro's eye; he said nothing, but she didn't have to guess which side of the debate he stood on.

"Believe what you want," said Caela. "We're on a mission."

"Oh, yeah—you use white magic so you must be good. The Shadow King is black magic, so he must be evil. Piss off."

"Don't think of magic in those terms. We just... *shift* the energies of the world from one place to another."

"Magic corrupts," Sir Adrian shot. "Always."

Everyone looked at him.

He stepped forward and repeated, "Magic corrupts. After the Orinul were vanquished, orders like mine were set up to protect the world against monsters and demons—we knew the Orinul might come back."

"Orders like yours were established to interrogate innocent people and assassinate threats," Caela said. "You're the guys who extract false confessions and burn women at the stake as witches. You're no better than the Confessors or the Mages' Guild."

"The Mages' Guild are traitors to the world. They removed every record of magic, every tool we had, and kept it for themselves. Magic is evil."

Gods above, he sounds like a fanatic.

"Magic isn't different from any other kind of power," Caela hit back. "*People* are corrupt."

"Tell that to the San Sirans."

"I will, right after I've saved 'em, like I did your friend."

Navarro's expression darkened at that.

"Believe me or don't." Caela turned and marched on. "You and I are gonna have a reckoning sooner or later, brave sir knight—make sure you're on the right side."

Thunder boomed and a light rain swept through the woods.

Jagged mountain peaks rose at either side of a flat valley, piercing the sky. Caela ordered them to stick to the woods as opposed to taking the roads through the valley to avoid being spotted from the sky. With her wrists still bound, Cassie didn't feel much like arguing.

Another crack of thunder rolled over the valley floor. If Navarro and the sorceress did come to blows, she couldn't imagine the reckless knight winning.

"Thought we'd have seen more San Sirans heading north," Cassandra said. "The way the *Cetro* tells it, hordes are piling into Phadra every day. The countryside is…"

"Strangely quiet?" Caela offered. "Yeah—been thinking that, too."

Yet more questions.

Varl whistled. "Found something."

He cleared vines from a rough, limestone rock.

No, not a rock—a building.

"What is that?" The ruins of an angular wall bore down on her, hundreds of years old. "It looks like the bastion of a... Gods above." Cassie's mouth fell open. "Is this Salvarado's lost fortress?"

"Wasn't he a tyrant?" Varl asked.

"That's putting it mildly." Cassandra stood in awe. "They say peace drove him mad—that he sat here in solitude until his mind broke. His diaries read like the fantasies of a paranoid madman who saw conspirators in every shadow. He wrote that Belios himself spoke to him in a dream, said the Gods commanded him to ignite another war between Phadros and San Sira. His troops cut off supply lines and he set up a blockade on the Phadril Sea. For fourteen days and nights, he sat here and got fat while San Sira starved. For two weeks, he stood atop the walls and laughed as brave San Sirans watered the soil with their blood."

"Yeah," Mara grunted, "'til the sneaky cowards dug the place from under him."

"They were *warriors*," Cass spat. "Salvarado burned their towns and villages. Only through Sato's ingenuity did they survive."

"Two weeks of sending people to their deaths? Yeah, Sato was a military mastermind."

"She sacrificed the few so the many could live—she sacrificed her own son. She bought her people time to dig beneath the fortress and wrest it from Salvarado. She broke the deadlock. She's a hero."

Mara bore down on her. "The San Sirans who lived here were lawless *savages*—Salvarado brought peace during the Age of Exploration."

"The Age of Exploration is what Phadrosi revisionists say

to help themselves sleep at night. It was an age of conquest. Of *bloodshed*."

"You ever thought that maybe the San Sirans were killed 'cause they needed killin'? Phadros saved 'em from themselves."

"By waging war and bringing death?"

"By educating the savages who thought that sacrificing humans and cutting their hearts out would mean a better harvest."

"Human sacrifice wasn't *nearly* as common as Phadros wants the world to believe."

"All this talk of human sacrifice and genocidal tyrants is fascinating," said Caela. "Tell me again, Sir Adrian, how *magic* is the enemy of the world?"

Navarro didn't respond.

"That's what I thought." Caela started off. "Keep moving."

After another two miles of trekking through jungle, an anguished mewling spilled from the trees.

Now what?

Caela stepped through a tangle of roots and vines. "Varl?"

The jungle bent to the Tarevian's will and created a clearing. At the centre lay the body of a creature wreathed in shadows. Slick, black liquid coated its coarse hair.

Caela knelt next to it.

"What is it?" Dante asked.

"A rupicabra—a goat-antelope." Caela patted the deformed beast. Darkness rolled from it and carried an acrid smell.

"Sure," said Dante. "A mite more *demonic* than the usual forest critters, no?"

Caela said nothing. Soft, yellow light flowed through her veins and into the animal.

"You should save your strength," Varl warned.

Without looking up, Caela said, "She's hurting."

Surrounding plants withered as Caela drew energy and

fed light into the animal. Its anguished cries eased and, bit by bit, the shiny, black corruption faded.

"It's okay," Caela whispered. "Just go to sleep. Just go to sleep."

The liquid shadow dissolved, and the creature stopped moving.

"You can't heal it?" Cassie asked.

Caela stood. Sorrow lined her eyes. "The corruption was keeping it alive—better to let it pass. Varl, there's another void nearby. I can feel—"

Thunder stole Caela's words. The air turned heavy and hot.

"Everyone, *down!*" the White Death commanded.

Cassie knelt. Her sweat-slick fingers knitted together and her hair prickled.

"What's happening?" Mara demanded.

Caela ignored her. "Magnus!" she called to the elderly Wielder. "Stay close."

Magnus nodded.

Cassie exchanged fleeting glances with Mara and Dante. Dread seeped into her stomach as the air shimmered and twisted.

Ramiro swore. "It's happening again."

Caela kept her eye on the darkening sky.

Then a howl tore through the air and the earth rumbled. The sky slashed open and darkness bled into the world, dripping like ink.

Screams and thunder filled Cassie's mind. Black tendrils descended and punched into the ground, churning the earth. Her knee seeped into the mud as the world threatened to crash in on itself.

Adrian looked at Varl. "They're coming." With a flourish, the rope on his wrists fell away. He held a hand out. "My sword."

Varl looked from Navarro to Caela.

"*Now!*"

More shadow demons bled out of the sky, accompanied by soft, murmuring laughter. Varl swore and handed Adrian the blade. In an instant, he darted towards the invading shadows, slashing and slicing. Orange light crackled within the shadows and they twisted and dissipated.

But more came.

With dark, elongated fingers, they rent the air, clawing at him, but Navarro moved like a ghost, flitting between attacks, striking hard and fast, anticipating every move.

Frozen, Cass watched the jungle turn black. Lightning crackled. She stood, willing her trembling legs to run but they disobeyed.

She stood frozen as a shadow formed before her—slick, oily, black. Its eyes burned red and black fangs formed within a cavernous, stretching mouth. She raised her bounds wrists as it slashed at her—

Dante shouldered her to the ground. Blood coated her tongue and she rolled and scrambled for purchase.

The shadow warped and stalked her with jerky, shuddering steps.

Dante kept yelling but Cass couldn't make him out—her world began and ended at the shade coming towards her, hands in the shape of scythes rising, rising—

Cassie screamed.

But instead of slicing her to ribbons, the demon hooked her and dragged her away, its cacophonous laughter worming through her brain.

Her heart raced. She thrashed and screamed but the demon gripped her tight and laughed. Dante ran towards her, panic etched over his face. She dug her heels into the mud but it didn't slow the demon.

Then the world changed around her.

The jungle melted away, transformed into a city—a *dead* city, hollow and silent.

San Sira.

Red and black, the sky above the city bled, like something out of a nightmare. She screamed again and—

And then she stopped and rolled in the mud, Dante running after her.

She twisted around to face the demon—bursts of orange-yellow lightning flickered within it. When it burned away Adrian stood in its place, clothes torn, his sword dripping black.

"*Hide*," he commanded.

"Protect Caela!" Varl yelled.

Rock and thick roots appeared around them, shielding Cass and Caela and everyone else, but the shadows bled through. Magnus stayed close to Caela, freezing demons in time and letting Adrian kill them, but before long, the old man dropped to a knee, exhausted.

Caela cried out.

White-hot light pressed against Cassie's eyes, like two thumbs pushing into her eyeballs.

The light flowed from Caela's fingertips, golden threads growing thicker and brighter. Sparks showered from the rift in the sky.

More demons descended. Adrian slaughtered them, their mouths stretching in agony, their shrill screams even worse than their laughter.

"*Protect Caela!*" Varl yelled.

A demon swiped at Adrian and clawed his chest over and over—but still he stood.

His sword danced and struck the darkness; the demon howled, twisted, crackled and faded.

White lightning burst across the black sky and the demons cried in anguish.

The scar in the sky sealed and shimmered. Caela fell into Varl's arms, weak and pale. The remaining shadows bubbled and faded into nothing.

Adrian stood, sword raised. His torn clothes exposed his chest, but he bore no wounds from the demons' claws—only strange, shimmering black tattoos.

"Damn the Gods," said Dante. "Another Cataclysm?"

Caela drew ragged breaths and steadied herself against Varl's thick arms. "Barely a tremor."

Cass pulled her eyes from Adrian's tattoos. "You did it, Caela. You sealed the rift."

Though weak, the White Death summoned a smile. "One down, a million to go."

"How?" Ramiro asked. "How did you do that? You can kill the shadow demons!"

The White Death shook her head. "I told you, I redirect energy. I need energy to create energy. I redirect life from the environment to heal, and I redirect magic into *different* magic."

Cassie frowned. "You can absorb dark magic and turn it into light?"

"We should go." Heavy breathing punctuated Varl's words. "The rift is closed but magic lingers. Darkness plagues this place."

Ramiro stood staring at nothing. "They were… *tangible*. The demons. They had hands like scythes, sharp as steel and *physical*."

Adrian tied his shirt closed and sheathed his sword. "The Shadow King's growing stronger. I need to stop him."

"*You* need to stop him?" Caela asked. "And how are you gonna do that?"

"Figured I might try killing him to death."

Caela peeled away from Varl. Sweat glistened on her skin. "It's all on you, yeah? You think you're the protagonist in some story—the brave knight here to slay the dragon and then we'll all live happily ever after? No; you're not a hero and we're not your sidekicks."

Navarro squared up to her. "And you can't fight the Shadow King on your own."

The shimmering scar in the sky fizzed and sparked. The two stared at each other, both ready to pounce.

"So we need to work together," Cassandra urged. "Right?"

"Bullshit," Varl spat.

Her eyes still on Adrian, Caela said, "The copper's right. Varl, unbind them. We're on the same side now—whether they like it or not."

If I wanted to march this long, I'd have taken the King's Shilling and a kiss from Carmen Caro.

Cassie's legs ached, more than when she'd run the stone steps connecting Lower and Upper Phadra.

Thick jungle surrounded her, identical to the Bermeja—it breathed the same clammy, warm air over her, sang the same song of buzzing insects and fluttering wings.

"In my view, folk who revel in magic should be staying in the finest inns and travelling in luxury," said Dante. "You should start charging the people you save, Caela."

"We avoid open expanses," Caela explained. "It's how we survive."

Is Vega prowling the skies now, seeking his escaped prey?

Gods, she missed the din of the city. Phadra had its own song, a rhythm Cass knew well. Its walls contained it all, gave structure to the chaos. Like a suite of Aurien tal Varaldo's symphonies, the rhythms could change and the tempo alter at any moment, but in ways that felt natural; out here, in the wilderness with strangers, there were no walls, no rules, no control. *More like sitting in the front row to listen to a group of children playing instruments for the first time.*

The sun sank beneath tall sentinel trees and pink streams stretched across the sky like fingers beckoning darkness. Sir Adrian wouldn't like that; he tried to hide it, and maybe

Dante and the others were fooled, but Cass saw straight through him. *He's afraid of the dark.*

A curious thing, for a soldier in a military unit that conducted assassinations and subterfuge by the light of the moon—and which named itself after a mythical beast of darkness. Yet he'd risked his own life to save her. So did Dante. Cowards they were not.

Cass, on the other hand, had frozen in fear. Gods above, being rescued once was embarrassing—twice was *humiliating.*

But not the worst of it.

Fear wrapped over her like a blanket of ice.

She'd seen San Sira, real as anything, dark and bloodied. Was it an illusion? The demon hadn't tried to kill her—it had dragged her away. Why?

Cass forced the question from her mind; no answer existed that didn't terrify her.

And she had a job to do.

She followed Ramiro onto a log that bridged a narrow fissure. "How many Wielders are there?" she asked Varl.

He gave her a sideways glance. "You think we all know each other?"

"I—"

"People are strange. 'Oh, you are from Tarevia—my neighbour is called Boris, do you know him?' Caela, you are from Aludan—you must know long-lost Uncle Jock, yes?"

Cass swallowed hard; she didn't like being made a fool of. She heard her sister's voice whispering in her ear. *"Oh, little Cassie, you are so stupid... They don't let idiots into the Watch. Why not sit in the corner with your silly books?"*

She cleared her throat, willing the voice away. "How do you do what you do?"

"Don't know."

"I… Okay. Are there different types of Wielder? And is the term offensive?"

"Questions, questions, questions."

"If we're going to work together, we need to trust each other. You manipulate the environment; can you heal, like Caela?"

"No."

"Don't blame Varl," Caela said. "The Mages' Guild's been hunting us. Makes it hard to trust."

"Why are they after you?"

Caela didn't respond right away. "Best I can tell, Wielders have been sprouting up all over. We've always been around, but since the ignicite crisis, there are more of us than ever. And the mages don't like that."

"No-one heard of Wielders 'til recently," Mara pointed out.

"It's just a name—there have been many. Wielders, witches, whatever. The Mages' Guild's been keeping a lid on it. They haven't been relevant for hundreds of years but now that there's no ignicite and magic is seeping back into the world, well... They want it all."

"How did you find each other?" Cassie asked.

"Met Varl in Ryndara. Found Magnus in Mercuria."

"We have to reach San Sira before the Mages' Guild," Caela continued. "They won't try to destroy the shadow demons—they'll try to harness them."

"You think the mages caused the Cataclysm?" Adrian asked.

"Makes about as much sense as anything else. Or it really was an accident and they're capitalising on it. Either way, Wielders are being hunted, captured and killed. They must be stopped."

Cass didn't know much about the Mages' Guild—no-one did.

"Your powers have limits, yes?" she asked Caela.

"Yeah." Caela brushed a curtain of vines away and stepped through a gap in the rock. "A Soulwielder, I'm called. At least, according to an old Mages' Guild book. Varl's a Windwielder —someone who can manipulate the environment. And Magnus is a Timewielder."

"He can travel through *time?*"

Caela smirked. "No. He creates these... bubbles. Stops time, temporarily. Then everything resets in a blur. Imagine an elastic band stretched to breaking point; it always goes back to its original form."

"And if it snaps?"

Caela's bottom lip jutted out. "Hasn't yet."

A Timewielder. Magnus can move so fast the naked eye can't see him... Or make everyone else move slow.

"Magnus is how we escaped the mages," Caela explained. "We reached Phadros—when the Cataclysm struck, I knew they'd blame us. I tried to warn your king but couldn't get to him. The mages hunted us—figured we'd go to San Sira and investigate ourselves. That's when we encountered the portals. Been sealing them on our way south... When we're not being accosted by reckless knights."

"I want to meet a Bloodwielder." Varl spoke and his eyes lit up. "A drop of blood is all a Bloodwielder needs to give him total command over victim. And Mindwielders, who can waltz through a man's head and make him think he *wants* to carry out the actions they're being made to perform—like the sirens of legend who once tempted sailors into the sea with their mesmerising song."

"Much easier to make someone your dancing puppet when they're not fighting back," Caela said. "Not sure they exist. Not that *we'd* ever use our powers for such assholery, of course."

The thought made Cass squirm. If people were out there with the power of the Gods themselves, what was to stop them from taking over? How do you arrest someone, interrogate them and put them on trial when they could walk into your mind at any moment? Or manipulate you into carrying out their crimes? In an age of magic, what did justice look like?

"When did you realise you were… You know. Magic?"

"Enough questions," said Varl. "Caela, there is something big nearby—I feel it. It will serve as cover."

Varl stretched his hands out. He grunted from the effort, but the jungle obeyed his silent command: Trees folded back like turning the pages of a pop-up storybook, revealing a slope that delved into a deep, circular pit—but it's what stood in the centre of the pit took Cassie's breath away: A tree, as monumental as some of the buildings in Upper Phadra.

Sweet Musa…

Eyes pinned on it, Cass followed Varl and Caela down the slope as the jungle settled back into place behind her. The tree bore a dense, upturned crown with thick leaves of every shade of green. Its pale, knotted trunk, on the other hand, resembled old bones fused together.

A symbol of life and *death. Good and evil. Light and darkness.*

She stood at its base and stared up at it. "Is this… Is this Eiro's Sorrow?"

"Huh?" said Caela.

"It is! *Eiros cinnabari*, to give it its scientific name. Been around for a thousand years or more."

"Wow." Dante grinned and put his hands on his hips. "It certainly is… a great big tree."

Cass caught herself smiling. Perhaps it was nerves from the battle with the shadow demons, but the skinny actor made everything seem less serious.

"There a reason we should give a shit?" Mara asked.

Her vulgarity made Cass uncomfortable. Dante possessed a certain charm when he spoke like a gutter rat; Mara had all the charm of a pimple on an ass cheek.

"We sleep here tonight," said Caela. "It's natural cover, which means Varl can conserve his energy. Vega might be looking for us—from above, this looks like every other tree."

"Why do they call it Eiro's Sorrow?" Ramiro asked.

"Its sap," Cassandra answered. "*Eiros cinnabari* is the only species of tree in the world to have red sap, and—"

"And it looks like blood." Adrian's voice came low and heavy.

"Yeah. Eiro is the God of Peace. When we fight, she cries blood."

Mara shouldered past Cass. "Then I reckon the forest will be flowing red soon enough."

The Wielders fed them with fresh berries that burst with tangy juice. The landscape shifted around them; roots snaked this way and that, creating walls and canopies. Rocks churned and formed defensive pits along the perimeter. Magnus examined Varl's work, and in an instant, ripe apples and pears materialised. Figs and walnuts and apricots, too.

That's how they've been surviving; going from place to place with nothing but the clothes on their backs, manipulating the landscape around them to create food and shelter. Miracles.

"These berries are delicious," said Cass. "Can't conjure chickens, can you?"

Varl almost smiled. "No."

Growing food in an instant, a man who can manipulate time... The Watch would do well to have a Wielder on its books—as would every organised crime gang in the world.

Caela stretched her limbs and drank three cups of fresh water, one after the other.

"Why does she do it?" Cassie asked Varl. "She risks her life for a world that hates her. You all do."

"Asked her same question myself. I was content to let world fend for itself. But Caela is... Inspiring. Regretting my decision to follow her now, but if I turn back, she'll kick my ass."

Magnus snorted in agreement. The old Wielder lay back in the mud, flicking stones high and suspending them in time. He watched them float against each other, like some sort of game.

"The Watch in Phadra spoke of a white light," said Cassie. "A white light that burst from the sky, triggering an earthquake, or volcano."

"Not her," said Varl. "Caela will *seal* the portal in San Sira. She is wielder of light; these voids in the sky are born of darkness—they reveal the Shadow Realm beyond. Caela will save San Sira. She'll save world."

Caela approached them. The breeze made her light, white shirt flutter like the wings of a dove. "Talking about me?"

"Interrogated, more like," Varl answered.

"Varl here believes you'll save the world," Cassandra said.

"I hope so." Caela stretched her arms. "The smaller voids drain me, but they're just aftershocks—the big one, the portal above San Sira… That's still there. I seal the big one, then no more aftershocks, no more demons."

"You've seen it?" Adrian asked.

"I *feel* it."

"You will save it, Caela," said Varl. "You are the brightest light in world."

"Nyr's tits." Mara rolled her eyes. "You sound like you're in love."

Varl reddened. "Just saying she is powerful, is all."

After eating, Varl took their weapons, for all the good that steel and bullets did against the shadow demons. The Wielder took great joy in taking Sir Adrian's glowing sword from him. Again.

"Can't have you killing us as we sleep," the Tarevian said.

"If you think I need a sword to kill you, you don't know what the Order of the Shadow Dragon is."

"Speaking of which," Caela started, "I've got some questions."

"And?"

She cocked her head. "And you're gonna answer them. Firstly, your glowing sword—is that ignicite?"

For a long moment, Adrian said nothing. Then, "Yes."

Caela nodded. "The demons are vulnerable to it—good to know. Your tattoos—they just for decoration or something more?" The white witch didn't elaborate, but Cass admitted to being curious, too.

Adrian glared at Caela. "They're a tool. That's all."

"If we're gonna work together, we need to trust each other. You know what *I* can do; I need to know what *you* can do."

"It's… a secret."

Gods above, he sounded like a schoolboy.

"The tattoos are magic, aren't they?" Caela said.

"*Magic?*" Half-chewed fruit burst out of Dante's mouth.

Adrian tried to keep his composure, but he squirmed at the word. "The Order of the Shadow Dragon—"

Dante laughed. "And people call *me* a fraud."

"They ward you against mystical attacks at the same time as giving you powers," Caela pressed. "I'm right, aren't I?"

"It's… complicated."

"Then simplify it."

His brow furrowed. "It's shadow ink. Don't ask me where it came from, 'cause I don't know. My order uses it to give knights powers—use our enemies' strength against 'em. The symbols offer protection against magic, inoculate us against mystical toxins, prevent possession."

Cass couldn't believe the words coming out of his mouth. *After everything he said about Wielders.* "But back in the jungle, Magnus bound your wrists, too."

"The ink doesn't affect the environment, only direct attacks —and even then, it takes a second to engage. Magnus used his powers to get close, not directly against me. Its protections are limited. I don't understand all of it—but I know that it works."

"Fascinating," said Ramiro. "It protects you from the shadows. You may be able to go against the Shadow King."

"Can we all use it?" Mara asked.

Adrian shook his head. "In the wrong hands, it's dangerous. The world can't know about it. And there's a price."

"Which is?"

"Turns you into an arsehole," said Dante.

"Are they permanent?" Cassandra asked.

"So many questions." Adrian cocked his head. "You sure you're with the Watch and not the Confessors?"

"I've an inquisitive mind."

"Best be careful with that," Dante started. "You know what they say: Curiosity killed the—"

"Cat?"

"Copper."

"Varl had a… friend," Caela started. "A man from Val Candria. He travelled all the way to Aludan and trained with a group called the Nyr-az-Telun."

"Assassins," said Adrian. "Killers."

Mara spat a wad of phlegm. "Not like the Shadow Dragon at all, then."

"They give their soldiers potions to make 'em stronger," Caela explained. "To heighten their senses. One of them had tattoos like yours."

Adrian frowned but said nothing.

Cass had only heard rumours of the Nyr-az-Telun; older watchmen used them as ghost stories to haze new recruits—she'd never believed they were real.

"I mean, *I'm* magic." Caela laughed. "But some of those stories are insane. If you die, do your tattoos disappear?"

Adrian held her gaze.

Was that a threat?

"Yes," he answered. "If I die, the ink disappears so that the order's new First Sword can bear the tattoos."

Caela put her hands on her hips. "Such a gallant knight, wielding lies and magic."

"Never claimed to be gallant. The Order of the Shadow Dragon does the dirty work so the rest of the world can sleep at night. We corrupt ourselves to keep everyone else safe. From Wielders. From monsters."

"But there needs to be justice," Cass said. "All the laws of mankind were written under the belief that we're born equal —that's obviously not the case, so we need to adapt. We need to consider what justice looks like in this new world. Running someone through with a sword just because they're different *cannot* be the answer."

"Justice?" The world seemed to quieten, and she heard Adrian's breathing, sharp and pronounced. "There's no justice except what we make."

"Justice and vengeance are separate things."

"Not always."

"You're a damn hypocrite," said Mara. "You use magic but demand that no-one else does."

He gave her a sideways glance; his hood set his features in deep shadow. "I'd rather be predator than prey."

A chill ran down Cassie's back like the caress of a dead man's finger.

"Enough debate," said Varl. "Rest. I'll take first watch."

Magnus caught his stones and thumbed his chest.

"No, first watch is *mine*," Varl answered. "Or I will wake up in different place with no clothes on. Again."

Magnus laughed, but only whispering breaths came.

"I have more questions," said Cass.

Varl stood. "Not tonight, you don't."

Cass lay beneath the canopy of Eiro's Sorrow, its thick leaves blotting out the moon. Varl had conjured strange bioluminescent mushrooms to provide light. They pulsed with a soft, enchanting purple. Cass watched the colour ebb and flow.

Together, the Wielders could solve the fuel crisis *and* save the people of San Sira—if Cass could only contact Lucien. Phadros would be safe—perhaps even the rest of Imanis, too, if the Wielders proved to be a deterrent against Idari aggression.

And, yes, Cassandra would benefit—Lucien would see to that. But ambition was healthy, and she'd do so much good in the higher echelons of the City Watch. Maybe even Arch Vigil one day.

"*Mycena Morada*." Dante's voice pulled her from her thoughts.

"Hmm?"

"It means, 'fungus of purple.'"

"Fascinating. Next time my Watch house has a cops versus crims quiz, I'll invite you along to give us a good contest."

"You know, I was almost named Morado on account of my exquisite purple eyes. As a baby, I charmed anyone who looked at me."

Cass almost made a jibe about Dante conning people out of their coin even as an infant, but she didn't have the energy. She had to give him credit—of everyone, Dante was the only person who didn't seem depressed, dejected or on edge.

"Why are you so calm?" she asked. "And optimistic?"

He shrugged. "Just my nature, I guess. I'm either full of sugar or full of shit. Right now, I have food and shelter— those things aren't always a given. The company could be a shade better, but two out of three ain't bad."

Sergeant Diaz thought she knew everything about the criminal underbelly. Dante wasn't violent or malicious; in that, if nothing else, Sir Adrian was right: There were shades of grey between black and white.

Mara and Ramiro spoke to each other in whispers; Adrian simply sat, his back straight, as if meditating.

The jungle thrummed with nocturnal sounds, like a midnight sonata. *Music is a magic that even Wielders can't surpass.* The first—and only—time Cass had touched the keys of a piano, her sister had ridiculed her. *"You're too stupid to play music."* Cass had blamed herself, but looking back, it was Mariana's own insecurities that had made her so bitter.

That's why she enjoyed Grandpa Luís' machines so much; they either worked or they didn't. Playing music in front of people meant you couldn't hide behind mistakes or make excuses—it made you vulnerable. Tinkering with her grandfather's Bride's Code machine in secret meant she could run tests and practice in secret, with only the occasional broken mechanism or singed eyebrow as evidence of a mistake.

"That was a brave thing you did," she said without thinking.

"Saving your life?"

"Oh, Gods—I haven't even thanked you for that."

"Best not—don't want people to see through my carefully-cultivated roguish persona."

"Still... Thank you."

"Welcome. I will *absolutely* cash that favour in if you ever catch me stealing."

"I hope that's a joke."

"Of course it is; you'd never catch me."

"Just when I was about to commend your bravery. No, I wasn't talking about when you saved me—I meant in the tavern. When you played the fiddle."

"Oh." Dante shrank. "Well, thanks, but... Yeah. Yes."

"It's not easy, to put yourself out there. We put up these walls, to protect us, but... I don't know. Ignore me. I'm tired and babbling."

"You know, I suspect your reputation isn't entirely

earned, Cassandra Coldheart. You're softer than the front you put up."

"Maybe I believe that you trap flies with honey, not vinegar." *Just like Inspector Mila—and look how she ended up...*

Cassie turned and stared at the glowing purple light until sleep came.

Morning slashed the sky in pinks and oranges. Life teemed around Eiro's Sorrow and the jungle smelled of rosemary and wormwood.

Caela, Mara and Sir Adrian were huddled over a map and talking about a place called Terra Puerta; Cass strode toward them before spying Dante sitting alone, scribbling something on a piece of paper.

"What are you writing?"

The pen stopped and Dante looked up. "A play. I think. I'm... Not entirely sure. Just letting the words spill out. Been a while since I've felt so inspired. Being away from the pressures of the city, surrounded by nature and seeing what Caela did for Mara... It feels... *nurturing.* Shadow demons notwithstanding."

Cassie noted the balls of crunched paper surrounding Dante. "Well, be careful you don't waste *too* many trees; Varl's power only goes so far."

"Very droll."

Dante was an enigma. He bounced between Phadrosi street rogue and dapper dandy with every word. Which was the real Dante?

"Have you always composed your own work?" she asked.

"I've always *tried*, but..." Sunlight sparkled in his purple irises. "The circles I ran in, it didn't do to have aspirations beyond the next mark, not unless the scoundrels could make use of it. I never belonged, not to the toffs in the Musicians' & Actors' Guild, nor to the cutpurses. I've always been a bit of both. I think that's why I like it among you lot—the Wielders don't belong anywhere, so they belong together. It… inspires one to confront their own imposter syndrome, no?"

Cassandra stared at him, stunned. Being a part of two worlds, belonging to neither… For Dante, it was his social class. For Cassie, her race. *And* career. Hadn't she suffered from the same doubts as she climbed the ladder within the Watch? How many times had she second-guessed herself as a rookie, or wondered if she'd been promoted only because of her San Siran bloodline, a way for the brass to show her off and prove how tolerant they were? How many times had a male superior put her down in front of his peers?

And so the enigma remains unsolved. Perhaps the rogue and I have more in common than I—

"But you *are* an imposter!" she yelled without thinking.

"What?"

"You pretend to commune with the dead."

"Yes, but I don't know if I'm ever any *good* at it; that's the difference."

"Gods above."

"I offer comfort and support." The response came quick, as if he'd rehearsed it a thousand times.

"You spin lies," Cass pressed. "You simply tell people what they want to hear."

"Yes, well, life is bitter; why not sweeten it with a little sugar?"

She rolled her eyes. Just when she thought she'd found common ground…

Adrian stomped over to them. "Got our next destination in mind—we're gonna secure transport in Terra Puerta. We leave in five."

"What transport?" Cassie asked. "What are you planning?"

Adrian's odd eyes glinted. "We're gonna steal an airship."

. . .

Grey clouds crept over the sky and light drizzle swept over the walls of Terra Puerta, a small town nestled in the foothills of south Phadros and surrounded by canyons.

Above the walls, two small airships bobbed, their tethering cables anchoring them to the ground.

Thank the Gods—half-expected Sir Adrian to attempt to steal them mid-flight.

Lightning flashed and illuminated their envelopes. They weren't first-generation vessels, but they had the same design; a large, oval envelope that housed internal ballonets filled with ignium gas. A simple gondola hung beneath the envelope.

No thrusters, just a single engine and propellors.

"How did you know they'd be here?" Dante asked.

"Every major settlement has low-tech vessels under the command of the Watch," Cassie explained. "Phadra's were requisitioned by the military—we're lucky these are still here."

"Not luck," Mara asserted. "Intel."

"From where?"

Mara gave her a sideways glance. "My unit. Terra Puerta is to be used as a forward operating base. The Lynxes would be here by now if the *Judgement* didn't crash."

"Ah. And there's the catch."

"We have a man who can stop and start time." Ramiro grinned. "How hard can it be?"

"They're tethered, just there for the taking, like plucking a berry from a bush." Caela tied her white-blonde hair into a ponytail. "But Magnus' power drains him quickly. We go in, Adrian climbs the cable, breaks into the ship and we *run*. Varl, you'll boost us straight over the walls at the southern side. All goes well, we escape before Magnus' power expires, gone in the blink of an eye. They won't even know."

Ramiro put his hand up. "And the rest of us?"

"You know you're not in school, yeah?"

Ramiro put his hand down.

"Your objective is to not die," said Varl. "And do as we say."

"The second craft poses a problem," said Adrian. "We need to disable it before we leave, or it'll be on our heels the whole way."

Varl sneered. "Let 'em come."

"*No*, we don't let them come. How in all hells did you survive this long? If you summon a storm to neutralise it, more'n likely you'll take us out, too. Remember, this ain't a colossal, igneus-fuelled warship—it's a balloon tied to a box. Stealth and subterfuge are stronger weapons than steel and magic."

"Didn't stop us from kicking your arse, did it?"

"What's your suggestion?" Caela asked.

Adrian pulled his gaze from Varl. "I sabotage the engine before sneaking aboard our vessel. It can't pursue us if it has no propulsion."

Varl laughed. "*I* will destroy second craft—can't pursue us if it doesn't exist."

Cass shook her head. "There could be people aboard."

"This is war. People die."

"My way is cleaner," Adrian pressed. "If something happens to Magnus, we'll need you to get us away quickly. Better you're on standby to get everyone out."

Caela stepped closer to Adrian. "Even if it means leaving you behind?"

Adrian raised his chin. "Nothing matters but the mission. We need to reach San Sira and time's running out. If you, Varl and Magnus need to bail and leave me behind, that's okay—they won't keep me for long."

Caela regarded the young knight. The wind moaned a sorrowful song. "Okay. We do it your way."

The sky darkened and slanting rain hammered the mud as they made their approach. The gates of Terra Puerta loomed out of a grey fog. In a dark purple uniform, a lone soldier stood, cradling a repeater rifle. He drew from a limp cigarette.

The Order of the Amethyst Lynx—they're already here.

Cass thumbed her Watch badge through her coat. "I'll do the talking, say we're investigating a—"

And the rain hung there, still and motionless.

"Go!" said Caela.

They ran through the gate, past the dim orange glow of the soldier's cigarette and slipped through the gate. Magnus wore a mischievous grin.

Time reoriented itself and the soldier blurred, his past self catching up with the present.

An elastic band resetting.

Townsfolk crowded the main square, packing supplies and erecting defences. Did they expect an invasion from San Sira?

Horse hooves clattered over cobbles, led by soldiers in purple. Cass spotted chestnut brown Aludanian Clydesiders and black Tarevian thoroughbreds. They carried crates and cargo labelled as food and other supplies. Beneath the airships, guards stood sentinel around canisters containing ignium and igneus.

They must be using the vessels to transport cargo.

Shouldering through rushing people, Mara led them to the town square, where a clock tower stretched towards the sky.

A small knot of people voiced their dissent but they were very much in the minority.

"The Amethyst Lynx has occupied this place," Ramiro said. "If they recognise us, they'll shoot us on sight."

"We've not seen the *Judgement*," Adrian pointed out. "Might not know what happened with the Shadow King."

Mara cracked her knuckles. "Vega will have got the word out."

Is that a note of hope in your voice? Of all the people in Cassie's ragtag crew, she trusted Mara the least.

"Split up," ordered Caela. "Walk with purpose. We'll unfurl the ladder and pick you up at the base of the clock tower in ten minutes. Don't stay idle—you'll stand out."

Dante and Ramiro headed towards the western side of the tower, while Adrian and the three Wielders disappeared.

The sun struggled to shine from behind thick, grey clouds. Hands in her pockets, Cassie followed Mara. Soldiers hauled fresh produce from stores and meat from butcher shops.

"King's orders," one of the soldiers told a protesting shopkeeper.

"This is wrong," Cassie said. "They're stealing."

"Quiet."

Mara carried herself like a soldier and walked with purpose. Where did her loyalties lie?

"We'll circle around, look busy." Mara motioned to a narrow alley. "This way."

No sooner had they rounded the corner than a yelp rang out. At first Cassie thought it was a dog, until she saw a hard-nosed woman with auburn hair tied into a tight braid—she wore the black coat of the Fayth Confessors.

Scrabbling at her feet, a scrawny middle-aged man begged and pleaded.

"You stole food." The Confessor struck the man again and a tooth bounced over the cobbles. "Who gave you the key to the storehouse?"

Cassie stepped forward but Mara pulled her back. "Leave it."

She followed the soldier, keeping her eyes on Mara's back as the man's pleas echoed behind her.

Cassandra Diaz would never make it in the Watch, not without Lucien's help. The Confessors' powers were legal, but not moral. To them, it didn't matter that torture didn't yield quality intelligence; it mattered even less that it was *wrong*.

Lucien had the right of it when he criticized the Order of the Shadow Dragon's methods—Arch Vigil Cassandra Diaz would see to it that the Confessors were abolished as well.

Mara took them down stone steps bordering the town square. It brought them out to the south face of the clock tower.

"I don't like this." Cassie pulled her collar up though it didn't shield her from the rain. "So much activity—Vega must be on his way."

Mara grunted in agreement.

Five minutes.

The seconds crawled by. They wove between alleys, acting like they belonged. Wind moaned between the narrow walls and rain muffled every footstep.

But Sergeant Diaz didn't need to hear footsteps to know they were being followed.

"You," the voice came.

Mara picked up her pace.

"You were aboard the *Judgement*."

Mara froze.

"She's with me." In an instant, Cassandra turned and faced a soldier of the Amethyst Lynx. She brandished her badge. "Watch business."

"Commander Vega has jurisdiction here." He looked no older than twenty and his voice sounded as smooth as the song of a starling. His fingers glided over the hilt of the sabre on his hip. A whistle glinted around his neck.

"I know." Cass put her badge away. "Any idea where I can find him? Found this one sneaking into the town, said she lost her papers. You said you recognised her? If she's supposed to be here, then we have no problem."

"Vega isn't here yet. Why don't you both follow me?"

Cassie's heartbeat spiked. "No can do—Watch business."

Don't do anything stupid...

The soldier unsheathed his sabre. "I told you the Lynx has authority here. King's orders. Why don't you—"

A stone flew through the air, smacked the boy square in the face, and brought him down. Blood bubbled from his nose.

Mara darted towards him. Though dazed, the soldier scrambled on the cobbles and blew three short, sharp breaths into his whistle. A chorus of whistling rose up and a shrill alarm pierced the air.

"Shit!" Mara yelled. "Run!"

Cass had no choice. She followed her down an alley, the soldier on her heels, wind and rain lashing her face.

They rounded a corner—and met three soldiers with repeaters.

"Move!" Mara charged through a weak wooden fence and into a stable. Horses snorted and reared back.

They fell through the door at the other side and back into the frenetic town square—one of the airships sailed overheard, a searchlight flitting over the ground.

The townsfolk scattered and soldiers yelled. Shots rang out.

Cass could only follow Mara.

The searchlight scoured the alleys and pinned onto them, but still Cassie ran, legs aching and lungs burning.

"On me!" Mara bent low and hefted a manhole cover. Shouts rang out and steel glinted in the dark.

Swift and silent, Mara disappeared into the sewer.

Cass followed. She landed on her hands, fingers splayed upon grimy stone.

"Move!"

She ran. Darkness permeated the tunnel and a cloying metallic stench filled her nose and throat. "Where are we going?"

Voices called out behind her and feet pounded stone. As

Cass ran, darkness closed in on her, deeper and deeper. She sensed the soldiers closing in behind her.

Lit by weak candlelight, three tunnels opened before them. Without slowing, Mara pointed to the right-hand tunnel and darted through it.

Cass didn't know what lay before her, solid ground or a sheer drop, but she kept running.

Ahead, a low light ebbed, breathing weak light onto a heavy iron door flecked with rust. Mara gripped the handle and pulled. "Shit."

"Come on, *come on!*"

"Wanna help? Then shut up and pull."

Cass pulled and the door scraped open and—

And the handle broke off.

"Shit." Mara wedged into the gap and tried to squeeze through. "No use."

"Keep pulling!"

A whistle cut through the air.

"Here!" one of the soldiers yelled. "On me!"

"Pull, pull!"

Grinding, the door opened and the two women slipped through. Mara grabbed the handle at the other side to haul it shut but the soldiers thundered down the tunnel.

"Leave it!" Cassie yanked her back.

"Fire!" a voice yelled.

Repeaters snapped and bullets pinged. The tunnel wound and twisted but the soldiers kept pace.

"There!" Mara climbed rungs in the wall and hefted the manhole cover above her away. Cass followed.

Cold air wafted over them. The alarm filled the air and the looming vessels' searchlights swept over the town, hunting.

"There's the way out!" Mara kept running.

"The others!"

"We'll figure it out!"

They ran and ran, slipping through alleys and behind buildings, weaving their way towards the gatehouse.

"It'll be locked, they'll have soldiers!" Cassie stopped. "Mara—"

"Listen," the soldier snarled, "if you wanna give up after all that, go ahead—but I ain't going down—not here."

"We'll never get—"

"On me!" Caela roared

Cass looked onto the thoroughfare—and there, upon a galloping Clydesider, teeth gnashing in fury, Caela rode.

Above her, one of the airships descended, its envelope wreathed in fire.

Stunned, Cass could only watch.

The horse thundered closer; Mara ran and leapt onto its back.

Cassie trailed after it. "What about—"

"Here!"

Atop a Tarevian thoroughbred, Dante raced towards Cass and held a hand out. The horse slowed and Cass grabbed Dante's hand. In a smooth movement, he hauled her up.

She held him tight as the horse galloped hard.

Bullets rang and confused voices filled the world.

Terra Puerta rushed past in a blur. The outer wall loomed bigger and bigger.

Soldiers dotted its surface, raising rifles and firing.

Cass held tighter. How long could their luck hold out? How long could the bullets keep missing?

Then the second airship loomed overhead.

A pit opened in Cassie's belly.

It descended, close, too close. The horse complained and fought against Dante. Acid lurched in Cassie's throat.

The craft's gondola sheared the ground.

"You're going to crash into it!"

Caela galloped ahead, lining up with the airship.

Then Cassie's eyes widened.

The rear ramp of the gondola opened and slammed into the ground. Varl and Ramiro stood in the cargo bay, beckoning them. Caela's horse thundered onto the ramp.

Heart rising, Cassie couldn't close her eyes.

"*Hyah! Hyah!*" Dante's horse charged and leapt onto the craft.

The ramp closed and Cassie peeled herself from Dante, dragging breaths into her lungs and grateful for solid ground.

"Not out of woods yet!" Varl said.

Ahead, Cassie saw Adrian at the pilot's station—Magnus sat next to him, blood weeping from a bullet wound in his shoulder.

With Dante and the others, she piled into the wheelhouse. The town walls loomed tall—the craft ascended but bullets struck its windows.

"Varl!" Adrian yelled.

Varl grunted. His hands rose as if lifting a great, invisible weight—

And the airship rose, and rose, and rose.

Wind hissed through the smashed glass and the craft surged over the walls and towards the great canyons ahead.

Mara brushed the horse's rich brown mane. The narrow cargo bay—if it could be called such—carried the metallic stink of spent ignium.

"How did you know about the sewers?" Cassie asked the soldier.

"Y'know, your questioning irritates me somethin' fierce." The horse snorted and wagged its tail.

"He likes you."

Mara stopped brushing. "They've not been taking care of 'em. These ain't war horses." Mara crossed her thick arms. "Terra Puerta filtered the runoff from Oro Lengua and other

137

mines, recycled the water. The sewers run beneath the whole town. With no ignicite mining, I knew they'd be empty. Happy?"

"You know a lot about Terra Puerta."

Mara frowned and shouldered past her. "It's where I was born."

Cass followed her, past two cramped bunk rooms. Though it carried no external markings, the papers in the craft named it *Justicia Ojo*.

In Phadra, officers would spend a full day or more aboard their patrol craft. Each craft had quarters for male coppers and female; Cass knew full well that separating their rooms did nothing when measured against the boredom of a full shift with nothing to do—meaning that, on occasion, she had to keep watch on both the city and the vessel while the others disappeared to check the perfectly fine ignium levels, maintain the perfectly fine engine, or some other task that required locking one of the bunk rooms from the inside.

For no reason at all, she pictured Dante; he'd cut a dashing figure on his horse.

The cramped craft didn't have much to it, just the small cargo bay and a passage leading to the bridge, where the steering column and navigator apparatus were housed. Everyone but the Timewielder huddled together there, relief plain on their faces.

"And Magnus?" Ramiro asked.

"In bunk," Varl answered. "Caela will heal him when we have more energy surrounding us. It was close—this was mistake."

"What's the next move?" Mara asked.

Without turning his head from the wheel, Sir Adrian said, "We need to ditch the vessel as soon as we clear the canyons. They'll be searching for it."

"By now they know we're heading to San Sira," Mara said. "Best move is to keep going, get there first."

Something metallic next to the pilot's wheel caught Cassie's eye—a Bride's Code transmitter.

Cassie cleared her throat and said, "Um, we could turn around. Go back to Phadra. Explain what happened with the *Judgement* and everything else. Lucien will listen."

I'll make sure of it.

Adrian shook his head. "We'll be gunned down before the walls are even in view."

"Gods above." Dante threw himself onto the navigator's chair. "I can't stand any more walking through endless jungles and forests."

Varl grunted. "I am not going back to Phadra."

"You've been before?" Cassie asked.

"Sons of Belios assaulted me. They were just street gang then, not legitimate political party. King Harnan has much to answer for."

"I'm so sorry."

"Hah! Yes, watchwoman, I am sure. They used words at first. Then bricks. Then fists. I escaped and ran to Watch… And watchman laughed in my face. I lost someone close to me. So save your pity—you can't help me. I will die before I go back to that place."

"We keep going," said Caela. "No turning back. No retreating."

Cass tugged at her coat, feeling for the familiar outline of her badge. "If Vega catches us, they'll arrest us and drag us back to Phadra, but if we get there first and explain everything—"

"They'll stick a dagger in our hearts."

"Caela's right," said Adrian. "We don't know who to trust. The king and the mages are plotting something, the Confessors have been interrogating every San Siran in Phadra—and the Shadow King is still out there. Only Caela can seal the rifts and only I can take him out. We're on our own, Diaz."

The badge didn't mean anything out here. It couldn't

protect anyone. Even Mara had seen the futility in staying loyal to a group that didn't want her.

Maybe I take my vows more seriously than she does.

"We're all here for one reason or another," Adrian continued. "Circumstances saw to that. Right now, we're all we have—and we have a job to do."

Dante clapped. "Sir Adrian Navarro, proving that a leopard *can* change its spots… If not its strange, mystical tattoos." The actor stood up and put his hands behind his back. "If we're going up against the Phadrosi military, the king *and* the Mages' Guild, we need to trust one another." A grin smeared over Dante's face. He conjured two bottles of Glenfortoshan whisky and set them onto a table. "I say we drink until we like each other."

"Where did you get them?" Cassie asked.

"Liberated it from Terra Puerta. Funny what people will leave lying around—even if I did have to pry a crate open to get it."

Dante swigged from a bottle and passed it to Varl. Cass waved it away.

Outside, Phadros' canyons grew more jagged and treacherous, lit only by the ignium-powered searchlight at the nose of the vessel, but Sir Adrian was a capable pilot.

When more than half of the whisky had disappeared, Dante and Ramiro sang songs, Mara and Varl traded war stories and Caela retired to a bunk.

"Drink with me, Cassie Coldheart!" The purple in Dante's eyes glinted brighter the more Cass gazed at them. "I promise I won't tell anyone that you lowered yourself to drinking with a rogue. C'mon—I don't offer single malt to *every* pretty watchwoman I meet."

Heat crept over her cheeks and she pulled her gaze away. "Not for me." Again, her eyes fell onto the bricode kit. "Someone has to relieve Sir Adrian."

The knight craned his head back. "No, they don't."

Basic flight training was compulsory in the Watch; non-rigid vessels with ballonets, an envelope and the most basic of gondolas were common in cities, hovering above to remind people the Watch were there—though it didn't seem to deter criminals much.

Like her, Adrian chose not to drink. A pity; she'd hoped they'd all be merry and unconscious. Sleep tugged at her own eyes.

"Rest up," Adrian commanded when the drink had run dry. "I'll take us as far south as we can but we've got more walking ahead of us."

The singing died down and the others left, leaving just Cass and Sir Adrian in the airship's wheelhouse.

"I really don't mind taking over," she said. "I need to brush up on my flying skills anyway."

"I'm fine. You should rest."

"I don't need to rest."

"That's a lie."

Sir Adrian was even more of an enigma than Dante. Each new thing she learned about him only posited more questions. He used magic. He didn't seem to eat. Or sleep. For all Cassandra knew, everything he'd told her since leaving Phadra was a lie—and once you witnessed a liar tell their fictions, it was hard to see them as anything else.

She scratched her head. "Honestly, after all the running and fighting, I'm wired to the moon. Come on, I've had to be rescued at least three different times—let me do *something* useful."

Adrian opened his mouth but hesitated.

"Come on. Don't you need to polish your sword or pray to Belios or something?"

He met her eye. "Okay." He gave her the wheel. "Keep an eye on the headlamp and watch the needle—the ignium runs out, we're dead."

"I know how to fly these things."

He regarded her for a long moment, his face betraying nothing. "Yeah. Sorry. Goodnight, Sergeant Diaz."

"And you."

Sir Adrian had been right about one thing; it's better to trust no-one than trust everyone. A hard lesson to learn, but a useful one.

I'm all for justice but we need to consider what that looks like in this new world.

That's what she'd said in the shadow of Eiro's Sorrow. Three months ago, Sergeant Cassandra Diaz had arrested two women for stealing a few aerons to buy food. The fuel crisis had driven many people into the same hole—igneus refineries had closed and the price of food inflated more each day. Without a thought, she'd arrested them and knew it to be the right thing to do. A few weeks in prison, sentenced to assist the military with recovery efforts. They'd have rations, she'd told herself. Shelter. The broadsheets said everything would settle after a month or so. Perhaps Dante had a point; he'd let that child keep his apple after he'd stolen it. If she'd known then what she knew now…

No.

Guilt was an indulgence of criminals and scoundrels; an officer of the Watch *acted*. An officer of the Watch didn't second-guess themselves.

As a constable, Cassandra had worked nights outside the Beaming Bull, identical to a hundred other drinking dens in Lower Phadra. Cassie had never touched alcohol, not after seeing what it had done to her sister, but sometimes she enjoyed the Bull for its noise and its music.

After hours, however, it became a nest of gamblers and cut-throats.

Cassandra would stand outside the premises until dawn, watching as men and women entered a hidden door by the alley. It rankled her, allowing such flagrant disregard for licensing laws.

"Greases the wheels," Inspector Mila had told her one morning, as the sun painted the Phadrosi sky the colour of amethysts. "Let the smaller fish swim free to bait the sharks."

Cass had helped Mila stagger back to the station that morning, but she learned to stop complaining and start *watching*.

The shifts had also taught her to stay awake for long stretches. The *Justicia Ojo* floated through the dark, like a blue marlin in an empty ocean.

The canyons widened before her. The RADIOM kit—a piece of technology that sent a pulse out and sketched contours onto paper to identify terrain and other craft—told her that the expanse wouldn't narrow for a few minutes at least.

After making sure that Sir Adrian was in his quarters, Cass sat by the bricode transmitter. It was a modern model, like a typewriter with keys and wires and antennae, though dents and cracks marked its mahogany-coloured casing.

Flaking gold lettering dotted its side: *Property of the Royal Phadrosi Air Force*.

With a gentle *click*, the device hummed to life.

This new generation of bricode device was rare; a closed transmitter had its own cipher, meaning even if the transmission was intercepted, it couldn't be read without access to the specific machine it was intended for. *You'd be amazed, Grandpa.*

She prayed it would work so far from Phadra—that the receiver in the Travelling Troubadour would pick it up and bounce it far enough north for the transmitters in Phadra to pick it up.

Her fingers hovered over the keys.

Fool. You're hesitating.

She could switch it off and no-one would ever know, but…

Sir Adrian would submit a report to Lord Lucien, and the

Gods only knew what version of the truth he'd spin. He was loyal only to himself and chose when to follow the rules—Cassie had to be the strong one.

She started typing.

Lord Lucien,

I will keep this brief. We encountered Wielders in Alma-Condenar. We fought but we are unhurt.

My lord, I fear that you will not believe what we have seen.

Caela—the so-called "White Death"—in fact uses her powers to heal. I have encountered a Tarevian who can manipulate the environment and summon wind. Most fascinating of all, one of the Wielders can slow time.

I would not believe these things had I not seen them with my own eyes.

The Wielders are benevolent. In fact, we are on the same side. Lord Lucien, I urge you to inform the king that a great danger is coming—demons from a realm of darkness have accosted us, led by a "Shadow King". They appear through mystical portals. This King of Shadows attacked and brought down Commander Vega's warship. Two of his troops are in my party now; we're travelling to San Sira so that Caela can reverse the Cataclysm; she has sealed the voids from which the demons emerge and it is only through her intervention that Commander Vega and his remaining crew survived.

My lord, our weapons are useless against this enemy. Lord Lucien, I urge you to send support.

Sir Adrian believes all Wielders to be evil; I hold no such prejudice. Bias is the enemy of any officer of the Watch—our duties must be performed with clarity and our investigation led only by evidence. With that in mind, it is my duty to inform you that

Her fingers faltered again.

Sir Adrian is an inexperienced leader whose recklessness almost got us killed. He keeps the company of a thief who boasts of enlisting to the military under false identities and deserting with a King's Shilling each time.

I recommend that the duties of the Order of the Shadow Dragon be folded into the City Watch, where investigations into mystical phenomena will result in speedier and more satisfactory conclusions.

I do not know when my next report will be submitted.

In haste,

Sergeant Cassandra Diaz.

She hit the Send key and hoped that it'd find its way to Lucien.

Or did a small part of her hope that it would disappear into the aether, never to be read?

No.

She believed in the law. In order. Places like the Beaming Bull may have their uses, but justice had to be the endgame. Somewhere along the way, Inspector Mila had forgotten that. She'd lost everything: Her money. Her job. Her family.

Once you witnessed a liar speak their fictions, it's hard to see them as anything else.

So what does that make you, Sergeant Diaz?

DANTE

Dante's stomach growled, sweat rolled off of him like Irros' piss, and his head pounded like a troupe of tap dancers atop a rickety old stage. *A small price for Glenfortoshan.*

Yet through all that, blood burned in his veins like liquid igneus—that joyful, unfettered buzz of *creativity.* Words and pictures swam in his head—Gods above, he couldn't wait to put pen to paper! To let his words be born onto a page!

He adjusted his clothes, cleared his throat and smoothed his hair down. Outside, morning fought against the last remnants of night. San Sira wouldn't be far, now; there was still time to disappear, to let the fighters fight and the Wielders... Wield. Dante tal Arata may cut a dashing figure when rescuing beautiful maidens, but that's where the fairy tale ended. He could disappear, start a new life, choose a new name...

That's the old Dante talking.

That, and he didn't want to prove Sergeant Diaz right.

No, the time for cowardice had long since passed; Dante tal Arata was on the side of the angels! He'd venture forth with the coppers and the soldiers and the sorcerers, a common person's eye amongst the heroes. *Someone* had to record their deeds, after all. He would tell the tale of San Sira, be the voice of the voiceless. And if that meant plunging head-first into danger, so be it!

In a matter of days, he'd gone from living a boring-but-relatively-safe life in Mrs. Herrera's poxy flat to battling demons and stealing airships. Yet strangest of all, *he'd made friends with the Watch*.

That last thought turned his stomach the most. He'd have to steal a dozen more King's Shillings to wash *that* stain from his soul.

He caught his reflection in the mirror and stopped pacing.

You're not him any more.

And that was good. Being uncomfortable and riddled with angst was *good*. How else to grow, to evolve? The best songs and the most renowned poems all celebrated love and beauty and joy and hope—but that was only *part* of the human experience. What about anger? And grief? And pain?

Let the poets wax lyrical about the beauty of a leaf on the wind or a single, floating snowflake; let the singers sing of everlasting love or the transcendent beauty of Musa, Goddess of Music; Dante tal Arata would use the tragedy of San Sira to inspire him. His words would be the words of the lost. He'd dedicate his work to San Sira and her sons and daughters—a charitable effort, one that the world couldn't ignore. He would shine a spotlight on it—and stand beneath it, back straight and proud.

Yes, he'd write a play, a play for San Sira. A *good* one. As epic as *Dalil and the Djinn* or *The Pharos That Shone Upon A Shadowed Sea*. He would tour the world, from Phadros to Tarevia, Aludan to Idaris!

Well, not Idaris, but still—a play! The very thing to cement his reputation. At just twenty years old, Dante tal

Arata would become Phadros' leading playwright and adopted son of San Sira.

Gods above, was a knighthood out of the question?

He started pacing again. *"The Thief and the Gentleman... The Rogue and the Knight...* Something along those lines."

A play based on his own life, to be sure—something to challenge himself, to confront his own issues... And sing his own praises. Something that pit the two leads against each other, only to reveal at the end of Act Three that they were, in fact, the same person! The audience would *never* see it coming. *Dante tal Arata*, they'd say, *master wordsmith! Genius! Virtuoso!*

Gods above, as lead actor, writer *and* director, people would say his name in the same breath as Aurien tal Varaldo's.

And musical numbers! Every good play had to have a musical number. What was Carmen Caro doing when she wasn't kissing new recruits? With her by his side, those damned fools in the Musicians' Guild would accept his applications. He'd show them—he'd show *all* of them!

He stopped pacing.

But...

But what if he wasn't good enough? What if they laughed at him, as they had all over Phadros? Wasn't it that very rejection that had driven him down a bad path and into the arms of Rav and his crew?

Not good enough to be an actor, nor deceitful enough to be a rogue.

That summed Dante up—neither good nor bad, mediocre to a fault, doomed to be anonymous his entire life.

No.

He'd escaped all that, made a new start. Didn't he bring comfort to the grieving? Didn't he offer hope?

Yes. Yes, I am *good. Not great, but willing to get better. Willing to work.*

That was the problem; he'd wanted everything in an instant but had always quit when the work got too hard. Well, not anymore—from now on, he'd put the graft in and work his fingers to the bone.

Metaphorically speaking, of course.

And he knew exactly who to ask to get his story out there.

Someone banged on the door.

"Yes?"

"Sun's coming up," said Adrian. "Waiting on you."

"I'm well worth it."

With one last look in the mirror, Dante perfected his smile.

Show time.

In the low light, the golden-red of the canyons looked more grey, like a mouth full of teeth capped with fillings.

The *Justicia Ojo* squatted atop bare brush, clay and sand. Everyone wore grim expressions—especially Cassandra. She twisted a curl of auburn-brown hair around her finger; for the first time, Dante noticed how small her ears were.

"*We're* hungover and Adrian is Adrian," Dante said to her. "Why are you so grim?"

A smile flashed on her lips, too quick and shallow to be genuine.

"Grab the horses and whatever supplies you can carry," Adrian ordered. "Varl, conceal the *Ojo* as best you can."

"We're not far from San Sira." Caela peered ahead to the horizon, where the canyons shimmered in the heat. "Move out."

Magnus and Ramiro rode the two horses at a gentle trot. They'd scout ahead and wait for the others to catch up.

They followed an old railway line snaking through the floor of a steep ravine. A mile in, Dante found a rusted, broken carriage sitting on the rails. Flaking green and purple lettering told Dante that had it once been grand, the pinnacle of ignicite-derived technology. Had it been left here because of the fuel crisis, or forgotten about as soon as air travel had rendered trains obsolete?

As a child, his mother had promised to take him on a train trip, from Phadra all the way to San Sira, then San Sira to Ancaster, and Dalthea, and Rhis, and all the other great cities of the world.

"We'll take the train and I'll show you the world," she'd said. That was before she'd abandoned him with his father. The young Dante had told himself that she'd got on a train and it had carried her away, that she was looking for a way to come back to him. He'd let himself believe that for years.

Mara nudged his shoulder. "Move."

Dante ran after the others. His sweat-soaked shirt clung to his skin; he recalled the days when he'd change clothes three times a day and douse himself in Dark Water, a peppermint and sandalwood cologne that promised adventure. *My signature scent.* When had he last worn it?

When audiences sing my name, I'll buy buckets of the stuff. And chests big enough to hold enough clothes that I'll never have to wear the same thing twice in a month.

"San Sira's a big place," Cassandra said out of nowhere. "Yet the only San Sirans we've encountered were in the tent city."

"People are proud." Varl spoke without slowing. "Home is home, whether it's verdant field or ruined hellscape."

The copper didn't look convinced. "Yeah, maybe."

Red sand danced on the horizon, like a velvet stage curtain. *And one must step through, even when the audience is hostile...*

Dante tapped Caela on the shoulder. "Um, hello."

"Yeah?"

Gods, how was one supposed to address a warrior-sorceress? He cleared his throat and puffed his chest out. "You know they call you the White Death?"

"And?"

"Well, it strikes me that that isn't an accurate representation."

"I don't care what people think of me, just so long as they don't hurt me and mine."

"Exactly why I wanted to speak with you. You may not care what people say about you but other Wielders will—what you've accomplished will have ramifications for years to come."

Caela let a yellow and white butterfly with stripes like a zebra's land on her finger. She smiled at it before it danced away. "If you're coming to a point, Dante, get there quicker."

"Have you ever considered recording your deeds? People are going to write about you, talk about you, whether you want them to or not—I wonder if getting your truth out first will save other Wielders a lot of grief?"

Caela's face pinched into a frown. "What the hell are you talking about?"

Dante strode in front of her. "You've seen so much, done so much—the *Cetro* portrays Wielders as malevolent and capricious."

"Maybe some of us are."

"The paper blames San Sirans for everything from the fuel crisis to the rise of Idari aggression—and probably Valador Ramos' tiny penis. But now it's shifting its focus to Wielders. It's easier to hate something unseen than fix what's right in front of you—I say you remain unseen no longer!"

"Uh, honestly, I just want to stop this and then disappear —the world hates me and people like me. I got more important things to do than launch a public relations campaign."

"What's more important than the future?"

"Huh." Caela slowed, then stopped. "What do you have in mind?"

Dante beamed and put an arm around her shoulders. "Picture this: A play, in all the great theatres of Phadros and beyond." His hand swept through the air. "Show Wielders that they need not hide in the shadows—that their gifts should be visible for the world to see."

"You're off your head… But you might be onto something. I haven't thought about what happens after San Sira. None of us have."

"Well, it's a long walk—I propose that *you* talk, and *I* listen."

And Dante did. He listened as Caela wove tales of adventure and derring-do on her journey across continental Imanis, seeking answers. Prior to the ignicite crisis, she'd concealed her powers and sought the help of the Mages' Guild in Ryndara; they'd offered conflicting advice, half-baked rumours and questionable facts, but one *magus aspirant*—a novice—had told her of a Tarevian man asking the same questions. From there, she found Varl and travelled south to a small town named Belon, close to Dalthea and the sea called Irros' Bounty.

"From there, we went west, through Mercuria. That's where we found Magnus. But then the fuel crisis hit, and airship ticket prices soared. Then air travel stopped altogether."

"How did you find him?"

"He saved us. As usual, Varl and I had gone to the local Mages' Guild chapter—by then, they'd seized the fuel crisis as an opportunity, spun the rumours of magic bleeding into the world. 'In these unprecedented times, only the Mages' Guild can guide you'. After that, they'd barely give us the time of day. To be fair, they weren't wrong; stories of demonic animals had started popping up. Varl and I chased every rumour, trying to track down more Wielders. One girl in Ryndara was arrested for making herself look identical to the Ryndaran king. They say that they arrested the king *and* the doppelganger because they weren't sure which was which."

"Now *that's* a stage show."

"Anyway, Mercuria. Panic set in after everything was locked down. Igneus was reserved for emergencies. Ignium was rationed. A mob attacked a Watch house, and when I healed a young corporal, the bastard tried to arrest me. Should've let him bleed out. When the mob saw what I could do, they forgot all about the Watch. We ran. Varl tried to fight but I pulled him back. They came at us with sword and bricks and glass bottles—anything they could throw. We ran through the streets, through alleys—ended up in a dead end. They cornered us. Still remember their eyes—the *hate* in them. They didn't know us, but they hated us all the same. Then they all froze, like statues. They just stood there, completely still. Mouths open, bricks floating in mid-air, flecks of spit suspended in time."

"Magnus."

"Magnus. Using his magic takes a lot of out of him but he saved us. We escaped Mercuria on a motorcarriage, but had to ditch it when we ran out of fuel."

"Fascinating. You know, I've yet to hear him speak."

"Yeah... He doesn't talk. Best we can figure it, Magnus was a Confessor who helped innocent suspects escape. The Confessors are just as bad as the Mages' Guild. When his superiors found out he was letting people go, they removed his tongue so he couldn't 'speak out against the will of the Gods' ever again."

"Gods above," Dante swore. "Not bad for a seventy-year-old."

"Magnus? He's only twenty-eight—he's just spent so long in his time bubbles that he's aged quicker'n the rest of us."

Dante froze. "That's tragic. And *fascinating!* Do you think he'd mind if I... Wait, you're messing with me, aren't you?"

Caela smirked. "Maybe. Anyway, we reached Phadra. I

wanted to warn the mages there… I felt something. I *still* feel it… Then the Cataclysm struck. The world's hurting, Dante. She's crying out in pain and I…" She stopped moving and drew a breath.

"Are you okay?"

Eyes closed, Caela nodded. "Yeah. Sorry, it's… It can be a bit much. Feeling the world's pain. Where was I?"

"Uh, you wanted an audience with the Phadrosi Mages."

"Right. Well, you know how that ended—more mobs, more fleeing. So, we headed south, towards San Sira. I sealed the rifts and fended the shadows off, but Ramiro's right— they're getting stronger. We need to reach San Sira. We need to seal the hole in the world."

Dante clapped his hands. "So much drama! There's a lot to tangle with, there—political intrigue, power struggles between religious and mystical fanatics, a white sorceress fighting to unite the world… Accompanied by a roguish, charming bard."

Caela held fingers to her head, as if massaging a headache away. "Yeah, and don't forget your band of knights."

Dante waved that away. "A chorus of comic relief."

Show me the world, Mum? Ha! I'll show the world a spectacle like it's never known.

The sun cowered behind grey clouds.

Dante came to a sign reading, "Welcome to Mar de Susurro" with a painted backdrop of a seaside. The words "Listen to the sweet whispers of the sea!" were scrawled beneath it in flaking white letters.

Oh, I'm the prince *of sweet whispers.* Art was its own sort of magic, Dante reflected. Words and music and pictures had the ability to take someone from one place and transport them somewhere else entirely. The best musicians, word-smiths and artists performed feats of magic every day—

people like Aurien tal Varaldo and the singer Genevieve Couressa. Even Carmen Caro possessed a hypnotic allure that made men act completely out of character, like mythical sirens. Why couldn't Dante do the same? He would weave illusions with his words.

A stone bridge crossed a shallow river, where boats bobbed in silence. "We're near the mainstem," Ramiro said from atop the Clydesider. "Always wanted to sail the Susurro with my father, drink that Glenfortoshan with him as the tide came in... Though he never did seem interested. He owns Alvarez Aviation, so perhaps convincing him to sail the seas was always a folly."

"Fathers and sons." Dante shook his head. "A conundrum impossible to solve."

Ramiro opened his mouth, but before he spoke, his horse tensed—Magnus', too. The animals' ears pinned back and they whimpered and snorted.

"Go on, it's okay." Ramiro spoke with a gentle voice, but when he spurred the horse, it refused and complained.

"Leave 'em here," Adrian said. "They sense danger."

"Maybe we should listen to them?" Cassandra asked.

"We check the area out," Adrian commanded. "All's well, we come back for 'em."

Magnus and Ramiro tied the horses to a post. Beyond the bridge, a cobbled town square sprawled open, skirted by two- and three-storey houses. No birds wheeled in the sky and no breeze carried through the town. A mansion loomed at the head of the town square, silent and empty. The entire scene was as still and silent as the picture on a postcard.

No-one greeted them. No-one came out of the houses or the stores or the mansion. No townsfolk. No-one from the Order of the Ivory Dove, no-one from San Sira.

Just... Nothing.

The silence reminded Dante of performing in an auditorium filled with empty seats. The memory made him shudder.

In the distance, a windmill poked above the houses, its lazy blades unmoving. Adrian stepped forward, hand hovering over the hilt of his sword. "Stay close. And keep your eyes open."

"It doesn't make any sense." Ramiro swept a hand through his blonde locks. "This is a perfectly good settlement—why didn't the San Sirans set up a checkpoint here? A place to co-ordinate and organise? And why didn't Vega have any orders for this place?"

"No signs of struggle, no signs of life. It's the shadow magic." Adrian stepped into the centre of the town square. "This place has been picked clean."

"You can't know that."

"He's right." Caela reached out, her fingers twitching as if playing the strings of a harp. "I can feel it. There's a portal nearby."

"Then where the hell are the bodies?" Mara demanded. "The *Judgement* was a slaughter."

"There's something I need to tell you." Cassie stepped forward and faced them all, though her eyes pointed down. She wrung her hands as she spoke. "I think the people here were... Taken. By the shadows."

"Taken where?" Mara demanded.

"I..." Cassandra's face turned pale, like she'd overdone the stage make-up. "San Sira. I think they've been taken to San Sira. I... I glimpsed the city when one of them grabbed me. I think it was going to take me there."

"And you're only telling us now?" Adrian demanded.

Dante held a hand up. "Steady on, she's clearly terrified—we can't *all* suppress our emotions, Adrian."

Read the room, you pig-headed fool. Honestly, how did Adrian Navarro ever survive without Dante?

"All the people of Mar de Susurro have been taken?"

Ramiro looked lost. "Every one of them? To what end?"

"I'll be sure to ask the Shadow King before I kill him," Caela said.

"Good plan," said Adrian. "He might even answer before he murders you."

"I don't intend on dying." With a fleeting glance at Dante, she added, "Some of us have a future to fight for."

The grey clouds turned as black as a funeral shroud. A ghostly fissure hung above the calm waters of the Susurro and gleamed like glass in sunlight, fading and re-emerging.

"It's like it absorbs the light," Ramiro said.

"Gotta get close to the water." Caela slapped Adrian's shoulder. "Hope you can swim."

For half a heartbeat, Dante hoped she'd shove him in.

A dirt path snaked close to a rocky shore with a jutting, makeshift wooden pier. Row boats sat as still as painted boats upon a painted sea. Trees loomed high, infected with the same black substance as the rupicabra that Caela had cleansed. Their bare branches stood out among the vibrant greens and yellows of surrounding leaves.

Their backs to the treeline, Caela marched to the fissure, the pier creaking beneath her steps. Varl, Magnus and Adrian followed close behind; Adrian swept his blade from side to side, anticipating an attack. Even the two other knights and Cassandra looked ready for a fight.

"I'll just stand between you all, shall I?" No-one answered Dante's question. "Right, then."

Caela stood at the edge of the pier and held a hand up. "The rift's exhausted."

Without turning to look at her, Adrian said, "Meaning?"

"Meaning I don't think it's gonna spew shadow demons intent on gouging us to death. Still…"

Light flowed through Caela's veins like molten gold and

surge towards the rift. Sparks rained and Caela growled in pain, but still she clasped the light.

Like a welder's torch, the light sealed the gaping void. No demons came, no Shadow King.

Dante let himself breathe.

Caela put her hands on her hips and panted. "Well, that was much eas—"

An arrow grazed her shoulder and sent her spinning with an arc of blood.

"Caela!" Varl yelled.

More arrows struck the pier. Terror froze Dante's blood.

"*Magnus!*" Adrian roared.

Another volley—this time they froze in mid-air.

Panicked, Varl kept saying Caela's name. Dante stood there, legs like jelly, unsure whether to run or hide or both.

The White Death stood, blood weeping from the wound in her shoulder. Varl unleashed a gust and blew the suspended arrows away.

Leaves rustled and figures shifted within the town's tree-line—people. Varl commanded the trees to shake and part, forming a clearing, and—

And revealed dozens of San Siran soldiers.

They charged. Dante's heart leapt into his throat. "What do we do? Adrian? *Adrian?*"

Mara readied her repeater but Adrian blocked her aim. "The rules of engagement—"

"Piss on that!"

Sweat beaded Magnus' forehead as he slowed another storm of arrows.

"They're innocent!" Cass yelled. "And Magnus can't hold them forever."

"To hell with surrendering," Varl growled. "This is war."

"The boats!" Ramiro yelled.

Caela pulled Varl by the shoulder. "We have to go."

"They could've killed—"

"Move!"

Caela ran across the shoreline, the others close behind. Dante sprinted but his foot struck a rock and he hit the ground. He rolled, blood in his mouth, and kept rolling until Adrian hoisted him up and threw him into a small boat.

"Row!" Mara roared.

Dante found an oar pressed into his hands. His muscles ached with every stroke.

Varl summoned wind and the Susurro awakened with the fury of Irros himself. Waves threw the boat this way and that, jouncing and spinning. Voices yelled. Magnus clung to the edge, one hand raised in defence.

They broke from the shoreline as arrows rained overhead.

"Varl!" Caela yelled. "Push!"

Wind shoved them and the boat scythed towards descending rapids. Dante's fingers clenched on the oar, knuckles whitening.

"Portside, reverse row!" Mara yelled.

Too late.

The boat spun and flew over the waterfall, then another. Wind and water stung Dante's eyes.

"Hold on!"

Carried by the Susurro, the boat scraped against rocks, white water drenching everyone. Cliffs blurred past and the world spun. Dante's stomach clenched.

"Let it run!" Mara roared.

The boat ploughed through choppy waters. Varl grimaced, struggling to rein his power in. The rapids wrenched Dante's oar from his grasp and snapped it in two. He threw up into the water and took in a mouthful of salty brine, then vomited again.

And then the wind died down, the water eased and the boat slowed.

"They're gone," Varl said. "But we're taking water."

Ramiro pointed to the sun. "What's that?"

Dante's eyes narrowed. Like a mirage on the horizon, a brilliant golden beacon formed out of nowhere, high in the sky. Warm, golden light swept out from it.

"It's a lighthouse," said Caela. "An island."

At its base, dozens of people stood beckoning the boat.

"San Sirans!" Cassandra laughed. "They're San Sirans! They're alive!"

"Probably think we're refugees," said Ramiro. "They can help us."

Cheering and laughter spilled out of the island. Dante didn't know how their voices could be heard from this distance, but he didn't question it.

Cassie beamed, the happiest she'd been all day. *Cassandra Coldheart has a soul, after all.*

"Wait." Adrian shook his head. "Something's not right."

"What are you talking about?" Dante asked. "We've found survivors, Adrian. This is a good thing!"

Adrian said nothing. He kept his gaze ahead and his hand on the hilt of his sword.

The lighthouse beacon shone as bright as the sun. So bright, in fact, that Dante had to shield his eyes.

"Row," Mara commanded. "Keep rowing!"

The boat inched closer and closer, and the lighthouse loomed higher and higher...

Until it didn't.

It faded away in fragments, bit by bit, all the light and colour draining away. The cheers and the laughter died with it.

A great pit opened in Dante's stomach. "A mirage?"

Adrian growled. "Magic."

In the illusion's wake, an ancient, giant warship sat proud upon the sea, the kind that had conquered the oceans in the pre-ignium age—like something from a storybook, yet all too real.

160

Beneath the steel-grey sky, a white flag fluttered bearing the coat of arms of the Grand Duchy of San Sira: Two birds of gold plumage and black wings facing each other on either side of a three-tined crown. The ship's broadside cannons were aimed and readied, and her red sails stretched wide.

Red sails, like the curtains on a stage—and I think they've just come down for all of us.

Dante climbed a rope ladder onto the vessel's deck. Upon her hull, in golden letters, were the words *Sato Bravura*.

Granite clouds crashed overhead and thunder rolled. Rain fell in a torrent. *Varl's work?* San Siran sailors in cream-white uniforms aimed crossbows as Dante and his allies were shoved onto the deck. Two of them even had repeater rifles.

What thoughts ran through Adrian's mind? Or Caela's? Were they gearing up for a fight, or were they among friends? Couldn't Magnus simply freeze time, tie the crew up, steal their ship, and sail to San Sira?

Adrian saved me, back on the pier. He could've left me behind, but he didn't. Makes a change. One day, they'd have to have a conversation about what Adrian had done. One day *soon*.

"Inside." The soldiers pushed everyone into the captain's cabin at the rear of the ship. *Or stern. Or is it aft? Or bow?*

The room smelled like a library, thick and musty. A broad-shouldered bull of a man peered up from a map on his desk. His hair and beard were black, peppered with white, and his grey eyes were hard as diamonds. He wore a cream white uniform adorned with various medals and insignia. Their meaning was a mystery to Dante, but judging by the way he stood with his hands on his hips, he certainly considered himself A Very Important Man.

Shorter and overweight, the other officer in the cabin wore the same uniform but with fewer accessories. From his attempt at mimicking his captain's stance, Dante figured that he *wished* he was A Very Important Man.

"I am Captain Nyralto." His San Siran brogue came thick and deep. "This is Lieutenant Arturo. Welcome aboard *Sato Bravura*. Now that the introductions are done—" The captain slammed both fists onto the table before him. "—tell me what in all hells you're doing?"

No-one spoke. Dante exchanged awkward glances with Cassie and Ramiro.

Magnus or Varl will do something.

They'll get us out of this.

Any moment now.

A false grin spread over Nyralto's lips. "Brave Phadrosi knights, lost for words. We can rectify that, I'm sure."

Adrian stepped forward. "No need for threats. I'm Sir Adrian Navarro, First Sword and Commander of the Order of the Shadow Dragon. I'm here to neutralise the source of the Cataclysm."

"And you have permission from the archduke to carry out military operations on his soil, yes?"

As usual, Adrian said nothing.

"Of course not. Lieutenant Arturo, arrest this man and throw him in the brig."

"Gladly." The other officer moved towards Adrian but Caela stepped forward.

"Wait," she said. "We're on the same side."

"I'd *love* to hear how you reached that conclusion."

"My people and I are not Phadrosi—that much you can see. Sir Adrian is telling the truth—we're here to stop the demons. We're here to reverse the Cataclysm—and we need your help, Captain."

"It's true," said Ramiro. "We're wanted by the Phadrosi military—we're on the run, we're desperate, and time is running out. If you don't believe what we have to say, you can toss us in the brig. But, please, just *listen*."

Nyralto did so. Caela, Mara and Ramiro told them of their journey—of the Mages' Guild, of Commander Vega and the *Judgement*. Every now and then, Dante shaded in details— Oro Lengua, the railroad that led them to Mar de Susurro, his recommendations on San Siran wine.

"A fanciful tale," Nyralto said when they were done. "Yet not the first we've heard of shadow demons."

"Captain," Caela started, "how did you survive the Cataclysm?"

Captain Nyralto shifted. "We were at sea, testing the *Sato Bravura*... And four other galleons. Relics from the arch-duke's private collection, you see—but it seems the world has need of relics. The earthquake damaged our hull, nearly sank us..."

"The other ships?"

Nyralto held her gaze. "We're all that's left. We've been sailing the coast, gathering materials to make repairs. Now that we're seaworthy, I intend on sailing into Phadra to request aid—perhaps Phadrosi prisoners, wanted by your own military, will help win King Harnan to my cause?"

"We waste time," Varl growled. "Caela, we can kill these fools in an instant. Just say the word."

Caela held a hand up. "We're on the same side."

"Alas, you have not convinced me," said Nyralto.

"I was sceptical, too," said Adrian. "I was tasked with assassinating Caela—but she didn't destroy your city. I know that now. And don't get your hopes up about King Harnan— he's amassing an army under the pretext of sending aid. Don't believe it."

"A Phadrosi knight speaking against his king?" Nyralto arched an eyebrow. "This is turning out to be a most inter-esting day."

It was Cassandra's turn to step forward. "Captain, I'm a sergeant in the Phadra City Watch. Sir Adrian is correct; King Harnan courts war with San Sira."

Nyralto looked her up and down. "A San Siran in the Phadra City Watch—that might just be the most peculiar detail in this farce."

"We've faced the demons." Panic made Ramiro's words tremor. "Barely escaped with our lives. They come out of nowhere and Caela and Adrian are the only ones who can stop them. Please, Captain, you must believe us."

Nyralto put his hands on his hips. "When we reach Phadra, I will speak with the king. Until then, you—"

"You need to turn the ship around and go back to San Sira City," Adrian warned. "It's only a matter of time before the *Judgement* is air-worthy again. What's left of San Sira will fall. You said it yourself—you sail a relic. You can't hope to stand against them."

Nyralto laughed without a hint of humour. "Only someone who has not seen the devastation of San Sira would suggest turning back. Believe me, if I could return home and save the dead, I'd do so. The city is lost."

"And who do you think is responsible?" Adrian snarled. "Harnan has isolated his own council, surrounded himself with sycophants and the corrupt Mages' Guild. Who stands to gain from the destruction of San Sira? Who has the resources to initiate a mystical attack? *They* do, the mages and the king. You sail to Phadra, you're playing into their hands."

"Only I can seal the rift," Caela pressed. "I can prevent another Cataclysm. We don't know what the demons want. We don't know their plan. All we know is that they're growing stronger."

"And we're gonna need to work together to defeat 'em," Adrian said. "Wielders, San Sirans, Phadrosi—all of us."

Nyralto considered it. "Wielders, join me in my quarters —if you have a plan, I want to hear it."

"Captain?" the one called Arturo said. "You can't be serious?"

"Am I in the habit of japing, Lieutenant? Escort the Phadrosi soldiers to the brig."

"Like hell," Mara grunted.

"Do not fret, I will not put you in fetters—but I can't have you running amok on my ship—I'd sooner trust a Wielder than a Phadrosi operative—let's see if your stories match."

"You want the Wielders' plan but to keep Phadrosi knights as bargaining chips," said Adrian.

"You would do the same. Arturo, when they're secure, send for the Ganaldi—he'll divine the truth of these tales."

"Ravinatro?" the lieutenant answered. "Sir, you place too—"

"*Now.*"

Ravinatro? Dante's stomach plummeted at the sound of the name. *No, no, I misheard.*

"We're wasting time," said Caela.

"Yet you'll indulge me if you want me to trust you. Otherwise, you can start fighting—but I promise you, no matter how strong you think you are, *we* are stronger. Lieutenant, make sure our Phadrosi guests are comfortable."

"Is this what 'comfortable' means?" Dante asked after Arturo punched Adrian for the third time.

In a chair with his hands bound behind his back, if Adrian was in pain, he didn't show it.

Steel bars in the hold made up *Sato*'s brig—far from the worst cell that Dante tal Arata had seen.

A hanging candle lantern swung from left to right, painting Arturo in a devilish light. "If you don't talk, your friend will." Arturo struck Adrian again and Dante flinched.

"*Brute.*" Dante struggled in his own chair. "You know everything already! Sweet Eiro, just *stop.*"

Arturo cracked his knuckles. "When the work is done." He raised his fist again.

"Far be it for me to tell you how to interrogate someone," Adrian started, "but you might wanna ask questions *before* you decide I'm not talking."

Arturo's mouth creased into a savage smile. "What do you really want in San Sira, and did your Wielder friends destroy my city?"

Adrian said nothing.

"Funny man." Arturo struck him again.

Gods, this is sickening.

Ten minutes felt like ten hours. Dante felt every punch that Adrian took. He flinched and cowered, yet Adrian maintained his resolve. Even living on the streets together—thieving and surviving by the skin of their teeth—Dante had never witnessed his friend suffer so much. *There must be some lie I can weave... Some illusion of my own.*

But under so much stress, Dante struggled to keep his train of thought let alone come up with a convincing story.

Arturo's breaths came quick and deep and pearls of sweat dotted his skin. "All this beating is thirsty work. You know, I've broken every bone in my right hand doing this over the years. And my left. One of my toes as well, but that's a long story. Takes a hard hand to keep a crew in line—no room for complacency. That's how you build respect, eh? How you build *fear*. Nyralto doesn't understand that; here you are, a Phadrosi knight on an illegal mission, and he wants to let you run loose? Not on my ship, says I. I'm good at what I do. And yet you, Sir Adrian... I been beatin' you yet you don't have so much as a bruise. Gets me thinking, that. Gets me thinking that *you're* a Wielder, says I. Go on, then—show me what you can do, Wielder. Eh? Nothing?" Arturo cocked his head towards Dante. "How about I start on your friend here? How long you reckon he'll hold up? Reckon he's more like to squeal before I bloody my knuckles on him. Let's see, shall we?"

Arturo raised a fist—

And an instant later, he hit the floor.

Adrian loomed over him. "You're up against a knight of the Shadow Dragon." Deep shadows filled the facial features that the lantern couldn't reach. "You think you're interrogating me? I'm interrogating *you*. And this is what I know: You're weak. And quick to anger. And lack respect for your captain. And you're as in the dark about the Cataclysm as we are."

Arturo staggered to his feet and spat out a tooth.

"But yeah, keep going—you wanna take bets on how many times I knock you on your arse before *my* hand gets sore?"

Rage filled Arturo's face—but when he opened his mouth to roar, no words came. A fleck of spittle flew and stopped in mid-air.

Magnus crept into the room. He wore a grin that only increased the depths of the creases on his face. Wordless, he pointed up.

"Thanks, Magnus," said Adrian.

Just as Dante stepped into the passageway, Magnus turned back, tied Arturo's laces together and yanked his trousers down. Laughter rasped from the Wielder's mouth and he winked at Dante.

Of all the Wielders, this one is my favourite.

Wind hissed through holes in the narrow passageway and puddles gleamed with candlelight. *Not sure this thing can reach San Sira, let alone Phadra.*

"Did Caela convince 'em?" Adrian asked.

Magnus held his hand out, parallel to the floor, and rocked it. *So-so. Fifty-fifty.*

"Better than nothing," Adrian said.

A clatter and a yelp came from behind, and Magnus laughed.

But then the laughter stopped.

Magnus' face twisted and his grey skin turned even paler.

"Magnus?" Dante asked. "Are you okay?"

The hatch at the end of the passageway opened. "He'll be fine," a syrupy-sweet male voice said. "He's just got to learn to play better with others, that's all."

Rav.

White bubbles frothed over grey, glassy water. Dante leaned over the ship's rail, staring down at it. The others stood in the ship's bridge, debating the virtues of this plan or that, but their words had gone into one of Dante's ears and out the other—and slapped him in the face on their way out—so he took to the deck. He had nothing to offer these people, nothing to contribute.

The water sloshed, calm after the recent storm.

Dante tried—and failed—not to think about Ravinatro. *How in all hells did he end up here? Is he really a Wielder?* His stomach churned. *Maybe he didn't recognise me... It's been a few years—*

"Little Dante." A hand slid around Dante's waist, accompanied by the smell of cedarwood and lime and vetiver, a scent that thrust a thousand memories rushing through Dante's head.

He pulled away and crossed his arms. "Rav."

"You look taller." Rav's voice sounded sickly sweet. He wore a short, black beard, and the sun had kissed his flawless ochre skin. His shiny black hair fell onto his narrow shoulders, and—as usual—the buttons on his black silk shirt were fastened one too low. "But still skinny. You eating enough?"

"You still stealing from the rich and not giving to the poor?"

Rav grinned and showed off his sparkling white teeth. "You're one to talk. Anyway, the past is the past! I have a proper calling now."

"What's that, then?"

"See for yourself."

Rav lifted a hand. An island broke the surface of the water, with a sweeping crescent beach of golden sand and trees with verdant crowns of pink and green. A pristine igneus-fuelled locomotive with gleaming crimson carriages rolled past, a stream of amber smoke trailing from its chimney.

"How...?"

Rav clicked his fingers and it all dissipated.

"You. The lighthouse illusion. You *are* a Wielder."

Rav laughed. "Ironic, no? Sightwielder, so your Tarevian friend calls me. Rav, a wizard! Just like the Gods themselves."

"Oh, *come on!*"

"Why not? Aerulus commands lightning, Terros is lord of the land. Why not call myself a god? We walk a broken landscape filled with death and suffering—I let people see the world in the ways it pleases them most. Isn't that beautiful?"

Dante couldn't form a thought, much less a response.

"Always knew I was special." Rav poked Dante's rib. "Knew I'd rise above you lot one day."

"But... *How?*"

"Hard to explain. Just happened one day. Rav felt it. Been smuggling refugees into Phadra—almost too easy with this new power. No sport in it any more. But got to make my money somehow, now that the old troupe's disbanded."

"Magic powers and still referring to yourself in the third person—it's a wonder you haven't built a temple dedicated to yourself yet."

"One day, maybe. Old Nyralto arrested me, kept me banged up—now he needs me. Funny how things turn out, isn't it?"

Dante stared at the sea. "Not the word I'd use."

"Rav thinks he's settled his debt to society—actually, I think I'm in credit. Rescuing people, saving lives—all in an honest day's work for old Rav."

"You've never done an honest day's work in your life!"

Rav slapped Dante's back. "And now I'll never have to!"

Rage flared in Dante's chest. The Gods were surely fools if they thought Ravinatro Bala deserving of their gifts. The same Rav who used to tackle people to the ground and spit in their mouths. The same Rav who once made his own moonshine with food colouring and piss, stuck a Glenfortoshan label on it and sold it to a collector for five thousand aerons. The same Rav who once conned a watchman out of his clothes and left him naked on the Bridge of Bone.

Dante had enjoyed that last one, but still.

And now he's a bloody god.

"Tell me," Rav whispered, "what's so special about the train?"

"What?"

"The train, all gleaming and chugging."

"You saw that?"

"I see what you see, if I choose to."

Dante hugged himself. "Nothing. Just a train."

"Something special about trains, to be sure. More romance than airships, if you ask Rav."

"I didn't."

"My grandparents were separated during Nom Ganald's Great Divide. They were young lovers, but revolution separated them. My grandfather fled by clinging onto a train for seven days and seven nights with nothing but the clothes on his back. They found each other decades later, at the very same train station from which they made their farewells. By that time, no-one desired to be bound to the land. Airships filled the skies, so the station was left to rot and ruin... But the love they bore one another didn't diminish."

Dante fixed his gaze straight ahead. "Nice story. Full of shit, though."

"Believe it or don't—truth is flexible, as you and I well know. I best see what miracles Nyralto wishes of me. Good chatting, Little Dante, I look forward to... re-connecting with you."

Dante stared at the horizon, refusing to watch Rav go.

Sunset stained the sky a pinkish-orange, like spilled rosé wine.

Gods, Dante was thirsty—though even alcohol couldn't dull the ache in his chest. A curious feeling, to be surrounded by people yet feel so lonely. Curious, but not unfamiliar. *Surrounded by soldiers and Wielders and people a* lot *more talented than me.*

Warm wind whispered and carried the salt smell of the sea. Dante stood on the deck, watching and listening as sailors hammered wood and hoisted fresh red sails. The *Sato Bravura* remained anchored but would soon embark on her voyage. To where, Dante didn't know.

Nyralto had ordered his men to set up makeshift quarters in the hold for his new arrivals—that meant sharing with Adrian and Varl and Magnus, and likely a horde of rats. *Not Rav, though; he gets his own room.*

A sailor barged past Dante without even acknowledging him.

Caela would save San Sira—Dante had no doubt about that. And Adrian and the knights would kill the Shadow King. Of course they would. Wasn't that how stories went? Maybe Magnus would replenish ignicite; find a core and turn back time to reverse whatever had happened to it. And Varl? Well, Varl could eliminate starvation with a snap of his fingers. He could summon wind and rain, obliterate poverty and suffering and...

...And where did that leave someone like Dante tal Arata? What happened to the side characters when the story ended?

Dante watched Rav regale the San Sirans with tales of his criminal exploits—he left much of the detail out, specifically the stuff that made him look bad, but he waved his hands as he spoke, painting illusions in his audience's mind. They adored him, and Rav looked proud as a peacock.

Dante remembered that feeling well enough; the pride that came with a job well done, the tension, the excitement, be it on the stage or in the street. He recalled the elation at the applause, the high that came with a successful lift; he remembered the aching disappointment that accompanied a silent audience or when a mark saw you coming. Like Glenfortoshan, the excitement intoxicated.

More exciting than living with a false name and peddling lies to pay the bills, certainly. Sure, life might be safer these days—but also *dull*.

The San Sirans worshiped Rav. Dante saw it in the way they looked at him, the way they spoke of him. They talked of how he helped ease the passing of those who were mortally wounded, filled their heads with happy memories as they closed their eyes for the final time. One sailor with an amputated leg told how Rav filled his head with sweetness to blunt the bite of the surgeon's saw. Rav wove illusions and falsehoods with more veracity than Dante could ever manage. All the years Dante had spent honing his skills, perfecting his talent, only to be made obsolete by someone who worked half as hard for twice the rewards.

Maybe they're equal to the Gods after all.

Anxiety gnawed at him, and every intrusive thought he'd ever contended with sprang into his head.

"You'll work in the ignicite mines, son, like me and my father..."

"You'll never amount to anything more'n that..."

"I'll show you the world, son, I will... One day..."

"You're lazy and stupid and ignorant..."

Wasn't too lazy or stupid to rob you blind without you even knowing it, old man...

But that was a long time ago. Dante tal Arata had changed since then.

"Rav says you're a medium." A San Siran sailor appeared out of nowhere. His pale blue eyes were dull and weary. He looked older than the sun and his uniform bore amateur stitching and patches.

"What?"

"Rav says you're a medium."

Dante groaned. "If I could go just one moment without hearing that name, I'd be in your debt."

The man's shoulders slumped. Wheezing, he said, "It's not true, then? You can't let me talk to Melinda?"

"Who?" Dante snapped.

"You… You're not a conduit to the heavens? You can't speak to the dead?"

Dante's blood flowed with the pressure of a rushing river. "*No.*"

"Only, Rav said—"

"Well, he was bloody lying then, wasn't he? One of his great illusions, yes? Rav and I tell lies and spin yarns so people too stupid to think for themselves can sleep easier at night."

The man stepped back. "S-sorry, I—"

"Oh, no, no, *I'm* sorry!" Dante's arms flapped up and down. "Sit, good stranger, and tell me whose spirit you wish to commune with! Dante the Deceiver will tell you all you want to hear and take a pretty penny from you for the trouble."

"Didn't mean any offence. I'll take my leave—"

"*Sit!* Ah, yes, I can see her now—your wife, Melinda!"

"Sister."

"She's terribly disappointed in you."

"I—"

"Nyr herself has decreed that Melinda's soul be damned until you make amends."

"What? Now, hold on—"

Dante held a finger up. "Your sister wishes to speak." He

rolled his eyes up and stood rigid. Then—slow, at first—Dante's fingers scratched his skin, growing fast and frantic. "I can feel them, brother... I can feel them all over... The mosquitoes! Oh, Gods, they're everywhere.... *Everywhere!*"

"Please, stop—"

Dante's eyes snapped open, fire raging in his veins. "Oh, not what you want to hear, eh? Want to toss a shiny penny to a medium so they'll sell you sweet lies and let you think your sister's soul is at rest in some magical paradise? Well, that's not how the world works. Nothing matters, the heavens don't exist and *your sister is gone.*"

Grim-faced, the sailor stalked away, leaving Dante with the bitter taste of a job well done.

Hours later, Dante sat apart from everyone else, a thin blanket wrapped around his shoulders. The moon shone bright and glared down at him.

Piss off, Lunos.

Damn the moon.

Damn the sun.

Damn the Gods.

A symphony of hammering and shouting filled the vessel. Sailors made wagers about who would finish first, betting their rum rations and other goods. *Tomorrow, then. Tomorrow, we sail to San Sira City.*

Dante smelled Rav before he saw him.

"You have to be so cruel?" Rav held a bottle of wine toward Dante—a San Siran white.

He stared at it for a moment. "Did you piss in it?"

Rav showed off his perfect teeth. "No, but Rav reckons that'd improve the taste."

Dante grabbed it. "Can't believe you're the one chiding me for being cruel."

Rav sat next to him and put a hand on his thigh. "Strange

days, for sure. Anyway, screw him. Who is he? Nobody. Forget him."

Nobody. Just like me.

Maybe he'd been looking at things all wrong. Wasn't there comfort in being anonymous? In never being who you'd always wanted to be? It meant that if you failed, then no-one would know. If you only ever had to be accountable to yourself, then what difference did it make? Who'd be disappointed in that?

No-one.

No-one at all.

Dante took a swig. The wine tasted like vinegar.

"Gods, you weren't lying."

"You just drink up, Dante." The moon filled Rav's eyes and made them sparkle like two silver coins. "Drink up, and I'll show you wonders you've never dreamed of."

ADRIAN

No friends, no weaknesses.

Adrian had believed that living by that mantra made him strong. *So did Amos. Look how it turned out for him. So much hate. So much anger.* But now…

The lantern-lit passageways of *Sato Bravura* creaked and groaned. Sailors sang songs of celebration. *We're on the move.*

Dante staggered from a cabin and stumbled into Adrian. The smell of stale wine rolled off of him. "Ow! What? Sorry."

"You look like shit. What did you have to do to get a real cabin?"

Dante paled. Before he spoke, Ravinatro appeared from the same room. He squeezed Dante's shoulder and a smug grin spread over his face. "Morning. Did we sleep in? I'll find coffee."

"What?" Dante said after Rav had left.

"Didn't say anything."

"You gave me a look."

"No, I didn't."

"You gave me a look with your weird eyes."

"When have I ever cared who you spent the night with?"

"You've never approved of Rav."

"Neither have you."

Dante hugged himself and rubbed his shoulders. "Yeah, well... It was a mistake."

"Don't need to explain anything to me."

"Stop going on about it, will you? Gods!"

Dante staggered off, bumping into two San Sirans before disappearing.

Adrian climbed the stairs to the deck. After spending the night in a cramped, makeshift cabin with Varl, Magnus and a bunch of sailors, the air relieved him. There, Nyralto summoned him to the bridge, where Mara and Caela were huddled over a table with him.

Caela, the White Death, or Caela, the Saviour of San Sira?

"Our repairs are complete," the captain proclaimed. "We sail south imminently."

"It's decided, then?" Adrian asked. "You're not going to Phadra?"

"Not in the first instance." Nyralto placed a wooden token of a ship upon his map of Imanis. The token sailed down the long, ragged edge of Phadros and San Sira. "We sail south, drop anchor here."

"Stop? Why?"

"That was my question," Caela said. "He wants to use longboats. Why can't we circle around to the southern banks? San Sira City is by the bay."

Nyralto shook his head. "Not so easy. The Cataclysm destroyed the harbours, but that's not the worst of it—if the reports are true, the city teems with shadow demons— possibly your Shadow King, as well. We must sneak in without being seen." Nyralto tapped on an inlet on the map. "The coast is a warren of caves; many of my people sought refuge here after the devastation. We can use this cave network to get into the city."

Caela crossed her arms. "We don't have the time. The shadows grow stronger every hour."

"A slow and sure pace is better than a quick and reckless one," Nyralto insisted. "And there is another reason."

Adrian waited for Nyralto to elaborate. He didn't. "No, please, take your time, Captain."

Nyralto glared at him. "You won't like it."

"Hardly been a vacation up 'til now. How's Arturo, by the way?"

"Chided and humiliated. He's in the brig."

"Give him my regards—and let him know that if he needs any more dentistry work done, all he has to do is ask."

"Never been in a unit where men could resist a pissing contest," Mara growled. "Captain, continue."

Nyralto scratched the back of his head. "You won't believe what I'm about to tell you—*I* didn't believe it until you came aboard. A week ago, a man from Phadros came to San Sira, seeking an audience with the archduke—he claimed to have urgent information; he claimed that a great devastation would befall San Sira... And the world. Madness, of course—who would believe such tales without a shred of evidence? Naturally, his request was denied and he was ejected. That was two days before the Cataclysm struck."

"How could he know?" Caela demanded. "Is he a Wielder?"

Nyralto shifted and straightened his cream-white shirt. "He's a mage."

Adrian stared at the captain. "You're kidding, right?"

"The Mages' Guild are assholes," Caela said. "Can't be trusted."

"That's what he said." Nyralto's knuckles rested on the table. "His name is Izan Suaro—I've not met the man, but Arturo found him among the civilians during the evacuations, ranting and raving. He claims he held the rank of *magus peritus*, if you can believe it. He absconded from the Phadra guildhouse and sailed to San Sira under cover of darkness. Arturo told me this mage was raving about Sol's

Kiss, that it shall open the doorway for the Shadow Realm. Why would anyone believe such ramblings?"

"What happened to him?" Caela asked.

"What do you think? The Watch tossed him into a cell and forgot about him. If I knew then what I know now... Well, no use in wishing."

"We need to find him," Adrian said.

"If he's still alive, then he's underground with the bulk of the survivors. He would not risk going back to Phadra—the Phadrosi military probably wants him more than they want you."

"He tried to warn the world, same as me," Caela said. "And the mages didn't believe one of their own."

"On the contrary—from what I have pieced together from Arturo, they knew the Cataclysm was coming but they wanted to silence Suaro before he talked."

"Of course they did." Adrian raised his chin. "Magic corrupts, and the Mages' Guild holds all the secrets. That's why they've been meeting with Harnan in secret; they knew it was coming and they didn't try to stop it."

Caela bristled. "Why? What do they gain from the destruction of San Sira?"

"Harnan gains the pretext to annex it, achieving what no other Phadrosi king could—and all without shedding his own people's blood. In exchange, who knows what he's offered the mages?"

Caela drew slender fingers through her white-blonde locks. "We don't know this man—if he's a mage, we could be playing right into his hands by revealing ourselves to him."

"Or he has all the missing pieces," Mara pointed out. "Might even know what the Shadow King wants."

"We don't have time to waste looking for him—people are dying."

"Which is why we work together." Adrian met her eye. "We're on the same side now—whether you like it or not."

A silken smile settled on Caela's red lips. "How long have you had that in your back pocket?"

"A while. I'm petty like that."

"Okay." Nyralto tapped the map again. "We take the longboats and enter through Zafiro Cueva—your watchwoman rides with me; a San Siran face will help foster trust with all of you I'll leave a skeleton crew aboard *Sato Bravura*. The Cataclysm has negated San Sira City's bricode capabilities, so we're on our own. No help, no back-up. We perish, Arturo takes *Sato* and seeks help elsewhere. She is provisioned for six months—more than enough time to circle Phadros and find a sympathetic territory."

"You said people have been taking refuge in the caves." Adrian tapped the map. "If they're alive, will you help Sergeant Diaz find her family? She risked everything by ignoring the Watch's orders and following me."

Nyralto frowned. "I wasn't aware, she has not spoken of family—but I'll do what I can."

"Thank you. Dante doesn't need to put himself in danger, either—I'd say the same for Ramiro and Mara, but—"

"But you'd rather keep your teeth." Mara pointed to the sprawling city of San Sira. It spread from a crescent bay. "From the caves, where's our insertion point?"

"It's not on the map, but the archduke has an estate north of the city, in the countryside," Nyralto explained. "There, he houses his private collection of curiosities—among them, vintage airships. They're just sitting there, waiting to be put to good use."

"Will he sign off on you taking them?" Caela asked.

"I don't even know if the archduke is alive, and it's better to ask for forgiveness than permission."

"Military vessels?" Adrian asked.

The captain shook his head. "Antiques, like *Sato Bravura*. First-generation. They won't move as quickly but they don't rely on igneus for propulsion, either."

"How do you know the archduke hasn't escaped the city in 'em?" Caela demanded.

"I don't."

"Don't like it." Mara put her hands on her hips, eyes narrowed in thought. "We need intelligence."

"This is the best way," the captain insisted. "Approach from too far a distance and the shadows will have all the time they need to swarm us as we approach. But if we get as close as we can before showing our hand—"

"We strike, swift and unseen," Adrian said. "Multiple craft, spread out, converging on a single target. That thins out their number—then it's all up to Caela."

"I can't fight while I'm sealing the rift," Caela pointed out. "I'll be vulnerable. Soon as I start, they'll come at me."

Adrian tapped Nightsbane's hilt. "I'll be by your side. Seal the rift while aboard an airship, make ourselves a moving target—I'll handle any shadows."

"It's risky."

"Doing nothing is more so."

Caela's eyes narrowed, though it didn't dim their sapphire glint. "This portal is the big one. Soon as I start, the Shadow King will come for me. You know that."

Adrian saw his own mismatched eyes in hers. "I'll protect you."

"We concentrate defences on one airship, then," Mara said. "The others are distractions."

"Lambs to the slaughter?" Nyralto shook his head. "My men have been through too much to sacrifice them—we have no weapons effective against these shadows."

"Caela's the key to all this," Adrian said. "I don't like putting all my eggs in one basket either, but Mara's right: Caela needs the strongest possible defence around her. The rest of us are expendable."

Nyralto met Adrian's eye. "I've heard stories about those who pledged themselves to the Order of the Shadow Dragon, but I did not believe them. You would throw your life away so easily, and the lives of others?"

"There's no other way. I get that you don't trust us, but all we're asking for is time to get Caela close enough to seal the void—we'll do the rest. You and your people don't even need to be aboard—as soon as Caela starts, the demons will converge on us—you only need to buy us time. The moment the demons realise what's happening, you can escape."

"I'll work with Phadrosi if I must, but I'll not cede command of one of my vessels to you. No, this is a joint operation. So be it—we find Suaro, take to the air, and seal the void. But know this—I will not risk my men to save you. And if you betray us, a cataclysm shall be the least of Phadros' worries."

So much hate.

So much anger.

Adrian raised his chin. "We have an accord."

The morning sun painted blades of gold upon the sapphire sea. Half a dozen boats peeled away from the *Sato Bravura* and towards San Sira's rocky cliffs.

Identical to the Bronze Coast. Identical to Phadros. So much animosity between two peoples—neighbours, cousins, separated only by the most minor of differences.

Skin colour, nationality, accents—people chose to hate others over the most innocuous things. *Even someone who looks the same and sounds the same yet dares possess eyes of two different colours.*

Adrian cast a glance at Caela, sitting in the boat in front. She pulled on the oars, strong as any of the sailors.

But Wielders...

Cave mouths yawned open along the stony shore, ready to swallow the boats. Adrian rowed with Nyralto and two other San Sirans, the oars beating the water in a slow, steady rhythm.

Worms writhed in his stomach as the boat slipped into a cave—but instead of darkness, the water turned a dazzling blue.

Francisco—a young San Siran sailor at the bow of Adrian's boat—craned his head back. "This is Zafiro Cueva—bioluminescent algae make the water glow. Beautiful! Who needs ignicite, huh?"

Ahead, Captain Nyralto called out, and a grinding sound filled the cavern, like the tumblers of a lock settling into place. Stone turned and shifted like clockwork and the cavern transformed, opening a wider waterway.

"San Sirans escaped your hero Salvarado through these caverns," Francisco explained. "Like a flower blooming in darkness, hope never dies, even in the direst circumstances."

Oars beat the water with the rhythm of a heavy heartbeat. Sometimes, in Adrian's most private moments, a fear nestled in his brain that threatened to tear his world down…

What if my life is a lie?

What if he was still the same scared little boy who was too helpless to save his father?

And what if I fall into the water and the darkness takes me?

What if I drown in the dark?

Days ago, Sir Adrian Navarro's resolve was as steadfast as an anchor. Now, though…

The boat slowed before a wall of rushing water. Nyralto whistled, and a gate rose into the ceiling, stemming the waterfall. The boats sailed through, into the light of a thousand candles.

The sailors stepped into the water and moored the boat to a protruding stalagmite.

"This way."

Adrian followed Nyralto, grateful for the candles. Light

pulsed like a beating heart. Voices ebbed and flowed like the sapphire waters.

He followed the soldier into a smaller cavern. There, more San Sirans embraced the soldiers.

"What is this place?" Sergeant Diaz asked Adrian.

"A haven." The displaced San Sirans looked healthy. Tired, maybe, but not malnourished and not injured. "Hope."

The San Sirans were apprehensive. Nyralto explained that these Phadrosi were here to help, but they kept themselves apart regardless.

Men and women wore bloodied rags and tended to their injured. Some wept, others stared into nothing. One woman prayed over the still body of a man.

And yet songs carried through the caverns, as did the aroma of salted fish and lemon. *They've turned it into a home.* Francisco was right: Hope never died, even in the direst of circumstances, and it had given these people the strength to survive.

But where hope fails, anger succeeds. And Adrian Navarro wielded anger as surely as he wielded Nightsbane.

"Wait here," Nyralto commanded. "I will find Suaro. Eat and rest while you can—it may be some time before you get another opportunity."

The San Sirans eyed them with suspicion and squabbled over returning to their home or pressing on to Phadra.

"The soldiers have ships but there are storms," some spoke.

"I have no money to pay the Ganaldi smuggler," others said.

Yet more wanted to stay in the caves, and all questioned Nyralto's leadership—and his wisdom in bringing Phadrosi soldiers into their midst.

That suited Adrian; he still had a job to do. As Cassie, Dante and the others ate, Adrian hunted for an empty space where he could practice his drills, but he found nothing suitable. After ten minutes, he gave up and joined Caela at the edge of a vast plunge pool, where men, women and children swam and laughed, all beneath the benevolent glow of hanging lanterns. It made the water resemble liquid gold.

"This is... breathtaking," Ramiro said. "Simply breathtaking."

Adrian stood by the edge of the pool and stared into the shimmering water.

But the gold only sits upon the surface. Beneath, the waters are murky and the light fades. Stare long enough at something dark, and deep, and empty for long enough... sooner or later, it'll invite you—

The pool rushed up and Adrian plunged into the water, bright and freezing.

He flailed for a moment before his legs kicked back and forth and he broke the surface.

On the ledge, looking down at him, Caela stood with her hands on her hips, laughing.

Adrian's face burned and words rose and fell in his throat.

Then Caela leapt into the pool, dived down and materialised next to him. She drew hair away from her face with slender fingers. "Gods, that'll wake you up."

"What..." But Adrian didn't know what question to ask. He simply frowned as a smile spread over Caela's face. "Caela—"

"Relax, you're safe here. And whether you like it or not, so am I. Don't you get bored of brooding? Can't just *exist*, brave sir knight; you have to *live*."

Adrian's head spun in annoyance and confusion, but the San Sirans were laughing alongside Ramiro and Cassandra. Even Mara mustered a smile.

"We're safe here," Caela repeated. "Not one person chose it, but we're all on the same side. After all the running and fighting, I'd say we've earned a break."

From the pool, he watched Varl entertain kids by making

a piece of paper dance on a breeze. Magnus conjured stones from behind their ears and suspended them in mid-air, much to the children's delight.

The only outcast here is me.

"I'd… like to get out of the pool now."

Caela floated away, graceful as a swan. "Is anyone stopping you but yourself?"

Shadow ink snaked around the body like a living thing. An optical illusion, of sorts; like any shadow, it stretched and contorted into any shape the mind conjured if you stared at it long enough.

Tucked into a cramped alcove with a cracked and dirty mirror, Adrian dried his dark clothes and cloak. The ink wound around his shoulders and down onto his chest, black but with a silvery sheen. To Adrian, the three sharp and elongated lines running from his shoulders to the centre of his chest looked like dragon talons—or the hideous, grasping fingers of the monster that took his father from him.

Receiving the tattoos had hurt like the hundred Idari hells, and their power came with a cost… But it was worth it. The ink numbed pain and allowed him to move like lightning. It unlocked the Order's secrets and amplified the ignicite in his sword. It made him *stronger*.

In the caves, the people ate quince fruit—hard, tart, golden-green pears. Once, before swearing fealty to the Phadrosi Crown, Adrian and Dante had chanced upon a crate of quince fruit in a Lower Phadra alleyway, behind a fresh produce store. The owner was well-known to visit a nearby brothel and barter with fruit—he'd visit the girls with young children and tease them with bright and colourful fruits, ripe and fresh.

"Ours now," Dante had said. "The kids'll think it's Wintercast."

They'd taken the fruit, left it outside the brothel and run off, laughter in their hearts. It had always bothered Adrian that he'd never got to see the look on the merchant's face, to make him know that Adrian had beaten him—but he and Dante spent the night on a rooftop, laughing and eating the share that they'd kept for themselves.

Even now, Adrian remembered its striking, bittersweet taste, the tang on his tongue, the texture. How long since he'd last eaten? The shadow ink sustained him now, suppressed his appetite and made food taste of nothing. Strange to think that he'd never eat quince fruit again, or drink fragrant plum wine, or bite into a succulent, rare steak seasoned with rosemary and pepper.

And nor would he know hunger again—the kind of aching, gnawing hunger that sapped the life from a person and dulled their mind.

In the Order's prime, each of its knights bore the tattoos. The ink remembered; it recorded their actions, their skills and their knowledge. And when they died, the ink faded and returned to the bottle, ready to be borne upon skin again with all the skill and knowledge it had accumulated from its previous bearer.

"It marks not just the skin—but the soul." Amos had said those words with fire in his eyes. "Be sure you understand what it will take from you."

Adrian didn't know how the Order had come by the shadow ink and he didn't question it; if it helped rid the world of corrupting magic, Adrian Navarro would use anything.

He pulled his shirt on but left the top two buttons undone, the edge of the tattoos just visible. That was the difference between him and Caela; he'd chosen his power and the pain that had come with it. He couldn't hide from the marks they'd left. Adrian Navarro knew *exactly* what he was.

Once he'd dried off, Adrian found Dante slumped against a wall, his fingers wrapped around a bottle of red wine.

"Only you could find a bottle of fine wine underground."

His eyes still closed, Dante said, "Well, at least I'm talented at something."

Guilt wormed in Adrian's belly—but what could he say? "Dante—"

"Don't." His eyes fluttered open. "Just don't."

"There he is." Rav's words dripped with molasses. He carried a sack over his shoulder. "There's the Dante I know."

"You going somewhere?" Adrian asked.

"Toledra Village, with whatever San Sirans can afford to come with me. If you lot seal the portal above San Sira, then it strikes Rav that no-one will need to be smuggled into Phadra any more. Best make my coin while I can, no? Came here to ask this one if he wants to come."

"Could use your help," Adrian told Rav—as much as it galled him to admit it.

Rav scratched his cheek. "Make it a point never to risk my skin for someone else. No, old Rav'll get the folk into Phadros—and escort them back as soon as San Sira's safe again."

"How enterprising." Dante swigged more wine. "Still forging your writs of passage?"

Rav hooked his thumbs into his belt. "Who needs papers when I can make the guards at the skyport simply see them?"

"Skyport?" Dante frowned. "You've still got the *Luna*?"

"Oh, yes. My second home. How about it, Little Dante? I'd make even more money if you wised up and joined—your silver tongue liberated more coin than any cutpurse's dagger."

Dante looked away. "I don't do that any more."

"Changed, have you?" Rav cocked his head. "Commune with the dead, like Nyr's ferryman, eh?"

Dante took another swig and muttered, "I offer hope to the grieving."

"*False* hope. Is that all you can give these people? People who've lost their homes and families? Rav may profit from misery but he still delivers. C'mon, Dante—didn't I promise to show you the world? Where's following this wanker ever got you?"

Adrian glared at Rav. "*Sir* Wanker to you."

"I aspire to be a good man." Dante set the bottle down. "Might never make it, but I'm going to keep trying."

"A good man is only ever a good man," Rav insisted, "but a rogue can be a *great* man."

"A great man should know when to piss off."

Rav shrugged. "My offer won't be on the table forever."

Adrian watched Rav leave. "Your old friend's an asshole."

"Seems I have a habit of making friends of assholes."

"Dante. I... I'm sorry. For a lot of things. Reckon I've gone about things the wrong way."

"Yes, can't imagine all the swimming with sexy witches was part of your plan."

"I should have looked for you, after the job. I shouldn't have left you to languish in jail. I don't know, maybe it's the shadow ink—it costs a part of your soul and—"

"I accept your apology, Adrian, but I won't accept excuses. We're not friends. *You* made that choice, remember? It's me who held out hope, fool that I am. Maybe I *will* go with Rav."

"I want to fix—"

"Just leave me be."

"I will—but one more thing: You're right, Dante—you *can* offer hope. After this, someone has to tell the stories of the San Siran survivors, not just Caela's. And that person ain't me."

Before Dante could say anything more, Mara appeared and said, "Navarro—we found him. We found Suaro."

. . .

A narrow tunnel wound into a larger, circular cave. Scraps of food and unkempt clothes littered the floor. Strange glyphs and symbols lined the walls in chalk, as though a child had been given free rein. Drawings clashed with each other in a senseless jumble. Rings within rings, hexagons, dodecahedrons and other shapes that Adrian didn't know the name of were all annotated with numbers and complex formulae.

Adrian followed Mara into the tunnel, where the voices of Caela, Nyralto and the others mingled.

Izan Suaro, former *magus peritus* within the Mages' Guild of Phadra, couldn't have been older than thirty—much younger than Adrian had imagined. He wore a tattered orange robe with numerous stains of varying colours. His narrow eyes were filled with suspicion and curiosity. Candlelight gleamed on his bald head, and a long, single-braided black beard swung from his chin. Lithe without being too skinny, he held a piece of chalk in two bony fingers, scrawling more symbols onto the walls.

The rest were already there: Varl, Magnus, Caela, Diaz and Ramiro. Dante sat apart, lost in his own thoughts.

Adrian stepped through and Captain Nyralto introduced him to the mage, but Suaro didn't acknowledge him.

"Tell us about the Cataclysm," Adrian demanded. "Tell me about the Shadow King."

The chalk halted. "Finally, someone asks the right questions."

"You'd better have the right answers. What's the Mages' Guild up to?"

"To manipulate the course of history. The Mages' Guild has roots in every country, every city, every town—but they are not yet unified. Most of the world closed our halls and removed our charters. Our numbers dwindled when magic became myth and the Indecim slipped into legend, but now a desperate world looks to us for answers."

Varl grunted. "They bend the truth to suit themselves."

Candlelight danced in Suaro's amber eyes. "Mm. Human nature—history is written by the victors, and Phadrosi conquistadors were most often the victors. But some legends don't die easy. There is a hole in the world, and magic bleeds through it."

"How long has this hole been there?" Adrian asked.

Suaro laughed, though Adrian couldn't see the joke. The mage paced, gazing up at his own calculations as if staring at an Aurien tal Varaldo masterpiece. "Before the age of ignicite, magic was rife. Records are almost non-existent, but there are too many similar cultural signposts across the world. No such thing as coincidence. No. Then the magic stopped. Became myth."

"Why?"

"Ignicite. Ignicite shields the world from extra-dimensional incursions. But mankind's ambition knew no bounds, hmm? We mined ignicite, sparked an industrial revolution. Ignicite dwindled—enough left to regenerate, yes, but the dampening effects were weakened. Bit by bit, latent magic seeped into the world and Wielders were born. Without ignicite to stanch it, magic seeps into the world as freely as blood from a nicked artery."

"Bullshit." Mara spat a wad of phlegm onto the floor.

"Can you… *not* do that, please?" Diaz asked.

Mara rolled her eyes. "If ignicite stopped magic, yeah, then how did *eleven* gods find each other and save the world? No-one mined ignicite two thousand years ago."

"Eleven Gods. Were they Wielders?" Suaro didn't take his eyes from the strange diagrams. "Magic has been dulled, like the edge of a blade without a whetstone. But it's been here all along. Weak, perhaps, but there."

"Forget the Gods," spat Caela. "Tell us about the Shadow King."

Suaro cocked his head, his beady eyes alive with wonder. "To exist in our reality, the shadow demons must become corporeal. For that to occur, the barrier between worlds must be shattered—the Cataclysm is the first step, but it took a tremendous amount of power."

"He's not corporeal yet," Ramiro said. "He's smoke and shadow."

"But his strength increases."

Adrian raised his chin. "Maybe we should let it."

Caela frowned. "Why?"

"If he bleeds, I can kill him."

"Or he'll kill *you*."

"But what does he *want*?" Ramiro asked. "How is he getting enough power to destroy a city?"

"Who can speak to the desires of a demon?" Suaro said. "As for gaining power, my theory is that the shadows draw the life force from their victims and store it as energy. The hole in the sky—that is where their souls go, crushed down, bent, twisted... Used to create more shadow demons."

"Gods above." Cassandra placed a hand on her chest. "That's why the demons take their victims to the portal in San Sira. He's creating an army."

"All I know for certain is that the Phadra Mages' Guild are allied with him. I *did* try and warn you all, but you tossed me into a jail for my trouble. The Mages' Guild attracts bright minds—the eccentric, wonderers, wanderers and thinkers. But also those with dark intentions... Those whose ambitions are not cowed by morality. These men and women work in secret, serving their own masters—dark gods and demons who seduce with promises of power."

"Sounds like a cult," said Mara.

"Precisely. Do you know the story of Zirun and Niamat?"

"Everyone does," said Adrian.

"*I* don't." Varl looked to Magnus, then back to Adrian. "Neither does Magnus."

"Niamat is the Phadrosi god of darkness," said Suaro. "And Zirun, the god of light. Zirun was tricked by a witch and lay with her, incurring the wrath of Niamat, his twin sibling and lover."

Varl sighed. "Sex stuff. Cults are always about weird sex stuff."

"Niamat discovered the betrayal and wounded Zirun—but he survived and fled. Niamat grew ever more wroth and vowed to drown the world in darkness, in mockery of Zirun."

Mara rolled her eyes. "A fairy tale."

"Fairy tales often contain a kernel of truth, but it's not a story's veracity that makes it matter—it's the power of *belief* in it. There are those among the Mages' Guild who worship Niamat, who want to bring her forth and usher in an age of darkness."

"Every country has their own legends that pre-date the Indecim," Adrian pointed out. "Their own Niamat and Zirun. Every nation had tribes who sat around campfires, coming up with stories to explain why the sun rises or the wind howls. It's fantasy."

The mage's face soured like week-old milk. "You belong to the Order of the Shadow Dragon, yet you are this naïve? If there is enough *belief* in a thing, then it's true."

"Guess that means Mother Snowfrost is real, too, huh?" said Mara.

"Why not?" Suaro asked. "Mother Snowfrost offers gifts of fresh fruit at Wintercast, hangs baubles of ice on trees to cheer children—is that so different to what Varl does?"

Dante stood. "What are you saying? That if you believe something hard enough, it'll come true? That every nightmare, fairy tale and story we've ever heard is based on reality?"

"I'm saying that it doesn't matter whether it's true or not—people will do great and terrible things if they *believe* in it. If it's a parent who gives gifts and hangs baubles for their children, everything that defines

Mother Snowfrost has come to pass—therefore, she is real."

"And these evil mages have only popped up now?" Caela asked.

"They've always been there, behind the scenes. Not just Phadra—I'd wager every chapter of the Mages' Guild has rotten apples. But most chapters are closed. Mages are laughed at, ignored. But that all changed the day that ignicite stopped replenishing itself; the mages' whispers turned into fevered discussion. Magic grows resurgent, and suddenly, they're relevant again. Who else to turn to when the unexplainable becomes the everyday? They consolidated their power in secret, even proclaimed King Harnan *grand magus*. The King of Shadows needs physical form—he needs a human host to exist on this plane."

"And who's that, then?" Ramiro asked.

"King Harnan," Adrian said. "Has to be. Why else ally himself with the mages?"

"Wouldn't that kill him?" Diaz asked. "Being possessed by a demon?"

"Or bestow upon him great power," Suaro said. "Perhaps the Mages' Guild has knowledge that would allow him to wield the Shadow King's power without sacrificing himself?"

"Well?" Mara folded her arms. "Do they?"

Suaro cocked his head. "Miss, if I knew that, I wouldn't have posited the question in the first place. If I need something punched in the head, I'll come to you—in the meantime, let the adults speak."

Adrian cracked his knuckles. "It's not the first time Harnan has tried. The Shadow King's been here before—nine years ago, during the last Sol's Kiss. But never when ignicite was so weak. The barrier between worlds shifts as the sun and moon are released from alignment. It's a narrow window—he'll throw everything he has at it."

Caela arched an eyebrow at Adrian. "How do you know all that?"

Adrian kept his voice low. "My order's records."

She didn't need to know that the Shadow King had murdered his father—none of them did. Would the Shadow King remember Adrian?

He will. I'll make sure of it.

"But there was no Cataclysm nine years ago," said Suaro. "Whether the Dark Mages—if I can ascribe them a cliché—conspired to remove ignicite or if they're simply taking advantage is irrelevant; what matters is that he is here. Truly, we live in exciting times."

Adrian's mouth tightened. "Not the word I'd use."

Captain Nyralto placed his hands on his hips and paced back and forth. "Harnan makes a deal with the Mages' Guild and they give him the secrets to inherit this Shadow King's power. Right now, he's sucking the souls from his victims in order to build an army of shadow warriors so that Niamat can invade our world. This is your theory?"

"That's the gist of it," Suaro said.

Cassandra's mouth hung open. "It'll be another Age of Conquest—Phadros against the world with an army of shadow demons at its back."

"We'll stop that from happening," said Adrian.

"I admire your confidence, Phadrosi." Nyralto stopped pacing. "But you're not from here. You haven't been through what we've been through. You're here to complete a mission —what about after? Who helps clear the rubble? Rebuild the city? Who digs through the dirt to recover the bodies so that we may say goodbye to our loved ones and grieve? We mean nothing to you."

"Not all of us," said Cassandra. "We're in this together."

"You're all insane," Mara said. "You're talking about going against the king. You're talking *treason*."

"They can behead me *after* I've saved the world," said Adrian.

"Yeah? You're gonna walk up to the king with your magic sword and slay him?"

Adrian raised his chin. "If I have to. The next Sol's Kiss is tomorrow. The barrier between worlds will be at its thinnest. We need to seal the void and kill the Shadow King before then."

"Alright." Caela crossed her arms. "When do we leave?"

Beneath a hazy, mid-day sun, the deck of the *Glimmer* creaked.

Adrian marched through the vessel; the San Siran soldiers exchanged curt nods with him. No salutes, though; that'd be a courtesy too far for a Phadrosi knight. *Especially once they hear about my plan.*

Men worked overhead in the tangle of ropes and lines, calling out to one another, patching the vessel's outer envelope.

The soldier called Francisco—the young man who'd led Adrian's boat into Zafiro Cueva—hefted a barrel on one shoulder and grinned at Adrian when he passed.

"You seem happy," Adrian said.

"I am—you've given us something to do besides sitting on our asses. I'll be with you when we reach the city, Sir Adrian —wanna see us win with my own eyes."

Adrian liked Francisco's demeanour, liked that he still had hope.

Voices called from the netting above. The archduke's airships were exactly where Nyralto had said they'd be, within the country estate. Three identical first-generation vessels, made of black walnut wood—hardwood, but light and durable. Nyralto had explained that these vessels were part of the first San Siran air fleet, that they'd been housed in a museum for decades until Archduke Anuelo took them for himself, much to the dismay of his people.

If he hadn't, they'd be deep below the earth right now.

A canvas envelope covered the vessels' ballonets. The archduke had kept stocks of ignium gas for lift; between the gas and Varl, ascending wouldn't be a problem, but without modern technology and liquid igneus for fuel, their propellors had to be operated manually. That drew some complaints from Nyralto's men, but most of them were happy just to be doing *something.*

Adrian stared out at the bare and broken San Siran countryside, untouched by the Cataclysm

No archduke, no people—no-one at all. Have they all been taken, moulded into the Shadow King's minions?

The soldiers had raided the nearby mansion residence for food, liquid igneus and ignium gas; Adrian figured that the archduke wouldn't mind.

At the bow, beneath the shadow of the looming envelope, Caela argued with Nyralto; he'd insisted on accompanying them aboard the *Glimmer* with a skeleton crew, including Francisco. Adrian didn't like it, but he understood the man's misgivings—he wouldn't trust Phadrosi soldiers and Wielders, either.

The *Glimmer* would be the key; Varl would assist with its ascent and Caela would seal the great void; Adrian and Magnus would defend her when the shadows boarded. Dante, Mara, Ramiro and Cassandra would stay aboard the *Cintila* with a contingent of San Siran sailors and soldiers, drawing the enemy away where they could. Mostly, Adrian needed someone to survive should he and the Wielders fall.

That left the *Incendios*; of the three vessels, she was in the most disrepair. Rot had crept into her hull and the sailors said that she'd never be sky-worthy. Adrian had an idea for that, one that had made Captain Nyralto laugh in his face. "You'd have me use up our most critical resource? Not to mention the *Incendios*, the archduke's most prized possession!"

"Then he should've taken better care of it."

If Adrian's plan worked, it'd buy Caela time to seal the portal and end the fight before it began…

And if it doesn't work, we'll all be too dead to notice.

He sensed Dante sidle up to him before he spoke. "Adrian."

"Dante. Regretting your decision yet?"

"To come with you?" Dante hooked his thumbs into his pockets and bounced on his tiptoes. "No. Have to see how the story ends for myself. If I'm gonna be on the sidelines, I need to observe. Need to listen. Some of the stories, Adrian… These people have gone through hell. Makes you appreciate what you have. Funny, that; I'd never looked back on my life and considered myself lucky before. Spent so long weaving tales to make folk feel better that it never occurred to me that the truth can achieve the same. Need to tell the good *and* the bad."

"Perspective matters. Being too narrow-minded blinds you." *And Gods, I've been blind.*

"The world needs to know what happened here, Adrian. Phadros will cover it up—you can't let 'em. And that means you need to survive, okay? So don't go rushing in and waving your shiny sword around."

"Noted. Dante…"

"Yeah?"

"When this is over, if we get separated… Meet me back in Phadra. At the Dragon's Lair."

Adrian wanted to say more—much more. If he didn't speak now, would he ever get the opportunity again? Words rose and fell in his throat. "The *Cintila*'s waiting."

Dante offered a theatrical salute. "Best make an appearance, then."

"Fortune find you." Adrian extended a hand, not sure that Dante would take it.

He did. "And you. I'll cheer you from the sidelines. Forget swords and magic, show this Shadow King how a Phadrosi street rat scraps."

Adrian's muscles tightened, primed for a fight. "I will."

Credit where it's due, Captain Nyralto has organised his men well.

The *Glimmer* would ascend in mere minutes. Adrian had never travelled aboard a first-generation airship before, and a childhood of reading Captain Crimsonwing had painted a romantic picture of them.

The *Glimmer* had a music to it, a rhythm; the creak of boards, the hiss of snaking ropes through iron loops. If her crew broke into a shanty, Sir Adrian Navarro might be tempted to join in.

Not knowing what to do with himself, he circled the deck.

"You should rest," a grizzled old sailor said. "A good soldier never wastes a chance to eat or sleep."

"Duly noted." But Adrian wasn't a good soldier—he was an *exceptional* one. Or, at least, ought to have been. Drills and theories were all well and good, but not even the Order of the Shadow Dragon could prepare its warriors for the first time they came up against demons and wielders of the dark arts.

When this is over, Lord Lucien will reinstate us. He won't have a choice. Magic bled into the world, and it wouldn't stop with San Sira, or even the Shadow King. The Mages' Guild wouldn't stop until they'd seized supreme power.

Adrian thumbed Nightsbane's hilt. *We're gonna be busy.*

He circled the deck again and again. Nyralto barked orders, men hoisted equipment and affixed cannons to the deck. Two sailors squabbled over whether "cannon" or "cannons" was the right plural, but Adrian didn't care.

Ahead, peering over the bow, Caela stood alone, the wind whipping her blonde hair. She looked taller, somehow. Adrian sidled up to her, not sure what to say. *Caela, the White Death. Caela, saviour of the world.* She was a woman, the same age as Adrian—too young to bear the burden of saving San Sira on her shoulders alone.

She's not alone. She has Varl, and Magnus, and...

Me.

"Caela."

She turned, but before Adrian spoke, Suaro sauntered over to them, hands behind his back as if he owned the world.

Wish Caela listened when I suggested tying him to the Cintila.

"Sir Adrian, Caela. Are you well?"

"Yeah." Caela cracked her knuckles. "Just keen to get started. It's the waiting that I hate."

"Agreed—waiting has a way of making one rummage through the darkest recesses of their mind, hmm?"

Seems I have something in common with the mage, after all.

Suaro frowned, as if seeing Adrian for the first time. "Sir Adrian... Your eyes."

"Yeah, I've got two of 'em. All my own teeth, too."

"Heterochromia, I didn't notice before... Did you know it was Phadrosi mages who convinced the world that people like you were corrupt?"

"One good reason among many to hate 'em."

"They say that—"

"That Amaya the Corrupter changed her skin to look like Niamat and seduce Zirun, and only when she birthed the first half-god, half-man did Zirun learn of the deception." Frustration, impatience and anger made Adrian's words spill out—but he saw no reason to stem the tide now. "We all grew up with the stories, Suaro. But you know which story I prefer? The one where there's nothing wrong with people who have different eyes, different hair or different skin—and whoever says otherwise is an asshole."

Suaro's little eyes narrowed. "I was going to say that in this battle between light and dark, it's ironic that it falls to one of the so-called Corrupt to save the world. As I explained, belief is a powerful thing; the Phadrosi Crown ordered Lucas Salvarado to murder every man, woman and infant in Phadros born with the eyes of the Corrupt, for fear of Amaya using them to carry out her will. One of the bloodiest chapters of the Age of Conquest. And now here we are."

Sir Adrian Navarro, First Sword and Commander of the Order of the Shadow Dragon—working alongside mages and Wielders. What would Amos think?

"Only fools have narrow minds." Adrian looked from Caela and back to Suaro. "Gotta learn to be more curious."

"Mmm, I wouldn't be so sure," Suaro said. "Curiosity has tempted many a mage down a dark road. Curiosity leads to obsession, and obsession drove us to find the answers to questions best left unresolved. Man harnessed science to make weapons of war, to kill the world a little bit every day in order to make our fleeting lives a touch more convenient. I wonder if—when it comes down to it—we're any better than this Shadow King."

"Curiosity also gave us art." Caela pushed a lock of hair from her eyes. "Gave us the capacity for empathy. It's how science is used that determines whether it's good or evil— been trying to convince our brave sir knight here the same thing about magic. Science explains the natural world, but art is how humans explain *each other*. And we've still a lot to figure out."

Adrian stared at her but found no words.

"Well put, Caela!" said the mage. "Naïve and trite, but well put."

Adrian cleared his throat. "*I* have a question for you, Suaro—how did you escape the San Siran jail?"

Suaro's eyes glinted. "Terros Earth-God delivered us, or so the other prisoners said. The Cataclysm opened the earth and half the city sank into the dirt. My cell had a window—I could only look on as the earth disintegrated and a wall of dirt and dust rose before me, a tide of destruction inching closer and closer... I thought I'd die, but when I opened my eyes, the dust had faded and a great spear of light cut through the wall of my cell. I simply walked through the gap. I had nowhere to turn, no-one to seek, so I followed the trains of refugees north. I walked for hours before realising I had no home to go to. After a full day, I ended up in the caves, so I got to work—started planning, thinking, developing theories. And then a gift—you."

"We arrived just in the nick of time." Caela gripped the wooden taffrail. "As if the Gods themselves willed it."

"A comforting thought—much less distressing than believing that man has free will and all we use it for is devising ways to torment each other."

"Prefer to own my shit," said Adrian.

"Aha, yes, a good and honourable knight. I am excited to see how this all plays out, Sir Adrian—most excited."

Men shouted and the *Glimmer* ascended, slow at first before picking up speed. The countryside shrank.

Sweat pearled on Suaro's forehead and he vomited over the rail.

"That bodes well," said Adrian.

"Please, uh, excuse me." The mage muttered an apology and disappeared, leaving Adrian alone with Caela.

"Maybe he has a point," said Caela.

"I'm sure he has many, in between all the riddles and self-obsession."

"If the Gods are real and we're just pieces in a game, then what's the point of worrying?"

"Because you might not like where they place you." Adrian tapped Nightsbane's hilt. "I'd rather fight back."

Caela leaned over the taffrail, peering ahead. Red dust filled the air as the *Glimmer* bobbed and weaved through canyons. "That man Rav possesses a great power, don't you think? To wield illusions. What would you choose?"

"What do you mean?"

"If you could live inside an illusion, what would you pick? I'd choose home. Such a cliché, right? But I miss it. I'm from a village on Loch Anam. You ever been to Aludan?"

"Never."

"You'd love it. Freezing, and it rains a lot, but it's beautiful."

The red dust thickened. Someone called for Varl and the *Glimmer* rose even higher.

"When did you know? That you were a Wielder?"

"When I was seventeen. Even when I was younger, I sensed that I was… different. I felt things. Like… The world around me. I heard it crying. Thought I was going mad. You know, I never got sick as a child. Not once. Didn't realise it at the time, but my mother feared me. Not at first, mind you, I had a great childhood, playing by the loch—but later…"

Caela's voice dwindled to nothing. Adrian didn't want to overstep by questioning, so he said, "Lock?"

"*Loch.*"

"*Lock.*"

"Purse your lips and blow."

Adrian did so.

"Good—now do that and make a *k* sound."

Adrian did.

"Now say it."

"*Loch.*"

"Okay, good. Bit less spittle next time and you've nailed it."

"I'll bear that in mind."

"One winter, I was walking along the banks of the loch. I found a red stag. He'd been shot. Hunting's illegal but the animals of Aludan attract poachers. Guess it's man's prerogative to destroy nature's beauty. Anyway, it was dying, and I grieved for it—this regal, majestic animal. I wanted to fix him. To comfort him. So I reached out and touched him… The next thing I remember is waking up in my bed, my mother looking down at me, concerned… Scared. The next day, I went looking for the stag, but I never found his body. I heard two men talking in the pub—one of them said he was convinced he'd shot a red deer. When he followed the blood, the deer was gone and he'd lost track."

"Did he find you lying there?"

Caela shrugged. "My mum said she found me."

"And you realised you were a Wielder?"

"I thought I was a witch. The Mages' Guild came calling—I didn't stick around to hear what they had to say. It was months before I even tried healing anything again. It drains me. Anyway, from that day on, my mum looked at me differently. Thought I was a freak. So I left town. But no matter where I ended up, I didn't belong. I hated my gifts for the longest time. They isolated me. I thought I was the only one, the only Wielder in the whole world. When I found Varl, everything changed."

Behind his back, Adrian's fingers knitted together. "He has a lot of love for you."

"He's family. Magnus, too." She fixed her gaze onto Adrian. "And I won't let anything happen to them."

"You… You don't need to worry about me. I won't hurt them. Or you."

Caela stared back over the rail. "You bear shadow ink."

"Yeah."

"You sacrificed something for it. A part of yourself. I've not said anything to Varl or Magnus, but… You'll understand."

"What are you talking about? Understand what?"

Caela drew a long, slow breath. "It's the voids—I absorb their energy when I close them. Same as healing—I redirect energy, let it flow through me and use it to heal others. But the shadow magic is different... I need to absorb it before I can reform it into light and seal the voids. Normally, once the energy is gone, it's gone, but this... It lingers. I can feel the darkness inside me, roiling like the sea. The portal over San Sira will be bigger. *Much* bigger."

"We'll be with you, Caela—all of us."

"It might not be enough. I don't want the shadows to corrupt me, Adrian. I don't want to be turned into one of those things."

"Caela, you—"

"You know what it means to sacrifice part of yourself for the greater good. We're different in many ways, but you're the only person who understands *that*."

"Speak to Suaro, he—"

"Can't be trusted. And neither Varl nor Magnus can do what needs to be done if I get turned. Adrian, I've been abandoned, chased out and vilified my whole life—fighting back is all I know—but this might not be a fight I can win. I get turned into one of those demons, only you can take care of it. You're a knight of the Order of the Shadow Dragon, right? It's your job to neutralise mystical threats." Caela kept her expression hard, but Adrian saw the fear in her eyes. "Can I count on you to uphold your vow?"

At once, the airship deck seemed too small, too cramped. "Yes."

Tension filled the bridge. Soldiers bounced on their feet, filled with nervous energy. The *Glimmer* hugged San Sira's broken, fractured ground, and more than once her hull scraped against rock. A strange red mist made the city warp and shift like a mirage.

"We need to ascend," Nyralto barked through gritted teeth. "Too dangerous."

"Not yet," said Adrian. "The mist works both ways. Stay hidden."

Nyralto swore. He pulled at levers and turned cranks. "This had better work, Phadrosi."

Looming above, the shadow of the *Incendios* slipped in and out of view. Wind shoved her gondola back and forth but didn't push the pilot ship off course. Lanterns hung on its rails—barely enough to keep the red fog at bay but Adrian wanted it as visible as possible.

"It'll work." He stood at the ready, stance wide, fists curled. His muscles tightened and his heart beat like a marching drum.

The *Glimmer* glided over the earth. The warping mist made things look either closer than they were or further away. The vessel could be sailing straight toward a sheer cliff and no-one would know; modern vessels had apparatus to detect proximity, but Adrian had to make do with what he had.

Behind the mist, mountains reached to the heavens…

But they weren't mountains.

They were buildings, reduced to ash and rubble. Stepped pyramids, like Phadra's royal palace, sat in ruin. Towers resolved from inky red—still standing but hollow and broken. Sinkholes swallowed streets and long, winding crevasses scarred the city.

Caela frowned and touched her chest.

She feels it. She feels the city's pain.

A sorrowful wind moaned through the bridge as if the city itself grieved for her lost. Still the *Glimmer* plunged through the red mist. The colour of the world drew in deeper, darker, stealing the sun and smearing her rays away.

The hull scraped against jutting stone.

Nyralto mopped sweat from his forehead. "Gods above, I need to ascend."

"*Not. Yet.* Let the *Incendios* lead."

"*Ow.*" Caela fell to one knee and pressed her palms against her ears.

Varl reached out to her, but she waved him away.

"I can hear it," she whispered. "I can hear the void…"

"Screaming?" Varl suggested.

Then Caela said a word that came as no surprise to Adrian. "Laughing."

"Stay strong," Adrian said.

"Gods, Adrian, every instinct in my body is telling me to turn back. It feels… Different. Deeper."

"Stay strong."

"Nyr, give mercy." Nyralto's words came weak and hollow.

When Adrian looked beyond the glass, he saw why; San Sira's dead littered the streets—thousands of bodies. Skeletons clung to each other or lay on the dirt, hands clasped to skulls. Others were decomposed, old, wrinkled and robbed of life.

"Most of them never made it out." Varl drew an eleven-pointed star across his chest.

Words caught in Nyralto's throat. "Genocide. This is genocide."

The *Glimmer* turned silent as a tomb. Adrian heard every creak of the boards, every tick of the dials, every draw of breath. "I can take over flying."

Nyralto shook his head. "This is not your fight. Not your home."

Minutes crawled past. No-one spoke but Adrian knew they felt it—the seeping dread.

Have we made a mistake in coming here?

"Gods above," Caela whispered.

From the crimson sky, dark tendrils spiralled through the ground like thin whirlwinds, churning the earth.

"The Shadow Realm," Suaro said.

Cold fear seeped through Adrian's veins. "It's bleeding into our world."

He scanned the epicentre of the dark tendrils. Shadows flickered and moved.

Adrian's heart raced. *They know we're here.*

Dark phantoms glided through the air like bats, soaring towards the *Incendios*.

"They've taken the bait."

"Is it time?" Nyralto asked.

"Not yet."

The demons swarmed the pilot ship and smothered her. One by one, the *Incendios'* lamps snuffed out. The vessel was unmanned, as part of Adrian's plan, but that didn't stop fear from gripping his bones.

More shadows scurried through the air and boarded the pilot ship.

"Sir Adrian?"

Adrian raised his chin. "Now."

"More ignium!" Nyralto roared. His men pulled levers and the *Glimmer* ascended.

Adrian looked to Caela. "White Death—you ready?"

"First Sword. I am."

The *Glimmer* soared and the serrated giggling of the shadow men cut through the wind. The red sky flickered and shifted.

"Wielders!" Adrian roared above the din. "On me!"

Adrian raced onto the deck, freezing wind lashing him. Varl, Magnus and Caela were close behind.

The demons concentrated on the *Incendios*—just as Adrian had known they would. They clung to it, slashed its envelope, ripped its hull.

"Are we close enough to the void?" Adrian asked Caela.

"I… I think so."

"Light 'em up."

She reached out towards the black and churning clouds and…

Nothing.

"Caela?"

"It's… It's not there. The portal—it isn't there!"

"What? It has to be."

"Then this is a hell of a time for me to start lying!"

"You said you can feel it!"

"It's not *there*, Adrian!"

"Shit." Adrian gazed up.

The demons tore into the *Incendios'* envelope, slashed at its cables, rent her hull. Without Caela's magic, Adrian's plan had failed before it began. Unless… "Captain! Get me higher."

"Won't make any difference!" Caela roared. "If the void's not there, then I can't absorb its magic!"

Adrian unsheathed Nightsbane. "*Nyralto!*"

Caela frowned. "Adrian? It's suicide. We can regroup—"

"Sol's Kiss is tomorrow." The vessel maintained its altitude. "Damn you, Nyralto. Varl?"

"On it." Varl raised his hands and a howling wind rocked the *Glimmer*. The gondola shook from side to side, but the vessel soared towards the *Incendios*, higher and higher.

"Higher!" Adrian roared.

The *Incendios* got closer. Adrian put one foot onto the rail, wind shrieking in his ears.

Are you there?

"Closer!"

Be there. Please *be there.*

The *Glimmer*'s envelope threatened to crash into the bottom of the *Incendios*—but it was close enough.

Adrian raised his left arm. The grapple uncoiled and bit into the *Incendios'* gondola.

Adrian arrowed through the air, freezing wind in his ears.

And the darkness noticed.

Nightsbane slashed as shadows descended upon him. Adrian shot onto the gondola and climbed onto the deck, cutting and slicing.

They charged at him, grinning, giggling. Adrian ducked and dodged, his blade flicking in and out like a snake's tongue. The shadow men burned and dissipated, hollow faces twisting in anguish.

Steel clashed with scythed hands.

Smoke swirled and reformed around him. Adrian twisted and thrust, rolled and slashed, felling demons left and right. He fought across to the stern of the vessel—where the igneus canisters were.

Nightsbane danced. The demons clawed at Adrian but the pain came and went within a heartbeat. The shadows screamed before Nightsbane's wrath.

Where are you?

More shadows descended from the sky, giggling, scything. Adrian spied the igneus, six canisters bound together— he snatched one, cracked it open and raced back across the deck, leaving a trail of acerbic amber liquid.

Come out, come out...

Demons fell from the red sky in a stuttering chorus of laughter—hundreds, thousands.

But no sign of their king.

Its steering mechanism locked in place, the *Incendios* kept sailing in a straight line over San Sira's tallest towers, never deviating from its path. Adrian pounded the deck, liquid igneus bubbling at his heels.

C'mon, c'mon, c'mon...

Below, the *Glimmer* descended to avoid the onslaught.

Damn it.

Adrian's blade swept through a score of shadows. They rent his clothes but fell before Nightsbane, flickering and fading like embers from a fire. Adrian dodged and deflected, redirected attack after attack, but the demons didn't cease. Hordes fell upon him.

Adrian let the canister fall and darted away.

Then he snatched a bag of sparkpowder, hurled it to the ground, and watched it snap and fizz and catch onto the igneus. A trail of brilliant amber fire raced through the *Incendios'* deck, toward the rest of the canisters.

Adrian leapt over the rail, stomach clenching as he fell towards the ground. Freezing air rushed through him, burned his lungs.

Heart in his mouth, he plummeted, twisted and—

And the grapple uncoiled and caught onto the *Glimmer*.

Adrian swung.

An instant of pain threatened to wrench his arm from its socket, but he swung up and rolled onto the deck.

Above, the liquid igneus flared. Flames licked the *Incendios'* ballonet.

"*Varl, push it!*"

Growling, Varl summoned a gale. The *Incendios* shot higher and—

And erupted in brilliant orange light.

Shadows screamed, aflame.

Adrian stared at the fire, mesmerised. He watched it spread through the shadow men, watched it climb and lurch.

The darkness burned, so bright it hurt Adrian's eyes but he kept watching—*made* himself keep watching.

"Was he there?" Caela asked. "Adrian? Was he there?"

"What?" Adrian tore his gaze away.

"The Shadow King—was he there?"

Adrian shook his head and turned back to the fire in the sky.

The light burned through the shadow demons like paper, their screams a song in his ears.

Then the world turned silent, the only sound coming from the pounding of Adrian's heart.

In one move, he'd taken out hundreds of enemy soldiers. The King of Shadows wasn't among them, but now Caela had space to seal the void—all they had to do was find—

Laughter floated through the air, a soft buzz at first, before forming into a full, discordant choir.

Adrian peered over the rail, to the shattered city below.

The *Glimmer* plummeted through the mist—and below, where San Sira once stood, a vast sinkhole expanded.

Shadow gushed out—hundreds. Thousands.

"It's not a void in the sky." Caela turned to Adrian. "It's a hole in the world."

The *Cintila* circled around. Streams of darkness lurched up towards it.

"We descend," Adrian said.

"You want to go *in?*"

"Is that where the void is?"

Caela's expression hardened. "Yes."

"Then we go in." Adrian faced Varl. "Tell Nyralto to signal the *Cintila*—they cover us, we go in."

Varl nodded and disappeared into the bridge. "Caela, go inside—Magnus, up for a fight?"

The old man's mouth stretched into a grin.

"I should be out here," Caela said. "If either of you get hurt, I can heal you."

"No." The laughter grew louder. "Don't use your magic on me. Ever."

"Adrian—"

"I made a promise to you—you make one to me. I don't want your magic to touch me. Not ever."

Caela swallowed. "Okay."

The first shadow demon climbed over the rail.

"Inside, *now!*"

And Nightsbane whirled.

Adrian stood by the wheelhouse door and fended off

wave after wave of demons. Magnus froze them and Adrian slaughtered them.

Cannons roared. The *Cintila* circled and hammered the demons as they ascended. The cannon fire didn't kill them but they dissipated and reappeared, buying the *Glimmer* time.

Faster and faster the vessel sank.

Demons clawed their way onto the deck, concentrated on Adrian. He dodged and deflected, spun and slashed, killing more demons than he could count.

Magnus tapped his shoulder and pointed to the *Cintila*.

She's abandoning the fight. Dante…

"Doesn't matter." Adrian struck at more demons. They were weak but countless.

Varl burst onto the deck. "Cowards abandoned us!"

"No!" Steel clashed in a shower of sparks, the demons' scythe-hands hooking and slashing at Adrian's throat. "There's nothing they can do!"

The *Glimmer* plummeted past collapsed towers. In a blur, the ground rushed up and darkness swallowed the airship.

Demons sparked and twisted and screamed before the wrath of Nightsbane.

And then they were gone.

That hateful, jagged giggling disappeared.

The *Glimmer* plunged into darkness, deep into the hole, deeper and deeper, until the opening above became a pin-prick in a black canvas.

Adrian swept into the bridge, breathing hard. "Captain, what's our rate of descent? How close to the bottom are we?"

"We… should have hit the bottom some time ago."

Seconds crawled past, punctuated only by the creak and screech of the ship.

Though vast, Adrian sensed the cavern close in around him, a hole in the world, vast yet intimate, empty yet full of malice.

"Brace!" Nyralto spun the wheel; the ship slowed but her keel struck the ground. Wood cracked and peeled away.

"All okay?" Adrian yelled.

"Damage report?" Nyralto called.

"No bugger knows because we haven't sailed on one of these before," Francisco said.

Nyralto cleared his throat. "Better to poke a hole in the hull than the envelope, or we'd be stuck down here, eh?"

No-one appreciated the comment.

"Sail on." Nyralto ordered his crew to turn the vessel's signal lights on to full power. The retrofitted ignium lamps would run low soon, but in the meantime, they illuminated the ship in a halo of soft light.

The *Glimmer* sailed underground in silence—a lone tiny firefly in an enormous expanse of shadows. Adrian's heart pounded.

"There." Caela pointed to a thread of light twisting in the dark, shimmering and faint.

"The portal," Adrian said. "Not gonna lie—thought it'd be bigger."

Caela's brow creased. "Something's wrong."

"Captain, take us closer."

The *Glimmer* hovered near the strange light. One hand on his sword, Adrian stepped out onto the deck with Caela and Suaro.

"That's it," Caela said. "The void that caused the Cataclysm."

"Can you close it?"

"I... Oh, no. *No.*"

"What?"

"The world's crying out in pain. But this portal... The magic's already extinguished, Adrian—just like Mar de Susurro. There's no power for me to take, it's all been used up. I can feel it."

"Meaning what? That the void that swallowed San Sira can't be closed?"

"No—that it's *already* been closed." Caela shook her head. "We're too late."

Ice crept through Adrian's veins. "We never had a chance. All this, for nothing."

Lucien...

Lord Lucien had ordered Adrian to come to San Sira. Had the king manipulated Lucien... Or had Lucien manipulated Adrian?

"Phadra's defenceless," Adrian said. "No Order of the Shadow Dragon, no Amethyst Lynx. Phadra's ripe for the Shadow King's army to attack. Sol's Kiss... We need to leave —*now.*"

Suaro opened his mouth but a great roll of thunder stole the words. The *Glimmer* shook.

Adrian looked up. "What now?"

Stone fell and another peal of thunder resounded through the vast cavern, as if the earth itself roared in anger.

"Back inside! *Now!* Nyralto, get us out of here!"

"Gods," said Caela. "Look!"

Then Adrian saw it—a tide of shadows, darker than dark, blacker than black, rolling towards the *Glimmer*.

"Suaro, get inside—get Varl and Magnus. Caela, we're on defensive duty. Nyralto, get us out of here!"

"Adrian," Caela whispered, "the only way out is back the way we came."

"I know."

Varl and Magnus strode onto the deck. The few San Sirans aboard scrambled to man the vessel's cannons.

The *Glimmer* turned and surged towards the tide of darkness. Laughter echoed, loud, discordant. It cut through Adrian's skin like a surgeon's scalpel. Cannons roared and darkness enveloped Adrian, suffocating his thoughts.

He slashed and sliced, driving the shadows away. More came, bounding towards him with shuddering, long limbs. Nightsbane swept back and forth, painting arcs of amber light.

Shadows stretched and grinned, that horrific giggling prickling like needles. The more that disappeared, the quicker the others came. Adrian's sword slashed two, three times before they dissipated.

"They're stronger!" Caela yelled.

Screams and laughter filled the world. Nightsbane painted mad orange arcs. Adrian fought, fuelled by a will to survive—to *protect*.

The phantoms raced to the tethering ropes connecting the gondola to the envelope—if they went, the *Glimmer* would crash.

Adrian climbed after them, swinging, slicing.

A horde fell upon him.

The demons pulled him onto the deck, steel clashing in a burst of sparks. Adrian spun and twisted, dodged and parried —but there were too many. They pushed him against *Glimmer*'s taffrail. Pain flared and faded.

The San Sirans screamed orders as cannons thundered.

Demons twisted in anguish, fading at Nightsbane's touch. Adrian found footing, stepped forward, felled enemy after enemy.

The shadows rushed him, claws rending his clothes. Nyralto raced out of the bridge, his sabre dancing but having no effect. A shadow cut him down and left a livid red line, throat to belly.

Adrian pressed forward, hate and fear and panic fuelling him.

But it made no difference. For every shadow vanquished, two took its place.

Adrian caught a blow to his face. Painless, but it sent him flailing back.

Giggling shadows descended on him, pinned him against the taffrail.

Roaring, Nightsbane thrust and stabbed. No room to dodge, no room to spin or slash.

Then Adrian faced the pin-prick hole in the ceiling, legs leaving the deck.

"Varl! Lift!"

Wind swept through the cavern. *Glimmer* juddered and rose and—

And the shadows threw Adrian over the rail.

He tumbled into the darkness, spinning, twisting. Bile filled his throat.

He thrust his left arm out.

Rope uncoiled and the hook struck the hull. Cool air washed over him as he swung, a human pendulum in the dark.

Heart pounding, Adrian zipped back up, climbed the hull and fell onto the deck. He slashed at a phantom, its coal-red eyes lingering as the rest of it faded.

The *Glimmer* bounced in the air, its envelope cables fraying and snapping.

Adrian drove the shadows away, but they swam around him, laughing, mocking, disappearing and reappearing at will.

Magnus froze enemies and Adrian killed them, but there were too many. The demons' delirious laughter filled the night. Darkness closed in around the old Wielder; Adrian fought to free him.

Though he didn't feel it, another slash drove Adrian to one knee, blood seeping from his shoulder.

A grinning shadow drew tall over him, readied its hooked hand—Adrian swung up and deflected it, like steel on steel. Adrian cut it. It howled in pain but didn't disappear. Black blood trailed onto the blade. Adrian drove it deeper and the shadow's grin twisted in anguish. It convulsed and bubbled into nothing.

He'd kill them all, keep killing until—

The Shadow King.

Shadows swirled and he materialised—huge, hulking, his three-tined crown of onyx shimmering like black liquid.

A black skull with empty, hollow eyes... Twisting and stretching, grinning...

The Shadow King towered above his soldiers. His huge, intangible blade swept San Siran soldiers away like wheat before a reaper's scythe, leaving blood and gore. The blade passed through their bodies like a gust of wind and stole their lives away.

Francisco charged with a sabre.

"No!" Adrian yelled.

Without pause, the King of Shadows' dark blade cleaved the young man in two.

Adrian's muscles burned with rage. His sword swung and spiralled, dissipating shadows in a blaze of fiery circles, steel shedding sparks on their tangible claws as he ran towards his nemesis.

The King of Shadows towered above Magnus and raised his sword.

On one knee, the old Wielder raised a hand.

The Shadow King froze, shimmering like metallic smoke.

"Magnus!" Caela darted forward and leapt onto the Shadow King's back. She plunged her hand into the deep darkness of his chest...

And the King of Shadows screamed.

Adrian fought forward but the demons flooded over him.

Caela screamed and fell to the floor.

Adrian's heart sank. Dark tendrils filled her veins and she gasped for air.

Enraged, Adrian fought towards her, slaughtering shadows without thinking.

Caela.

He had to get to Caela.

He had to destroy the Shadow King.

Magnus got to his feet and staggered back, hands held out, holding the Shadow King in place.

All Adrian had to do was cross the deck and slit the bastard's throat.

Hissing laughter spilled from the demon's skeletal mouth. Air shimmered around him and shattered like glass—and the Shadow King broke free of Magnus' prison.

Magnus fell onto the deck, hard, gasping for air. The Shadow King loomed over him.

Adrian darted forward, Nightsbane raised, and—

And the King of Shadows brought his blade down.

Magnus died at once. His skin melted away and his bones turned to dust.

Adrian fought forward, cutting through shadow after shadow.

The *Glimmer* shook and convulsed, throwing Adrian from side to side, but he kept his footing and slashed out at him.

Steel sang.

With heavy swipes, the King of Shadows lashed out. Adrian rolled and dodged, slashed and poked, fuelled by hate.

But the demon absorbed Nightsbane's fury.

Adrian flipped and wove between the Shadow King's attacks, slashed at the back of his legs, but the demon reformed and warped around Adrian, its giant blade swishing like a painter's brush.

Nightsbane wove amber patterns, but the demon flickered in and out, reappeared, and—

And Adrian stood, vulnerable, as the Shadow King deflected Nightsbane.

Swift and sudden, the demon's sword swept through Adrian.

It felt like a cold breath passing through him, a bitter whisper from Nyr herself.

Ice filled Adrian's veins and he fell to the floor.

Then the pain erupted—brilliant, blinding and terrible.

Blood filled his mouth and the world flicked in and out. Adrian tried to stand but his legs refused.

Darkness fill Adrian's eyes. His father's killer loomed before him—a grinning black skull with empty, hollow eyes. He raised his sword—

Blinding white light cut through the darkness.

The King of Shadows staggered back, and brought his sword up to shield against the storm of light.

Adrian flitted in and out of consciousness. Cold fingers dug into his skin.

Stay alive...

The Shadow King's giant blade swept and cleaved but still the light punished him.

...Stay alive... just long enough...

The Shadow King screamed, howling, discordant.

Just long enough...

To see him die.

The Shadow King dissipated.

Caela stood in his place, ragged and bloody.

The Shadow King... Vanquished by the White Death.

The demon faded into nothing, as intangible as a coil of smoke.

With a scream, Caela convulsed, her back arching, anguish painted over her face.

A bright, golden light emanated from her and filled the world, burning the Shadow King's legions.

Adrian wanted to laugh.

The White Death banished the demons. She killed my father's murderer.

As death claimed Sir Adrian Navarro, it came as small comfort.

DANTE

The *Cintila* glided through the red mist like a drunk stagehand fumbling through a velvet curtain. The wheelhouse creaked and groaned but her crew stayed silent.

Cass whispered something to herself. "…and into darkness, I descend…"

"Definitely the right moment to be muttering creepy whispers."

Cassandra cleared her throat. "Sorry. It's from *Captain Crimsonwing and the Mad Baron's Mechanical Menace.* He says it when he dives into a bottomless pit to confront Baron Midnight, like… A way to steel himself, strengthen his resolve, you know?"

Dante patted her shoulder. "How about you just *think* it?"

"Quiet!" the brute Arturo yelled at the vessel's wheel.

It turned his stomach, but Dante forced himself to look upon the devastation below; bodies littered the streets and buildings sat in ruin.

Arturo barked orders to his men; there were more soldiers aboard the *Cintila* than the other two vessels but their presence didn't offer any reassurance.

"The plan has to work, right?" Ramiro asked. "It has to."

The young knight wore his emotions on his sleeve; Dante pitied him. "Fear not—Adrian Navarro's far too stubborn to fail."

"Fear?" A weak smile formed on Ramiro's lips. He tugged at his collar. "Never. Hey, uh, did you hear the joke about the three sailors and the priest of Nyr? A Mercurian, a Phadrosi and a Ganaldi come off the boat in Ancaster—"

"Quiet!" Arturo roared again.

Dante very much wanted to punch Arturo in the face, but Mara would be best suited for that. Ramiro resembled a dashing stage actor in the role of a knight, but Mara was the real thing. Even without speaking, strength radiated from her, wild and angry.

Knots of people filled the ship's cramped wheelhouse. Too many people for a small vessel, but no-one wanted to stand on deck—not when a strange crimson mist smothered the city and dark, twisting tendrils spun out from the sky like a spider's web.

"Captain!" A young soldier with a gleaming brass spyglass peered out of the bridge's window. "The shadows—they're converging on the *Incendios*!"

"Let's show these bastards how San Sirans fight. Increase speed, bank to port—let's see this light show up close."

"Wait..." The soldier handed the spyglass Arturo.

"What in all hells are they playing at?"

"What's happening?" Dante asked.

"See for yourself." Arturo pressed the spyglass into Dante's hand.

"Gods above." Through the smudged glass, Dante watched the *Glimmer* ascend. "Is that... What in all hells is he doing?"

Dante tensed as he watched Adrian zip towards the *Incendios*, the amber glow of his sword flashing in and out. The shadows smothered him but he fought through them.

"Why isn't Caela sealing the portal?" His stomach quivered. "What's Adrian doing?"

Arturo snatched the glass back. "Getting himself killed."

Dante's heart thudded. He lost track of Adrian but glimpsed Nightsbane wink like a star before darkness snuffed it out.

"Do something!" he yelled. "Mara, Ramiro, can't you—"

An explosion detonated and blazing orange light filled the sky. Fire raged through the darkness, terrible and beautiful all at once.

And the shadows burned.

A cheer erupted in the bridge.

Arturo shielded his eyes. "Your boy's got balls, I'll give him that!"

"He did it," Ramiro said. "Adrian did it. He killed the shadows. No way the Shadow King could survive that... Is there?"

The *Cintila* circled the city as fire rained from the *Incendios*' wreckage. Dante followed the embers as they danced downward—and, illuminated by the tide of blazing igneus in the sky, his eyes fell upon a vast hole. Darkness looked back at him.

"A hole in the world," said Mara.

The site of the immense pit stole the words from Dante's mouth. *Oro Lengua is a speck of dust compared to this...*

"You hear that?" Ramiro asked. "It sounds like..."

Ragged laughter cut beneath the crew's cheers—inhuman laughter.

"Demons." Mara narrowed her eyes. "Coming from the ground."

Sure enough, streams of black phantoms soared up from the ruins of San Sira.

Arturo paled. "Battle stations!"

Alarm bells blared. Soldiers spilled onto the tremoring deck as demons glided towards the vessel. Her cannons roared, but the demons disappeared and reappeared, howling in amusement.

The spectres swarmed the *Cintila*, clinging to her hull, ripping men apart in showers of blood and dragging them overboard.

And all the while, they laughed.

"Maintain fire!" Arturo yelled. "Evasive manoeuvres!"

"Remember the mission," Mara snarled. "We protect the *Glimmer*!"

"I'm not dying for Phadrosi! *Evade!*" The *Cintila* banked, cannons thundering, yet not loud enough to conceal the screams of men.

"Sir!" someone yelled. "The *Glimmer*! She's sinking!"

Dante's heart rate spiked. He ran to the window, fingers white against the glass as Adrian's vessel plummeted into the pit.

Then, one by one, the shadows ceased their assault. They dived overboard, blood dripping from their scythed hands, and chased after the *Glimmer*. They followed it into the pit.

"Do something!" Dante yelled.

Arturo's eyes widened and his mouth opened and closed.

"Wake up!" Mara struck him with the back of her hand. "Protect your ally!"

"Retreat! *Retreat!*"

"You kiddin' me?"

Arturo pushed Mara away. "We have no effective weapons, the Wielders are gone! The battle is lost."

Words choked in Dante's mouth. "We... We have to save them. We have to save Adrian."

But Arturo wouldn't hear it. The *Cintila* turned, cannon fire covering her retreat.

"Turn back!" Mara yelled. "Ramiro, back me up."

Ramiro stared at the floor. "He's right, Mara—we lost. Captain, sail for Phadra, we'll—"

"Bullshit!" Mara yelled.

"Stay calm," Cassandra said. "We regroup, plan—"

"Piss on that. Arturo, I'll slaughter you and all your buddies. Turn back." Mara squared up to the captain. "*Now.*"

The low sun shone upon Dante like a spotlight on a stage. He didn't know how long he'd been walking, or where he was walking to.

He slouched and faced the dirt as he passed trees and rocks and other pointless things. The landscape here was as anonymous as him, the wind and sun indifferent and uncaring.

Every time he closed his eyes, bright, flaming amber light pressed against his head. He couldn't shake the sight of Adrian dwindling into nothing, screaming shadows tearing after him. More likely than not, Adrian lay dead at the bottom of the pit, along with Caela and the rest.

Dante trudged through the mud, wordless. Even Mara remained silent. She had ranted and raged after Arturo had kicked them off of the *Cintila*, but now...

Accepting defeat is never easy—even when you're used to it.

Cass sidled up beside him. "I'm sure Adrian's okay."

Dante didn't see how he could be, but he couldn't bring himself to voice his opinion.

"We'll find him," the copper continued. "We'll find a way back to Phadra and bring more resources into San Sira. The Gods saw fit to let us survive."

Dante laughed, bitter and humourless. "The Gods don't give a shit about us."

"Good," Mara spat. "Don't need 'em. Don't need permission to fight back."

"Mara's right," said Cass. "We can't give up just because we got beaten."

"Again," Ramiro added.

Mara punched the young knight on the arm. "Your attitude ain't helping."

"I pledged to the Order of the Golden Griffin—I didn't ask for any of this."

"*None* of us did! You wanna crawl back to the Griffins and sell your sword so rich merchants can keep their coin, go ahead. Your daddy got you into the military, Ramiro—it's *his* business that bought you a knighthood. Belios' balls, Navarro might have been half an asshole, but at least he was on the right side."

Ramiro turned red and seethed. "You think my father helped me in any way? The 'right side'? We're Phadrosi, Mara—we conquered half of Imanis and put anyone who rose against us to the sword. Maybe it's about time we stopped picking fights. Your head's so far up the Amethyst Lynx's arse that you can't even consider that you might be wrong!"

"Shut up, both of you!" Cassie growled. "I've lost my *home*. I've lost everyone I've ever cared about—and if King Harnan gets his way, the next Age of Conquest will be ten times bloodier than the first. The *world* needs us to stop him, so stop arguing and start *thinking*."

Ramiro walked away, shaking his head.

Mara crossed her arms. "Any bright ideas, then?"

Cassie scratched the back of her head. "We're all we have. San Sira's gone—we need to find a way back to Phadra. Sir Adrian made a deal with Captain Pedro—the vessel that took us along the Bronze Coast will be waiting for us. We just have to reach it."

Not for a moment did Dante believe that Pedro and the *Solnadar* were waiting for them, but he dared not argue with Cassandra. She had heart, and courage, and—

Wait a minute.

The others kept talking but their words came and went.

I recognise this place.

The seeds of a plan formed in his mind. Had he been leading everyone here without realising?

"We need to head north," Mara said. "And find supplies to camp outdoors."

"You want to *walk* to Phadra?" Ramiro asked.

"I know how to get us home." Iron filled Dante's words.

"We can climb the foothills, stick to the forests," Mara continued. "The Watch in Terra Puerta might still be looking for us. But it'll be days; we'll never make it back before Sol's Kiss."

Ramiro scratched his chin. "Vega may still be downed—we can try explaining everything to him?"

"He'll arrest us before he listens to us."

"I know how to get us there!" Dante said, louder this time. "I can get us to Phadra before the eclipse."

"What?" Ramiro asked. "How?"

His heart beat harder. "We're near Toledra Village."

"And?"

What was it Cassie had said? *You trap flies with honey, not vinegar*.

Ravinatro didn't see Dante as a threat—no-one ever did. *I'm just Little Dante, their performing puppet, wheeled out when they need me and then put away again.*

"Dante?" Ramiro pressed. "Do you have a plan?"

Excitement kindled in his belly. "Damn right I do."

Let the soldiers and the Wielders fight—Dante tal Arata had talents of his own.

It didn't matter if the world never learned his name—he only had his own standards to live up to. For Adrian—for *himself*—he'd save Phadros and tell Caela's story. He'd do all of that *and* screw Rav over in the process.

And that was better than any adulation.

Three plunging waterfalls surrounded the scrap of dirt

known as Toledra Village. The settlement perched atop a circular island that rose from a pit in the earth; just seeing it made Dante squirm—for the old memories, and the new. The waterfalls spilled down into the darkness, and a precarious, rocky path offered the only way across.

Dante knelt by a rock and peered across to the village, the music of cascading water in his ears. The town had changed its name a dozen times, so the story went, passed between various governors and councillors and self-styled outlaw kings—but that was before the age of ignicite. Twenty years ago—or so Rav had once told Dante—an ignicite vein had ruptured and swallowed the earth, sending the Toledra River flowing in different directions. The only thing untouched was the town itself, now crowning a pillar of rock. "Blessed by Terros," the locals had claimed, but the trade brought by the river soon dwindled away, and the fissures in the ground made landing any large airships precarious. The townsfolk abandoned their home for Phadra, leaving Toledra a ghost town—a place where you could be anyone, a place where you could choose your name and change your identity, just as the town had done in centuries past.

All that made it ideal for smugglers and runaways. It was the closest thing to a home that Dante and the crew of the *Nueva Luna* had ever known.

"Haven't heard of this place," said Ramiro.

"No." Dante's heart drowned out the sound of the waterfalls. "I don't expect you have."

Ramshackle townhouses sprawled out upon a field of pale grass and muddy trails—and there, at the north side of the town, Rav's decrepit manor squatted. Dim, fuzzy light edged its windows and highlighted the reds in the crimson door below.

And in the broken streets, two dozen San Sirans lingered.

Not many—is that why he's still here? To pick up stragglers?

"What's your plan?" Cassandra asked.

Dante inched forward and pointed. "Do you see that?"

Next to a church dedicated to Aerulus God-King sat the *Nueva Luna*. Streams of paint exploded over her hull, purple, green and orange. Inside, her cargo hold housed a stage and cabaret tables. Memories of hazy red light and the sweet smoke from exotic tobaccos floated into Dante's head.

"Of course." Mara snorted. "Can barely go a day with you lot without stealing an airship."

Dante rubbed his hands together. "Prefer to think of it as *reclaiming*."

Gods, how people cheered as the *Nueva Luna* sailed out of the sun, ready to bring entertainment and joy, songs and music, distractions from the drudgery of everyday life. *Why was that never enough for you, Rav? Why did your greed get the better of you?*

"No guards?" Ramiro asked. "Why don't they just take the vessel?"

"They don't know where the key is," Dante answered. *But I do.*

"Right." Mara rubbed her hands together. "We don't know how many are in the mansion; Ramiro and I will—"

"Not many." Dante didn't take his eyes away from the manor. "Rav doesn't keep friends for long."

Mara frowned. "Alright, we can make 'em think we're a bigger force than we are by—"

"No, no." Dante held a hand up. "I'll take care of this."

"You can't go up against 'em, you're not a fighter."

"Nor will I have to be."

"Whatever you're planning, get on with it. We need to get to Phadra before the eclipse."

"And take the San Sirans with us," Cassandra added.

Mara eyed the copper. "Agreed."

Dante grinned. *This is going to be fun.* "Okay—wait for me by the *Luna*."

He strode through the uneven path, towards the red manor glowering at him. Forlorn eyes followed him.

Keep calm, keep calm.

He reached the red door and teased it open. Candlelight throbbed and warmed the empty hallway. From the darkness, two of Rav's men approached. One looked younger than twenty, sandy-haired and strong, while the other looked middle-aged, rake-thin, and stood a good head taller.

The thin man's hand rested upon a dagger in his belt. "Who the hell are you?"

"Why, I'm Dante tal Arata, surely Rav has spoken of me?"

"No."

Dante slapped his thigh. "Hah! Typical—head in the clouds, that man." He stepped forward but the guards blocked his way.

"This is where you piss off, mate—we got cattle to herd and don't need no distractions."

Cattle? They're human beings.

Dante's face contorted in mock affront. "Me? Listen, friend, this is my operation as much as Rav's—I'm a Wielder, just like he is."

The younger, shorter man laughed. He had two purple irises that glinted brighter than Dante's. "If I had a shiny aeron for every man who told me he was a Wielder, I'd be rich. You'd think half the San Sirans out there were wizards."

Of the two, the younger, muscular one wore finer clothes. In particular, his boots looked brand-new.

"Rich?" Dante said. "Rich enough to afford a pair of boots from Mateo's, eh?"

The young man frowned. "How the hell did you know that?"

Because their brass buckles are stamped with a bull insignia, a royal mark that only one man in Phadra has earned: Mateo Moreno.

Dante cleared his throat. "*They* told me."

"Who did?"

"The spirits, of course."

"You talk to the dead?" the older one said.

"I told you, I'm a Wielder. And the spirits say that *he* is Ravinatro's favourite."

"*What?*" the older one said. "Bullshit."

"Ignore him." The young one shifted, uneasy. "He's lying."

The thin man glared at the young one. "Is he?"

That didn't take long.

Dante held his palms up. "Sorry, I mean no offence."

The young one cocked his head and drew his own dagger, a simple blade with a plain hilt, and pointed it at Dante. "Talk to the dead? Forgive me if I don't believe you."

Dante eased the point of the weapon away. "A Wielder, my friends. You've heard the San Sirans tell their tales, yes? Of shadow demons? I'm connected to the afterlife, just as these monsters are. I can prove it to you—I'll look into the spirit realm and divine your future. You first, um?"

"Alfred," the old skinny one said.

"Alfred. Or perhaps you have a loved one that you'd like to speak with?"

"Go ahead." The corner of Alfred's mouth crinkled. "Prove it or bleed."

"I shall! A caveat, however; sometimes the images are unclear, and sometimes they're clear as crystal yet mean nothing to me but are significant to you. With your help, we can unravel the secrets that surround you."

"Alf, he's a liar."

"Shut up, pretty boy." Alfred's eyes narrowed. "Get on with it, Wielder. Prove yourself."

Dante made a show of listening to secret voices and nodded. "Where in Lower Phadra are you from, Alf?"

"What?"

"The Harbour District, yes?"

The guard tensed. "Half the bastards in Phadra live in the Harbour District. A lucky guess."

When Dante had danced blindfolded upon the streets for a bet, he had relied on his ears and his nose. The scent of fresh fish, the taste of salt on his tongue—and the mongrel accents of the sailors. This man was Phadrosi through and through. "The spirits of the sea surround you, my friend—fret not, they mean you no harm."

"And what are they saying, then?"

"That you didn't live by the water—no, you stayed towards the rear of the harbours, no?"

Almost imperceptible, but the guard's eyes widened. "A guess."

"Alfred?" the young one said.

"Shut it, Cedric."

The one called Cedric shifted from foot to foot. *Nervous—and that means he's starting to believe.* Cold reading, the charlatans and mystics called it. Tease out small details to paint a bigger picture, convincing the mark that you know everything about them.

"Alfred? Yes, yes…" Dante muttered. "Oh, I don't know about *that*."

"What are they saying?" Terror shone in Alfred's eyes but then he steeled himself and said, "Never mind, you're full of—"

"The Lynx and Pheasant."

"What?"

"The Beaming Bull."

"You're full—"

"The Black Stork."

Alfred paled.

We have a winner.

"Yes, the Black Stork," Dante continued. "I see it now—the sign hanging and wavering in the wind, squealing on its hinges. When was the last time you were in your local tavern?"

"I don't know, a month or—"

"Recent but not *too* recent. Did you get tired of the ale or did…" Dante cocked his head to listen to more unseen phantoms. "Ah, yes, *that* makes sense."

"Stop that. *Stop*."

Guilt all over him. "The tavern banned you?"

"*No*. I, I just stopped going in."

Close enough. "The spirits are laughing at you for what happened—they wouldn't want to be in your shoes."

Alf's face turned red. "I had too much to drink is all. Carmen Caro was in and offered to give me a King's Shilling." Without looking, he tapped the left pocket of his jacket. "No man has ever said no to her, what was I supposed to do? I kissed her in front of everyone. I swear I was going to report for duty the next morning, but I was hungover. I missed the call and—"

"And that's why you're here, because the Phadrosi military don't take too kindly to deserters." Dante stepped closer and squeezed the man's right shoulder, while his free hand glided over his jacket. "Don't worry, the spirits may judge—but I don't."

Alfred's shoulders dropped and his chin hung low.

"Bullshit," said Cedric. "Any man could figure all that out, all you did was let him talk!"

"All I did was let the *spirits* talk."

Cedric raised his chin. "Go on, then—do me."

"Yes—you're the money man, eh?"

"What?" Cedric's turn to look uncomfortable. "How did you know that?"

Because your friend only had one coin. "The spirits see all, my friend. You're Rav's favourite because you're young and pretty—much easier to part people with their coin."

Alfred turned sullen. "Pretty don't last forever."

You're a creature of habit, Rav. Recruit those who need acceptance and validation—then move on to the next one.

Cedric huffed. "Shut *up*, Alfred—don't give him any more—"

"Who's Sofía?" Dante asked.

Cedric frowned. "I don't know a Sofía."

A hundred thousand women in Phadros named Sofía, and I meet the one idiot who doesn't know any of them.

Dante fake-stifled a giggle. "Oh, my friend, I'm so sorry—she must have given you a false name. She's young, she knew you from a while back… For one evening, I believe?"

"One night? That dusky slattern with the big…" Cedric paled. "How did she die? Wasn't the pox, was it? I knew it, I *knew* I shouldn't have—"

"Hush, hush, it wasn't the pox that took her. She wants to thank you—she died not long after you both… *connected.* She wants to thank you for leaving her with a happy memory in her final moments."

Cedric stood about three inches taller after that. "Well, I, I… Tell her she's very welcome."

Dante squeezed Cedric's shoulder and let his hand brush over his pocket. "Oh, she knows. Now, if I could just—"

"Fancy tricks don't mean we're gonna let you pass," Alfred said.

"Oh…" Dante's eyes widened. "Oh, my."

"What now?" the older man growled.

"I, um. I shouldn't say."

"You're so full of shit," said Cedric.

Alfred grinned. "That explains why he thinks you could please a woman."

"Shut *up.*"

Dante cleared his throat. "I, um… Perhaps I should leave."

Alf's lips curled into a snarl. "Make up your mind."

"Cedric? Are you going to tell him? The spirits tell me you've been very naughty indeed."

Cedric reddened, though Dante couldn't divine the specific reason why—but that was half the fun of cold reading.

"*Very* naughty." Dante cleared his throat. "Alfred, he has something that belongs to you."

Alfred frowned. "What?"

"Seems your King's Shilling is weighing down his pocket, he and Rav plan on selling you out to the military as soon as you reach Phadra, get themselves a nice little reward."

Alfred fumbled in his jacket. "Empty! Son of a—"

"The spirits say that... Splitting the San Sirans' money two ways is better than three. Does that mean anything to you?"

Alfred shoved Cedric against the wall and turned his pockets out. His King's Shilling rolled onto the floorboards.

"You little bastard."

"I didn't take anything!"

"So you're denying it, eh? You and Rav haven't made any plans?"

Cedric turned redder than the manor's crimson door. "I swear I didn't take the shilling, but—"

"But you and Rav are gonna screw me over, huh?"

"How did you know that?" Cedric spat at Dante.

Because Rav is a creature of habit. "Because the spirits told me. They also think that Rav made the same offer to Alfred— a split of forty-forty and leave the rest for you. Not that you'd know."

"*What?*"

Now it was Alfred's turn to go red. "Aye, well, you get the gifts, the glory, the fancy shoes—only right that I get a bigger share of the take."

"I'm the one who does all the—"

Alfred punched Cedric, and Cedric punched Alfred. They hit the floor, rolling and scrapping.

Dante marched towards Rav's room and pocketed

Alfred's King's Shilling. It'd make a nice addition to his collection.

How long before they realise I've lifted all the San Sirans' money, too?

Rav's bedroom reeked of incense, but it didn't conceal the multitude of stale odours. Tattered curtains hung over filthy windows, but precious antiques dotted the floor and tables. Just like the *Luna*, the humble and the extravagant clashed with the pristine and the filthy.

A web of fairy lights hung over a king-size bed, breathing, a soft, warm halo of light over it. Rav lay there, like a saint bathing in the glow of the Gods, flicking through a burned and tattered book. "Do you know, I've started reading more books than I can count, but I can never seem to finish them. Guess I'm more interested in action." He tossed the book away and sat up, a smug smile on his lips. "I knew you'd come."

"Oh, yeah," said Dante. "I'm sure you can read me like a book."

Get hooked by the promise of the blurb and then toss it halfway through because you got bored. But that means you don't get the full story. Just when you think you know what's going to happen, BANG.

"Your crusade with Nyralto reach a premature end, did it? Or did your quest for hope and joy and world peace reach a successful conclusion?"

"You underestimate hope, Rav. Hope can take you far." Dante stopped his eyes from flicking to the thin chain glinting around Rav's neck. "It can lift you higher than any airship, take you farther than any train—and it can kill you sure as a knife to the heart. I'm here because I'm done. Adrian and the Wielders are gone. I wanted to see their story end, and it did—bloody and brutal. I've seen where hope takes you. I want to take you up on your offer." Here, Dante lowered his head. "If you'll still have me. I want to travel on the *Luna* and swindle the rich and foolish. Before long, there will be war—I mean to line my pockets while rich Phadrosi are still too fat and docile to notice the ill wind banging at their door."

Rav slithered off his bed and took a bottle and two glasses from a broken bookshelf. "A peace offering."

"Not for me, thanks."

"This is an añejo tequila, my friend, meant to be sipped and savoured. Never known you to say no to the finer things in life."

The chain around Rav's neck charmed the light from the fairy lights. "Only when they're bad for me."

Rav eased onto a battered leather couch that would once have been luxurious. "Tell me what you have in mind, Little Dante."

Dante squirmed. Over the years, he'd rehearsed this moment a hundred times or more. There was much he wanted to say to Rav, but now that he was here…

He sat next to him. "Sweep it all away."

"What do you mean?" Rav's voice came low and sweet and rolling, like seeping treacle.

"This place has bad memories." He inched closer to Rav. "I mean to make new ones, before the world burns. You showed me a train—show me what *you* want to see."

"Oh, I will—but I won't need magic."

"A manor, then. Bigger and grander than this."

"I don't use my magic lightly, Dante, you don't—"

"Understand? I understand better than you, Rav. I've watched Wielders manipulate time, command the earth like Terros himself. What, are you scared that your pretty pictures won't be as miraculous as all that?"

Rav's head tilted and he raised an eyebrow. "Since it's you."

237

The bedroom peeled away, bit by bit. The ragged curtains melted and the cracked and peeling ceiling gave way to an expanse of blue sky. Gulls wheeled overhead and an island of green and grey formed. Men and women laughed and an ancient lighthouse towered high.

"You're repeating yourself!" Dante said above a whistling breeze. "Why the lighthouse?"

"Heard a story once, before I knew I possessed the power of the Gods." The soft crash of waves brushed against a winding, golden beach. "Of an island that housed dragons and sirens, a haven for the lost and the misunderstood. Only they can see the lighthouse, everyone else just passes straight through."

"It appeals to you."

Rav inched away. "Just a story."

"Show me the *Luna*."

Rav did. The phantom island dissipated, and in an instant, Dante stood on the deck of the *Nueva Luna*. He floated over the grand castles of Ryndara, the rolling emerald hills of Aludan, the crystalline ice fjords of Tarevia. Gentle wind and warm laughter surrounded him, the music of an adoring audience.

Dante slid closer to Rav and drooped an arm around his shoulders. Sweat dotted Rav's forehead, just as it did when Varl and Magnus overexerted their power.

"I waited for you, Little Dante, but now we should go."

"Just a little longer."

Together, they sat on the deck, gazing up at a starlit sky, surrounded by music. The world floated beneath them—and in a swift, smooth motion, Dante whisked the chain from around Rav's neck.

The illusion warped and faded. "I grow tired, my friend."

Dante's arm snapped back. "Of course." He stood up. "You know what? I *will* have a drink." Dante tossed a shot of tequila back. It had notes of vanilla, dried fruit, and what he imagined flaming igneus tasted like. He shivered. "Hard stuff."

"I did tell you to sip it."

"I've never counted patience among my virtues—one of the few things we have in common. And on that note, this is farewell, Rav."

Rav frowned. "What?"

"You will never see me again. You won't look for me, and you won't come after my friends."

"You don't have any friends."

"I'm done with you, Rav. Never needed you in the first place—I just didn't realise it 'til now. I could've taken the *Luna* and disappeared—probably should have. But I want you to know—I want you to know that I beat you."

"Dante, Little Dante—"

"That is not my name."

Rav stood, his face paling. He fumbled for the chain around his neck.

"Looking for this?" Dante held it up. The *Luna*'s startup key swung like a pendulum.

"That's only half," Rav spat. "Without the flight sequence—"

"You mean the one you keep in your copy of the *Analectus and the Great Gospels*?"

Rav's eyes narrowed.

"You always treated me like a kid. All of you. While you were laughing at me, I observed. I absorbed. You taught me how to walk around without being heard nor seen—who do you think I practiced on? I bet you thought you were so clever, hiding the code in a book you knew no-one would read. But I saw how your eyes would flick to it whenever the Watch inspected us. I saw the panic in your face that time we had those Dalthean nuns come aboard with their orphans and one of 'em picked the *Analectus* up. The *Luna*'s mine, your guards are done, and the San Sirans are safe."

Rav's mouth worked as he figured out his next move. "You won't get far."

"Been hearing that my whole life."

Rav swept a hand across the table and sent the tequila bottle smashing onto the floor. "*All* of you needed me! I was the brains, you were all too dumb to think for yourselves. Who saved you all? Who fed and clothed you? Who planned jobs, came up with strategies?"

Dante stepped close to him. "And where's your old crew now, Rav? Gone. Your two guards are at each other's throats because they don't trust you. No-one wants you. You've been left behind, mate. You want to live on a magic island because you have nowhere and no-one. You didn't want me back here for my silver tongue—you wanted me here because you're *lonely*."

Rav's face burned red. "You won't get out of here alive. I won't let you."

"Of course you will—because you've never been in a fight in your life, you always had other people to fight your battles. And if anything happens to me, you'll answer to my friends outside—one of whom is a knight with *severe* anger issues." Dante put his hands on his hips. He exhaled, long and satisfying and cleansing. "Feels good to get all this off my chest. Funny how we can't help but rebel against the lies we build around ourselves, isn't it?"

Rav laughed, low and sinister. "I know you, Little Dante. I know the *real* you."

"No—you knew a *version* of me. This is goodbye, Rav. Forever."

"I'll find you."

Dante turned and walked away.

"I'll find you! You know what I am now? *A god!* I know you, Dante—I know what you love. What you hate. What you *fear*."

The world melted away and turned black.

"What you *fear*." Rav's voice echoed through a long, winding tunnel.

Dante's heart thudded. "This is just an illusion. You can't hurt me."

Rav laughed again. "I can make you *beg* me to hurt you."

Dante kept walking, the hairs on the back of his neck standing up.

White light flooded the tunnel, an engine chugged, and a train barrelled towards him. His mother leaned out and waved, her chestnut-brown hair sweeping behind her. Gods, she looked young. It felt real, so *real*—the sound, the rush of warm air, the smell of leaking igneus.

"Take my hand!" his mother called. She stretched out, reached towards her boy, and—

Dante kept walking.

"Come back!" Rav roared. "Get back here! Dante! Little Dante!"

The train rattled away and shattered like a mirror.

A shadow resolved before him as the illusion changed. Of all the strange, shadowy fiends Dante had seen recently, this was the worst.

His father.

Words tumbled from his mouth, harsh and cutting.

"Yeah, yeah, sticks and stones." Dante passed through without flinching.

That was the thing with illusions—they could be terrifying, powerful, deadly—but they were never as bad as the terrors that one's own mind conjured.

Rav threw memories at Dante—or Rav's own version of his memories. Dante watched himself as a child, letting his bladder go onstage when he flubbed a line and struggled to get back on track. He watched his teen self vomit all over the *Luna*'s deck after Rav and his crew plied him with ale and spun him around two dozen times.

Every embarrassment, every humiliation, he relived over and over.

And the strange thing?

Most of them aren't that bad. Dante chuckled to himself. *Some of it's even funny!*

The illusions flickered like a guttering candle. One by one, they melted away.

"Just as I was starting to enjoy the show."

Sweat fell from Rav's brow. "I'll get you back for this, Dante. I swear it."

Dante yawned. "Swearing revenge is so passé. A word of advice, Ravinatro, that I should have given to a better friend than you: Let the hate go."

Alfred and Cedric's war had taken them into the manor's drawing room. Dante heard furniture breaking, glass smashing and a tumult of very bad language. It sounded better than the music in Rav's illusions.

Once outside, he tossed the key and money to Ramiro. "Let them aboard and give them their money back."

It didn't take long for the survivors to board the *Nueva Luna*, but one little girl stood apart from the others, no more than eight years old, a toy bear clutched in her hand. She wore a tattered green dress and her light brown hair was tangled and matted.

Dante looked at her for a moment, trying to tell if she was real or one of Rav's illusions.

"It's safe aboard the airship," he said. "I promise."

"I don't want to go to Phadra." Her voice sounded weak and scratchy.

"Have you lost someone?"

She gave a weak nod.

"Your parents?"

Another weak nod.

"What did they do, your parents? For work?"

"Doctors. Stayed behind to help after the earthquake, but they got lost."

Dante's stomach knotted. "What's your name?"

"Sofía."

He smiled. "Of course it is. Did you know that Nyr's ferryman takes souls across the Grey River, Sofía?"

She shook her head.

"If a soul's been bad, the ferryman will steer towards the Black River. If they've been good, he'll take them to the White River to live in Nyr's grand palace. It certainly sounds like your parents were good."

"They'll go to the palace?"

"Oh, I've no doubt."

"But... I'm sad. What if I forget them? What if I don't remember their faces?"

"It's okay to be sad sometimes. And for as long as you live, you'll never forget them." Dante tapped his chest. "They'll always live in your heart, see? They'll always walk with you."

"Sofía!" an old man called from the *Luna*.

"Is that your grandfather?" Dante asked.

Sofía nodded.

"Off you go, then—and whenever you think of your parents, do so with a smile."

Dante stretched and took a deep breath and climbed the stairs into the belly of the airship—*his* airship.

The smell of rosewood and incense hit him and ushered in a hundred memories. Most of them bad, but not as bad as all that.

Dante took to the stage to address the San Sirans; he remembered the stage being a lot bigger. Cassandra waited for him there, her arms crossed and a smile on her lips. "What did you do?"

"Gave the performance of a lifetime."

All around, the desperate throng stirred in their seats.

Dante put one foot onto a crate, cupped his hands to his mouth and yelled, "All of you—my name is Dante tal Arata, and today is a new dawn! None of you are indebted to Rav. I'll take you to Phadra and I'll keep you safe. You don't need to be scared any longer."

Calls of "Dante! Dante!" rang through the auditorium. In the front row, the little girl Sofía beamed at him, which lifted his heart higher than the chanting.

The *Nueva Luna* ascended. Through the cargo hold's windows, Dante saw sunlight sparkling like diamonds on the waterfalls surrounding Toledra Village. Rav's false kingdom dwindled away, small, insignificant, nothing. Toledra was a home, once, a refuge, but Dante knew that he'd never return. He wouldn't need to.

He turned to Cassandra and asked, "How's *that* for a fireball show?"

CASSANDRA

C assandra held a well-worn costume dress before her, all sequins and shiny thread.

She dropped it onto a pile of similar clothes. Chests and trunks dominated the backstage area of the *Luna*, filled with old outfits, props and stage make-up. *All the things a liar needs to become someone else.*

It must be an easy way to live, switching identities whenever one felt like it. Gods knew there were days when Cassandra wished she could change who she was, shed all her responsibilities and become someone new. Responsibilities, like her sister...

It wouldn't be long before they landed in Phadra. Cassandra would make sure that the refugees had food and shelter, then have Mara and Ramiro convince their commanders to form a search party and find Adrian and Caela.

And in the meantime, pray that Lord Lucien hasn't received my bricode message.

She drew a filthy curtain away and revealed a small, smudgy window. The sun caught her gaze and she pleaded to Sol, like a defendant before a judge.

"Any answer?"

She cleared her throat and straightened herself. "Dante. Didn't hear you. Any news?"

He stuffed his hands into his pockets and shook his head. "Ramiro's sitting by the bricode kit."

Cassie's stomach knotted. "Perhaps no news is good news." In truth, she didn't want to think about bricode messages. She'd sent a message to the skyport in Phadra and received no response—part of her wanted it to stay that way; if no-one had read that bricode message, then perhaps Lucien really hadn't received the one she'd sent after escaping Terra Puerta...

Dante eased onto a large trunk, chin resting on his knuckles. "Do you think Adrian and the others are alive?"

"I do." She eased down next to him.

"Yeah. I mean, he's with Wielders, right? They'll look after him. He'll be fine."

"You care a great deal for him, don't you?"

"He's a friend. Not had many of those in my life. Not *real* ones. But I screwed it up."

"What happened between you two?"

"I..." Dante scratched the back of his head. "I found him on the streets, one day. After his father died. We looked out for each other. It's a long story, one that I have no intention of divulging to a member of the Watch, but one day, I told him about a job—with Rav and my old crew. It was danger-ous, Adrian begged me not to do it. I tried to get him onboard, but he refused. A smuggling job, Rav had told me— our old friend Captain Pedro. You remember when Idaris tried to invade Dalthea? It caused the price of igneus to rise, made everything more expensive. In Lower Phadra, people starved. This shipment of food would feed them, Rav said, but..."

"But it wasn't food."

Dante shook his head. "Scuzz. Rav spun the story to get me to rejoin his crew. Anyway, Adrian followed me to the harbour. He tried to pull me out at the last minute, but the Watch spilled out of the warehouses and arrested us all. Adrian escaped but not me. After I got out of jail, I went to him… He was balls-deep in the military by then, said he didn't have time for friends like me—for liabilities. Can hardly blame him—he saved my skin more times than I can count—I'd have got tired of me, too."

"Dante… I had no idea."

"He doesn't speak about his past much. He was orphaned. His father was murdered by shadow demons—funny how normal that is to say now. Obviously, I didn't believe him the first time he told me, but I'd spent most of my childhood with madmen and sociopaths, so I didn't press it. No-one ends up on the streets through choice, and his story wasn't the most outlandish I'd heard."

"And *your* father?"

"Alive, I'm sorry to say. No, Adrian was my *real* family. I blamed him for leaving me behind, but it wasn't his fault—it was my own. I swear I didn't know what was in those crates. Guess I got what I deserved—and can't ask for any more'n that."

The vessel's engine hummed and her wooden beams creaked. "We don't always get what we deserve," Cassandra started, "but the Gods ensure we get what we *need*."

"Is that why you sold your soul to the Watch?"

"I joined the Watch because I don't like bullies. My mother was San Siran, my father Phadrosi." Cass frowned. "He was a distant man. Not cruel, not unkind, but… cold. My mother fell in love with someone else, so my father brought us to Phadra. Being San Siran children in Phadros wasn't easy. My father tried, but I don't think he ever truly recovered from losing my mother. Looking back, I see that he was sad. And lonely. That's what sent Mariana down a dangerous path, I think. She took her frustrations out on me."

"Families." Dante's fingers drummed the chest. "A conundrum impossible to solve."

"I tell people I joined the Watch to help others. In reality, I'm angry. At those who prey on the weak. At myself for *being* weak."

Dante nudged her with his elbow. "If only we could change who we are, eh?"

Sailing aboard a theatre ship, pretending to be someone different every night...

What happened after the performance had ended and the last echoes of applause disappeared? Maybe it wasn't as easy as Cass had believed, continually changing and pushing parts of yourself down in order to survive.

As if reading her mind, he swept a hand out and said, "You know, I never was very good at all this. Oh, I was fine for what we were doing—fleecing people out of their money. But acting should be about more lying—it should be a different kind of *truth*. Reckon I was always scared of failure, so I didn't bother trying in the first place. Seems so insignificant now."

"Your skills helped us escape, Dante. You saved lives."

He brightened at that. "Yeah. Yes, I did. Funny thing—a performance is only good if you put *yourself* into it. Maybe that's why Rav was always so good at manipulating the rest of us?"

"Don't let what that fool did rile you, Dante, he's—"

"An asshole—but he was only ever himself. That's where I've gone wrong my whole life."

Cassie frowned. "I don't—"

Hesitating, Dante's fingers floated to his eyes...

And peeled the purple contact lenses from them.

"Dante?"

His eyes were brown, deep and earthy.

"I'm not what I say I am. Never have been." He blinked tears away. "It was an act, like everything else I do. I wanted... to be something else. Some*one* else. Even when I wasn't on stage, I was always pretending. Do you know, I don't even remember my real name?"

"Dante... Why?"

He leaned back, beneath the absent glare of an empty spotlight. "I don't know. I grew up surrounded by talented people. I was sick of being the useless one. No matter what I tried, I kept failing. So I ran away, feigned an aristocratic accent when I needed to and a commoner's idiom when I didn't. If I constantly changed who I was, then I didn't need to confront the truth: That I'm nobody. That I'm nothing. If I was a red-haired clown who dipped people's pockets one day, then I didn't need to feel guilty, because the next day I'd be a prince from a faraway land, regaling crowds with tales of heroism. I wasn't guilty because it wasn't *me*. I'd change my identity from one day to the next as if it were one of these costumes. It's an easy way to live... For a while. But each time I did it... It got worse. Stripped away my sense of self. The truth is, I'm no leading man—I'm a follower. I go with the crowd but always keep my distance in case they reject me. Gods, I was so angry at Adrian for walking away from me, even though I'd done the same thing myself a hundred times over. Too scared to be alone, too scared to get close to anyone."

"Dante, I..." Cassie reached out but drew her hand away at the last moment.

"Funny how things turn out, isn't it?" A sad smile caressed his lips.

"We're in a ship, safe, heading for home, bringing injured people to safety. *You* did that, Dante. *You* saved their lives, and ours."

Dante's eyes glistened again. "Didn't think I'd ever have a conversation like this with the cold-hearted Diaz, iron fist of the City Watch."

"Yes, well... Reputation has its uses. Even if it's a lie."

"What?"

"Since we're being honest... I did not arrest my own mother."

"Excuse me?"

"I did not arrest my own mother."

Dante frowned. "Gods above. Then why let me go on at you? Why let the rumours endure?"

"Did *you* ever think to question them?"

"Well, I... When you hear something often enough, you figure it *has* to be true. Gods above." Dante's face softened. "This might mean nothing coming from me, but... Sometimes you have to stand up for yourself, make yourself vulnerable to—"

"It was my sister. And I didn't arrest her—I sent her to a Fayth retreat."

"Oh. That's worse."

Cassie laughed at that. "She had a laudanol habit... Among other things. I sent her away for her own good. She begged and pleaded, almost clawed my eyes out. It broke my heart to bear her hate, almost as bad as seeing her in her stupors. But after a month, she resembled her old self. She thanked me. At first, I hated the stories about me, but it made it easier when people saw me as cold. Helped me keep my distance, keep my head down. The Watch isn't an easy place to be when you're San Siran. Or a woman. At least this way, I had some measure of control."

"Cassie... All this time, you've carried that. I... I don't know what to say. I thought you were a stuck-up copper who only knew how to follow orders."

I am—but I hope it's not too late to change.

She looked into his teak-coloured eyes, and he held her gaze. "First impressions are often wrong, it seems. You don't have to be tied down by circumstance, Dante. You have the strength to be who you *want* to be. And... so do I."

Eyes pinned to each another, her little finger brushed his.

He didn't pull away. He drew closer to her, and she felt his warmth. The touch of his skin sent electricity up her arm.

"Dante," she whispered. "There's something I... need to tell—"

"Hullo!"

Ramiro's voice startled her. She yanked her hand away and stood. "What? Yes? What is it?"

The soldier arched an eyebrow. "We're here."

The peak of the palace dominated the horizon like the tip of a spear in the centre of a battlefield.

Phadra looked unscathed, unblemished, unchanged—but things *had* changed, hadn't they? When she'd left, she was Sergeant Cassandra "Coldheart" Diaz, striding out of the city with her head held high, a single purpose on her mind and fire in her heart. But she'd returned on a stolen airship and consorted with thieves and Wielders. She'd cheated, lied and broken the law.

The Wielders weren't evil.

The law hadn't protected the San Sirans.

And Dante...

Dante was so... *unlike* anyone she'd ever met. His humour. His heart. His dual habit of being charmingly offensive and offensively charming. He...

He was a thief. And a liar. And a con man. But... He wasn't *bad*.

The *Luna* sailed over Phadra's walls, over monuments to famous conquistadors. The statues stood tall, with straight backs and raised chins, all surveying their glories with stiff upper lips and swords in their hands.

A celebration of conquest and murder.

Old first-generation vessels crowded over the circular walls of Phadra's skyport. The *Nueva Luna* slowed and joined them.

Cassie gripped the rail tight.

It'll be worth it. I'll explain everything to Lucien. He still wants to improve the city. I'll get my promotion and I'll effect real *change.*

But it wasn't Lucien who awaited them.

Cassie shrank. In the skyport yard, a troop of watchmen awaited.

"Guess they got our message," Ramiro called at her back.

I guess so.

Ramiro set the gangplank onto the ground and ushered the San Sirans to safety. Behind them, heart racing, Cassie strode down, hoping she looked more at ease than she felt. With a mocking smile, a watchman she didn't recognise grinned at her. Bald and broad-shouldered, he stood with his legs apart and fists on his hips, like he owned all of Phadra. Glee filled his features, as if struggling to stifle a belly laugh, and when Cass got closer, his dark, purple irises sparkled.

Isn't he...

"Arch Vigil Valador Ramos." The rough accent of Lower Phadra gave his words a jagged edge. "You must be Sergeant Diaz."

That stopped her heart dead. "Yes. I—"

"Boys." With a nod, his men seized the San Sirans.

Mara shouldered past. "The hell are you doing?"

"Every San Siran in the city is to be detained and interrogated."

"Um, Cass?" Dante said. "Why is the leader of the Sons of Belios a copper?"

"Sir, these people are survivors," Cassie pleaded. "They're not dangerous!"

"Then they have nothing to fear from interrogation. I believe these are your words?" Ramos produced a piece of paper and read, "'Bias is the enemy of any officer of the Watch—our duties must be performed with clarity and our investigation led only by evidence. With that in mind, it is my duty to inform you that

Sir Adrian is an inexperienced leader whose recklessness almost got us killed. He keeps the company of a thief who boasts of enlisting to the military under false identities and deserting with a King's Shilling every time.' Sounds to me like you've spent too long in the company of criminals to judge the San Sirans."

"Cassandra?" Dante asked. "What's he talking about?"

Her skin burned. "Arch Vigil, that information is out of date."

"Cassie?" Dante repeated. "What did you do?"

"Sergeant Diaz, the information you provided is the only reason you're not in chains with the rest of the San Sirans, thieves and half-bloods. I recommend you hold your tongue. Seize their vessel, lads." Ramos pointed to Dante. "And take him."

"Sir, *please*—Dante has saved—"

"Dante tal Arata is a known thief and deserter. I got arrest warrants for him under six different names—a pity the hangman can only tie a noose around him once."

"The *hangman?*" Dante squealed as two watchmen grabbed him. "Now, please, just a moment—Cass?"

"There's been a mistake!" Diaz yelled. "If I could just speak to Lord Lucien, I'll clear this up."

But the watchmen didn't let up. The San Sirans begged but the coppers clamped them in chains, put sacks over their heads and tossed them into waiting wagons.

"Cass? *Cass!*" Dante called, but a baton to his stomach had him doubled over. They covered his head and dragged him away with the others.

"Are you insane?" Mara demanded. "Listen to her!"

"Ah, yes, the soldiers." Ramos glanced at his papers. "Sir Mara Doncella de Hierro and Sir Ramiro Alvarez—you're both to report to your units for the expedition to San Sira. Reckon you're on the front lines."

"We've just *come* from San Sira."

"Sir," Ramiro started, "with all due respect, we don't take orders from the Watch. If you could simply—"

Ramos scowled. "If you want, I'll arrest you both as traitors—been a while since we've exercised the death penalty on our own, reckon we're due an example."

Mara brimmed with fire, but Ramos and his watchmen were too numerous.

"Do you need me to repeat your orders?" Ramos asked.

"C'mon." Mara dragged Ramiro away. "We'll figure it out."

"Sir," Cassie urged, "*sir!* With all due respect what *the hell* is going on?"

"Refugees from San Sira are to be charged as collaborators with Wielders. Their government's been using 'em to attack Phadros. Reports of portals and dark magic striking our warships."

"Bullshit!" Cass spat. "Sir, let me talk to Lucien, I can explain it all."

"The lord is busy—all matters concerning Wielders fall under my remit, *Sergeant.*"

Cass swallowed the bile in her throat. "Sir—if I could just speak to him, I can clear this up—we have new information—"

"Sergeant Diaz, if it was up to me, you half-breeds would be in chains with the rest of 'em, but Lucien wants you in the Watch. Question me again in front of my lads and I'll arrest you for treason."

Her fists tightened. "Screw you, screw the Watch and screw Lord Lucien, I'll speak to the king!"

"You may have difficulty with that." Ramos cocked his head. "The king is dead."

Stale beer and liquor permeated the Beaming Bull tavern. At first, the minutes crawled by. Now, the sun threatened to disappear and turn into evening—and that meant Sol's Kiss. But what could she do?

The king is dead. Killed by a San Siran Wielder.

That's what the broadsheets said; Cass didn't believe it, but what did the truth matter? If Phadros didn't hate San Sirans before, it did now.

She stared down at the glass of amber-brown liquid. "The best whisky in the Bull," so the barmaid had said. "Glenfortoshan, 18 years old."

At first, her sister drank the best liquors. Whisky, champagne, premium gin. As her friends abandoned her, so she abandoned her taste. Expensive liquor became cheap beer, homemade spirits... And an alcoholic solution from a medical kit.

It was walking in on Mariana in her bathroom—unconscious with a bottle of rubbing alcohol lying on the tiles—that steeled Cassie's resolve. She poured cold water over her, slapped her face and dragged her outside. Cass recalled the scratches from her sister's long nails.

Why do we hurt ourselves in the ways that we do?

Cass had never touched the stuff, and never planned to. She believed in control. Believed in order. Believed in the law.

She slid the glass across the table and examined her Watch badge instead. Candlelight glinted over its dents and bumps. She'd clung to it as a symbol of justice for so long—clung to it as her sister did the bottle—but now it seemed flimsy and malleable. Corruptible. Just a worthless piece of tin.

In a few years, she could've been Arch Vigil. She could've changed the system from within, made *real* progress for the people of Phadra. The way Lucien always smiled at her... She'd appreciated it at first, an avuncular superior taking her under his wing. Now she saw it for what it truly was: He smiled at her like she was his pet. He knew where her sister was and had even sent her money. *Not much, but enough to buy my loyalty.*

The Wielders had treated her as one of their own, and even Adrian, Mara and Ramiro had accepted her in a way that the Watch never had. Outcasts, every one—like her.

And Dante…

Dante was a liar. A thief. A con man who fleeced people out of their money. But…

There was good in him. She'd seen it. He'd helped people, put their welfare before his own. When was the last time she'd seen a copper do that? Or do *anything* that they weren't ordered to do?

At the end of the day, that's what the Crown wanted of its Watch: To be filled with mindless instruments, an extension of their will, a way to get the dirty work done without muddying their own fingers.

Need to collect tax from old widows who can't afford it? Send the Watch.

Hordes charging at the city walls? Send the Watch.

Need a spy who'll blindly follow orders if you dangle a carrot in front of her, then when she betrays her friends, pat her on the head and call her a good girl? Send Cassandra Diaz. She'll do it, and she'll bloody thank you for it.

Well, not any more.

She sent her badge clattering over the table, stood with her back straight, and tossed her drink back.

ADRIAN

Six months ago

Adrian sat at a table, hunched over old papers. An ignium lamp painted the piles of books around him in autumn gold.

The entrance to the Dragon's Lair swivelled open and Amos' feet pounded the floor. *Great.* Perhaps he'd give Adrian a very important mission to sweep the floor or collect another bottle of rum.

"You been here all night?" The commander sounded like he'd eaten razor blades for breakfast.

"And most of yesterday." Adrian didn't look up from the giant tome before him. "You never told me you had all these books."

"Didn't reckon I had to."

"There are editions of *The Analectus and the Great Gospels of the Indecim* that I've never seen before—the Order of the Ivory Dove makes its knights memorise it, but this is twice as long as any of their copies. There are entire passages about hunting down evil sorcerers and how to kill 'em. 'The Sword of Light wards against magic'. What does that mean?"

Amos stifled a cough. "Can't says I know."

"And this one." Adrian tapped the crisp page of the book lying open before him. *"Schiehallion's Breath: A Comprehensive Guide on Aerulian Gods & Daemons, and Orinul Myths and Monsters.* It's not as old as the others. Gods, is this *real?"* Adrian flicked to a page describing mischievous imps. "Devils, goat-men, and sirens who can control men like puppets? It even talks about shadow dragons."

"Might have been real once." Amos yawned. "Not any more."

Adrian remembered the shadows that killed his father. Hard to forget them when they plagued his dreams every night. *"Just a child's imagination making sense of trauma,"* Lord Lucien had told him.

Amos threw himself onto a battered chair. Before the inevitable snoring, Adrian asked, "What's in your safe?"

Amos groaned. "What safe?"

"The one behind the bookcase. It's the one lock I can't pick."

Amos laughed. "Too clever for your own good, boy. Who the hell taught you to pick locks?"

"Were you born a knight of the Shadow Dragon?"

"No."

"Neither was I. Is the safe where you keep the best weapons?"

Amos didn't speak for a moment. "It's where I keep my best whisky."

"No, it isn't." Adrian turned the page. "That was under the kitchen floorboards."

Amos chuckled, then stopped. *"Was?"*

"I've hidden it."

"Where?"

"If I told you, it wouldn't be hidden."

"And if you *don't* tell me, they'll never find your body."

"No-one'll look anyway."

"Little bastard."

"Better than being a big one." Adrian slammed the book shut, stood, and met Amos' eye. "Open the safe and I'll tell you where your whisky is."

Amos regarded him in a way he'd never done before. "Why the hell are you here, boy? What is it that you want?"

"I want to know about magic. Monsters. How to find them. How to kill them."

Amos' eyes narrowed, as if deciding whether or not Adrian was lying to him. "Tell me why you're obsessed with all this. Tell me why you're different from the rest."

Adrian didn't know this man, not really. The only person he'd ever confided in was Dante tal Arata, and Adrian very much doubted he'd ever see him again. *Don't need friends—I need answers.* Commander Amos was the closest thing to a custodian of the knowledge Adrian sought. Anyway, he'd said it himself—no-one took the Order of the Shadow Dragon seriously. Who would Amos tell?

"People don't believe in monsters," Adrian started. "Don't believe in the things that go bump in the night. *I* do. And I learned that it's not a *thing* that comes out of the night—it's the night itself. It's darkness and shadow. There's power there—I've seen it. Darkness took my father. I need to know how. I need to know why."

Lines creased Amos' brow. He looked at Adrian as if weighing his soul. "Follow me."

Amos pulled a bookcase out and revealed a grey steel safe as tall as a man. A Burston & Macaro unit, to be sure, but it looked different to the others Adrian had cracked; for one thing, the dial had strange symbols instead of numbers.

Amos touched the dial. The markings glowed and formed into numbers, then—

of its own accord—the dial spun left and right with muted *clicks*.

Right 36.

Left 10.

Right 59.

Right 97.

The door swung outward, revealing an unlit room.

"Magic." Adrian's stomach tightened. "You use magic."

Amos glowered at him. "Knights of the Shadow Dragon do what's required of them. We weave illusion and lies to keep people safe. We use our enemies' strengths against them. Knowledge is our chief weapon against the darkness, and we use that knowledge to—"

"Turn yourselves into monsters?"

"To turn us into whatever the world needs us to be, boy. You know this."

"But I didn't know you use *magic*."

The usual hint of humour faded from Amos' eyes. "Magic is science unexplained. If you're serious about learning all there is to know about the Order, then I'll hear no argument. If you're like every other initiate only here to tick a box so you can parade yourself in the taverns like a damn peacock, then Amos'll sign it right now and throw you onto the street. Up to you."

Adrian peered into the unlit room. "Let's go."

Amos stepped through the door. At once, small ignium lamps sparked into life. "This way."

Adrian almost said, "There is only one way," but for all he knew, hidden staircases would jut out of the walls or an unseen elevator would ferry him to some unknown basement.

They came to a wide, circular room, filled with dusty shelves and chests. Piles of books lined the shelves in no discernible arrangement.

"This is the Order's vault," Amos explained. "Its library. Its armoury. Gods, I haven't been down here in years."

"Most of the boxes are empty."

"Aye. My commander told me that after the Gods saved us from the Orinul, the threat of magic disappeared, so the Order found other uses for its treasures. Reckon the Crown had the Order carry out assassinations and the like, depleting our resources instead of saving 'em for real threats. All speculation on my part, of course—that's the thing about working in a secret sect: No-one writes a bloody thing down."

Amos rummaged through a pile of old books and coughed, harsh and hacking.

"You okay?"

Amos waved the question away. "Overdid the rum last night. Most of the initiates that walk through my door are only here to get their writs signed—three months in each military order then the Crown calls you a knight. But this stuff takes *years* to master, boy. Amos reckoned you were another wide-eyed, green kid with delusions of chivalry. Simple-minded men will do a lot when a lord sticks a 'sir' in front of his name."

"I didn't become a soldier to blindly follow Lucien's orders—he's a good man, but—"

"Lord Lucien is many things—*good* ain't one of 'em."

"He's a war hero—he piloted rescue vessels when Idaris attacked Imanis."

"Yet none of his men came back with him—makes Amos think, that. Here we are." Amos turned and held a piece of parchment out to Adrian. "There's a vow we make, boy—a secret one. Not to the king and not to Phadros, but a vow to the world."

Adrian scanned the parchment:

I am a knight of the Shadow Dragon

I am its tool, its servant, its sword
My deeds are measured in a flash of the blade
I bow to neither king nor lord

I am a knight of the Shadow Dragon
I will fight until my dying breath
I know no glory and shall rest in a nameless tomb
In deference to death

I am a knight of the Shadow Dragon
I know only the eternal fight
To defy the kingdom of the worm
That place which knows no light

He handed the paper back. "Cheery bit of reading."

"You're serious about facing the darkness? You're serious about being a knight of the Shadow Dragon? Then you'd best be serious about these words. The Order amassed materials here for years, boy, before the Crown squandered it. This is all that's left. You want to know our secrets, you'd best be sure. Not gonna lie—it won't be easy. Committing to the order will stretch you to breaking point. Your body, your mind—your soul. You'd be a lot happier just going through the ranks like the rest of 'em, blissfully ignorant."

Adrian raised his chin. "Ignorance was taken from me a long time ago. What materials do you have? More books?"

Amos' mouth curved like the blade of a scimitar. "Not quite."

The commander pulled a thick, black curtain back and revealed a smaller side room. Weapons lined the walls—swords, axes, even guns. Some of the firearms resembled unfinished prototypes, others were adorned with ornamental flourishes and polished to a mirror sheen. Amos' fingers glided along a tri-barrelled rotating repeater. "This uses igneus—coats bullets in the stuff. Never been tested, but I always wanted to see it in action."

Adrian spied vials of glowing igneus sitting on one shelf. "Half the ingredients, at least." But what snatched his gaze was an empty spherical bottle, sitting inside a simple wooden box with velvet lining.

"Fond of empty bottles?"

Amos pulled away from the firearm. "That's where I keep the shadow ink, drawn from the blood of a shadow dragon."

"What?"

Amos winked. "That lesson comes later. You gonna stand outside all day?"

Awed, Adrian stepped into the side room; of the dozen swords hanging there, one stood out: A shortsword with a shallow-curved tip, ribbed leather grip and a plain guard. It was identical to the Phadrosi slashing sword that horsed soldiers would wield during the Age of Exploration, typical in every possible way except one: The amber shimmering within the steel.

"Ignicite," Adrian said. "Is this the Sword of Light?"

"Some called it that. Some believe that's another weapon." Amos brought it out of its bracket and sliced the air with a satisfying swish. It left a faint afterglow in the air. "The first weapon forged by the Order of the Shadow Dragon, well before the world knew what to do with ignicite. Some say Aerulus used it to slay the Orinul, others say it predates even the Gods. The blood of a thousand demons washed this blade, yet never stained the steel. My master didn't know who brought it here or how it was forged, nor his master before him—we've lost most of our secrets; all we know is that this sword wards the world from darkness."

"How?"

Amos stared Adrian in the eye. The sword's glow grew brighter and brighter—so bright, Adrian had to shield his eyes.

"Belios' balls."

Amos chuckled. "Aye."

He handed the sword to Adrian; his fingers tightened around the grip. The swirling, shimmering amber in the steel mesmerised him. It felt almost weightless. He slashed the air; the blade had a keen edge and perfect balance. "Surprised the Crown hasn't drawn the ignicite from it."

"Remember, 'we bow to neither king nor lord.' The Crown doesn't know about this vault—and nor will it."

Adrian's pulse quickened. Finally, after all these years, he had something tangible—a tool to drive the darkness back.

"How do I make it glow brighter?" he asked.

"We'll get to that."

"And the guns?"

"Nothing much to say that you don't already know; when the ignicite revolution kicked into high gear and firearm production became profitable, my master made these—his theory was that if ignicite could be folded into the steel of a sword to drive the darkness back, then ignicite-based bullets could, too. He produced this rotary rifle but he died before he did anything with it. The Crown came and confiscated most of our gear, put me out to pasture—but no way in a hundred Idari hells was I telling 'em about the vault."

Adrian caressed the tri-barrel with his free hand. "Looks heavy."

"And never been tested in the field, so don't get any bright ideas, boy."

"So, this sword's all we have?"

"Amos reckons so. Boy, if your mate Lucien finds out about this stuff, the Crown'll take it. Make no mistake: They ain't our friends."

Adrian straightened. "We won't let 'em."

Amos coughed again, and this time Adrian saw blood on the old man's sleeve.

"Commander?"

"It's nothing. But it strikes me that you're the only candidate ever likely to take up my position here."

Adrian frowned, but before he spoke, Amos said, "You're serious about fighting the darkness? Then make the vow. Not an oath to me but a *vow* to the world. There's a difference. Take your time. Say the words slowly. Let 'em sink in— the world is listening."

"Alright." Adrian swallowed hard. "I am a knight of the Order of the Shadow Dragon." The words came slow and his heart rate spiked. "I will fight until my dying breath. I am its tool, its servant, its sword..."

As he spoke, the ignicite within the sword brightened. Surely just a trick of the light, or Adrian's imagination?

"You've made your vow, boy," Amos said when the words had been spoken. "You're a brother of the Order of the Shadow Dragon."

"I..." Strength radiated from Adrian's chest. "Thank you, Commander."

"You won't be thanking me when the training begins. Now, that blade belongs to the First Sword of our order." Amos snatched it back. "Which happens to be me."

Now

A tide of fire...
  The Shadow King...
  His sword...
  Caela...

Agony exploded through Adrian's body. Bright light pushed against his eyes, harsh and painful.

The stench of stale sweat and blood filled his nostrils. He shot up, fists raised. Shadows stretched before weak lantern light.

"Mornin', sunshine." Caela's voice sounded calm. She sat next to him, her eyes red and tired.

The world rocked and he fought the urge to vomit. His fingers caressed his chest, the spot where the Shadow King's blade had struck—but he found nothing. "Caela, what did you do?"

"Adrian—"

"What did you do?"

For a long moment, she didn't speak. Then, "Nothing."

"The Shadow King cut me down. I told you never to heal me."

Her eyes narrowed. "Open your shirt."

"What?"

"See for yourself."

Adrian opened his shirt and found no wound, no weeping red hole…

And no tattoos.

"What was it you said about the ink?" Caela asked.

Adrian's heart pumped with slow, sluggish beats. "That it protects against mystical attacks."

"And it disappears when you die." Caela stood. "I didn't heal you. You died, Adrian. Or close enough that your dark magic thought you had."

"How…" A thousand different questions choked in his throat.

"We escaped the pit, but the *Glimmer* took damage. The shadows killed Nyralto and the others."

"Varl? Suaro?"

"Alive."

"The fighting… You killed the Shadow King. How?"

"Same way I seal the portals—I absorbed his power and turned it against the demons." Caela's fingers fidgeted. "Near killed me. Then Varl got us out of the pit. We flew for miles but the *Glimmer* crashed near the Bermeja Forest."

"We're in Phadros." A peal of thunder exploded. The boat

rocked and Adrian almost tipped out of his bed. "And we're not in the air."

"No. You kept passing in and out of consciousness. You said, 'find Pedro' and 'take us to Bermeja Port.'"

Pedro. "We're aboard the *Solnadar*? He's taking us to Phadra?"

Through tight lips, Caela said, "He's dead."

"What?"

"This boat was moored but empty. I found Pedro in the captain's chair, all the life drained out of him."

Adrian's chest turned to stone. "The shadows got him. I made him stay. And if they're in Phadros already... We have to reach the capital. We have to stop the Mages' Guild."

"We flew over the tent city before we went down. Looked abandoned. Hopefully the San Sirans are all in Phadra, but..."

So much death. So much needless devastation.

Adrian tried to stand but fell back.

"Sol's Kiss is tonight," Caela said. "You need rest."

"How far are we?"

"Couple of hours, Varl reckons. And then we fight."

Nightsbane slashed the air and left a faint orange trail, but pain blazed through Adrian's chest with every movement. His muscles ached, hunger gnawed his stomach and sleep tugged at his eyes. It made him slow and unsure.

And weak.

When the aches grew too sharp, Adrian climbed onto the *Solnadar*'s deck. A thick fog clung to the Phadril Sea and dulled the sun. Soon, Sol's Kiss would blot it out completely.

Suaro leaned over the rail, vomiting. Caela stood by the mage's side. "Apologies, my lady," the mage started. "Seafaring disagrees with me more than air travel."

"My fist will disagree with your face if you call me *lady* again."

"Suaro," Adrian greeted.

"Sir Adrian. It's a relief to see that you're alright." The mage's eyes sparkled. "What was it like when the Shadow King struck you down? Did it hurt?"

"You have a strange sense of priority, Suaro."

Suaro's lips pulled back into a grin that showed off all his teeth. "A curious mind."

"We're going back to Phadra. The Mages' Guild will be looking for you."

The mage stared out to the water. "They won't find me."

Adrian peered over the rail, refusing to gaze into the black, glassy sea. "Suaro, how do we stop them summoning Niamat?"

"Easy! Simply prevent the moon from getting between the earth and sun."

"And if we had to come up with a Plan B?"

Suaro's face soured. "I don't want to say 'regicide', but..."

"We'd never get close enough before the eclipse. Can you get us inside the mages' guildhouse?"

Suaro shook his head. "I have no intention of going anywhere near the Mages' Guild."

"Then what exactly is the point of you?"

Suaro cocked his head and narrowed his beady eyes. "You think I can simply unlock a door and let you in? They're hunting me—and I'm afraid tales of mages wearing glamours to conceal ourselves are greatly exaggerated."

"You have inside knowledge."

"I risked my life to escape them; I'll not squander it by letting them get their claws into me. You have your priorities, I have mine."

Goddamn mages. "Then I'll speak with Lucien, convince him to evacuate the city."

"Can you trust him?" Caela asked.

Adrian's grip tightened on the rail. "I'll find out."

"Please do," said Suaro. "The Shadow King was bad but if

Harnan succeeds in bringing forth the Shadow Realm, then an army of untold evils will invade. Niamat herself may step into our world. What happened to San Sira will be a mere bruise upon the world."

"I'll stop her. I'll stop all of 'em."

"Not alone," Caela said.

"No." The muscles in his fingers grew too painful to keep a grip on the rail. "Not alone."

"Is there anything you can tell us?" Caela asked the mage. "Any weaknesses in the guild? Anyone who might be sympathetic?"

"Not much, I'm afraid. I studied botany and potions. If you're having trouble clearing your bowels, I can make you a tea of rhubarb and senna. I only joined the Mages' Guild to impress a girl I liked."

Caela arched an eyebrow. "Did it work?"

"Oh, she was *most* impressed when I let her try my tea. Poor girl didn't leave the bathroom for two days."

"What *can* you tell us?" Adrian asked.

Suaro let out a long breath. "You don't know what it was like, when we discovered dormant magic reawakening. There's so much I don't know, and if you're not in the inner circle of Niamat worshippers, well..." Suaro almost vomited again. "We don't have enough information to divine truth from myth."

"And Wielders aren't born with an instruction manual explaining how their magic system works," said Caela. "Truth is, Adrian, you might be the closest thing we have to an expert."

Adrian flexed his fingers. "So we're on our own."

"Excuse me." Suaro clutched his belly. "I believe I'll try and rest before my next bout of vomiting."

Caela watched him go and said, "He has a habit of doing that."

"I'm sorry."

"For what?"

"When I woke up, I was angry. I thought you'd used magic on me. I should've trusted you."

"You *died*. You're allowed to be grumpy."

"No excuse for being a dick."

"I forgive you."

The Phadril Sea spread out forever, dark and grey and indistinct.

"The Shadow King murdered my father." The words hung there, heavy as the fog. "For years, I wondered if it was my imagination. But the shadow demons are real. It's all real. There's so much I don't know, Caela. I don't know why the Shadow King targeted him. I don't know if he was a mage, or a cultist, or just summoned the Shadow King by accident. Guess it doesn't matter." Adrian stared out at the darkening sea. "The state sent me to an orphanage, then a boarding school. Didn't stick. I ended up on the streets, where I met Dante. He saved my life. But it's always *there*, Caela." Adrian tapped his chest. "The rage. The *hate*. I see the shadows everywhere I look, like they're following me. In the Bermeja, at Oro Lengua… Always darkness. I was obsessed… For years, I hunted for any information on the demons. Nothing else mattered. I abandoned the few friends I had. If I'm not training, I'm poring over the order's books. Texts from the Mages' Guild, each one contradicting the next, their authors pushing their own agendas… Gods, I *hated* magic. And I hated my father for dabbling in it. For dying. For abandoning me. And I hated myself, for being so weak. I figured if I got strong enough to fight monsters, maybe one day I'd see him again… So I could tell him how much I hated him."

"Adrian… Hate is toxic. The longer you hold on to it, the more it poisons you."

A scratching sensation caught in Adrian's throat and a weight pressed on his chest. "I… don't hate him. Not anymore. The only useful thing I learned from all those books, all those years of collected knowledge is… Magic isn't evil. And it isn't good, either. It's people. People are good. People are evil. You were right, Caela, and I was an idiot for thinking things were black and white. Guess it makes life easier when you view things through that prism. Light or dark, good or evil. But life takes place in the grey spot in between. If Suaro's right and the mages are behind all this, then it means we're not up against some mystical force— there's a person behind all of it. King Harnan's working with 'em, but it was Lucien who sent me to assassinate you. It was him who ordered the Amethyst Lynx to march south. Caela, I don't know who to trust. And I can't go up against them all on my own." Now Adrian looked into Caela's sapphire eyes. "Will you help me?"

Wind sang over the sea and through Caela's silver-blond hair. "Yes, Adrian. I'll help you."

DANTE

D ante lay on his bed, hands beneath his head, eyes closed. His cell reeked of piss, but at least it wasn't his.

So, this is how it ends—no applause, no encore. Just the final curtain.

His cellmate wailed like an infant.

Dante cleared his throat. "Begging your forgiveness, friend—but could you shut up? Some of us intend on dying quietly. Thanking you."

"Excuse me if I ain't ready for Nyr's ferryman to take me away just yet."

"By all means, pray, beg, plead—just do it quietly."

The other man marched back and forth, back and forth, muttering, "Must be some way out." He slapped the wall, punched it, raked his fingernails over the stone. "It was an accident. *An accident, you lot hear me?* Didn't mean to kill the old bastard. Not like that, anyway. There must be some way, *there must be!*"

Dante sat up and opened his eyes. Shadows smothered the corner of the bare, grey room. "If you don't shut up, you won't even make it to the gallows pole. Anyway, you've no idea what's coming—the noose might be a gift."

The man wore a sour expression on his weathered, grey face. His back hunched over and skin clung to his bones as if he hadn't eaten in weeks. "You know what they're gonna do to us, don't you? They call me a Wielder collaborator. They just passed a law to make that punishable by death. *Execution!* Never even met a Wielder!"

"Quite aware, yes." After all the running and fighting, after cheating death and losing friends, it was Cassandra's betrayal that preyed on his mind.

"And what?" Sourface asked. "You don't fear the Death God?"

"Nyr? Gods, no! In all of Phadros, there's only one woman who has ever struck fear into my heart." Footsteps slapped the floor and Dante's stomach squirmed. "And here she is now."

Sergeant Cassandra Diaz glided into the cell, face hard and eyes narrowed, a burly watchman at her side.

Dante swung onto the floor and put his hands behind his back. "And to what do I owe the pleasure? You wanted to give the knife one last twist, Sergeant Coldheart?"

"Something like that."

No flinching, no remorse—no sign of guilt whatsoever. *Gods, I'm a fool.* He wanted to ask her if it was all a lie, if anything she'd said aboard the *Nueva Luna* was true. But he swallowed the words; if he was about to die, he'd die with a bit of pride.

"Open the cell," Cass ordered.

The watchman stepped forward. "Backs against the wall. Now!"

The other man raised his fists, and Dante rolled his eyes. "You're optimistic."

"Wanna go down fightin'."

The big watchman smirked, strode forward and drew his baton. "Happy to oblige."

Sourface lunged at the guard, fist outstretched, and—

And the big watchman collapsed.

Dante yelped. "Belios' balls! *Are* you a Wielder?"

"No, I, I don't think so?"

Coldheart yanked Dante through the doorway and locked it behind her. "Drugged his ale."

"Cass? I—"

"Come on! Before he wakes up."

"Wait!" Sourface yelled. "Let me out! Please!"

Hauled away by Cass, Dante looked back and said, "Alas, friend, she only has eyes for me."

"What's going on?" Dante asked after they'd cleared the cells.

"*Sh!*" Cass peeked around a corner. "Stay quiet and do as I tell you. If we're discovered, we're both dead. Move."

Dante followed her, hands behind his back, playing the part of her prisoner, but no coppers filled the Watch house, no magisters, no inmates.

"Quiet in here. Guess hanging really is a spectator sport."

"It's not that." Cass shook her head. "Something strange is going on."

"You're bloody telling me." They slipped outside, and warm evening air kissed Dante's skin. "Cassandra, *what is happening?*"

She spun towards him. "For the first time in my life, I'm *choosing* who I want to be. If my last act is saving you… Then it's a good one."

Outside, music played and drums thundered. Lines of revellers wove from street to street, hefting banners high in celebration of Sol and Lunos.

Dante followed Cassandra through a tight alley. Wind kicked a can across the cobbles and steel-grey clouds crashed overhead.

"*Sh!*" Cassie knelt behind a crate of glass bottles. "Get down."

Dante knelt. Drums thudded in his chest. *Boom, boom, boom.*

A procession marched past—dozens, *hundreds* of San Sirans in chains, flanked by men and women of the Watch. Phadrosi, too. Dante watched as an old Phadrosi woman fought against a brutish watchman and got a fist to her jaw for her trouble.

"Gods above." Cassie's eyes widened. "We have to do something."

"They'll take you for a San Siran and clap you in chains. Where are Mara and Ramiro?"

"I don't know."

"What's the plan?"

"*I don't know!* I haven't thought my treason through yet."

"Look—they're taking them towards the palace. Why?"

"Oh, Gods." Cassie held her hand against her chest. "A sacrifice. Didn't Suaro say that the victims of the Cataclysm were being turned into the Shadow King's army? This city is teeming with people!"

"Right, right—Harnan was going to seize the Shadow King's power, but he's dead!"

Cassie met his eye. "So who's taken his place?"

Dante's whole body tensed. "We need to reach the Dragon's Lair."

"What? Why?"

Dante grabbed her hand and ran. "Because that was the plan!"

Thunder, drums and shouting crashed over the city. Dante darted from street to street, alley to alley, and came to Lower Phadra's Tanners' District. Upturned carts and decimated stalls choked the streets.

"Oi!" a watchman called at him. "Stop!"

"This way!" Dante hauled Cassie through hidden lanes, dangerous backstreets and over rooftops.

"I know the quickest routes!" Cassie cried. "I run through the city all the time!"

"And I run *from* the city all the time! Trust me!"

Every step of the way, soldiers, coppers and the Sons of Belios dragged protestors through the streets, slung them into horse-drawn wagons and took them away.

Coppers fought against each other in a clash of steel and blood. Bricks and glass and stone flew overhead; something struck Dante and he fell to one knee, but within a heartbeat, Cassie called, "Up!" and dragged him to his feet.

As they ran, the sky darkened and the shouts turned into screams.

ADRIAN

"**C**ome on!"

Adrian led Varl and Caela through the bustling harbourside, twisting and turning. Lightning flickered, wind lashed the world and lanterns cast greasy light through slanting rain.

Musical instruments, costumes and tattered banners littered the ground, the signs of an abandoned parade. Soldiers of the Ivory Dove galloped on horseback, clashing with troops from the Golden Griffin and Amethyst Lynx. Watchmen dragged San Sirans across cobbles, kicking them and bundling them into wagons. Adrian moved to intervene but Varl pulled him back. "Got your own battles, boy."

Adrian's stomach clenched. He had to reach the Dragon's Lair.

He pressed through the madness. Lightning flashed and thunder boomed, loud and hard.

"Damn the Gods." Suaro pointed to the royal palace. Darkness gathered above its peak as the sharp edge of the moon slashed the sun.

"Sol's Kiss." Adrian's heart pounded. "It's starting."

He cut through a knot of civilians. Crowds sprawled over

Phadra's wide avenues, too entranced by parades and dancers to notice the carnage creeping in from the side streets and back alleys. Singers praised Phadros and her bloody history, and purple banners celebrating the Sons of Belios flew high. Two wagons pulled a gigantic likeness of Lucas Salvarado carved in ice.

Adrian led his team down a back road, weaving between alleys to avoid the crowds. A fight between watchmen broke out and San Sirans fought off their tormentors and bounded towards the harbours. Adrian glimpsed Phadrosi men and women locking arms and form a ring around San Siran kids, but knights of the Golden Griffin rode them down.

Again, Adrian started forward, and again, Varl pulled him back. "Focus!"

Adrian roared a response—but then his hairs stood on end.

Even beneath the wind and the rain, the laughter pierced his ears, shrill and terrible.

"They're coming," said Caela.

Adrian clenched his fists. "We fight our way to the Dragon's Lair. Suaro, you'd better…"

But the mage had gone, lost in the crowds.

"Treacherous little bastard."

The laughter grew louder and louder, and the sky turned darker and darker.

"On me!" Adrian commanded. "C'mon, run, *run!*"

Pain stabbed his heart and lungs. Adrian stopped and doubled over, retching. Without the tattoos, everything felt more *real*.

"Keep moving!" yelled Varl.

Monsters crawled out of shadows; Adrian unsheathed Nightsbane and cut them down. "This way!"

He cut across the Bridge of Bone. Wagons and food stalls sprawled across the road. Shadows feasted on civilians and soldiers alike.

With every step, the demons crawled out at him, striking with precision. Steel sang on steel. Adrian sliced and slashed, the shadows stretching in pain as they faded into embers.

"There!" He pointed to the Lair's entrance. "Inside, quick!"

With shaking fingers, he fumbled for his key, turned it once, twice—

There.

The door opened and he fell inside.

Varl wiped sweat from his brow and leaned on his knees. "What are we looking for?"

Adrian didn't have time to explain. He strode towards the swivelling bookcase and hauled it open. The grey-black safe greeted him. Without shadow ink to bypass the warding, the symbols on the dial refused to change into digits—but memorising their corresponding numbers was the first thing Adrian had done after reciting the order's vow.

The safe opened and he stepped inside. Musty air hit him, that stale aroma of expired incense and old books.

"Varl, keep watch." Caela followed Adrian inside. "We need to talk."

"Now?" Adrian tumbled into the side room. There, on a shelf, the shadow ink swirled and roiled inside its circular glass bottle like a storm cloud.

"Yeah—about *that*."

"The ink's my best weapon."

"The Shadow King is dead, Adrian. You don't need to curse yourself or—"

"Don't be so dramatic." He snatched the bottle. "It makes me stronger."

"Makes you an asshole."

"Yeah, well, sometimes having friends is selfish."

"While you're alive, you're young. Isn't that what you Phadrosi say? You use that stuff, you're selling your soul. You got a second chance, Adrian. How old are you, twenty?"

The swirling darkness enchanted him. "Nineteen."

"You're still young. Adrian, listen to me; you spend your days obsessed with revenge. You don't eat. You don't sleep. You don't feel pain. You don't *live*. Do you want your fear of the dark to be your whole identity forever?"

"I deny myself to become stronger, to *survive*."

"It's not enough just to survive," Caela said. "It's not enough to exist—you need to *live*. After everything, you've still not got it—the past doesn't need to define us, we can choose who we want to be. Dante convinced me to think about the future—reckon you should, too."

Adrian stared at his knuckles and his calloused hands. He didn't *feel* young. He couldn't remember much of his childhood before his father's murder, and the details he could recall were fragmented, like a reflection in a cracked mirror. The memories might as well belong to someone else. "For years I didn't know if the King of Shadows was real or just my imagination. You don't know what it's like, Caela. I'm not sure what's worse—knowing I'm not crazy means he's real. It means it all happened. And if the Shadow King is real, what else is? Who'll protect us from the darkness?"

"Keeping people at arm's length doesn't make you strong." Caela stepped closer to him; her perfume smelled of candy apples and vanilla. "And being close to someone doesn't make you weak."

He kept staring at the bottle. "But what if you… What if they get hurt? Because of me?"

She stepped closer still, her scent almost as intoxicating as the shadow ink. "That's what being with someone *is*, Adrian. It's trust. It's fear. It's love and it's anger and it's sweetness and pain. It's all of that. And it's beautiful. Numbing yourself to everything because you might not like a small part of it ain't living. You may as well be dead."

His heart raced. "Caela, I—"

A roar tore out of the Dragon's Lair.

"Varl!" Caela raced out of the armoury. Adrian tucked the shadow ink into his cloak pocket and followed.

But then Caela froze.

She tensed, her arms pinned to her side, skin drawn and veins popping.

Adrian reached out to her—

But his limbs refused to obey.

Screeching filled his head. He wanted to scream, to fight, to *move*, but he couldn't—invisible iron rings clenched around him, pinned his limbs together, squeezed his lungs.

He fought to take another step, to pass through the armoury towards Caela.

She screamed as she twisted and shot toward the ceiling, her voice scratchy and raw.

No.

She remained there, pinned to the ceiling—just like Adrian's father.

Metallic black coils wrapped around her and sank into her pale skin—Caela fought to summon light through her veins.

"I think not."

Caela's light faded.

That voice...

Lucien.

Caela thrashed and twisted. She saw Adrian and her eyes widened. "V... *Varl!*"

Wind howled and thick, stony vines punched through the floor, concealing the armoury's entrance and sealing Adrian inside. Dust and stone rained over him.

N... No!

Then the tremors ceased and the world turned silent.

No wind, no screaming, no noise.

Adrian fell to the floor, muscles frozen, lungs aching for breath.

He fought to move, but all he could do was stare at the darkness.

Hours passed, or maybe minutes.

The shadows came for him, formless, like a dark mist. They tugged and pulled, rent skin and sucked his blood. His father looked down at him, shaking his head before turning his back and leaving Adrian behind.

Again.

Cold and numb, Adrian didn't feel their steel fingers gouge his skin. Better that way. Better to die in silence. No pain, no noise...

He screamed and the world sharpened. Fire filled his lungs and throat.

No shadow demons—just the dark.

But he could move.

Steadying himself against the wall, Adrian stumbled past withered roots and staggered into the Dragon's Lair. "C... Caela?"

On the floor, Varl's body lay mangled and twisted, eyes frozen open in horror.

Adrian bent low and closed them.

"Adrian?" Dante came tumbling into the Dragon's Lair with Diaz at his back. "*Adrian?*"

"Dante! You're alive."

Dante hugged him. "Mate, what happened?"

"Lucien." Adrian pulled away. "Varl used his magic to conceal me in the armoury—and Lucien killed him. His last act was to protect me."

"Adrian?" Diaz said. "Where's Caela? Suaro?"

Adrian spoke—the words came out slow and steady, like sliding a dagger into the flesh of a downed enemy.

"Gods above." Cass looked like she'd weep at any moment. "Lucien's a Wielder. I'm so sorry, Adrian. I, I didn't know. I sold you out. I told Lucien everything for… I'm so sorry."

"Reckon he's one of Suaro's dark mages," Adrian said. "But none of that matters—he has Caela."

"We'll find her." Dante's brown eyes narrowed in defiance. "We have Mara and Ramiro."

At that, the door crashed open and the two knights barrelled inside, accompanied by a chorus of chaos.

"You find him?" Mara asked.

"You should get out of here," Adrian said. "All of you."

"Like hell," said Ramiro. "We've just fought our way through half the city to get here!"

"Why?" snapped Adrian.

"Because that was our plan," Dante answered. "We said we'd meet back in the Dragon's Lair. Here we are."

"The shadow demons are back," Diaz said. "And you wield the only weapon known to hurt them."

Outside, voices screamed louder and louder.

"You hear that?" Mara demanded. "We need to be out there."

Adrian's head spun. All at once, he wanted to fight, wanted to scream and to weep. "Need a plan first. Lucien took Caela—he killed Varl but he took her—he must want her power. I'm goin' after him. I'm gonna end it. You should leave, all of you."

"Piss on that," said Mara. "You got any idea what we went through to get here?"

"Didn't ask you to."

"To hell with that."

"The palace," Ramiro said. "The darkness is focused there. Adrian, we're in this together."

"Valador Ramos is Arch Vigil," said Diaz. "The Sons of Belios have control—they won't let anyone leave the city. They're bringing every San Siran to the palace."

"Lucien's endgame." Adrian eased a crick in his neck.

"Suaro's gone but if he's right, then Lucien needs a tremendous amount of power to summon Niamat—he needs mass casualties."

"We'll end up like San Sira," Ramiro said. "All of us just… lying there, dead and withered."

Diaz shook her head. "Or bent into shadow demons."

"A hole in the world," Adrian said. "A tear in the fabric of reality, stretching from San Sira to Phadra. Lucien planned it all. 'A whisper in an ear is more effective than barking at a crowd.' He said that to me. He used my prejudice against me, took advantage of my hate and fed me a story of the Mages' Guild manipulating the king and a white witch causing chaos. I kill Caela, Cassie arrests me. Lucien jails me or kills me. Either way, there's no Order of the Shadow Dragon to stand in his way. Loop closed."

"But if he has Caela now, why send you to kill her in the first place?" Cass asked.

Adrian rolled his shoulders. "I'll be sure to ask him."

"Alright, let's tool up," said Mara.

"Wait!" Ramiro held a hand up. "What about the Shadow King? He's still out there."

Adrian shook his head. "Caela took him out, but who knows what else Lucien has under his command?"

"*So let's tool up*," Mara urged.

"She's right," Dante said. "I'm all for fighting, but I'd rather be armed with something other than quick wit and harsh language."

Adrian looked from Dante to Diaz, from Ramiro to Mara. "Wait here."

He hauled weapons from the hidden armoury and set them onto an old, scarred table. "Aside from Nightsbane, this is all that's left of the Order of the Shadow Dragon's arsenal."

"Just like Wintercast morning," Mara said. "Mother Snowfrost's real, and she's a little guy with a magic sword."

Dante pointed to a vial of glowing amber liquid labelled

Dragonfire. "It's true! I heard knights drink Dragon's fire to stifle your emotions. This explains a lot, Adrian."

Adrian glared at him. "That's Amos' homemade rum—if anything, it makes you *more* emotional. And makes your piss glow orange. Figured you'd want it."

"I do." The liquid disappeared up Dante's sleeve.

Diaz looked at daggers, knuckle dusters and sparkpowder. "Is any of this imbued with ignicite?"

Adrian shook his head. "Only Nightsbane."

"Great," said Mara. "Then thanks for the cutlery collection."

Adrian unravelled a bundle of rags and revealed Amos' tri-barrelled rifle and three vials of glowing liquid igneus. "This is the only working firearm I have—it uses standard repeater ammunition but it coats them in igneus and sets them on fire when the trigger is pulled. It's dangerous and—"

"Mine." Mara snatched it from the table.

"Fair enough. If Nightsbane works against the demons, reckon that will, too. If not, a bullet's still a bullet—and the Sons of Belios have declared war."

"What will the rest of us use?" Ramiro pleaded.

Adrian shook his head. "Nothing—this isn't an assault, it's an escape. Find as many civvies as you can and leave the city."

"The *Nueva Luna* is locked down at my Watch house," said Diaz. "Every copper's on the streets, it's just sitting there."

"Good. Take it and leave."

"Like hell," said Mara. "Should be hunting those things."

"There are too many demons," Adrian countered. "Fight only when you have to. And when you run out of bullets, fly."

"Where to?"

"Anywhere—as far as the *Luna* can take you. If I go up against Lucien and fail, the rest of the world has to know what happened. Dante, that's your story to tell."

Dante's chest swelled at that.

"You can't go up against Lord Lucien alone," said Diaz. "What about the civilians? Lucien won't stop with the San Sirans."

"The only way to save 'em is to stop him. The *Luna* can carry, what? Two dozen people? A drop in the ocean. That won't stop Lucien."

Mara took her own bullets and fed them into the tri-barrel. "But *you* need a plan, Navarro—the Wielders kicked your ass last time you charged in without a clue."

"I have a plan." Adrian withdrew the shadow ink from his cloak and turned it in his fingers.

"Chuck a bottle of ink at him." Dante stuck his bottom lip out. "You'll have the element of surprise, at least."

"It's for me—my shadow ink is gone."

Dante frowned. "I thought—"

"The Shadow King killed me—or close enough to remove the ink's protection."

"Um, are you sure you want that burden again?"

The roiling, stormy liquid folded in on itself, undulating, pulsing—alive. "I can't go up against Lucien without it."

"If it makes you stronger, we should *all* use it," said Mara.

Adrian shook his head. "It costs a piece of you. No knight of the Shadow Dragon has ever lost their shadow ink and come back. I don't even know if it'll work."

"All the more reason to let someone else use it," said Ramiro. "Mara could kick Belios' arse without it, give it to her and Lucien won't stand a chance."

"I've done the training. I've got the knowledge." He needed the ink to defeat Lucien... Didn't he?

"Do you even have time to disinfect a needle?" Dante motioned to the door. "It's chaos out there."

Who said anything about a needle?

"Regardless, the plan's still half-cocked," Ramiro said. "Use it or don't, we still need to think."

"No time, no choice. Lucien's growing stronger and Suaro turned tail and fled the first chance he got."

"Who could have foreseen *that* betrayal?" Dante asked, raising a hand.

"The plan is simple," said Adrian. "You take the *Luna* and get out. I kill Lord Lucien. Listen, we're talking high treason —the Order of the Shadow Dragon was founded by men and women who were willing to break the rules for the greater good. Loyal to no-one but ourselves, not shackled by the will of kings and queens who would use our power for their own ends. Our differences highlight who we are—and highlight what we have in common. Like an alloy, the different properties are what make us stronger. Wielder, warrior, San Siran, Aludanian—doesn't matter. This fight affects all of us. Lucien is just another enemy. Any of you have doubts, walk away now."

Dante put his hands on his hips. "I'm used to playing rogues and miscreants—seems like your order's a good fit."

Ramiro stood straight, almost as tall as Mara. "To hell with fighting so someone else can make coin—I want to fight for what's *right*."

Mara drew a slow, deep breath. "My whole life, all I've wanted is something worth fighting for. I'm in."

Adrian's lungs filled. "I'd... be proud to have you at my side. All of you."

Mara nodded towards Diaz. "And the copper? She betrayed us."

Outside, the wind carried the chorus of screaming voices. Diaz stood there, face drawn in guilt.

"Misfits, oddballs and rejects," Adrian started. "The kind of people the Order of the Shadow Dragon attracts. Sergeant Diaz—*Cassie*—gets a second chance, same as us."

Mara shook her head. "Figured you'd say something dumb."

"It's easy to hate." Adrian thought of his father. "Forgiveness takes strength."

Mara slung the tri-barrel over her shoulder. "Let's go."

"Not so fast." From his pocket, Adrian withdrew a piece of parchment. "There's something you need to say."

THE ORDER OF THE SHADOW DRAGON

L ike the curved, black blade of a scimitar, the moon edged into the sun.

Black clouds rolled over Phadra and swept the stars away. Riderless horses galloped through the streets, accompanied by thunder, and shrill, terrified screams filled Sir Adrian Navarro's ears.

The stepped pyramid loomed over Phadra, ignium lamps illuminating it like a polished jewel set into a rusted crown.

"You sure about this?" Dante had to shout to be heard.

"I am! Get out of the city! Go, now!"

"Adrian…" Even in the darkness, Dante's teeth gleamed. "See you on the other side!"

Adrian darted forward, past the lopsided tenements of Lower Phadra. Shadows dripped from the sky like droplets of ink. Demons bounded over cobbles, scurried across walls, their elongated fingers clawing into people and leeching the life from them.

Nightsbane danced in Adrian's hand. Demons sparked and twisted and faded like ash floating on the wind.

"Run!" Adrian yelled to a mother and daughter. "Find somewhere safe and hide!"

Demons giggled and lashed out with hands as sharp as razors. Adrian dodged and spun, his sword clashing and painting dizzying amber arcs.

Bit by bit, he inched closer to the palace, keeping it in his sights—and from its peak, he sensed darkness peering back at him, inviting him in.

Adrian pressed forward.

Dante flinched.

The demons burst into flames, accompanied by a chorus of screams.

Mara reloaded. "Oh, I like this."

The sour smell of spent igneus filled his nose. He ran through alleys and narrow lanes, wending towards the skyport.

"You sure we're going the right way?" Ramiro asked.

"Best to stay off the main streets, quicker to—"

Glass smashed above him and a man tumbled out of a high window and hit the ground. The demon on him sank its scythed hands into his chest. The man aged and withered before Dante's eyes.

"Down!" Mara pulled the trigger. A *hiss* and a bang and the igneus-coated bullet burned the demon to ashes.

Frozen, Dante stared at the blood running over the cobbles.

Mara grabbed him. "Nothing you could do, but if you stay here, you'll be next. *Move!*"

The harbours blurred past. Fire clung to sails and tore through vessels. Coppers ran back and forth, but they had no water, no—

"Gods, they're not saving the ships, they're *burning* them."

Cassie pulled him. "Have to keep going!"

More screams, more rioting.

Cassie looked away, and then back to Dante. "Listen, I—"

"Save your apologies—when it's all over, we can see where we stand with one another."

"And if we die?"

Dante straightened. "Then it will have been the performance of a lifetime."

A horde of people filtered through Phadra's alleys and streets, fighting to escape—but the Watch stood in their way, fighting back.

Cassandra rushed at them, barking orders. The coppers didn't listen—instead, they drew swords. Ramiro engaged first, his sword a silver blur. The watchmen fell in heaps.

"No time to fight these assholes!" Mara decked a Son of Belios with one punch. "Move!"

Watchmen filled the main roads, so Dante bolted through Harbourside and Ratcatcher Alley, past Maggie's Den and Fivepenny—all the safe havens that he'd hidden in, all the broken buildings and the slimy cobbles that he'd led watchmen past in merry chases with Adrian, all the glowering tenements which were as much part of his soul as they were Phadra's landscape.

An explosion rang out behind him. Dust and dirt and broken wood rained onto Dante's back. He stumbled but kept his momentum. He crashed through an iron gate, through empty crates and barrels, watchmen on his heels.

Fire filled his chest and lungs but still he kept going.

"Cass?" he panted. "Mara?"

But they were gone.

"Keep going... Keep going..."

The *Nueva Luna* called out to him.

Dante ran towards a warehouse and hauled a door open. The song of coppers' boots on cobbles resounded behind him.

"Keep going, keep go—"

Pain coiled around his leg and he hit the ground, blood bubbling from his lip.

He flew over the ground, over jagged stone and broken glass.

Dante thrashed and wriggled onto his back—and when he looked up, a demon of shadow and steel looked back at him.

∽

An explosion blew a wall away.

Cassie's sword blurred and whirled, deflecting a watchman's blade. He forced her onto her back foot but she feinted left then right and scored his sword arm.

He spat and swore, but her fist silenced him.

Where she slugged it out, Mara and Ramiro fought with savage efficiency. Watchmen and Sons lay on the ground, bleeding, unconscious—or dead.

"Where's Dante?"

Mara wiped blood from her lip. "Ran ahead!"

"Here!" Ramiro waved at Cass. "Past the debris!"

Cass followed, the discordant strains of screams and laughter ringing in her ears.

Ragged flags belonging to the Phadra City Watch writhed in the wind, like snakes in the throes of death.

To think she used to love it. The flag. The badge. The symbol of the City Watch looking over Phadra's sons and daughters.

Now she knew it to be a symbol of oppression and corruption.

Bullies.

Thunder exploded and lightning lashed the sky. Men and women ran in different directions, clashing, trampling one another.

Another scream.

She ran towards it, skidded around an alley and into a warehouse. A hulking mass of glassy darkness glowered over a shrieking man—Dante.

Roaring, Cassie thrust, but her blade did nothing.

The beast giggled and glared and scythed at Cassie's sword, shearing it in half.

She stumbled back but the thing had her in its sights. It slithered towards her, this thing of smoke, coming to take her away, to steal the life from her and drag her into the pit she once called home.

It swung a bladed fist—Cassie ducked beneath a shower of sparks as it tore through brick. It stomped towards her, swinging its razor-edged hands in a frenzy.

"Down!" Mara roared. A *hiss* and snap and a bullet punched through the demon, burying into brick and turning the monster to cinders.

Cassie dragged Dante to his feet. "You okay?"

"As long as you believe me when I say that the puddle on the ground was there before it attacked me, then yes."

"Good. Move!"

Darkness closed in on Phadra. Rampaging demons spilled through the streets, cutting, thrusting, slaughtering. Ramiro deflected their bladed hands and Mara's rifle cut them down. *Boom-boom-boom.*

Cassie buried her broken blade into any copper or Son of Belios that came at her. Blood and gore splattered her skin and clothes.

Dante spat blood. "Anyone ever tell you that you're cold as ice?"

"Yes." Cassie booted a door down. "And I consider it a compliment."

Nightsbane blurred and whirled, deflecting scythe and claw

—but more demons spilled out of the sky, red eyes glowing, jaws extending big enough to swallow someone whole.

They flitted through people like smoke, steel claws and teeth rending flesh, sucking the life from their victims and leaving withered husks behind.

And the noise.

They howled in anguish at Nightsbane's touch, terror tearing from their elongated mouths. Adrian ran, fighting them off, saving who he could—but they were everywhere.

The shadow-men grew stronger, more tangible. Adrian engaged a towering demon, its bladed hands whirling. Sparks burst from his sword as he deflected. It struck him in the chest and he hit the ground, head smacking against cobbles.

He rolled as its scythed hands sheared through stone, then leapt back and dodged, but the demon didn't stop.

Adrian scrambled away, leapt onto crates, scaled a wall and climbed onto a bridge—but the thing warped and materialised in front of him, slicing, scything. Its blades cleaved scars into brick, and the laughter, that terrible, manic laughter...

It drove Adrian against the wall of a chapel dedicated to Musa. Adrian reached to the sky—the thing leapt at him, claws held high, and—

And the grapple snaked up and bit into a stone gargoyle. Adrian zipped away as the demon crashed into the wall.

Midway through the ascent, Adrian stopped, dropped behind the demon, and thrust Nightsbane through its back. Its agonised howl sounded as sweet as the note from a harp.

The demon bubbled and twisted and disappeared. Relief filled Adrian's lungs—but it didn't last.

A deafening boom rang over Phadra. The moon passed between the earth and sun and crowned the world with a dark halo.

The world trembled before Sol's Kiss—and the sky tore open.

⁓

The *Nueva Luna* barrelled through the air, past the crooked tenements of Lower Phadra and over the harbours.

Frenzied first-gen airships crowded the sky—two collided and sank to the earth in a tangle of rope and wood. On the streets, people scurried, civilians and the Watch alike.

Cassie's muscles ached. She pulled levers and shoved the steering column. On the deck, Mara's bullets rang, *boom-boom-boom*. It killed Cassie to flee, but what could she do?

Ramiro's hands knitted together. "We should be helping Adrian, not—*watch out!*"

Cassie pulled on the column and the *Luna* scraped against a wall. Shadows bled onto the vessel's window, grinning, giggling. The glass cracked and a bolt of fear ran through her spine.

"Pull up!" Ramiro yelled.

Gritting her teeth, the *Luna* shot high and swept the shadows away. The craft spun over Upper Phadra, facing south, where the pyramid palace glinted like an orange topaz. Every captured San Siran stood in the palace's shadow.

Cassie wanted to throw up. "He's going to sacrifice them all."

"Let's see that he doesn't." Dante put his hands on his hips. "Take us down, we'll save as many as we can get aboard."

Ramiro opened his mouth to protest, but a peal of thunder stole his words.

"That was close," said Dante. "*Very* close."

From the south, black clouds rolled out of the sky.

Ramiro gasped. "Belios' balls. That's…"

Cass saw it, too. "The *Judgement*." The warship resolved from boiling clouds, angry, fearsome—and it had the *Luna* in its sights.

The warship's cannons roared.

"*Shit!*" Cassie yanked the column and the vessel spun. Ordnance blitzed the streets.

"Whose side is Vega on?" Dante asked.

In answer, the warship unleashed another barrage. Shot and shell blasted past the *Luna*.

Cassie engaged the igneus-fuelled thrusters. "We'll never outrun him! We're running out of fuel!"

She wove between first-generation airships. One crashed against the *Luna*'s hull, sending both vessels careening in different directions. Alarms blared.

"Vega's getting closer," said Ramiro.

"That's not what I'm worried about—*look!*"

Outside, the moon stabbed in front the sun, birthing a circle of fire high in the sky. Thunder exploded as if the world itself screamed.

A void crackled and formed in the air, wreathed in silvery white light. A dark shadow wrapped in a leathery membrane descended from it, accompanied by a crescendo of crimson lightning.

It reshaped, reformed before Cassie's eyes, dark and terrible.

A dragon.

Bleeding from the black clouds, the dragon twisted, barrelling towards earth. Its spine straightened and its leathern wings unfurled.

Its roar silenced the world and its wings battered the sky. Its black scales shimmered with a silver sheen—a monster as black as a starless night, made of smoke and shadow. A real, tangible *shadow dragon*.

Adrian watched it flit behind steeples and tower tops. Voices cried but the words were a jumbled, meaningless rabble.

Then the dragon soared into the sky, hung in mid-air for half a second…

And opened its monstrous jaws.

A stream of fire swept through Phadra's streets. In an instant, flames engulfed the city's museums and galleries, its ancient churches and customs houses, its slums, its offices and its industrial yards.

Adrian froze.

Intense heat scorched the air. Tenements blazed and smoke filled the sky. The envelopes of first-gen airships caught fire and danced towards the ground in a dizzying, fiery spiral.

No… No…

Riderless horses rampaged and people choked the streets. The dragon's silhouette flitted behind Esperanza's belltower and tongues of fire lurched into the sky.

Caela…

Caela can seal the void. Caela can absorb dark magic and turn it into light…

Find Caela…

Adrian ran towards the palace, Nightsbane gripped tight. Demons fell from the sky. Wreathed in darkness, amidst the dust, one stood alone, huge, hulking…

No.

Adrian sheathed his sword.

A war horse stood before him, black and muscular and standing still amidst the chaos. Its saddle bore the sigil of the Order of the Amethyst Lynx.

Adrian leapt onto it, pulled the reins, and galloped towards the palace—towards Lord Lucien.

The *Luna* swept over a phalanx of watchmen and sent them scurrying.

Another volley of cannon fire smashed the ground. The *Judgement* closed in, and Dante pictured a cat toying with a mouse.

The San Sirans at the foot of the palace scurried free, but too many of them lay on the ground, unmoving. The shadow demons stole their life force and ferried it to the top of the palace, orbs of light zipping back and forth.

A building collapsed and dust and rubble filled the air. Dante ran onto the deck, where wind and searing heat threatened to flay his skin. "Mara! Get inside!"

Fastened to the taffrail, Mara kept shooting at the shadow men clawing their way aboard the *Luna*. Afire, they shrieked and twisted.

"Gotta get outta here!" she roared.

"Not without you!" Dante sensed the *Judgement* nearby. "We have to go!"

The *Nueva Luna* circled above a tide of fire. Smoke blanketed the city.

"Need to take out that dragon." Mara reloaded.

"Are you mad?" Dante coughed into his arm. "It'll burn us out of the sky before we get near!"

Out of nowhere, the dragon swooped past. The sight of it froze Dante's blood.

Fire climbed the Tower of Esperanza. Its bell tolled like an agonised moan and the tower toppled, throwing a wall of dust and dirt and rubble into the air. The *Luna* swerved to avoid it. Its bell bounced through the streets, tolling with every touch.

"Oh, Gods…"

"*Inside!*" Mara roared.

But Dante stood frozen to the spot, gripping the taffrail,

fire and blood and smoke and death filling his eyes. Jets of fire lashed the sky and buildings fell before the dragon's wrath.

The *Luna* circled and soared—straight towards the dragon.

"Cassie?" Dante whispered. Then he shouted, "Cassie, what are you doing?"

The *Luna* shot closer to the dragon. Mara took aim. *Boom-boom-boom.*

If she hit the beast, it didn't react.

"Closer!" Mara reloaded.

"It's useless!" Dante cried. "We need to leave!"

"One more try… Just one more…" Mara reloaded—but the shadow dragon surged towards the *Luna*.

The deck juddered.

The dragon's jaws widened. Mara steadied herself, took aim, and—

A cannonade cracked the sky and struck the dragon. It howled and retreated, roaring in fury.

The *Judgement* unleashed another volley. Its cannons roared, and blazing, smoking ordnance struck the dragon. The beast disappeared behind a wall of smoke, hissing and growling.

The *Luna* descended and Dante laughed. "She did it! Cassandra led the *Judgement* to the dragon!"

Mara cheered. She grabbed Dante and hugged him so tight that she threatened to break a rib.

Ramiro tumbled out of the bridge and stared up at the monstrous warship. "He did it, Mara—Commander Vega saved us!"

Like a serrated blade sawing Dante's eardrums, the dragon screeched out of the sky, high above the warship. The *Judgement* attacked it with cannon and ballista. Bolts pierced its wings and cannonballs struck its scaled, silver belly.

But it bore the warship's fury. Its wings shot open and it hung there, above the *Judgement*.

Oh, Gods...

It opened its mouth and a jet of fire scorched the *Judgement*'s hull.

It returned fire but the dragon swooped past, over and under, flames scouring the warship at every turn. The *Judgement* descended and turned, but too slow and lumbering.

Horrified, Dante watched as men tumbled from its deck, their backs on fire, spinning in the air and disappearing into the smoke and fire below.

Blackened steel shrieked and spun away. The inferno raged and the *Judgement* plummeted to the ground, its guns silent.

Then the dragon turned its sights on Phadra.

ADRIAN

I am a knight of the Order of the Shadow Dragon...
     The horse thundered over the Bridge of Bone. Fires danced upon the Rio de Sangre like a thousand candles. Sweat rolled off Adrian's skin and smoke caught in his mouth, but still he rode.

A building collapsed and the bridge buckled and swivelled. The horse reared and snorted but Adrian spurred it on.

Stone and smoke choked the city. Within the blanket of dust, fire leapt onto silhouettes and made them dance.

Adrian pushed on.

I am its tool, its servant, its sword...

Stone plummeting at his back, he rode harder and harder, cleared the bridge and ploughed through two Sons of Belios. Ahead, the palace emerged, untouched by the carnage. Shadow demons flitted overhead, carrying the life force of their victims to the palace's apex, like tittering magpies with shiny trinkets.

Adrian charged through half a dozen watchmen and galloped through the palace gates.

...my deeds are measured in a flash of the blade...

He swung Nightsbane, cutting down demons left and

right. From the heavens, the dragon screeched and roared. The *Judgement* crashed, crushing the mansions of Upper Phadra and the slums of the lower city alike.

...I bow to neither king nor lord.

Screams filled Adrian's head, like the choir of the damned from the Book of Nyr.

I am a knight of the Shadow Dragon.

The horse thundered up the palace steps.

I will fight until my dying breath. I know no glory and shall rest in a nameless tomb, in deference to death.

So much pain. So much death and suffering.

He had to end it.

I am a knight of the Shadow Dragon.

I know only the eternal fight.

To defy the kingdom of the worm, that place which knows no light.

He had to finish it. Here, now.

For his father.

For his friends.

For Caela.

Silence filled the palace hallways, punctuated by the occasional scream or roar from the shadow dragon. Adrian's heart thudded against his ribs.

Darkness reached out and touched him, but still Adrian marched, fingers wrapped around Nightsbane's hilt.

The portraits of Phadra's old kings and queens glowered down at him. Cruel King Carlos, Cortes the Butcher King, Esperanza the Angel Queen. Some were good and some bad, but all had profited from the Age of Exploration. *The Age of Conquest.*

Adrian climbed a winding staircase, the darkness whispering to him. He didn't know what would happen after this night—all he knew was that Lucien would die, or he would.

And Caela.
She's there.
Caela is the light.
All I need to do is find her.

His feet slapped the stone steps. Windows offered glimpses of the carnage reigning throughout Phadra.

He'd last been here just days ago, but so much had changed since then. He thought of the boy Nerris and the drunken lout behind that tavern. What had happened to the kid? Adrian had been too focused on beating the thug to offer any real help to the boy—had been having too much *fun* fighting.

Quiet and grey, the throne room sat empty, its stillness broken only by motes of dust flitting through a thin shaft of light. Servant quarters, dining rooms, kitchens, all silent as a tomb.

Heart rising, Adrian climbed and climbed, until he reached the peak of the palace, where an ornate claret-red door loomed high and strong. Beyond, Adrian would find the palace roof, where dead kings and queens would rest for their bloodletting ritual.

Two guards awaited Adrian, wearing the plain, dark purple shirt and trousers of the Sons of Belios. Their boots were polished black and their violet eyes glinted with malice. They were armed with Watch-issue swords and batons; when Adrian strode towards them with his sword raised, their faces lit up.

Adrian's heart hammered. The military trained its soldiers not to see its enemies as human, but Amos had a different view: "Killing a living, breathing person is different from killing a monster, boy—it costs a piece of you."

Adrian had been surrounded by death over the last few days, but he'd never killed a human. He didn't relish the prospect.

Caela is through there.

The two Sons circled Adrian and mocked him for his size, and for his two mismatched eyes—but when he'd finished with them, the only words leaving their lips were their final ones.

The red door creaked open.

Light throbbed against Adrian's eyes. When they adjusted, he saw her—Caela, lying on a sacrificial slab, as still and silent as a porcelain doll. Candles surrounded her, wavering in the wind, bathing her in golden light.

Pillars surrounded the perimeter of the open roof. Cold wind howled through them.

Lucien loomed over Caela, gazing up at the widening black wound in the sky. His dark robes fluttered in the wind, a shadow made flesh.

Demons flitted towards the portal, feeding it and giving it power.

"Beautiful, isn't it?" Golden threads connected Lucien's left hand to Caela, while dark tendrils spun from his right hand and into the void. Red gashes wept on Lucien's skin before closing over and healing.

Adrian's grip tightened. "What have you done to her?"

"I am glad that you survived, Sir Adrian—truly."

Adrian roared and darted forward, sword raised, but Lucien conjured a blade of shadows and blocked Adrian's strike. He sent Adrian flailing backwards.

The golden threads and dark tendrils dissipated as Lucien adopted a fighting stance.

The two men circled one another. Wind lashed Adrian's skin and the cries of the city filled his ears. The dragon roared.

Adrian lunged again but Lucien parried and deflected, and Adrian worked to dodge the lord's backswing.

Adrian reset his grip. "If I was to ask you why, would you tell me?"

The swords chimed, a blade of light and a blade of darkness.

"Would you believe me?"

Adrian drove forward, prodding, slashing.

A gust of wind guttered the candles surrounding Caela. For a split second, Adrian's eyes fell on her—Lucien struck and blood seeped from Adrian's shoulder.

Adrian grimaced and retreated.

"The darkness is my domain, Navarro."

Adrian slashed but struck nothing.

"You'll die in agony, Adrian. She won't, but you will."

Lucien cut and thrust, the dark blade leaving a trail of shadows in its wake. Adrian deflected but a punch to the jaw sent him reeling.

"You'll die in the dark, boy."

Lucien punched the air—and an invisible grip seized Adrian. Lucien lifted him and slammed him from pillar to pillar, into the air and onto the ground. Blood filled his mouth. Lucien thrust him over the edge of the roof, the wind gripping him—the moment he released, Adrian fell—and unleashed his grapple, swung around a pillar and landed back on the roof.

A smile slashed over Lucien's lips. "Very good."

On one knee, Adrian spat blood. "You're the Shadow King."

"I am an instrument of the Goddess of Darkness—a pity you won't see her reign. She'll restore Phadros." Lucien's thin blade swiped and slashed, clashing with Nightsbane and sending the ignicite blade clattering to the floor. "Magic is a weapon we should never have neglected. How do you think we conquered half the world?"

Lucien moved with unnatural speed, putting Adrian on his back foot, driving him back, cutting, slicing. Adrian rolled, retreated, acid in his mouth, fingers searching for something he could use, *anything*—

White light filled the air.

Lucien howled and his shadow blade dissipated. A force flung him against a pillar and pinned him there.

Caela stood, one hand outstretched, the other clutching her chest. Sweat matted her hair.

Adrian ran to her.

"How... embarrassing."

"Don't talk. Save your strength."

"Being rescued from the Dark Lord by a young orphan knight with a magic sword... Like some helpless damsel. Gods above."

"Sh. Rest."

"No time. You need... to listen. I only have... part of his power. I saw *home*, Adrian. A garden, vast and verdant. Loch Anam." A smile brushed her lips. "I can see it, Adrian. It's beautiful. It's..."

"I'll get you out—"

"No, Adrian—it's... too late. I can't seal the void, he's taken too much and filled me with dark magic... I feel it... Slithering inside me. Did you use the shadow ink?"

Adrian swallowed. "No, but I need it—"

"You don't. Here."

She pressed a hand into Adrian's. Her veins lit up, golden light flowing through and into Adrian.

His back arched and fire filled his veins.

"It's the last of my power... I can only turn so much of his magic to light... He's powerful, Adrian." Sweat beaded Caela's pallid skin and darkness ran through her veins. "Use it, Adrian—*live*. And... kill that son of a bitch."

Caela sank to the floor, and her eyes closed.

With a groan, Lucien hit the ground.

Adrian retrieved Nightsbane and marched towards him.

Standing, Lucien conjured another shadow blade.

"You're an idiot, Lucien." Despite the pain, Adrian laughed. "What if I'd killed Caela, like you wanted me to?"

"I seize opportunities, Navarro—if the White Death had died, I'd have carried out my plan without obstacle. I am a Darkwielder, connected to a power you cannot comprehend."

Redirecting energy, Caela once said. "The shadow men—they steal the life force from victims and feed it to you."

"It takes a tremendous amount of power to open the gate. It should have killed me—but then you handed her to me. You think my life means anything compared to what Niamat will accomplish? I never intended on living—truthfully, I'd hoped you'd kill each other, but even if you had succeeded, Sergeant Diaz would have given you to me and I'd have removed the last potential threat." The corners of his mouth sharpened. "Then my eyes on the streets told me you were back in the city—you handed her to me, a healing Wielder. She didn't have to die, Navarro, but you saw to it by bringing her here. I'd gladly have given up my life to bring Niamat into our world, gladly have died to see Phadros restored to glory—but Caela's power will allow me to see the new Phadra. For that, I thank you."

"Willing to sacrifice yourself 'til you saw that someone else could take the fall for you." Adrian attacked. "How very human of you."

Nightsbane flicked and stabbed, unable to penetrate the lord's defences.

"You've *no idea* what I've sacrificed for the greater good. People I cared for, people I loved. Men who trusted me. I've sacrificed myself, my *soul*. All for Phadros."

Lucien's invisible grip tightened around Adrian's chest and squeezed his heart but Caela's power thrummed through him—he roared and shattered Lucien's grip.

Golden light sparked within his clenched fist. Adrian channelled it into Nightsbane and the blade glowed brighter and brighter.

"Dead in the dark, all alone—just like your father." Lucien

struck—Nightsbane absorbed the strike and sent bolts of pain up Adrian's arm.

Nightsbane spun and slashed, its ignicite burning bright, fuelled by Caela's strength. Lucien staggered back.

Adrian stalked towards him. "All my life I believed my father to be a coward. Why? Why did you kill him?"

Lucien said nothing.

"You murdered him." A shower of sparks as the swords clashed. "Twisted his body, *tortured* him." Steel and shadow collided. "And me. You stopped me from saving him. You pinned me to the floor, made me watch as you broke him bit by bit."

Lucien's brow furrowed. "Boy, I didn't even know you were there."

Adrian attacked but Lucien dodged and countered, sending Adrian sprawling to the floor with fresh cuts. Blood seeped over his skin and Nightsbane clattered away.

Lucien loomed over him.

Trembling, Adrian crawled away, fingers fishing in his pocket.

"Sparkpowder, is it?" Lucien pointed his sword at Adrian. "A child's trick. The Order of the Shadow Dragon was once filled with warriors. And what are you now? A boy playing soldier. Scared of the dark. A coward, weak and alone." Lucien struck, but Adrian slipped away at the last second.

When he stood, his fingers curled around the vial of shadow ink.

Sorry, Caela.

He tipped the bottle to his lips and swallowed.

The shadow ink slithered down his throat, burning, corrosive. Adrian convulsed.

The ink flowed through his veins—Adrian felt it clash with Caela's power, a duel between light and shadow.

And as it burned, invisible needles cut his skin, drawing

blood. Adrian screamed. Thin scars etched upon his skin and turned black, before settling into tattoos.

He rolled, snatched Nightsbane, and pressed forward, driving Lucien back.

"You think your enemy is evil, yet you use dark magic." Lucien retreated, grinning at Adrian. "*Darkness* gives you power." Then he turned the point of his sword to Caela. "And darkness always demands a price."

The blade plunged down—swift as lightning, Adrian slid and deflected the blade—but it left him vulnerable.

Lucien struck.

Cold ice passed through Adrian's chest, and for a moment, the world turned black. Pain wracked him, blunted only by the shadow ink.

But it didn't kill him.

"Darkness gives you power..."

A chuckle escaped his throat, then full-blown laughter.

Caela absorbs dark magic to turn it into light...

And now I have both.

Like Caela had done to seal the portals, Adrian summoned burning light. He drew power from the shadow ink, and the shadow ink drew power from the light. Adrian trembled as immense power flowed through him. He punched out—light swept over Lucien and his sword of shadows shattered. He flailed like a ragdoll, blood seeping through his dark robes.

The shadow dragon flitted past, its colossal wings beating like thunder.

"I'll slay you and your pet."

The lord laughed. "Niamat is coming and she will usher in an age of darkness—the dragon is a herald, the first soldier among many. The shadow legions will march over Phadros and beyond—and there's not a thing you can do to stop it."

Lucien lay there, bleeding and breathing ragged breaths.

Adrian wanted to stain Nightsbane with his blood, to get revenge…

He pressed his palm into Lucien's forehead. Bright light flowed into the lord's skin, through his veins, into his very bones. Lucien howled and convulsed in agony. Darkness flowed from Lucien's veins into Adrian's, mixing with the light. Dark power tightened in his chest, so hard it threatened to snap Adrian's spine.

But Adrian fought. Caela's power gave him strength.

And the darkness burned away.

Caela absorbs dark magic… Shadow ink protects against magic attacks…

But stealing Lucien's power wasn't an attack—it was a choice.

Adrian pulled away, breathing hard, heart racing.

Wrinkles lined Lucien's face, his skin drew tight against his bones, and his black hair turned grey. He tried to speak but only thin, ragged breaths came.

Adrian loomed over him. "Why did you kill my father?"

Lucien's skin paled. He cowered back, his wide, fearful eyes looking past Adrian.

"Why?"

Lucien shrank away, eyes clenched in terror.

"Why?"

Lucien's eyes sprang open. He lay there, shaking, terrified, and when he spoke, the words came in a whisper. "Because she told me to."

Adrian's blood froze.

The black dragon swept past again. The void still crackled in the sky, shadow men tumbling out in a torrent.

Adrian gripped Nightsbane tight. Light flowed from his veins and through his sword, bright as burning igneus. Caela's light, bright and golden, channelled through the sword.

And the shadows burned.

"My... work," Lucien whimpered. "My legacy..."

"Legacy? You killed my father—you didn't kill me and now I'm here to repay you in blood. *That's* your legacy."

"The darkness is in you now."

The shadow dragon circled Phadra's towers and spires, roaring and setting the night on fire.

Adrian stood at the edge of the roof, cold wind on his face. "It always was."

The dragon's red eyes met Adrian's. It surged towards him, a stream of fire washing over the ground.

Adrian's heart raced. The beast closed the distance and he leapt towards it. The grappling hook uncoiled and wrapped around the dragon's leg.

His heart leapt into his mouth. Adrian swung, icy cold wind and intense heat washing over him. The dragon thrashed and corkscrewed, trying to shake him off. Adrian gripped its iron-hard scales and climbed.

The beast snorted and howled, gouts of fire erupting from its jaws. Adrian summoned light into Nightsbane and thrust it between the dragon's scales. White light flowed from his veins and channelled through the blade.

He rode the dragon higher and higher, barrelling through the sky towards the void. Then white-hot, scorching light shot from his hand and burned the hole in the world— burned it to nothing. Demons howled in anguish and the dragon roared.

Adrian kept it up, hand outstretched, golden light shearing the darkness away. He glimpsed the Shadow Realm, a place of black fire and darkness. He sensed something coming—something *big*.

The sky screamed and the world tremored.

Roaring, Adrian pulled the sword from the dragon's back and slashed at the portal, slinging a blade of light towards it.

The sword turned white-hot, searing Adrian's hand, but still he gripped it. The light melted the shadows tumbling from the void. Adrian's body begged him to stop, but he kept going.

For my father.

For vengeance.

For my friends.

For Caela.

The dragon howled. Searing light sealed the void and the very darkness screamed. The void turned into a second sun and bathed Phadra in light, burning the shadow demons to embers.

Light sparked and flickered, but the seal remained tight.

When the void dissipated, Adrian plunged Nightsbane into the dragon and again summoned Caela's power to burn it from the inside out.

The dragon dissolved and Adrian tumbled through the sky, towards the flaming city below. The grappling hook bit into stone and he swung hard into the palace walls and climbed.

Lucien's ancient and withered corpse faded into dust. Caela lay in peace, soft, weak breaths coming from her—but darkness filled her veins.

Adrian fell to one knee and placed a hand upon her, but his light couldn't penetrate the darkness. He couldn't heal her.

Adrian carried Caela in his arms. She weighed almost nothing.

Chaos filled Phadra. The Watch ferried water and first-gen airships doused the fires from above, but Adrian couldn't hear any shouts of victory or anguish—he heard nothing and felt only the cold radiating from Caela's skin.

He couldn't meet the lingering looks from the people all around; he kept his head bowed, gaze fixed on her. If he looked away, she might disappear.

I won't let you go.

I won't let you go.

Adrian floated through the streets. Caela looked so fragile, so peaceful. No worries creased her brow, no blood or bruises blemished her skin—just the shadows in her veins. If only he'd been quicker, stronger...

Adrian marched aboard the *Nueva Luna*. Ramiro opened his mouth but Mara put a hand on his shoulder and shook her head. Cassandra's eyes shone and sobs wracked Dante's chest.

He set Caela down on a bed in the *Luna's* captain's quarters and drew a lock of white-blond hair away from her eyes. The world stilled even further.

"Rest." Adrian's voice sounded foreign to him. "I'll take you home, Caela. To Aludan. To Loch Anam." He held her cold hand. "I'll find other Wielders. I'll carry your mission. I'll protect them."

Did Caela hear him? Where was she now? Where was her essence? Her soul? Adrian carried her light inside of him. He couldn't bring her back, but part of her was still alive—and any glimmer could be nurtured into a radiance, bright and strong and *living*.

"I'll bring you back," he vowed. "I won't let you go."

It had been easy to hate the Wielders—too easy. Hatred made things simple and gave Adrian fire. But fire couldn't heal—it could only burn.

"It's inside me, Dante. I can feel it. The darkness. Niamat will try again. Lucien's dark magic is inside me now. She commanded him... And she'll come for me. As long as I live, I'm a threat."

"So you'll stop her again." The two men stood in the *Luna's* empty auditorium, surrounded by silence. "Caela gave you her greatest gift, Adrian—she gave you her power. You're a Wielder now, and that's not something to be scared of. None of us are who we thought we were."

"No—but we get to choose."

Dante scratched the back of his head. "You, uh, you may not have noticed but my eyes are, um…"

"Brown. They've always been brown—and I've always known. You're a good friend, Dante."

Dante beamed.

Cassandra had the right of it, back in Ignarribia. She didn't make snap judgements on people. Neither did Dante. Both accepted people as they were. Amos had told Adrian that friends made a warrior weak, but Adrian had been weak to start with. Weak, and blinded by ignorance. No, just as an alloy inherited the strengths of different metals, so, too, did Adrian's allies make him stronger.

"It's done?" Ramiro asked when Adrian stepped into the vessel's small bridge. "Lord Lucien is…?"

"Dead."

"How did he do it? How did he summon the darkness?"

"He's the King of Shadows—reckon he borrowed power from Niamat so she can exist in our world, just like Suaro said. The shadows drew the life force from everyone they touched and fed it to Lucien. Kept him young and powerful. He needed their life force to keep the void open long enough for Niamat to step through. He capitalised on existing prejudice against San Sirans, knew he could pen them in and sacrifice them without question. By the time the shadows stole the souls of anyone else, it'd be too late."

"But you stopped him."

"And Caela. That was his mistake—he planned on dying tonight to summon his goddess. But when he realised Caela's power could keep him alive, he changed his mind." Adrian's fingers curled into fists. "Sacrificed her instead. But she's strong… She bought me enough time to stop him and seal the void."

"You saved Phadra and stopped Lucien." Dante squeezed his shoulder. "She'd be proud of you."

"What about this hole in the world?" Mara asked. "Is it done? Or is it gonna reappear at the next Sol's Kiss?"

Adrian flexed his fingers. "Niamat has more disciples. They'll try again."

"And if they succeed?" Cassandra asked. "If they open another portal?"

"I'll seal it."

"You're sure you can go toe to toe with a god?" Mara asked.

"I am." Adrian met Dante's eye. "I have my friends around me."

"Suaro was the expert," Ramiro started, "and Valador Ramos will blame the Order of the Shadow Dragon for what happened today. Commander Vega attacked us—if he's alive, he'll try again."

"Not so worried about Vega," said Dante. "We're talking about a man who managed to crash the same airship *twice.*"

"We need to leave," said Adrian. "We need to find Suaro. If anyone knows how to save Caela, it's him. We leave Phadros. Now. While things are still chaotic and—"

A mechanical whir rocked a table in the corner of the bridge. The Bride's Code machine puttered. Cass translated its message onto the unit's notepaper. "From Ryndara."

"On an open channel?" Adrian asked.

Cassandra frowned. "I… It doesn't make any sense."

"What does it say?"

"It… There are more voids opening… Shadow demons."

"What?" Mara said. "But we closed it."

Cass handed her the paper. As she did so, the bricode machine hummed to life again. This time, Adrian wrote the message down: "This is an official communication from Karina Taliana Konstantin of Tarevia, sent to all open channels. The sky is splitting. Shadows invade. Request immediate assistance from all nations of Imanis. Repeat: The sky is splitting. Shadows invade."

The machine didn't stop. It hummed and whirred, its red lights pulsing in warning. Similar messages poured out from Mercuria and Nom Ganald, Val Candria and Aludan.

Adrian's heart thudded like a battering ram.

"Adrian?" Dante asked. "What's going on? What do we do?"

"We're the Order of the Shadow Dragon." Adrian tied his sword belt around his waist and clasped Nightsbane's hilt. "We get to work."

ACKNOWLEDGMENTS

Writing is a hard slog, and the first book of a new series is no different—so eternal thanks, as always, to Zoe, my wife (!) for putting up with the long hours and the longer rants.

Big thanks and huge appreciation to Michael Schaefer, whose wisdom knows no bounds, and to Travis Riddle and Phil Parker for their perpetual enthusiasm. Huge thanks yet again to Andi Marlowe at Andromeda Editing for tightening the manuscript, and for Paul at Trif Book Design for that gorgeous cover!

I raise a glass of whisky (Talisker or Laphroaig, please. Or both) to all my author brethren, and to the amazing readers, bloggers and reviewers out there—you are the unsung heroes of the publishing world who deserve much more glory than you get.

Fist bumps and hugs to the friends and family who were all neglected while this book was being dragged into life. I would apologise, but I've already started work on a new project, so…

Specific high fives to Alan, Sinéad, Callan, Robbie and Jason; Ryan and Rachel; and the clans of Martin and Mann. Big love to my mum, Jeana, and to Ross Bullen and Auntie Sally.

To my granda, you were always there to offer encouragement and support. And to my gran and my da, you're both still always in my thoughts—but we'll meet again. Until then, I'll miss you all.

ALSO BY STEVEN MCKINNON

The Raincatcher's Ballad

Symphony of the Wind

The Fury Yet To Come

Wrath of Storms

Choir of the Damned

Legacy of Light and Shadow

Order of the Shadow Dragon

Other works

Boldly Going Nowhere

The Vividarium, featured in the anthology *In Memory: A Tribute to Sir Terry Pratchett*

GoogleFuture, featured in Issue 6 of The High Flight Fanzine

ABOUT THE AUTHOR

Symphony of the Wind is Steven McKinnon's first fiction novel, and is Book One of The Raincatcher's Ballad. *Wrath of Storms* followed in 2019, and the concluding volume—*Choir of the Damned*—was released in 2021.

The Fury Yet To Come is a prequel novella set in the same world.

His first book, the true-life tale *Boldly Going Nowhere*, was released in 2015.

Steven is 35 years old, and was born in the bathroom of a high-rise flat in the year 1986.

He has since moved out.

 facebook.com/shrmckinnon
twitter.com/SHRMcKinnon
instagram.com/stevenmckinnonauthor

Printed in Great Britain
by Amazon